I0745581

PURSUING GENEVIEVE

Novels by Mellyora Ashley:

**A LADY IN DISGUISE
A HERO'S HEART**

Georgian Sister Series:

**FORBIDDEN ARABELLE, Book 1
PURSUING GENEVIEVE, Book 2**

**THE ROGUE AND THE ROSE
THE INSTANT HEIRESS**

My heartfelt thanks to **Sharon** for this

Advance Reader Review:

"It was refreshing to have some of your characters quote Scripture. You had a moral to your story that needs to be told, and you included it convincingly. The ending showed how good prevails over evil when people follow God's will."

PURSUING GENEVIEVE

By Mellyora Ashley

England and France, 1754

Georgian Sister Series, Book 2

Coachman
Publications

First edition 2020

Coachman Publications
PO Box 220, Yamhill, OR 97148 USA
Printed in the United States of America

All characters in this book are purely fictional, and have no existence outside the imagination of the author except for the following historical characters portrayed or mentioned:

Francois Premier, King of France
Emperor Charles V
Maurice de Saxe, a Marshal of France
Leonardo da Vinci
Lord Hardwicke

Dedication

I dedicate this book to you, dearest **Myriam**, friend of my heart. Over the years, you and **Gérard** have given me so many joyful experiences in châteaux, cathedrals, and the glorious French countryside, including our walk on Chemin de Saint-Jacques de Compostelle, that I cannot thank you enough. By showing me these places, you inspired me to set Genevieve's story in Château de Chambord, Cathédrale de Chartres, and Château de Villebon.

Merci et bisous, ma Belle Grâce!

Acknowledgement

A heartfelt thank you to Monsieur and Madame de la Raudière for the private invitation to your fairy-tale home, Château de Villebon. It was a joyful privilege to hear your story of life in the castle, and the historic dramas of centuries past.

It was lovely to see the bed where Kings of France have slept, and to watch the working of your drawbridge over the moat.

Thank you for welcoming us so graciously to your romantic château. It still feels like a dream.

Author's Note

Strange as it may seem, the beautiful Château de Chambord was truly empty . . . for sixty years.

Chapters

PURSUING GENEVIEVE

By Mellyora Ashley

England and France, 1754

Georgian Sister Series, Book 2

CHAPTER 1

Genevieve's Mistake

"Are you *nervous?*" whispered Genevieve Lamar as the coach veered around a corner of Bloomsbury Square.

"If your father finds out, he will strangle me!" Shrubsole Curling replied, looking apprehensively out of the window.

Genevieve thought her illicit swain looked almost attractive for the first time, but that was due to the golden light bathing him from the carriage lantern. Before sneaking out of the house, she had borrowed one of her father's lace jabots and boldly tied it around Mr. Curling's throat to give him a bit of elegance. Otherwise, he lacked any.

He lifted the lace and added darkly, "Lord Bastwicke could easily choke me with his own jabot."

"I suspect he might like to," she agreed, "so we must rattle on to Fleet Street as fast as we can. Then he won't know about our marriage until it is too late." A prickle of guilt caused her to let go of

Shrubsole's bony fingers. "But although he would thunder," she added, widening her eyes, "the worst repercussions would come from Madam, my mother. But," she sighed, "I simply must get away from her." Now it was fear that encroached upon the joy of Genevieve's idealistic elopement. "Madam, when crossed, strikes out quickly and sharply, like lightning."

"I know! Frightening lightning! She didn't like the way I combed her hair once."

In the slowly jolting coach, Genevieve eyed Mr. Curling's profile. He had straight brown eyebrows, a long, narrow nose with a high bumped bridge, and a wide mouth that often smiled.

He was not smiling now. Below his three-cornered hat hung a sparse and tangled queue of light brown hair, which seemed ironic to her, considering his profession. He was a hairdresser much in demand with the most fashionable ladies of London. He said, "You will soon be a widow if she strikes me for this. But how long do we have, I wonder? How long can we stave them off and live in wedded bliss?"

Though feeling jittery, Genevieve decided to maintain a semblance of audacity. "Who cares?" she threw back as they rolled by a lamp-lighter with a flaming torch. "We are leaving Madam—and without permission! I have longed to do this for two years!" She hung onto the remains of her triumph. "This is a marvel of courage for me, Shrubsole. It's been a sore trial being the eldest girl since Arabelle married and left." A certainty crept into her mind that her beloved sister would not approve of this horrendous scheme. Eloping with a man—and from such a low rung of society—was absolutely contrary to their family's precepts. Truly, she should not be doing this.

Shrubsole pulled Genevieve back from pressing her nose to the window. "Be careful! Someone in your house might see you. We are not safely away by any means since we have to circle this confounded square to get out of sight, and that lamplighter has everything lit now." The wheels clattered much too loudly over the flagstones for any kind of a clandestine getaway. He rapped sharply on the ceiling and shouted, "Hurry up!" which caused the coachman to set the pair of horses from a fast walk to a ringing trot.

Genevieve bit her lip as she looked back at her four-story home. She no longer felt like laughing. There were candles burning in Lady Bastwicke's boudoir, but what was worse—and which instantly doused her euphoria—was the sight of a familiar-shaped horseman approaching from up ahead.

"Shrubsole, look!" She gasped. "My father is coming home! Oh, I hope, hope, *hope* he doesn't see us! Duck!" She moved her face away, which had been in the full light of the lantern when she spied Father.

Shrubsole gave a quick look out the window, and swiped his hat off his head to hide most of his face. "Isn't this earlier than normal? I thought you said he works late!"

"This is very early for him. I thought he would be gone until ten o'clock! He has been toiling every night on that Marriage Act to see it into effect. Shrubsole, I feel afraid!"

"Duck down farther!"

She did so, her pulse thudding in her ears as she cowered and clung to the seat.

"We'll soon be out of sight," said Mr. Curling, patting her head.

"Can he see you? Are you in the shadow?"

"No, yes, but he's turned his horse around and—oh no, now he's following us! This is not good!" He pounded on the ceiling with urgency.

Genevieve tightened her fingers around his wool-clad arm. "What should we do? Quick! Are we out of the square yet?"

"Yes, but here he comes, straight after us!"

Genevieve rose to peek. Mr. Curling pushed her down again.

He rearranged his position so that he sat completely in shadow. "I'll cover our lanterns," he decided. "How stupid of me to keep them lit. He could recognize our faces." He slammed down each side window in turn, and with a deal of difficulty, performed the operation through one open window while Genevieve impatiently rose up to do so with the one on the side away from Father.

She said under her breath, "I imagine he saw you do that, in full light."

Shrubsole yelled, "Speed it up!" but it was doubtful that the coachman heard over the clattering of the horseshoes and wheels. As they swerved, his voice became terrified. "Blimey! He's almost upon us!"

Genevieve listened to the hoof beats. "He is pursuing me! Oh no, now what?" Serious doubts drummed through her head. "My father is rarely angry, but when he is—oh, Shrubsole! I don't want his wrath turned upon you!"

"Confound it! I never should have suggested this. We should not have tried to elope. Why did I not listen to my better judgment?"

Genevieve grabbed his lapels and loudly whispered, "Because you said we would never be allowed to marry each other unless we ran away, that's why!"

He shook her off and muttered, "I have always been one for a challenge."

"Do not blame yourself. Not entirely."

"Now Genevieve, you must realize that if Lord Bastwicke catches us before we are married, it will not happen. I will never be allowed to see you again. I won't even be able to arrange your hair, or your mother's either, I presume."

The thought that flicked into her mind was that he was giving up very easily. "You are right," she said, eyeing him with dawning disfavor. "Face it, Shrubsole, if Father catches us, it will be good-bye to you and me."

"Oh, well," he said on a sigh, fingering her long copper-colored curls that hung in silky glory beneath her tiny lace cap. "It felt too wonderful to ever come true for me."

"Shrubsole! Whyever not?" Genevieve demanded.

"Because you are such a beautiful, wonderful, and wealthy daughter of a Peer, and I am just . . . nothing."

When the cantering hoof beats caught up to them, Genevieve felt a rush of terror. She gave her former fiancé a quick kiss on the cheekbone—the first she had ever given him—and said, "Then why don't we just stop? It will go much better for us if we do."

"You have likely said a true thing," conceded Mr. Curling. The horses slowed and the coach swayed as the coachman tried to maneuver into a place where he could halt.

Genevieve said frenetically, "Loosen that jabot, quick!" She received it from him and thrust it deep into her bodice, explaining, "My father is working on a very important change to the marriage law. He calls it *An Act for the Better Preventing of Clandestine Marriage.* Have you heard of it?"

Shrubsole's eyes widened incredulously. "The one they will read in church once a month? Do not tell me that it passed into Law!"

"Yes! It is to prevent marriages like the one we wanted performed tonight! Oh," she wailed, "how far is Fleet Street? Maybe you should tell the coachman to whip them up again. That law is not enforced yet, but it will be. Very soon, I think."

Mr. Curling fearfully watched Lord Bastwicke through the window. "Blimey, Genevieve, I am a dead man!"

Next to the coach window, Lord Bastwicke roared in his forty-acre voice, "Halt this vehicle! Do as I say, Coachman! You have a child inside!"

Genevieve looked through the glass, and jumped back when she saw the whites of a horse's eyes, its black mane flicking, and then her father's dark coat draped over his white stocking. She looked up, and there was Father's white-wigged bulk in all its authority. There came the sharp rap of his riding crop on the coach body.

The wheels ground to a halt. *A child,* she thought, and instantly felt like an extremely naughty one with no hope but punishment.

"Emerge from that coach at once, sir!" came her father's second shout as soon as Shrubsole cracked opened the door, keeping all but his terrified eyes covered.

"Father! Please don't worry!" cried Genevieve, pushing past Shrubsole. "I come willingly!" Climbing over his legs, she kicked the round carriage step down and stepped onto it. She jumped down, snapped it back in, slammed the door shut, and imperiously motioned the staring coachman to drive away.

This he did with no hesitation after noting the menacing brows of Lord Bastwicke, an enraged father and a Peer of the Realm.

Genevieve had urgently instructed Shrubsole to hide his face in the hope that Father would not see who her fellow eloper was. So it happened, for Genevieve caused a distraction when she fell against her father's moving horse. The animal shied and backed, causing her to tumble to the ground. As she knew he would, her father moved his horse away, dismounted hastily, and lifted her up.

"Oh, my little Genevieve!" he crooned in dismay. "Thanks to God on high, I have you safe!" The coach rattled away and diminished down the dim street. "What were you thinking, minx? You gave me the fright of my life! Where were you going with that man, and at this time of night?"

Genevieve, astonished, and most gratified at her Father's change of tone, said, "I thought I was in love with someone, and I wanted to go off and marry him tonight—do not glare at me like that, Father!—but now I know it was very wrong, and—"

"Absolutely wrong!" he exploded.

Painfully, she added, "I am so relieved that you stopped us."

His eyes widened. "Are you, indeed?"

"Yes! Ow, my palm is scraped."

"Continue!" he demanded, pulling her along and lifting her white hands to look at them in the light from the street lamp. Though his voice was intimidating, his touch was gentle as it always was.

Genevieve, surprising herself, started to cry. "He is not the man for me after all!"

"How do you know that so soon after leaving the house, which is approximately a three-minute journey?"

She felt foolish, but she blurted out the truth that she had just discovered. "He did not act decisively! He was too scared of you, Father."

"He should be! Why is that a drawback?"

"I learned that I cannot feel much respect for him. You see, he cringed."

Her father let out a guffaw. "Is that so! That is a major drawback. Well, I am delighted. He does well to be scared of me, and lose your respect. I hope he remains thundering terrified for life!"

"He will, I am sure." Genevieve vowed that the man she married would have far more backbone and dignity than Mr. Shrubsole Curling had demonstrated. How blind she had been, and how childishly impulsive.

As they walked homeward, her Father led his snorting horse behind them. Suddenly he said with fervor, "This, Genevieve, is precisely why we need the Marriage Act. Most young people do not see past the whirligig of romance to the real character or suitability of the marriage partner they think they want at a certain moment."

Humbly, Genevieve said, "I am sure that is true, Father."

He shook her arm. "I am relieved beyond measure that I caught you from making a tragic mistake. I shudder to think! Added to your own plight, I would never have been able to hold my head up had my own daughter succeeded in an elopement, and just as the Marriage Act becomes Law!"

Genevieve felt a rush of remorse. "Oh, Father! Please, please, *please* forgive me! I have been utterly tempted against my better judgment. I was totally thoughtless of how my actions would affect you. It makes me sad that I am such a worm."

He stopped their progress and took her into a bear hug. "There, there, my precious, let us say this is forgiven and forgotten, and you will promise to forget that sprig, Mr. Curling. I will not tell your mother if you promise me that."

So he knew the name of her partner in crime. Wiping away a tear, she drew a deep breath, feeling much relieved, and nodded. "Yes, Father, I promise. I will think seriously from now on before I even *like* another man, much less think of marrying one."

CHAPTER 2

The List of Men

Bloomsbury Square, London
13th March, 1754

My dear Arabelle,

How are you, my ardently-missed sister? I wish I could recount to you what happened in person. You heard a little in my short note of yesterday.

Father, after his initial interrogation about my aborted elopement, has not told Madam that I tried to go to Fleet Street to be married clandestinely, and to such a lowly man, one who works for a living. What a relief! I cannot imagine what she would do to me if she knew. I know that Father is hugely relieved that he stopped us before any harm was done. We agreed that we would keep it a secret until we die—as long as I promise not to see the man again. I promised. Thank God for Father's good heart. He has forgiven me all my sins, so I am glad beyond measure to our Saviour, and can report that I am free of that awful load.

Here's something curious, Arabelle: Father said, 'When I was a young man, I made a mistake, but I was not as fortunate as you were to be rescued from it.' I didn't think it was the moment to ask him for an explanation, and he didn't give one, but I am still curious. Have you ever heard what that was about?

To answer your question, yes, I am definitely over Mr. Curling. When I met him, I was missing you terribly. Since I had no other friends around, I talked to him when he came to do my hair for a ball, two plays, and a concert. We talked the most on the day he created my coiffure for my Court appearance. At that time, I thought it was lucky that Madam's special-occasion hairdresser (not Bertha) died, because the word went round that, when one lost one's hairdresser, Shrubsole Curling was the man to summon.

He made me feel uncommonly beautiful, so that must be why I fell in supposed 'love' with him. I am ashamed to say this, but I think that, on very slim evidence, I imagined greater qualities in him than he actually has. I am much too much of a romantic. I even thought he cut a dashing figure for awhile, especially in Father's lace jabot when we were eloping! I know you're laughing at me, Arabelle. Don't worry, I grabbed the jabot back.

Shall I tell you a truth about him that I have realized since then? It is this: I saw him from a shop window yesterday. He was running through the street, his green coattails flapping.

His knees and elbows looked so gangly, and his own thin hair was slipping out of its queue. He was frowning as if something vexed him. I did not admire him anymore. How could I have been so foolish as to fancy myself attracted to such a woefully inferior man? He does not have enough self-respect to command anyone else's admiration, except in ladies' hair dressing.

I think the observations that you or Aunt Claracilla might give me are that he listened to me, and he talked convincingly about my good qualities. That is how he gets so many customers—being complimentary and listening with interest. To find myself in the hands of such a man—any man—when Madam was being so irksome to me day after day was such a relief that I started imagining all kinds of romantic thoughts about escaping this place with him.

Oh, Arabelle, I have vowed never to admire, as a possible suitor, any other man who has a few good qualities. I must take thought to what the hidden bad ones might be, and investigate.

Aunt Claracilla wrote that sometimes we bestow virtuous qualities onto people we want to admire, but they often do not live up to our ideals of them. Do you agree, Arabelle? I find that so disappointing.

Your devoted sister,
Genevieve

When she gave the letter to Welford, the young

Bastwicke footman, he assured her that he would keep the mailing of it a strict secret. He would run it to the mail coach at the George Inn for dispatch that day. Genevieve urged him on no account to let Lady Bastwicke see any evidence of it.

Upon his return, he knocked softly on Genevieve's bedchamber door, and gave her a missive that had come. He knew that Lady Bastwicke snatched letters directed to her daughters and read them first. Welford made a practice of hiding Genevieve's letters until moments when he could put them into her own hands unseen. For this, Genevieve was grateful, and she always gave him sixpence.

The letter Welford had just smuggled to her was from Aunt Claracilla at Fawnlake Hall in Kent. She wrote that her dear *must not do anything unbecoming to a lady,* and that she should get to know a gentleman very well before she ever considered giving her heart and hand to him. *Do not be in undue haste to marry,* she warned, *not even for love, but especially not for the sole reason of monetary gain.* She had written similar advice to Arabelle before her marriage, giving her courage to deflect their mother's opposing dictates.

Genevieve had read those letters many times over, but, to her shame, she had not followed that wise counsel. She knew that what Aunt Claracilla said to the sisters was always in their best interest, for she loved them dearly. After all, she had been their practical mother for eleven years, when they lived with her and Uncle Trent, Lord Shepley. When Lady Bastwicke, upon her husband's command, finally returned from living on the

Continent, she plunged her two oldest daughters' lives into chaos. She advised and pushed them in opposition to the values they had learned from Uncle Trent and Aunt Claracilla. The result was a major upheaval in their lives, especially in her elder sister, Arabelle's, before she married and escaped from under Madam's roof.

On this sunny winter day, Genevieve hid her aunt's letter inside the pillow slip in her yellow curtained bed. She descended to breakfast by the oval staircase beneath the sunbeams streaming from the sky-lit dome.

Lady Bastwicke sat in the dining room, fully dressed at eleven o'clock, so Genevieve suspected that something new was afoot. "Which man is it?" she demanded of Genevieve with a glare from her small green eyes, just as if they had been carrying on a heated discussion already.

"Which man is it who has done what?" inquired Genevieve nervously, pouring coffee from the china flowered pot.

"Won your heart, if that's the way you want me to put it. If you even have one," she added acidly. "Which man have you decided you would like to marry? If you must have a say, let us settle this now."

At nineteen, Genevieve had developed just enough assertiveness to withstand some of her mother's intimidating assaults. Not about to be cowed by her on this personal subject, Genevieve flipped her long, coppery curls over her shoulder as she sat down. "No one I know."

Lady Bastwicke slammed her hand onto the lace tablecloth, making the cups rattle. "If you do not name one, *I* shall choose a husband for you!"

"No, Madam, please do not!"

"Oh yes, and I will pursue him until he gives in."

"Gives in?" Truly alarmed, Genevieve begged, "I implore you not to arrange any man for me!" She wondered what Father would think if he heard this.

Lady Bastwicke's close-set eyes narrowed beneath her ginger eyebrows as she glared at Genevieve. Without looking where she set it, she clattered her china cup onto the edge of its flowered saucer. It tipped sideways and coffee spread, staining the tablecloth. Ignoring it, she snapped, "Whyever not?"

Grabbing the silver bell on the table and ringing for the footman to clean up the mess, Genevieve whispered loudly, "Because it would mortify me to be the object of such a desperate search!"

"Then stop acting like a scared little ninny and tell me who—of all the men you met in the past year—you will deign to marry."

"I repeat: none of them." In face of her mother's increasing ire, Genevieve stabbed out, "Why must I be in such a hurry to marry? I am not yet twenty."

Lady Bastwicke rose in a rustle, her extremely wide olive green gown causing the tablecloth to pull after her. Genevieve grabbed it, just preventing the cups and coffee pot from tipping off the table.

Her mother gave it no mind, for she was working up to a verbal explosion. "You are impossible! Arabelle was considered quite old to marry at nineteen. You must get on with this business before it goes round London that we have a hard time shifting our daughters. Stop shilly-shallying!"

"How am I shilly-shallying?"

Lady Bastwicke rounded on her, pointing a skinny finger. "You are much too quiet amongst my friends, and far too timid when talking to men of rank. *We* have rank! Your father is a Viscount! You have no reason in the world to shy away from people. We are getting nowhere with you!" She added a rider as she fiddled with a quill pen at her marquetry escritoire, "I'll have you know that I am weary of taking you everywhere with me."

Genevieve looked her surprise. "Why, I am weary of it, too . . . Madam," she tacked on, for her mother dictated that her children call her so. That way, if they were amongst company who did not know them, she would not be pegged as their mother when she wished to appear much younger.

Lady Bastwicke put her hands on what might have been her hips were they not buried under a six-foot width of wood farthingale, petticoats and quilted silk gown. "Then get married and out of my way!" She waved one hand wildly toward the door.

So that was part of it. Genevieve rang the silver bell again with emphasis.

Granted, Genevieve had never wanted to be close to this flighty mother of hers, for she had only come back into her life a little over two years ago. For more than a decade prior to her forced return to Lord Bastwicke and their four children, Lady Bastwicke had gallivanted around Europe. She was assumed to have been cavorting with other adventurers or idly rich people from France to Belgium, Switzerland, and who knew where else. Lord Bastwicke had finally tracked down her whereabouts through a bank. He wrote and demanded that she return home and "Be a mother for a change." She came back, but Arabelle and Genevieve had suffered great emotional duress under her worldly influence.

Before that, they had lived a blessed, nurtured life with Lord and Lady Shepley in the Kentish countryside. There, they had learned from the Bible, and taken all their other studies from their aunt and uncle's wise tutelage.

Now Genevieve inwardly admitted that she would welcome getting out of Lady Bastwicke's way because whenever she was *in* her way, she felt completely unlike herself, and miserable. She had an idea, and asked, "May I go to visit Arabelle, then?"

Lady Bastwicke made a grandiose picture, seated before her French escritoire. It was draped from high above by aqua silk curtains and golden tassels. She shot back, "Whatever for?" Lady Bastwicke had often shown jealousy at the two sisters' closeness, which she could not penetrate nor diffuse.

Genevieve drew a breath for courage and said, "For introductions. They often entertain very nice gentlemen, so perhaps there will be someone different in their circle that I could ... get to know."

"Not good enough! No, you may not go to Arabelle. She lives too far away and too close to Claracilla. I will procure a wealthy man with a title for you. Claracilla is not to be trusted. Though she is a Viscountess herself, I know hardly anyone in her country circles. She even entertains a vicar every Sunday. Hitch you to him regardless of rank might be what such a dumb goody-goody would try to do."

Genevieve hotly interjected, "Aunt Claracilla has my best interests at heart! She always has and always will!"

The searing glare that Lady Bastwicke turned upon Genevieve was followed by intense words. "Forget that woman! She has done you too much damage already. I bet God was punishing her when He took her voice away. Hah! If only she were prevented from writing letters, too. Oh no, you will not heed her nor step foot under her roof again. Not until you're safely married."

As Genevieve's heart thumped hard, her mother added, "You are fortunate that I am even asking you who takes your fancy. Many of my friends just pick someone of benefit to their family, and make their daughters or sons marry them. But your father has made this ridiculous edict that his daughters get to be in on the choosing." She yanked opened a drawer and pulled out a page on which she had written lines of text. "Now sit there," she pointed at a pink gilt-legged chair, "and answer my questions." With sarcasm, she asked, "Would you *consider* marrying Lord Danville?"

Sinking to the seat, Genevieve, with her mouth going dry, asked, "Who is he?"

"Oh, an old flame of mine. Fie! I suppose that would never work because he still finds *me* attractive." Her lips curling in sly pleasure, she crossed him off and asked, "Do you like Admiral Maurice O'Leary?"

"The limping Irishman with the bawdy jokes?" She had heard him outside Drury Lane Theatre telling her Father about the horse-racing track he had built, but Father had left him with disgust, saying, "Foul-mouthed, and a boastful upstart!"

Genevieve looked straight at Madam and said, "Never."

"There you go, throwing away good money again! What about Sir Babbitt Prycross? I believe he has a massive estate in Cumbria."

Genevieve took a deep breath and let it out in a huff. "Is he not the one with seventeen children?"

"I think he does have quite a pack of those. But lucky for us, his wife just died. Now he is one of the most eligible widowers around. Who cares about the brats? You could send them all to schools and get them out of your way if you didn't relish the smells and the noise."

Genevieve did not dignify that with a reply. Her temples were pounding with rage. That was Madam's method of dealing with children. Though she had four of her own, she did not like them. She considered them great hindrances to her freedom and enjoyment of life. Therefore, Arabelle and Genevieve had not had her presence in their lives for most of their formative years. Even now, little Lenora and Jerome had to live most of their hours up on the top floor with Fanny, their nurse.

Lady Bastwicke continued, tacking a smile to her lips, "Here's one you know and like. I've saved him as a treat."

Genevieve blinked and looked warily at her. "A treat? Who could that possibly be?"

"Why, Sir Pomeroy Chancet!"

Genevieve jerked her spine straight.

Her mother effused, "Oh, those big, brown eyes!" Passing a hand over her high-piled pale orange hair, Lady Bastwicke said in an excited timbre, "I had a letter from him this morning. Look!" She lifted a folded billet with a broken purple seal.

Genevieve saw, in her mind's eye, the flamboyant peacock of a man who had bantered with her mother when he was in London during Arabelle's coming-out season. He wore pastel wigs, and his heavy-lidded eyes and speech were saucy, to put it mildly. His rouged lips had kissed London society women on their mouths as his customary greeting, but Arabelle had made him cease that with her. He used creativity in his gorgeous dress and placement of his face patches. His way with flattery and charm had made him a sought-after man in many drawing rooms.

What set Genevieve dead against him were his lewd actions toward Arabelle. He had been a major scourge for her to deal with. Genevieve icily asked Madam, "What could possibly be the subject of his letter?"

"Well, if you can't figure that out, you need to see more of him."

"No!" expelled Genevieve with finality.

"Whyever not?"

Genevieve felt it was unthinkable of Madam to mention his name after what he had done. "I could never, ever marry such a creature!"

"Stop calling Sir Pom a creature. He is a Baronet, and he was received everywhere, even at Chesterfield House, remember? All my friends love him."

"Is it not true that he dashed to France to escape punishment for his crimes?"

With an affronted lift of her pointed chin, Lady Bastwicke blinked defensively and said, "He has been much misunderstood. He wrote me that he has now acquired a château! Think of it! A French one!"

"Has he? How odd. The last I heard, he had declared himself very low on money, and was asking some from . . . you, Madam." If nothing else would convince her mother to forget him as a possible husband, lack of money should do it.

Her mother looked flushed and excited. "Not any longer! He has found great means, as he hints broadly in this letter. I, myself, can hardly wait to see him again, and hear how he got it." Lady Bastwicke drew the feather quill across her smugly-smiling lips.

Genevieve stabbed out, "See him again?"

Lady Bastwicke waved her away with her quill pen. She looked about to write a letter, so Genevieve left the room in mingled dread and disgust. Apparently Madam was planning to see him somewhere. Genevieve told herself she would not cooperate by joining them, so Sir Pomeroy could be no threat to her. Father would back her in that, for he could not stand the man.

What worried Genevieve was a much more eligible man—a man whom she kept trying to avoid. She needed to discuss her whirling thoughts about him with someone. In her bedchamber, she uncorked her ink bottle and grabbed a quill. Though she made globs of her looping letters, she wrote with angry zest.

15th March 1754

Dearest Arabelle,
    Now I am plunged into a quagmire. It is

all to do with Radford Laurence, Lord Ashby. I am still jittery around him. Please do not support Madam if she wants me to marry him because I feel utterly under scrutiny whenever he looks my way.

Would I be able to endure that nervousness all my life? No! Especially not when he turns that amused look upon me. I think he means it nicely, but it instantly conjures up the day when I was at that tailor, Mr. Dupper's, establishment being measured for corset bodices. Unbeknownst to me, Radford Laurence was forced, by my entrance, to hide away in a closet just a yard from where I stood. As a gentleman, he did not throw open the door to surprise me in my undress. He waited until he thought I was gone, and then he emerged and saw me standing there, wearing only my chemise! I have told you how mortifying that felt.

When I formally met him at the Chesterfield Ball, he looked as though his eyes were brim full of that sight of me. While he may think I have taken a lighthearted look at what happened, I have not. After he apologized on that embarrassing day, he told me, "I hope to see more of you!"—remember? You were as scandalized as I was. But I saw you choking on a laugh. To me, it wasn't a whit funny. It is painful to face him still because that's all I can think of.

Madam is in a tizzy because she frets that he will never call upon me. She is desperate to push me into his arms—that much I've seen clearly, although today she read out a list of what she called eligible men, and every one was a nightmare. As with you during your debut, she wants me to marry the loftiest title or the heaviest purse in England. She doesn't care how awful they are; she will not have to live with them.

Regarding the invitation to your soirée on Saturday, I have to say that, since you wrote that Radford will be there, I am not coming. Besides, Madam will not let me come anyway because she said Aunt Claracilla might marry me to her vicar or some other low person. Where does she get these ideas?

Finally, I hate to bring this up, but Madam has received a letter from Sir Pomeroy Chancet, that villain. Why in the world would she hear from him? She is heavily hinting that I consider him as husband material because now he has money! Can you imagine? He gives me the shudders after what he tried with you. We know how Father was glad to see him booted out of England. But he apparently has a château in France now. I'm worried. Why would he write to Madam? Worst of all, why is she looking so sly about his letter?

I miss you, Arabelle. I wish you were here to support me in this chaotic world of Madam and men.

I remain
Your loving sister,
Genevieve

That evening after dinner, Lady Bastwicke was still focused on the subject of men for her burdensome daughter, Genevieve. Consulting her paper, she said, "Let us continue to go through this list of eligible husbands for you. How about Lord Bitterhill?"

Genevieve widened her eyes in horror. "Madam! That man is sixty years old, pock-marked, grossly fat, and—"

"And what?"

"He reeks!"

"Reeks?" She waved that away. "He used to be good-looking, and is very plump in the pocket now. You must take that into serious consideration. Buy him perfume, or better yet, get him to bathe as we members of Lord Chesterfield's circle do."

Genevieve shuddered. She could not believe this train of conversation. Though their family did bathe several times a week as inspired by Philip Stanhope, Lord Chesterfield, Lady Bastwicke was not of his vaunted circle. Nor would she ever be, despite the fact that she had desperately cottoned onto the polite and timid Lady Chesterfield when Arabelle was invited to stay with them. Lord Chesterfield, in his dignity, had caused Lady Bastwicke to behave in a silly, insecure manner every time she pushed herself into his presence. It had been especially agonizing for Arabelle, when she was a guest of Lord Chesterfield's, to have her mother invade the house with her embarrassing prattle born of self-aggrandizing motives.

Genevieve longed for Arabelle, and she longed for them to be living with Aunt Claracilla and Uncle Trent, back in their secure, loving care. Her eyes grew wet and made lovely blurs of the six girandoles of candles around the room.

Quietly padding in silk slippers, seven-year-old Lenora appeared in the doorway, her blue eyes lighting on Genevieve. She ran across the Persian carpet, her pink gown ruffles fluttering.

Genevieve received her little sister in a protective hug. It was just what she needed, loving warmth and closeness. She kissed her soft cheek and hugged her close, breathing against her silky blonde hair. She smelled faintly of lavender. Fanny, the nurse, kept the children very clean.

Lenora cupped her hands and whispered, tickling Genevieve's ear with her breath, "What is she talking about?"

Their mother was holding the list farther away, squinting in order to read the next name, as the sun had just set and deprived them of good light.

Genevieve whispered back to Lenora, "A man for me to marry. She wants to know who I like best. They're all impossible!" Genevieve rolled her eyes.

Lenora looked at her speculatively. Then, with a look of resolve, she took a step toward their mother. "Madam," she asserted, "Genevieve likes Radford Laurence the best." With a look back at Genevieve, she showed a dimple.

Genevieve's heart began to thump. At the Chesterfield Ball two years ago, Lenora had taken a great liking to Radford Laurence. He had fed her a flavored ice, and she had sat on his lap and fed him back. The family had been startled to discover that he bore the title of Lord Ashby. He made such an impression on little Lenora that she had adored him ever since.

One night last month, when her mother discovered him in London, she had herded Genevieve and Lord Ashby into the opera box. After their formal courtesies of greeting, she directed them to sit next to one another at the front of the box for all to see. Chagrined, Genevieve had kept her eyes and ears riveted on the performance. She dared not turn her face toward him, for he had smiled at her quizzically, and she knew not what to do.

Seated close behind them, fanning down their necks, sat Madam and her particular acquaintances, two women and three men whom Genevieve did not know. They chatted and chortled all through the performance. It had been a horrendous evening to live through, and a resounding failure toward getting to know Radford Laurence any better.

So Genevieve had risen and excused herself. He rose politely to watch her leave the box. Outside, with the door shut behind her, she breathed deeply and made a purposeful dash for the ladies' retiring room. She sank onto a chair in the corner beside a mirror, but would not look into it. She had already glimpsed how flushed her cheeks were. There she stayed, sucking a sweetmeat, until the noise of chatter heralded ladies bursting through the door.

Genevieve thanked the attendant, gave her a coin, and made her exit past primping women. Before she could leave, one of them whirled toward her and said, "Your mother is looking for you, Miss."

"Yes, I imagine she is; thank you."

Outside the door, she almost collided with Radford Laurence, who steadied her by the elbow.

Genevieve felt alarm at the grip of his hand, which he quickly released as soon as she stood stable.

"Do not touch me, or pursue me!" she said in a rush, locking eyes with him for an instant. Then embarrassment overwhelmed her, so she hurried into the crowded lobby.

What had made her blast those words at him? She could not even explain to him that, if Madam saw them talking, that would rekindle her plan to shove them together.

He respected her wish, and did not return to their opera box.

Between the next acts, when most people surged again into the lobby, Lady Bastwicke could be seen fanning and smiling upon a short man in a black wig with diamonds flashing on his fingers. She spied Genevieve and imperiously motioned her over.

Genevieve let people impede them so she did not move forward at all. She saw that the man was about to part from her mother, but she grabbed his arm and turned him toward Genevieve with a significant look. Thereby she saw his pock marked face, squishy nose, and big lips. Genevieve shuddered, and let more people pass in front of her. Backing up, she bumped into someone.

A familiar male voice said, "You do not wish to meet that man?"

Genevieve whirled to meet Radford Laurence again, looking interested in her situation.

"What do *you* think? This is not your affair, My Lord, but will you please help me anyway?"

He had done so with brilliance. He bowed a little, took her hand, and kissed the air above it.

Genevieve knew it was important for her mother to witness this, so she smiled and made a little courtesy in return. Lord Ashby could not have done a more effective thing to keep her and the gnome-like prospective swain at bay. So it proved, for Madam had ditched the old man. She strove to move toward them through the crowd in her cumbersome *robe à la française*.

Genevieve, grasping courage, looked up at Lord Ashby. "Thank you!" Urgently, she added, "Now, do not let her come hook you into conversation. Flee, My Lord!" She motioned him quickly off in the opposite direction.

It made her giggle to see how he did it. There was a theater props man coming through the throng with a paper fire screen. Lord Ashby ordered, "Follow me! Take that end!" to the man while lifting the other. Radford hid his upper half behind it and carried it away toward a dim corridor, the stymied servant bearing the trailing end.

Since then, Genevieve had learned that a bit of opposition to her mother sometimes brought results.

Today, Genevieve still wondered what Radford Laurence thought of her. When coerced into that opera box, had he assumed that she was the one who wanted to be thrown into proximity with him? If he had thought so, he could hardly have been mistaken by the end of that evening. Had she actually told him bluntly not to pursue her? How mortifying it was to think about, for perhaps he had no such motive at all.

Lady Bastwicke had railed at her all the way

home, telling her that she must learn some conversation, wit, and a flirtatious attitude in an opera box or she would never, ever attract a man on her own. She blamed her for letting Lord Ashby escape in the lobby, not knowing that Genevieve had ordered him to flee. Genevieve giggled at that little *coup*.

"This is no laughing matter!" her affronted mother had exploded. As the coach clattered homeward, Genevieve heard all about her failure to use her wiles to keep a man by her side—a titled one like Lord Ashby at that!—and how she was dim-witted, naïve, and totally without the knack to attract men.

It was, therefore, no surprise to Genevieve when she saw Madam take up her pen and open her inkbottle. As she drew the feather across her lips, Genevieve asked fearfully, "What are you going to do?"

"You go away. Never mind."

That boded ill.

"I beg of you, do not write to Lord Ashby!" Genevieve quavered desperately. "Or Sir Pomeroy! Or anyone else about *me*."

"I said go away! Scat! I can't think with you two in the room. Why don't you go to bed? You could use some beauty sleep."

Apprehension dragged Genevieve's feet. She could hear the scratching across the paper. Madam pursed her thin lips, and her bony chest heaved as she deliberated, dipped the quill, and continued. The look on her face could only be called calculating.

Genevieve let out a huff and hurried out.

Lenora grabbed her hand and vaulted up the grand staircase with her. "I like him," she said, turning her blue gaze up at Genevieve. "I'm sorry I said that to Madam, though. Why did you not like me to?"

Genevieve squeezed her hand and said, as they rounded the oval staircase to the third floor where the nursery rooms were, "You may like him all you want, Lenora, but I will not be maneuvered at him again. It's embarrassing."

"Oh," said Lenora. "Arabelle told me that ladies do not chase after gentlemen. So you want my good friend, Radford, to start following you?" She cocked her chin and twinkled hopefully up at Genevieve.

"No!" Genevieve expelled, goggling in alarm at her young sister's idea.

* * *

Father came home just after she blew out her candle for the night. She heard him and Madam coming up the stairs, so she threw aside her warmed bedclothes, slid down from her bed onto the wooden step, and dashed to the door. She opened it a crack to listen.

Lord Bastwicke sounded well pleased as he said in his rich, carrying voice, "Lord Hardwicke and I have decided to call it simply The Marriage Act. We and the committee worked on it since early this morning to finish up what we believe is the final version of instructions to all parish Clergy."

Petulantly, Lady Bastwicke said, "So that is why you did not appear for dinner or supper tonight?"

"Oh, Regina, food does not matter at an exciting time like this. We popped out for some steak and kidney pies at the Olde Cheshire Cheese, and returned to write a clean copy. Now we have it ready." Lord Bastwicke sounded thoroughly proud of their accomplishment. Genevieve wished Madam would praise him for it.

Instead she snapped, "I am thrilled to hear that you get gratification from such a long and stuffy exercise! Meanwhile, I am left to sit at my own table alone."

"Why, weren't the children here?"

"The girls were, but they don't count as people to dine with."

Lord Bastwicke chided her as he ambled by the door where Genevieve listened. "But Regina, they count very much! You should enjoy them."

"Enjoy children? I've suspected that you have been steadily going mad, and now I see that you have finally gone round the bend. Children have nothing to say—unless it's contradictory!" she added bitterly.

Lord Bastwicke's footsteps stopped at his chamber door and, by the sound of his voice, turned to face his wife at hers. "You have to admit that you fire orders at them in a pretty stiff volley, my dear. They have little chance to relax and talk naturally to you. As for contradictory, who has been so?"

"That Genevieve!"

Genevieve winced.

"On what subject does she contradict you?"

"She opposes Sir Pomeroy Chancet as a suitor! And many others as well."

There was a startled silence. Then Lord Bastwicke's deep voice drawled with an undercurrent of iron, "That affected Baronet weighs nothing in the balance. With regard to manhood, he's about as light as one of his lace handkerchiefs. And don't forget what he did to Arabelle! And to me! He is well out of this country, so do not bring that criminal to this family's notice again!"

Lady Bastwicke lifted her chin and hurriedly told him about all of the other men on her list, naming a few she had not even mentioned to Genevieve. "But that stubborn girl won't consider any of them!"

Lord Bastwicke chuckled in a weary way and said, "Good for Genevieve! I heartily agree with her."

That enraged Lady Bastwicke, who exploded, "You always agree with your daughters instead of me! I'll have you know that it's not just Sir Pomeroy she resists. No one on my list is good enough for her!"

"Your list? I told her she can choose her own husband—within reason—so why have you made a list of your own?"

Lady Bastwicke ignored that and rushed on, "I got Lord Ashby, mind you, to join us in the opera box the other night. It wasn't easy. I put him next to Genevieve, but she left!—with him still sitting there! And in the lobby, when he found her again, she let him slip. I could strangle her! She is utterly hopeless."

Lord Bastwicke sounded tired as he said, "I still say, good for her. She's not ready."

Lady Bastwicke screeched, "I am your wife! I decide when daughters are ready to marry or not.

You should always support me, not them! I won't put up with your disloyalty!"

Lord Bastwicke was a man usually slow to anger, but Genevieve wondered how he would handle this. True to his nature, he merely said, "It is not true, my dear, but since you think it is, what will you do with me?"

"Do with you? I shall take you by the scruff of the neck and—"

He interrupted her laughingly, "Scruff of the neck? And what is scruff? I hope I haven't got any."

Genevieve choked on a giggle.

Lady Bastwicke hated his jokes and laughter, especially when she suspected she was the butt of them. Furiously, she cried, "That girl has to marry somebody! Soon! You, as her father, are doing nothing to help. You are gone from home all the time, toiling on a Marriage Act, but acting not at all on plans for your own daughter's marriage. So," she added with redoubled zest, "I will do what I have to do—whether you or Genevieve like it or not."

He drawled ominously, "You will?"

Lady Bastwicke snapped, "Just wait and see!" She slammed her door with resounding vehemence.

After her father's door clicked shut in the distance, Genevieve silently closed her own. That sounded bad indeed. In her moonlit room, she dropped shakily to her knees on the bed step and thanked God for her Father's support. With her forehead against the silken coverlet, she prayed that nothing terrible could transpire from her mother's threats. She thanked God for all her blessings, and finally prayed for a good husband. *Make him a true*

Christian, Lord, because no other kind in this wicked world will understand me, or be of the same mind, or love me without selfishness. Is there anyone for me, Lord? I ask in Jesus' name, amen.

As she settled into the curtained bed she used to share with Arabelle, she wondered what her mother's *Just wait and see* would bring about. What had she written on that paper today? Certainly it was a letter, but to whom? Could it have possibly been to Lord Ashby? No doubt it was already posted, for Madam was never one to delay when she hit upon an idea. Arabelle had been the innocent victim of her impulsive whims, and Genevieve did not want to suffer from that treachery herself.

CHAPTER 3

The Terrifying Lord Ashby

The next afternoon, when Genevieve was bent over in the garden cutting yellow daffodils to match her mother's dinner headdress, she heard the clattering of shoes on the flagstones.

Welford, the young, blond footman, hurried toward her, looking purposeful. "Her Ladyship needs you at once in the drawing room, Miss Genevieve," he said after she acknowledged him. "I will carry those for you, Miss," he said, taking the basket of flowers and the cutters from her.

"Thank you. Will you please cut a dozen of those white ones with the orange centers bobbing by the wall there?"

"I will, but Miss Genevieve, I suggest you wash your hands and tidy your wisps before you go in, if you'll forgive my saying so."

Curiously, she asked, "Why?"

"Because I know that you must look your best for gentlemen callers. Especially Lords." Welford grinned and wiggled his eyebrows.

Genevieve groaned, for her mother had all the servants trained. Genevieve hated to be shown off to men. Madam expected her to shine with allure and sparkle with wit . . . somehow. She also knew that, if she did not appear immediately when Madam summoned, she would call up the staircase in an artificially sweet voice until Genevieve did appear. That had happened before. She could not pretend to be absent from the house, or asleep in her room, or out of earshot up in the nursery, for Madam would hound her to the top of the attics or depths of the wine cave if necessary.

As she drew near the drawing room, Genevieve paused at the gilt-framed mirror in the hall and licked her palms. She pressed them to the sides of her head, trying to slick back her untidy hair. She wound the coppery curls hanging from her chignon around a finger to make them neater. They were falling out of curl because of their weight and because she had been outside in the damp breeze. Drawing a determined breath, she glided between the fringed curtains of the doorway into the drawing room.

Gleefully, her mother was exclaiming to someone, "How fortunate that you will be in France when we are! I, myself, have a recent invitation to absolutely the grandest château in France. I leave soon, and will take Genevieve with me. Will you, also, be in the Loire Valley or thereabouts?"

Genevieve's jaw dropped. Madam was taking her to France? To whom was she telling this news, and hoping he would be there? She thought Sir Pomeroy Chancet was already in France. Her heart thumped wildly. The yellow feathers topping

Madam's coiffure curled forward toward a man standing behind the potted palm, his back to Genevieve. Moving forward, she saw a sleek brown wig that lay smooth over the crown, the queue tied with a black bow and a silver buckle. He turned his head and she saw his profile. Radford Laurence, Lord Ashby.

He turned, smiled, and bowed his head to her. "Good afternoon, Miss Genevieve."

She curtseyed to him while her mother eyed them like a falcon.

"Miss Genevieve," he said in his well-timbered voice, "what an enchanting afternoon this is." His hazel eyes told her that he found her to be what enchanted it. "Is it the same for you?"

"Yes, it was, Lord Ashby," she returned contrarily, looking away from him to the French windows, where narcissi backlit by the sun swayed in the windy garden.

"Was?" he repeated. "The afternoon *was* enchanting?"

To foil her mother, she said, "While I was out there cutting flowers, yes."

She saw her mother's fiery eyes boring into her.

"Pardon me," Genevieve said toward their visitor, not looking at him as she forced herself to take a chair. She dared not say any more to pull herself out of her pit. Had he uttered a little chuckle? She did not dare to look at him to find out. She sat rebelliously regarding her shoe tips. One green brocade shoe had mud ground into it. She pulled it back beneath her flounce.

Lady Bastwicke sat stiffly with her rust and yellow print gown arrayed for many feet on either side of her. She said, "Are we not fortunate to have Lord Ashby call on us, Genevieve dear? His Lordship has been telling of his plans to travel to France again. Ask him where he is going."

Genevieve cocked her chin and quizzed him with stilted obedience, "Yes, please tell us, Lord Ashby, where in France you plan to go."

Looking faintly amused, he said, "I will visit Chartres mainly."

Genevieve, because it was expected of her, pressed on, "When do you travel?"

"In three days, I believe."

Lady Bastwicke smacked her hands together and exclaimed, "That is exactly when *I* am planning to leave! My, how fortuitous this is." She leaned earnestly forward, appealing to him. "Can we travel together?"

He looked rather stunned.

Genevieve tried to hide her smile, but she knew he saw it anyway. Her mother had obviously made up this plan on the spot.

He said, "That is certainly an interesting thought, Lady Bastwicke. Hmmm. My plans are already laid, but, ah . . . may I consider your offer until, say, tomorrow afternoon?"

"Of course, Lord Ashby!" she gushed. "I will continue packing for the journey, but you must know that my outriders will be well armed, and the baggage coaches will have extra space for all of your trunks. You could send them here tomorrow evening for packing."

Genevieve did not know where to look. His Lordship was being herded into a plan. It would be fascinating to see how he extricated himself.

Resolving suddenly to help him out if she could, Genevieve rose when he stood to leave. "I shall see our guest out," she said to her mother.

Lady Bastwicke looked nonplussed. Then, apparently thinking that Genevieve might be adhering to her orders to put herself forward with this prospective suitor by snatching a private interlude, she smiled widely at the bachelor Earl, waved him off, and stayed where she was.

He looked pleased as Genevieve lifted his tri-cornered hat from the hall table and handed it to him. He murmured, "Here's my hat, where's my hurry?"

She couldn't resist a grin. "Thank you for calling upon us, Lord Ashby."

He said behind his glove, "You know I prefer Radford."

She could not sustain contact with his admiring eyes, but she was determined to have private words no matter how ill-at-ease she felt. She heard a creak, and smelled her mother's perfume behind the draped doorway, so she walked out the front door, which Welford promptly opened wide. On the outside steps, Genevieve motioned for him to close the door.

Thus, she and Lord Ashby were alone, overlooking Bloomsbury Square, where the cool breeze wobbled the tree branches and set the yellow daffodils dancing. A dog barked, and the clip-clop of a rider's horse sounded from across the square.

Lord Ashby said, "I am honored that you have seen fit to send me off in this gracious way yourself."

"It's not that I am so gracious," she returned. "In fact, I believe you must think that your visit to this house has been unnerving. I am sorry that my mother tried to maneuver you into her plans. No, let me finish while I can," she added breathlessly. She glanced back over her shoulder at the window beside the door. Only the footman's back was visible.

Genevieve found that she earnestly wished Radford Laurence the best. He was actually a good man, and so close to Arabelle's husband. He should not have to knuckle under to Madam's dictates. What could she say to him? She decided to blurt out the bald truth. "Radford, she wants you as a suitor for me." Genevieve looked him in the eyes for a truthful instant as a hot blush rose up her face.

His brown eyebrows lifted. He seemed to be tamping down his reaction. "Is that so?"

Though it pained her, she said, "Yes! She has just yesterday asked me whom I will accept as a husband—from a list! Because I did not latch onto any from her list, I am undergoing the rack."

"I am very sorry that that is the case. I can see you do not like the rack. And I suspect that I am part of the torture."

"It is harrowing!" she threw back. Meeting the glint in his eyes, she laughed weakly and looked away.

He moved a step closer and asked quietly, "How would you, yourself, wish the business of arriving at marriage to be arranged?"

Genevieve burst out, "Not to be arranged at all! I want to fall in love—I mean I want to choose my own husband." She crossed her arms and met his interested look with a flash of spirit. "I know it is unusual in society such as ours, but my father has assured me that I *may* have a say in choosing with whom I share the rest of my life. His only concern—and it is a very big issue with him—is that he should approve the man before I marry him. That is as it should be," added the daughter who had tried to elope a week earlier.

"Well said," approved Radford. "Your father obviously trusts your judgment."

Genevieve bit her lip and blurted out, "I do not deserve that, but he does trust me now. Madam, however, has lost patience with me. She declared last night that she will *do something* to make a marriage happen for me."

"I sympathize with you."

"You do?"

He nodded. "I do. You are living in dread."

Genevieve could not tell if he was serious or not. "Thank you, Radford," she said cautiously, flicking a shy glance over him and reaching for the door lever. "Now I must go, for I see my mother's earrings glinting through the window. Will you help me to see that she will not win in her terrifying plans for me?"

Genevieve could not be sure what his small salute meant. She wondered if she had left him confused, hurt, or chuckling.

CHAPTER 4

The Marriage Act

Lord Bastwicke entered the house that night and called, "Regina! Come see your husband, if you please." His voice resounded up the staircase, sure to be heard in every room provided the doors were open, and in some rooms with the doors shut. The latter was Genevieve's case, so she flung it open and hurried out.

Lady Bastwicke emerged from the drawing room in stately grandeur, petulantly asking, "What is it now?"

Lord Bastwicke's jubilant voice matched the odd hop and skip he made. "The Marriage Act!" he boomed.

Genevieve, watching from the landing, giggled to see her father display the joy he felt in such a physical way. Was this her dignified father? She hurried to the top of the stairs where she could see him better. He grinned broadly up at her and waved his arms. "The Marriage Act is final, Genevieve! It's ready to go into effect on the twenty-sixth! Woo-hoo!"

Genevieve felt glad for her father that his task with Lord Hardwicke and the rest of the committee had reached a successful end. Then a pang of guilt assailed her. She knew that her own attempted elopement had given him a burning impetus to see an ironclad law against marriages taking place without parental and congregational consent. But she was quite certain that he had forgiven her for her childish mistake. She felt that she had grown up since then.

Crisply, Lady Bastwicke said, "Oh, goodie. Now I won't have to hear about it every time I happen to glimpse you. Will you be home for dinners now instead of working with your cronies on that thing late into the nights? Can I invite people to dinner parties here with you actually seated at the head of your table?"

Lord Bastwicke looked momentarily deflated. "I promise to be home a little more, Lady mine." Lady Bastwicke found herself snatched by the waist and kissed resoundingly on her rouged cheek.

She drew back instantly, frowning into his face. "What are you doing?"

"Kissing you! Wildly hoping that you'll share my joy. I am so relieved that our Genevieve, there," he met her eyes over Madam's head, "will not be able to contract a marriage without our approval. No one in England can marry her without calling the Banns for three weeks in a row, in church."

"What does that mean?" asked Lenora, bounding into sight. "Calling what bands, Father?"

"Banns, Lenora, banns!" cried Lord Bastwicke. "Public proclamation is what it means. You could also say that there will be a ban on your marrying some dicey bloke I don't approve of, young lady," he continued, letting go of his wife and scooping up his child. "The clergyman will stand before the congregation when the sermon is concluded, and announce that Lord So-and-So of Such-and-Such a place wishes to marry Miss Lenora Lamar, spinster, of Bastwicke House in this parish. If there is anyone in the congregation who knows of an impediment to the marriage, they must say so during the three times in three weeks that this announcement is made."

Lenora stared at him.

Lady Bastwicke gaped. "All that has to happen before the congregation?"

"Naturally."

Lady Bastwicke cried, "But that's terrible! How embarrassing to be called a spinster, eh, Genevieve? Even if it fits?"

Little Lenora patted her father's face and looked thoughtful. She asked, "What if somebody objects, Father?"

"Aren't you the smart little thinker? Then they cannot be married until the reason is investigated. This prevents unsuitable marriages from taking place behind parents' or guardians' backs. And if there is a legal issue, a couple cannot be married unless the legal impediment is removed."

Genevieve asked, "What if someone objects, and there really is no legal reason to prevent the wedding after all?"

"They'll be put in gaol for wrongfully disturbing the proceedings."

Lenora nodded. "That's good, Father. You did a

wonderful job on everything, I can tell."

Genevieve laughed, but corroborated by saying, "You've obviously covered all eventualities."

Father was smiling widely. He nuzzled Lenora's little nose with his big one, making her giggle. She poked at it and said, "Pickle-nose!"

He pinched hers and retorted, "Gherkin-snout!"

Lady Bastwicke drawled, "How life does change! Why *you* have to be one who changes it so ludicrously is beyond me. Will it not sound ridiculous to have such things announced in church, of all places? Why not read the social gossip there, too, and ask if everyone approves of Lady M's meeting Sir Q on the bowling lawn behind the Mansion House at midnight?"

That had been the end of that conversation, for her father blew out a breath, set Lenora down, took off his wig, scratched his closely-shaved head, opened his powder room door, threw the wig in, and headed up the stairs.

Lady Bastwicke shooed Welford, who was standing in the hall, away to the servant's hall, for she was mortified every time her husband removed his wig. She journeyed up the stairs after her husband, hissing, "For mercy sakes, can't you wait until you're in your bedchamber to take that off?"

When Lord Bastwicke rounded the corner and doubled back at the landing, Genevieve saw that his face still looked happy at his success with the Marriage Act. She winked hugely up at him, and he winked back.

Genevieve knew that he had saved her from a precipitous marriage, an ill-advised one to boot, and she was humbly grateful that he had also kept it quiet from her mother.

* * *

With the first post the next morning, letters arrived from Arabelle. Genevieve received one privately from Welford's hand. She gave him his sixpence and sneaked upstairs to read it since Lord and Lady Bastwicke were each opening their letters at the breakfast table.

17th March 1754

Dearest Genevieve,

How I miss you! Try not to worry about Sir Pomeroy pursuing you since he is out of the country. I know, because my husband told me. He said that Sir P is not allowed back in England.

As I will ride to visit tenants in a few minutes, I will dash down this news. There is a young lady whom Aunt Claracilla feels some pity for. After hearing about you, Genevieve, this lady would like to come and stay with you. She is a Miss Doyle, but that is all I know about her. We played with her when you were about nine, she ten, and I eleven. Do you remember her? I have not seen her since then.

I will tell Father and Madam about her in my letters today, but I wanted you to know in case they forget to mention it to you. I would recommend that you keep our bedchamber, which is now yours, as yours alone. If Miss Doyle stays with you, have Madam give her a guest chamber. That way, you will still have a place to call your own. I am cautious because I don't know if this girl has improved in character or not. She is the guest who poured water down my neck instead of into my mouth when we were playing doctor's visit—remember? You used to call her 'That girl who poured water down your neck.'

Please come and visit me whenever you are carted to Bastwicke Chase. I am enjoying your letters so much, so keep them coming.

My Love sends you his love, as he has just put his head over my shoulder to snoop into what I am writing. This is the reason for the ink spots!

Kiss Lenora and Jerome for me. The kitten they gave him has kittens! I hope they can come and see.

Your loving sister,
Arabelle

* * *

The Bastwicke house was cast into a mild uproar later, with Lord Bastwicke remarking, "Wasn't that a bit presumptuous not to wait for our reply? I certainly don't want some strange woman invading our premises without a by-your-leave!"

Thereupon he left the house, for Madam flew into a flurry. She fired orders at Bertha Blumm, the dour Scots abigail, to get a room ready "since we're to be saddled with some little charity chit. I shall send her back tomorrow, so she'll only need a room for the night."

It was that very evening that Dorcasta Doyle arrived. She was a fresh-faced lady, short and plump, of twenty years. Her wiry brown hair was pulled back, and small corkscrew curls flipped out from her thick chignon in many directions. She kept uncertainly smiling when she was introduced to each family member. Genevieve could see that she felt overawed by the group they made. Furthermore, she arrived just as they sat down to dinner, which caused Welford to hastily make a place for her. He whisked a plate, goblets, and silver, a linen napkin and salt cellar, and gestured for her to be seated in the chair he held. She looked bewildered when he waited for her to rise a bit so he could push her chair closer to the table.

Lady Bastwicke said witheringly, "Miss Doyle, our footman is waiting to push your chair in."

Looking panicked, she eventually figured it out. By then, her face was red. Nevertheless, she tried to smile at them from time to time, hunting for a friendly face amongst those curiously looking her over.

Genevieve gave her a smile or two, but she could not force a genuine one due to the fact that she knew nothing whatsoever about her character, and that was what mattered most. She kept wondering what induced this young woman to come here uninvited.

Lady Bastwicke talked loftily over Miss Doyle's head, directing her statements at her husband at the opposite end of the table, prosing on about vaulted persons whom their guest could not possibly know.

Miss Doyle's demeanor improved when she was alone with Genevieve in the drawing room. She looked around the richly furnished expanse with wondering eyes and exclaimed, "I am so privileged to stay here!" She gazed at the paintings, squinted at the flaming chandelier above her, and gingerly stooped to examine the glass items from Venice on display. She exclaimed over the orange silk gown that Lady Bastwicke had worn at dinner, and even the red silk poppies in Lady Bastwicke's hair, as well as her pearl eardrops with the matching brooch, necklace, and four rings.

Lady Bastwicke, walking in upon her gushing, looked highly gratified. She began to play the patronizing Viscountess to the hilt. She let drop to the girl that her silk had come from the Far East, and none of her friends had seen such a print before.

Miss Doyle cast down her eyelids and said, "What a high lady you are, Lady Bastwicke. I only wear cotton or wool, as no one has ever bought me anything finer."

"You poor thing," remarked Lady Bastwicke without conviction.

Genevieve decided it was time to usher Miss Doyle up the two flights of stairs to a guest chamber overlooking the back garden. As soon as their guest walked in, she exclaimed over the pale blue walls and the flowered blue and white bed curtains.

Genevieve said, "I am glad you find this chamber suitable."

"Oh, far more than suitable, Miss Lamar!" she exclaimed. "It is too good of you to give me such a magnificent room!"

"Not at all, Miss Doyle. Ah," she added, seeing Welford carrying a trunk and bandbox up the stairs, "I see that your luggage has arrived. I shall leave you now."

The next morning, they chatted at breakfast, with Miss Doyle revealing that she lived with an elderly aunt in Rye on the southeast coast because her father died when she was very young. Her mother was ill and in bed these days. Dorcasta had been educated at a local school from age seven to ten years old, but not since. "Like I told Lord and Lady B, I have never been nowhere or seen nothing. Until now." She spread her arms and smiled widely at Genevieve. "Now I am suddenly in London!—with your wonderful family. I must pinch myself."

CHAPTER 5

A Musical Interlude

"The fault with you, Genevieve—one of them— is that you have no idea how to interest men." Upon the words, Lady Bastwicke snapped her fingers. "You need to take some quick lessons."

"Lessons? From whom?"

Her mother looked affronted. "From me, of course!" Covered with a muslin cape, she leaned toward her vanity mirror and powdered her pale red hair carefully with gray powder dipped with a brush from a silver pot. "You must come with me and learn from my style. First, go get dressed." She continued to apply the smoky powder all over her hair in front. "Bertha, you must coat the sides and back."

It fascinated Genevieve that her mother was coating her hair with gray powder. It was rumored to be the new style for ladies of quality. That was what Shrubsole Curling had told them, and she had, in fact, seen two ladies at the opera who obviously used it. Madam herself had tried it once before.

Genevieve asked with sinking spirits, "Must we go somewhere?"

"Yes, I am going to Mrs. Ellwood's soirée and you are coming with me. Don't just stand there staring—hurry, scurry! Wait! Bertha, what am I wearing?"

The broad-shouldered Bertha was stooping over a drawer at the bottom of Lady Bastwicke's enormous armoire, pulling out stockings and ribbon garters. "Ooof!" she expelled, rising. Her angular face was ruddier than ever with her exertions. "I laid out the apricot with blood-red stripe, My Lady." She lifted the lace-embellished sleeve of a gleaming gown lying in an enormous pile on the bed.

"Good. Genevieve, go put on something that won't clash with me."

"Yes, Madam," Genevieve concurred meekly, backing out of her chamber. *Or take the eye away from you,* she thought. Therefore, she donned an ivory and aqua print silk gown with a brocade corset to match. Aqua *échelles* in a neat row ran down the front in slightly smaller bows until the one at the V below her waist was but an inch wide. The lace ruffles cascading over her forearms were edged where they met the sleeve with aqua ribbon. The effect was quite pleasing. She put on the aqua brocade shoes that William Chamberlain, their skillful cordwainer, had made for her a month ago from the same fabric as her corset stomacher. The effect in the full-length mirror was harmonious. If only her hair could be dressed by the best . . . but she banished Shrubsole Curling quickly from her mind.

"I will do your hair," said Bertha after a quarter hour, lumbering into the room, making the floorboards creak.

"That's good. I was certain you would have to spend all of your time on Madam. Is she ready and waiting for me?"

"All but her rouge and eardrops," replied Bertha, snatching the hairbrush and pulling Genevieve's hairpins out, "but she can do that herself." Bertha brushed hair remarkably nicely for such a rough-edged woman. That fact had never ceased to amaze Arabelle and Genevieve, for, by the belligerent way Bertha usually talked and the ungainly way she moved, one would expect her to yank one's hair, but she did not. She seemed to like arranging hair. It seemed to be her best creative effort.

Soon Genevieve's hair was smoothly pulled back and securely pinned. When she lifted her mirror to see the sides and back, she found that her chignon was looped around in an intricate new way. It coiled and twisted from her nape to her crown at the back of her head.

"How did you do that?" Genevieve asked, impressed. "The design is so artistic."

"Your hair is longer now. It can take an extra loop, and it gives you a better profile." Bertha pulled stray hairs out of the brush and threw the brush onto the vanity, screwed the hair around her finger, and shoved it into a round wooden box where she saved her ladies' hair. Later, she would arrange little pictures in frames by using it.

Genevieve felt much more grown-up in the new style. "Thank you, Bertha. It is very comely. I like it very well."

The woman blushed and turned away to bang the armoire door shut.

When Genevieve entered the carriage after Lady Bastwicke's enormous skirts, she was astonished to see that Dorcasta Doyle sat inside. She was dressed in one of the gowns Arabelle had left at home. Genevieve did not dare to comment, but her first outraged thought was that Madam had not told her of this inclusion. She wanted to remark that the vivid blue gown was too strong a color for Dorcasta Doyle's freckled skin, and that Arabelle's gown should not have been loaned without her permission. Even Genevieve did not wear Arabelle's things, but saved them in her armoire for when her sister came to London. It saved her packing so many trunks. But apparently Dorcasta did not have an evening gown suitable in which to accompany Lady Bastwicke out on the town.

Genevieve decided to be kind, and said, "I hope you had everything you needed in your room."

"Oh, much more than I needed!" Dorcasta cried. She suddenly stopped, her nose twitched, and she sneezed into her sleeve. "Oops, pardon me! I have come away with no handkerchief!"

"How could you?" Lady Bastwicke quizzed her. "You must always, but *always,* carry two in your pocket."

"Yes, My Lady. I am sorry; I am such an idiot."

Lady Bastwicke said starchily, "Well, yes."

Genevieve handed her second embroidered handkerchief to Dorcasta. "Here, you may take one of mine tonight."

Lady Bastwicke, reprovingly smug, said, "There,

Miss Doyle, is one reason why every lady should carry two. After you use one, you will need another one. But in this case, Genevieve must relinquish one of her supply to a poor planner." Lady Bastwicke eyed her sternly.

Their guest cringed. "Yes, My Lady. Thank you, Miss Genevieve. I will not let it happen again. I think I will have to make some somehow." She reverently fingered the pristine cotton with embroidery upon it in Genevieve's own golden stitches. It was a Copperplate style forming the quote, *Be still, and know that I am God.*

As they rounded a corner following the outriders who carried flaming torches ahead of the coach horses, Dorcasta said, "I promise I will give this back to you." With a burst of an idea, she added, "But I will wash it first."

Genevieve caught her mother's eye, and they both lifted them heavenward. It was rare that they saw eye-to-eye on anything.

When they were announced at the house in Berkeley Square, Genevieve placed herself behind her mother and succeeded in remaining unseen by the male eyes that riveted curiously toward them. Dorcasta received their full glare, however; and as the butler trumpeted, "Lady Bastwicke, her daughter, Miss Genevieve Lamar, and Miss Dorcasta Doyle," the latter gasped in pleasure. It took her no time at all to smile in awe at all the attention. Madam was receiving the bows, but Dorcasta reveled in reflected glory. She kept bobbing jerky curtsies with both knees at everyone she looked at. It was embarrassing to watch.

The dark and diminutive Lady Chesterfield

smiled invitingly at Genevieve, so she moved to her side and gave her a graceful curtsy. It was while telling her news of Arabelle that Genevieve saw Radford Laurence walk in. Tall and attractive in a bottle green brocade fitted coat, long waistcoat, and breeches, snowy jabot and lace cuffs, he smiled at her even before he was announced. While people were greeting him, he moved past them all until he stood before her and Lady Chesterfield. After bowing over the older woman's hand, he took Genevieve's fingers and kissed them. "How good it is to see you," he said.

Genevieve flushed. In her vivid memory, she felt again the chagrin of standing before him in only her undergarments, and his saying, "I hope to see more of you." Why did that statement always have to leap into her mind and fluster her?

Behind her fan, she asked him, "Is there any chance that you could refrain from saying such things to me?"

"I beg your pardon?"

Genevieve wanted to hedge and retract her daft request, but since a man had moved to talk to Lady Chesterfield, Genevieve decided to be frank with Radford. "It always puts me agonizingly in mind of the first time we saw each other," she said, feeling her face heat up.

"Ah! And to what did you object in my behavior just now?"

"Don't talk of *seeing* me!" Genevieve threw at him.

His lips curved. Thoughtfully, he queried, "May I get down on my knees and beg your forgiveness once and for all?" To her horror, he made as if to descend to one knee.

"No!" She grasped his arm to stop him, and felt eyes looking at them. "What must those people think?" she whispered, turning her shoulder slowly away from the crowd while eyeing him sidewise with warning.

Lady Chesterfield was giving them her full attention now.

He said, "I'm sorry, I thought I was being funny. Walk with me, please." He led her toward the French doors that stood open. "Were you afraid that they all thought I was about to declare myself? —in such a public setting?"

"Yes! Possibly! Don't do such things in view of others; it will be misconstrued. There are the most pernicious gossips in London!"

"Would it be acceptable in private?" he threw back with a saucy smile that she had never expected from him.

"Lord Ashby!" she expelled under her breath, glancing warily at him. Past his shoulder, she could see people edging toward them, and one man was watching them through his quizzing glass.

Lady Bastwicke spoke animatedly to another woman behind her huge fan while her small eyes remained pinned expectantly on Genevieve and Radford.

Genevieve whispered, "What do they all think? Please, lead me out of here! But no, if we disappear outside, they will press their noses to the windows, thinking we're up to something."

"Would that be so bad?" he asked quietly, searching her eyes for an instant as he moved her nonchalantly away from the French doors and straight to the alcove where a page was ladling out punch.

Genevieve did not reply, but cast him a half-fearful, grateful look before accepting a cup. She lifted it in thanks, and walked away from him. He looked dismayed, but she did not like being thrown into a situation with him under all the inquisitive stares.

The evening gave her a legitimate respite from talking with him more, for it was a musical evening. Guests were invited to take seats in a fanned-out arrangement. Lady Bastwicke took a chair without arms at the front, where her grand striped gown spread out over three of the seats. Her gold jewelry glowed in the light of several flaming *girandoles* upon the sideboards and walls. She preened her high feather headdress, keeping it in constant motion.

Next to her gown sat Dorcasta, looking squeezed into the blue evening gown. The crisscross lacing in front looked near to bursting and fit very ill. Genevieve, in her aqua and white ensemble, sank next to her, collapsing her panniers neatly. A portly, perfumed gentleman in a long, old-fashioned curled wig came to sit beside her with his lady.

While the chamber music played, a woman sang, and Dorcasta sat transfixed. Genevieve leaned over and said behind her fan, "Do you like her aria?"

"Is that the lace thing she has on her head?"

Genevieve choked back a laugh. "No, an aria is the musical piece she is singing. It's from the opera, *Florindo and Daphne*, by Handel."

"Oh!" Dorcasta said, all at sea. She turned her head to look at whoever it was taking a seat behind her. Genevieve felt that to crane one's neck to look back was vulgar in any setting, and felt chagrined by Dorcasta Doyle, who alerted to look at anything and everything that moved. After inspecting what was going on over her shoulder, Miss Doyle suddenly sat up straight. She schooled her countenance into a beatific expression with her eyes upon the singer. When the soprano came to a sad portion, Dorcasta grappled for her faded cotton pocket, loosened its strings, and plunged her hand inside, groping until she withdrew the handkerchief that Genevieve had loaned her. She dabbed at her eyes. Genevieve failed to see any tears there, and realized that she was performing for some person behind them.

When applause broke out and people rose to their feet, Dorcasta made an about-face and intensified her smile. Genevieve casually stood and turned to see who on earth it was who affected their guest so. It was none other than Radford Laurence.

He smiled at Genevieve and said, "If you will walk this way with me, I have something to give you."

"You do?" She stepped through the gap he had made for her by removing a vacated chair.

Dorcasta watched her and Radford jealously. Perhaps she should have introduced them, but it was too late now, Genevieve decided, since he had not cast even a curious glance in her direction.

Revealing what he had been hiding behind his back, he produced a sweetmeat to Genevieve on a tiny porcelain plate.

"Oh, thank you, I like these," she said with a smile. "Where did you find it?"

He grinned. "I took it from the table before I sat

down, and have been looking at it longingly through that ear-splitting performance."

She giggled. "Then why didn't you eat it?"

"Because I was manfully saving it for you. It was the last good one."

She was biting the sugared cherry anchored in a chocolate square when he said that. She halted mid-chew and flicked a remorseful look at him.

He burst out laughing. "No, it's yours! Eat it with joy."

She swallowed and objected, "But you said it was the last good one. What did you mean?"

"Only that the others had flaws."

"What kind of flaws?" she asked, savoring the rich chocolate and burst of cherry sauce inside.

He said, looking solemnly at her, "The squares were not square."

"Oh! And I just ate mine without remarking upon its perfection."

"Yes, you did, and I am crushed."

She laughed, and liked the way his eyes crinkled at the corners.

Behind him, she saw Dorcasta Doyle watching them intently. Someone should tell her that it was *gauche* to stare.

* * *

That night, when Genevieve was cleaning her teeth, she heard a knock at her bedchamber door. After rinsing with water, she went to see who it was, and there stood Dorcasta Doyle. She wore a nightcap and was huddling in an unbleached muslin nightrail, holding her candlestick. "I thought I should come and visit you," she said, tipping her head and smiling.

With hesitation, Genevieve said, "Come in for a minute, Miss Doyle. Why don't you sit there and wrap yourself in that shawl? You look like you're shivering." She pointed to the shawl on the pink and yellow striped settee beside the fireplace with its glowing coals. "Is there something I can do for you?"

Settling her candle down and pulling her feet under her, she said, "Oh, please call me Dorcasta. I loved the musical party tonight so much, Genevieve. I wish I could sing like that."

Genevieve stifled a yawn. "Do you sing at all?"

"Oh, yes, all the time! But I never dare to let anyone hear me."

"Why is that?"

"I'm too afraid that I don't sound good."

Genevieve thought that here was a girl who, though older than she was, had never had the encouragement of someone like her own Aunt Claracilla, who had given her and Arabelle all kinds of lessons, including singing. "You can sing for me, and perhaps I can tell you if you could become better by practice."

"You would really do that? For me?"

"If you like."

"But I am terrified to let you hear my voice. Not after the voice we heard tonight."

"She has had years and years of training, and many performances. Do not contrast yourself with someone like an opera singer. Just sing some little thing for me."

Dorcasta took a few deep breaths, but her eyes,

though uncertain, glinted with something like gratification.

"Anything you like," prompted Genevieve, wanting to crawl into bed.

"But won't other people hear?"

"Who? The children are sleeping in their room at the top of the house, and Father is not come home yet."

"What about Lady Bastwicke?"

"She is gone out again with her friends. I expect she won't hear from the middle of London."

"All right." Dorcasta took a deep breath and sang in a quavering, high voice,

"Ah, love, how can I leave thee?
The sad thought deep doth grieve me;
But know, whate'er befalls me,
I go where honor calls me.
Farewell, farewell, my own true love!
Farewell, farewell, my own true love!"

Genevieve said, "You sang that nicely, and I like the way you echoed that last line softer."

"Truly?" Dorcasta was alert in every line of her body, so great seemed her delight at Genevieve's praise. "Can I really sing, do you think?"

"Why not?" Genevieve yawned hugely behind her hand. "You should sing more since you enjoy it."

"So I have a nice voice?" Dorcasta jumped off the settee and ran to Genevieve, flinging her arms around her. "Thank you so much!" Leaning back and gazing up into her face, she declared, "You don't know what it means to me to have you say such good things about me. I cannot believe it! About *me*.”

“Well, I hope you’ll try to believe what I say.” Genevieve said, with exhaustion compelling her to move toward her bed and throw off her wrapper. “Good night.”

Looking deflated, Dorcasta finally left.

Thereafter, she seemed to take Genevieve at her word, and could be heard singing in her bedchamber at odd times the next day. She seemed to become louder and more confident because Lady Bastwicke heard it echoing down the corridor. She asked Genevieve, “Why is that girl singing? Does she think she has a voice?”

“She was so impressed by the musical soirée that she said she would love to sing herself. So I told her to do it. I gave her leave to practice all the songs she knows. I hope you don’t mind?”

“Mind? It sounds horrible, but today it might do us very well,” said Lady Bastwicke, who appeared to be forming a plan. “Send her down to entertain us. I do not have any wish to talk to the ancient spinsters in the drawing room, but I want to talk to their brother. That’s why they’re coming; he arranged it,” she said slyly. “Have Dorcasta come down and sing to the ladies so I can talk to him without those hens listening. Hurry, scurry! I think they’ve arrived.”

Genevieve hurried back up the white marble stairs and soon escorted Dorcasta down them despite her terrified whispers of protestation. “You are good enough to sing to these ladies. One will probably talk the whole time, and the other is practically deaf. You can do it.”

After urging her with more praise and nudges, Genevieve introduced her to the two garish old women. Soon she was singing "The Soldier's Farewell" to them. At the end, one of them, who had joined in with a croaking voice, sniffled sentimentally into her handkerchief. When they had clapped Dorcasta's efforts and asked if she knew another song, she launched into "Gaily the Troubadour."

Lady Bastwicke was flirting with the man called Mr. Wylie Hobbin, for Genevieve riffled through the calling cards on the salver and saw his name. While she was so doing in the entry hall, the knocker sounded, making her jump.

Welford sprang to open the door. In walked Radford Laurence, removing his tricorne. When he saw her, he smiled.

Genevieve gave him a little curtsy. "Lord Ashby! How do you happen to honor our house again, so soon?"

"Am I not fully welcome, then, Miss Genevieve?"

"Of course you are welcome, but what brings you?"

"Did you forget already? I am to travel with you to France."

Genevieve's mouth formed an O.

He chuckled. "You did not think I would accept the invitation?"

"No! I thought you were being politely evasive, and I was silently applauding you."

His eyebrows lifted. "Well, something about the trip excites my dull imagination, so I came to deliver my trunks as bidden."

Had he said *excites* his imagination? His cheerful

bearing confirmed that he looked forward to it because of her.

There was a bit more to this Radford Laurence than she had realized. Her thoughts flitted from the fact that she would be in his company for several days, and the regret that he should see what her mother was like on a day-to-day basis. He could take a dislike to her, too, tarring them both with the same brush. But perhaps he would remember that Arabelle, whom he knew better than he knew Genevieve, was the complete opposite of their mother. That should carry some weight.

Trying to relax in that thought, Genevieve said, "You are astonishingly good to escort us all the way to France, Lord Ashby."

"Please, leave off calling me Lord Ashby, will you? You know that my Christian name is Radford, so please do me the honor of calling me by it, as I have just used yours. Do you have any objection either way, Genevieve?"

She flicked a look his way and said, "We shall see." She truly did not want, or dare, to allow herself a nearer relation to any man until she knew much more about him. She felt that Father would agree with her new resolve.

* * *

Genevieve was almost asleep that night when she heard rapping at her door. She wondered, as she rose, if it was Lenora. She already had little Jerome in bed with her, for the children sometimes said they were scared of lightning and thunder, and came to spend the night with her. Tonight, Jerome said something was knocking on the nursery window. Even though it was just a tree branch in the wind, Genevieve gladly took him to snuggle with her.

It was Dorcasta who stood there again in the silvery light spreading from a high window over the landing, for the moon was sailing past the treetops. "What do you need?" Genevieve whispered.

Dorcasta looked up at her beguilingly. "Just you to talk to, if you do not mind. I am quite alone with my thoughts."

"I see. Aren't we always? Well, come in for a few minutes, but since my mother and I leave early in the morning, we must get as much sleep as we can."

"Oh yes, of course! I'm sorry. Shall I go?"

Genevieve yawned and said, "A few minutes shouldn't hurt." Mentally, she rolled her eyes.

When Dorcasta came in and settled on the settee, Genevieve stood and waited, eyeing Jerome's bundle and hoping he wouldn't waken. Furthermore, she was not in the mood to sit down for a comfortable coze with this uninvited guest.

Dorcasta seemed to struggle for words. "I—I just want to say, first of all, how beautiful you are. I so admire you, and I can see that everybody else does, too."

"Indeed!"

"Oh yes, especially men," continued Dorcasta.

"How can you possibly tell that?"

"I have seen how their eyes light up when they see you, and how they follow you across a room when you have no idea."

"It is certainly true that I have no idea," said Genevieve, tapping her foot.

"I especially noted how that handsome Lord Ashby came to sit behind you at the musical sorbet, even though there were many other seats he could have sat upon."

Genevieve, fighting to control her giggle, said nothing.

Dorcasta continued, "I do wish that I could be interesting to men, but I do not have all the expensive clothes, rich relatives, beauty, height, skinniness, or any of that!" She ended on a tragic note.

Genevieve went to press her shoulder. "You possess prettiness, especially when you smile," she said, being exceedingly generous. "If you want better gowns, you could acquire some more, could you not?" She hoped that was true, but she vowed that she would not let her keep wearing Arabelle's gowns without her knowledge or approval. "Gowns of your own size, not someone else's, would help you."

"Really?" Dorcasta cried, rising in pitch. "I have a pretty smile?"

Jerome sat up, startling Dorcasta by his presence. He rubbed his eyes and stared at her, his dark hair sticking out every which way.

"Yes," affirmed Genevieve, going to snuff one bedside candle so Dorcasta would take the hint.

"Oh. But I wish I had more talents, and everything that you have."

"You can sing."

"Well, at least *you* said I could . . ."

"The ladies enjoyed it today. Why not practice

every day where no one can hear you? Your voice will get looser and better, and you will feel happier, too, I believe."

Dorcasta leaped up and assaulted her with a hug around her elbows while Jerome stared. "I will! If you think I should, I will. I want to be like you, and you know what to do, so I shall be your pupil and practice what you say."

Jerome piped up, "Genevieve always knows what to do. She's smart."

Genevieve smiled at him in amazement, and then wearily turned to Dorcasta. "I hope you feel better now. Go get some sleep."

Jerome echoed authoritatively, "Right! Go get some sleep. A lot of it."

Dorcasta's mouth fell open as she looked at the handsome boy. She moved toward the door. "Thank you so much, Genevieve. You are now a friend to me."

"Good night." As she closed the door and locked it, Genevieve missed her sister, Arabelle, more than ever. It had not felt right with Dorcasta in her room, forcing herself into some sort of intimacy.

She vaulted up the bedside steps and grabbed Jerome. "You little wiseacre!" She kissed him on the cheek.

He giggled and said, "I got rid of her!"

Tucking him under the covers, she whispered, "Aren't you clever! Thank you, Lovey."

CHAPTER 6

The Purpose is Men

Genevieve greatly regretted that Father was not going to France with them. He had come to Genevieve's room to kiss her good-bye the morning of their departure, saying, "God go with you, precious. Listen to your conscience in everything."

"Yes, Father; with God's help, I will."

"Remember not to give in to anything that feels wrong. Pray daily for wisdom and guidance, and remember Philippians 4:13, which is?"

"*I can do all things through Christ which strengtheneth me.*"

"That's the one. Write to me, my dear, as soon as you get to your destination in France, and keep on writing. One or two letters might reach me before you come home." He put his arm around her shoulder and drew her close. "I'm sorry that I cannot be there to watch over you, but I am so tied up in my work that my presence is vital this month. We are all toiling every waking hour to prepare the parishes for this new law."

"I am glad, Father, that your work progresses so well. I wish you and Lord Hardwicke and the rest of the committee resounding success."

"Thank you, Genevieve; you're a good girl. You understand. Yes, we want to put a final stop to those clandestine Fleet Street marriages, and make calling the Banns understood all over our country. For too long, hasty marriages have caused untold grief, not only to parents but also to the unthinking couples who marry in haste and repent at leisure."

After Genevieve hugged him in farewell, she hurried down the stairs after him, and grabbed him again on the doorstep, quite to his surprise. "Father, I will miss you!"

"There, there, Genevieve. I will miss you, too, my girl. You always gladden my heart." They looked into each other's eyes, and there was love and understanding between them. "I have told your mother to return in three weeks. That's not so long, is it?"

Genevieve wondered. Some hours with her were interminable.

* * *

When she entered the travelling coach, there was a bandbox under the seat that she did not recognize alongside her mother's and her own. She realized whose it was when she saw Dorcasta emerging from the house. She was dressed for travelling in Arabelle's curvy bottle green jacket over the matching skirt. It angered Genevieve to see Dorcasta wearing another of Arabelle's garments.

She could see that it did not fit well enough to close the black buttons across the bodice, which showed much of her chemise and an inferior tan vest underneath. The straining waist bulged in an unsightly mess. The length dragged so that she tripped on it as she descended the stairs.

But the overriding question was: how had Dorcasta gotten Madam to include her on this trip? Or had it been Madam's own idea for some reason? Or—and this was the only positive thought that flashed into Genevieve's mind—perhaps they were dropping her at her home in Kent on the way to Dover. Lady Bastwicke had told Genevieve, "Since we don't have room for maids along, take gowns that you can do up yourself." Would not even one maid have been more essential than this Miss Doyle?

As Radford arrived on a fine mare with a small coach following, Genevieve suddenly felt better. He rode to her window and smiled. "Good morning, Miss Genevieve."

Dorcasta turned and smiled showily up at him from under her floppy linen cap, and declined to take the groom's hand to enter the coach. She looked pointedly at Genevieve as if to say, *See? I remembered that you said I have a nice smile.*

Genevieve felt annoyed, and opened her window.

As Dorcasta approached the step of the carriage, she looked back at Radford and smiled again. He, however, was looking at Genevieve.

She called, "Take good care of us, Radford. Shoot all highwaymen and bandits, and scare off anyone who looks interested in us."

"Orders noted. I will be busy." His lips twisted

into a grin as he saluted her.

It felt better than before, this meeting with him. She found she was no longer terrified of him—at least not at this distance—since their frank chats had opened up some understanding between them.

The groom tried to help Dorcasta up into the coach, but had to ask her to back down so he could remove the skirt hem from the step, as she had her foot planted on it. Dorcasta went red, and Genevieve thought it served her right for wearing what did not belong to her. Why was Madam allowing such thievery?

Out from the house came Lady Bastwicke, gushing at Radford. "Oh my, Lord Ashby! Don't you look smart?" As always, it took some time for the groom to maneuver and settle her huge, creaking gown and cloak within the confines of the coach. "Will you ride inside with us, Lord Ashby?" she called loudly as two neighbor women walked by.

"No, thank you, Lady Bastwicke. I will ride. I am on lookout duty."

Dorcasta looked disappointed, letting her eyes drag after him.

Genevieve wondered how she dared to raise her eyes to such a man, a Peer of the Realm. Was the encouragement she had given Dorcasta dangerous? Did it multiply in the girl's mind until she now thought that, because she rode with a Viscountess, she could claim glory for herself? She was sadly out of her depth, and Genevieve wondered what would come of it all.

* * *

Genevieve enjoyed the first two hours of travel after they passed out of London and onto the Maidstone-London road because it was such a fresh, sunny day. She had to admit that it was uplifting to look out and see Lord Ashby's fine figure in his dark brown coat and breeches, shiny boots and straight shoulders riding next to them or on the road ahead. At times, she carried on an interrupted conversation with him through the open window. What made her self-conscious was her awareness of her mother's watchful eyes upon the two of them.

Lady Bastwicke often burst in with her own tidbits of wit, as she supposed them to be. She rarely listened to others' complete monologues, but usually jumped in to interrupt with her own thoughts on every subject.

Genevieve felt chagrined by the trio of females all fawning, as it might seem, over their handsome, titled, and wealthy male escort, so she strove not to do anything that remotely resembled fawning herself.

Dorcasta watched him fervently, even while she kept up a flow of chatter with Lady Bastwicke. Genevieve marveled that her mother seemed to have taken to the girl, even after her initial disparaging words about her. The two discussed the latest songs and fashions, and Dorcasta listened, agog, to Lady Bastwicke's gossip about people she did not know.

Finally, when Genevieve closed her eyes to try to sleep against a little cushion, Dorcasta asked sweetly, "So, Lady Bastwicke, what will we do in

France?"

Genevieve realized, with a jolt of her heart, that their guest was coming with them all the way there. Her eyes wanted to pop open, but she forced herself to keep them shut. Perhaps Madam would talk more if she thought she was asleep. Trying to keep her eyelids still, she wondered why her mother countenanced Dorcasta's presence at all. Madam was usually not interested in others, let alone young people who got in her way and cluttered up her life.

Lady Bastwicke said promisingly, "We shall have such amusing soirées, card parties, plays, and you can't imagine what all. You will meet all sorts of eligible people when you're with me."

Dorcasta sighed deliciously and asked, "What are eligible people, if you don't mind my ignorant question?"

Genevieve was wondering the same thing.

"Why, single men, to be sure!" said Lady Bastwicke as the coach shuddered over uneven ground, making Genevieve's head vibrate against the glass. She moved slightly to a more comfortable position.

Dorcasta asked, "Men? Ah . . . for whom?" She lowered her voice and whispered, "For the Honorable Genevieve?"

Lady Bastwicke replied, "For her, naturally, but why not for you, too?"

"Me?" Dorcasta held a tongue-tied silence for a few ticks.

Genevieve mentally gasped, and wondered why her mother would care about Dorcasta's future. What could she gain by that? Madam had never, as long as Genevieve had been with her, done anything that did not further her own interests.

The coach slowed, and Lady Bastwicke said quickly, for she seemed to be distracted, "Well, why not? You're . . . young, and in need of a husband. Then you can go off on your own with him. There will be many servants of other people's to choose from. Ah, I see we're slowing through a village. I need to make a stop." She rapped sharply on the roof with her parasol handle.

Genevieve let the commotion seemingly rouse her, and she opened her eyes and sat up.

Dorcasta was fingering her mouth, looking speculative. A husband for herself in France could have been filling her head. Genevieve wondered what she thought about serving-men being the eligible ones Madam indicated for her.

Radford trotted back and slowed his horse. "Would you ladies like to stop for a few minutes? There's a good inn up ahead."

"Yes, of all things," agreed Lady Bastwicke, sounding urgent.

At the inn, Genevieve eventually found herself alone with her mother at the luncheon table, for Dorcasta had excused herself. Genevieve asked, "Why is Dorcasta Doyle coming with us to France?"

"To keep you company."

"I do not understand. I am with you, Madam. Is that not company enough?"

"I shall not be saddled with a daughter twenty-four hours a day. I want to spend time with my friends, and you require a companion. She will also be useful to us."

"I do not need a companion!" Genevieve

objected, horrified. "Do you think I will venture into impropriety without one?" Seeing her mother's irate reaction, she added, "Dorcasta is only a year older than I am. How could she be fit to be my companion in a foreign land? She has scant knowledge of anything! Please explain why I should feel secure with her. She's a stranger, and doesn't know our ways. And I'm quite sure she can't understand French."

Lady Bastwicke seemed to prevaricate as she said, "We shall be in the same château, so never fear. Dorcasta will be company for you; two girls together, and you much the prettier. That will be a good visual magnet for men."

Genevieve's jaw dropped incredulously.

Dorcasta came into the parlor with a lively smile on her face. "This is so pretty and charming," she said, fluttering her hands about at the half-timbered room with its chintz-covered chairs and watercolor pictures of roses and Bodiam Castle on the walls. She continued to extol the virtues of almost everything she saw on her way back to her seat, even the horse brasses and the dusty fabric flowers in a cracked vase. "I am becoming educated to the ways of the world."

"How so?" asked Madam.

"I have just learned that Lord Ashby is an Earl, which is higher than a Viscount and a Baron and other things. I am to call Lord Ashby *My Lord* instead of Your Earlship—right?"

Genevieve caught Lady Bastwicke's eye in rare amusement that this girl was pitifully naïve indeed.

Lady Bastwicke said, "You will learn a lot more with me. Where did you learn those facts, by the way?"

Dorcasta blushed as she gestured back toward the courtyard. "I, well, I bumped into My Lord—backed into him, actually—as I left the privy." She gave a sharp laugh. "I asked him outright. And a lot of other questions about nobility, too."

"What was he doing by the women's privy, may I ask?" queried Lady Bastwicke, eyeing Dorcasta suspiciously.

"Oh, he wasn't there, I was at the wrong one, but I—well, I wandered toward the fountain and washed my hands there, and he was quite nearby, taking something out of his trunk. He did not hear me behind him. He was so polite, even after I made him jump and drop his papers when I bumped into him, accidentally, of course."

"Of course," snapped Madam, with a needle-sharp look at the girl.

* * *

Lady Bastwicke made the crossing to France mostly sleeping on the boat to diminish her seasickness. At every stop in France, she emerged with orders all around for the servants, sending them to procure this or that for her comfort. She spoke some French, but Genevieve detected that her accent was odd and her word choices often bizarre. When the French did not understand her, Genevieve clarified the situation. She and Arabelle had learned French from Aunt Claracilla, who had learned from a French governess, so the accent she passed down was very understandable. Genevieve found that as she spoke to French people in the inns along their way from Calais to Paris, and from thence to their destination, she received warm responses.

Her mother, however, raised antagonism in those to whom she made her high-handed demands. The French were not as cowed by her grandeur as Lady Bastwicke wished, and while they were inherently polite, Madam was not. "Don't they know who *I am*?" she fumed.

Genevieve tried to smooth out the ruffles her mother left behind with positive expressions of gratitude to those who served them, and felt better when that helped.

When she was not dipping into their food basket along the way, Lady Bastwicke regaled Genevieve's and Dorcasta's ears with chatter about her anticipation for their stay at Château de Chambord. She talked mostly about men whom she hoped to see, and how she had been admired in this gown or that headdress, and in this play or that comedy-reading in her past travels. "I am excited to see the friends I miss so much! I know that they are dying to see me."

As a carriage of young men passed by, she said, "Ah, Genevieve, you will meet someone so good looking at our destination." She looked at Dorcasta next to her, and tittered.

Genevieve eyed them askance. "Oh? Am I expected to give him my admiration, or what?"

"Naturally. He has big brown eyes."

"You have a love of big brown eyes, I know. Where did you meet him?"

"Where was it? Anyway, he is now residing near one of my best friends, Madame Mortinette. She recently wrote to say that she's taking him along to rendezvous with us, or rather, with you." Her mother looked cunning and secretive.

Rubbing her forehead, Genevieve sighed heavily. She did not want to be thrown together with any man whom her mother liked.

When the Bastwicke equipage and Lord Ashby clattered into an inn yard for their last night on the journey, he said, "This is where we part company, Genevieve."

Surprised, she asked, "We do? Are you going somewhere else?"

"I am. But I have promised your mother that I will look in at the château in a few days."

"I see. Where are you going now?"

"On my tour of Europe, I made friends in Chartres. I am invited to be godfather to their new son, and the baptism is this coming Sunday."

Genevieve felt relieved. "I wish you a very pleasant time with your friends and your new godson," she said with a smile.

"Thank you. I wish you *bonne chance* where you are going. When do you plan to return to England?"

"Father told Madam to be back in three weeks."

"*Au revoir* for today, then."

She gave him her hand, and he kissed it.

Dorcasta, who emerged from the parlor doorway, came smiling widely to offer her hand to him. He took and shook it, but did not favor her with the kiss she expected. She said, "We will look forward to you joining us in a little while, I hope, Earl. As early as you can, I hope. She kept her bright-eyed, determined smile pinned on him. "Your Lordship,

I mean. Is that right?"

Radford cleared his throat and sent Genevieve a speaking glance before he rode away.

CHAPTER 7

Whose Guests are We?

"Here is our destination!" sang out Lady Bastwicke, putting her pointed nose to the coach window. "My stars!—it's even grander than he wrote."

Dorcasta, too, was exclaiming over the sight, so Genevieve sat up to look as they rolled along a tree-lined lane.

Château de Chambord lay majestically before them in the morning sun, a white plethora of curved wedding-cake corner towers with others placed gracefully at intervals between them. Those were all topped by dark gray conical roofs with cupolas at their points. Amongst them, a great number of lavish white chimneys in myriad shapes clustered closely in profusion above the third storey. Long windows in beautiful proportions glistened, reflecting the pink sunrise. The elegance of the wide château took Genevieve's breath away. Chambord was certainly a fairytale edifice of unimaginable magnificence.

Birds chirped and twittered as their coach approached the closest corner of the château.

The one-story circular end, which was part of a wing projecting from the tall palace, was, as its matching counterpart on the other end, a harmonious structure. It gave no outward sign of being a domicile of animals because it was so refined. The only clue that it was the stable wing appeared when they saw a young man emerge from it, leading a horse.

How green and tranquil lay the countryside in which the grand edifice was set. It was beauty beyond what Genevieve had ever imagined, and it was real. It thrilled her to realize that she would have the pleasure of admiring it from all sides, and of going inside.

The coach door opened and the step was folded down by a servant who had run to greet them. His eyes blinked against the sunrise as, in French, he asked Lady Bastwicke who they were. Oddly enough, she had opened a folded letter and replied to the servant by reading some words to him in a whisper. He said in French, "That is correct. You may follow me."

Genevieve eyed him and her mother. A code or password had just been exchanged, but why? Perhaps it was for security so that not just anyone could gain access to this jewel of a palace.

Lady Bastwicke struggled down from the coach, her wooden farthingale creaking in the stillness as it burst loose from its confines. She swayed perilously, but the groom propped her up until she was safely on the grass.

Genevieve descended next, and patted down

Madam's enormously wide skirt and arranged its draperies for her.

Dorcasta, grasping the skirt she wore up much too high for her descent from the coach, appeared indecisive about whether to let the skirt go and take the groom's offered hand, or stumble down on her own, lifting the skirt up. Trying the latter course, she tumbled sidewise onto the servant, who strove to break her fall, but she still landed with one knee in the grass. She moaned, and cried, "Oh, fie! Now my shoes and stockings are wet, and so is my lovely skirt!"

Genevieve swiveled a questioning look at her.

Dorcasta flustered, "I mean this borrowed, lovely skirt! Oh, I am such a clunk!"

Lady Bastwicke sniffed and ignored Dorcasta as she made her grand way through the central door into the interior. They passed through, and emerged outside into a cobbled courtyard. What a grand view there was upward, with rows of windows rising to the sky in the white expanse of the palace, and a plethora of different chimneys atop it. The servant escorted them through an immensely tall wooden door.

In the echoing white interior, Genevieve stood transfixed. The ground floor corridors formed a giant T with graceful white arches and ceilings. In the center, like a crown jewel rising from the expanse of floor, was an ornate white open-work column with a spiral staircase.

It had handrails and balusters that reminded her of balconies, but they graced the stair steps which were shaped like shallow pie wedges, white and inviting. As Genevieve moved to the bottom step to admire the elegance above her, a man's silver-buckled black shoe appeared on the stairs above. Then came shapely calves in white hose decorated with silver clocks. This materialized into an energetic form clad in red knee breeches and a matching coat of tomato red. Above the pale waistcoat spilled a cloud of white throat lace. Wearing the finery was, alas! –a familiar face!

Her mother had been right: he was still a resident of France. He had fled here to escape punishment for his London wrong-doing. Her father and other influential men had made certain of that, or he would likely have landed in Newgate Prison.

With smiling red lips, Sir Pomeroy Chancet hailed them with an exuberant wave of a lace handkerchief. His heavy-lidded brown eyes looked mightily pleased as he neared them, breathing, "O, my lovely ladies! It is Lady Bastwicke and Miss Genevieve Lamar, as I live and breathe! What a divine feast for my starving eyes!" His voice throbbed as he thoroughly took in the vision of Genevieve from head to shoes and back.

Lady Bastwicke shrieked out a laugh. "Oh, Sir Pom, I wrote to you that we would come!" She moved forward and kissed him coquettishly on the lips. Though he returned her lavish attention with smiles and gushes, he managed a clandestine wink at Genevieve in between.

She turned away, utterly dismayed that Sir Pomeroy Chancet was here. It nearly killed her that she would be forced to associate with him in this otherwise dreamlike setting.

Madam was chattering, "Isn't this the most beautiful château in the entire world? And to know that our friends occupy it now is too, too marvelous! What a *coup!*" She turned. "And we are to benefit by staying here, Genevieve!"

Dorcasta, who hung back, was frantically adjusting the wet, unsightly skirt front and keeping hidden behind half of Madam's wide gown. She lifted her chin and smiled uncertainly at the flashy Sir Pomeroy. She stared at how he was posing on the bottom step with a hand on one hip and a lace handkerchief upraised in the other.

He ignored her until Lady Bastwicke said, flicking her hand toward Dorcasta, "That's Miss Doyle." Quickly, she pressed him, "Who all is here so far?"

He regaled her ears with a list of names, none of whom Genevieve had ever heard except Madame Mortinette's. At the men's names, her mother lit up or simpered, but at the other women's, she either groaned or flared her nostrils. Genevieve surmised that some of them must be beauties, for Madam did not like to be in the same company as any of those.

At the end of his catalogue, she asked, "Will there be any charade parties or play readings?"

"Oh yes," he promised, "if *you* instigate them. There are endless rooms here for a myriad of heart-leaping activities. I will help you organize them, of course." He slid an assessing look over Genevieve. "We can make lots of creative fun for Genevieve."

Intent on his every move, Dorcasta moved her shoulders from side to side, smiling up at him, striving to draw his attention. He said, "And, ah, Miss Boil, was it?"

Genevieve couldn't stop her laugh.

"Dorcasta Doyle." Dorcasta shot a dark look at

Genevieve.

Lady Bastwicke was whispering urgently to Sir Pomeroy, "But in my circle of friends, they have been only for adults!"

"Are Genevieve and that one not entered into the adult category yet?" His eyes traveled up and down each of them as he added covertly, "They *look* to be—"

"Genevieve is out," snapped Madam, "but that Doyle girl is not, nor does she expect to be, in the way we mean. Now, we need bedchambers for them, as Genevieve must have beauty sleep. For obvious reasons." She tittered.

Sir Pomeroy turned a rueful eye on Genevieve to see her reaction.

Genevieve, while steaming inside, repeated, "Obvious reasons? Why yes, traveling has tired us abominably this morning. We have been on the road about an hour, and I feel the grueling effects of the journey. I can hardly stand."

Sir Pomeroy's eyes danced with mirth.

Swiveling her shovel-shaped gown several degrees, Lady Bastwicke frowned at her, and immediately smiled at an advancing group of clattering, echoing ladies and gentlemen.

"*Bonjour, bonjour!*" she called. She was suddenly in alt, kissing and talking in her clumsy French with a portly gray-wigged man and others. Then she ran in little jerky steps toward a woman with a green and purple feather headdress and three face patches. After shouts of greeting and loud kisses, they put their heads together behind the woman's huge fan and laughed in shrieks. The woman seemed to be thrusting gossip into Madam's ear.

Lady Bastwicke pushed her arm, her eyes alight. "No! Can you believe it?" and they both went off into cackles of merriment.

Genevieve asked Sir Pomeroy, "Is that Madame Mortinette?"

"Oh yes," he said. "I hear they are two peas in a pod."

Dorcasta hurried to stand behind the stair rail, curiously watching everyone.

Sir Pomeroy sidled closer to Genevieve. "What do you look forward to doing here in France?" She could smell perfumed powder on his wig. Back in London, she had seen him wear a kaleidoscope of styles and colors. There had been those despicable incidents involving wigs that had shown him to be far less of a nobleman than he strove, even now, to appear. He awaited her answer, his eyes never straying to the noisy group, though they easily distracted Genevieve's attention.

What did she look forward to? She took a step up the staircase and turned back, saying, "An increase in my knowledge of French ways and culture, for a start." When she stepped upward, he kept pace with her. She kept ascending, interested in the staircase, running her hand along the cool marble rail; anything not to have to look at him. But when she reluctantly turned his way, he offered her his arm. Not wanting to offend in such a watchful company, she placed her hand upon his sleeve and they kept slowly ascending the white staircase under its arched ceiling.

"I want to look at many places such as this," she replied, "and maybe even see Chartres Cathedral. I wish to dip into the past. I know already that the

French make beautiful dinners and *pâtisserie.*"

"Oh, yes, that they do!" he corroborated, smiling his red lips over yellowed teeth and nodding. "You will not have long to wait until I bring you some," he promised. "Many of the guests have brought not only chefs but also bakers and *pâtissières* with them."

"Why naturally?" she inquired.

Sir Pomeroy cocked his chin. "How else would we live?" he asked airily, flipping his handkerchief.

Genevieve was puzzled. "Doesn't this château have its own kitchen staff?"

Sir Pomeroy ignored that and fiddled with the large bow at the side of her gown. She pulled away from him. Gazing around at the top of the staircase, she murmured, "I would like to explore this château."

She could have bitten the words back, for he pounced on them with glee. "I shall give you the tour, but only a partial tour it can be because we think there must be some seven or eight hundred rooms. There are dozens upon dozens of staircases, too. Some people have gotten quite lost already. And, oh joy, we can go onto the roof!"

"Oh? I saw a profusion of artistically-shaped chimneys, some huge and very elaborate. It seemed like none were alike."

"Oh yes, their shapes vary from cupolas to steeples and all kinds of towers with and without windows. You can walk between them as in a city. It is like another world up there, Genevieve." He leered at her.

Running her hand up and down a cool support column, she decided to gain some information from him. "This staircase is most unusual."

Dorcasta inserted from behind them, "Yes, I think so, too. At least, I've never seen any like it in Kent."

Sir Pomeroy ignored her and said to Genevieve, "It is! Did you notice what makes it so?"

"Well, it looks to have two tiers of stairs, one on top of the other."

"How observant you are! Other people haven't noticed that, but that is the case. We are walking over the other set now. We think that Leonardo da Vinci designed it." Sir Pomeroy's brown eyes watched her reaction.

"*The* Leonardo da Vinci?"

"Yes, and it was none other than François Premier, the first King of France, who commissioned him to build *Le Grand Escalier*, as this is called."

Genevieve looked down and admired the stairs in their shadows, the light touching them all from the windows in the distance. "This is truly a breathtaking view, but it is even more fantastic from the sides, as I noted when I walked in. I feel privileged to be allowed to stay here and traverse this treasure of a staircase," she said with feeling.

If only she could do so without the likes of this troublesome Baron at her elbow, stinking up the place with his perfume and his dissolute manner. This was the kind of a realm she wanted to experience for herself, and by herself, or with Arabelle.

"Ah, Genevieve, it is so good to have you here!" Sir Pomeroy's voice throbbed. His warm breath assailed her cheek as he leaned close.

"Why so?" she countered, turning pointedly away.

"Because you are so beautiful, young, and fresh!

You are different from all the other ladies here. You are unspoiled. I love your dress, all white with that intriguing tied white vest over the top, and such a lovely shell pink sash in such a jaunty big bow. It makes one want to pull it!"

"You are saying that the other ladies are spoiled? How would they like to hear that?"

Her challenging look seemed to encourage him, and he laughed low. The next thing she knew, he ambushed her from behind with his left hand grabbing her ribcage.

She slapped his hand down and whirled away. "Stop that! Do not even *think* of touching my person again!"

Prickling with unease, she realized that it was not wise to have left the others to end up alone with him. Dorcasta was no longer in sight below them. What an effective companion. She must have given up on gaining Sir Pomeroy's attention. Genevieve turned to descend the staircase and rejoin the throng.

Sir Pomeroy, hurrying next to her, remarked, "It's just that you, Genevieve, are devoid of dissipation and all kinds of sin."

"All what sin?" she threw back, shocked.

He murmured, "I should not regale innocent ears such as yours with such goings-on. Perhaps later."

Genevieve challenged him over her shoulder, "Why later? Do you expect that you will have made me more sinful in a hurry?"

He gaped at her, and guffawed gleefully. "You are so witty! These people will love you, especially if you know a little French."

Fuming, she did not answer him. The loud

gathering of people watched them descend. Many halted their conversations. Someone called to Sir Pomeroy to present the lovely ingénue.

He introduced her as "Miss Genevieve Lamar, newly from London. She has just arrived with Regina, our treasured Lady Bastwicke." Genevieve noted that he did not make them known as mother and daughter because he followed Madam's wishes in keeping the myth alive that she was much younger than she was. They would find out, anyway, so Genevieve thought her mother's practice absurd.

When introduced, she curtseyed slightly to each person in turn, and received many kisses on or near both cheeks. What a variety of scents she inhaled from overdressed men and women. By the time the third person kissed her, she had learned to plug her nose until they retreated, for she did not like perfume or fetid breath in such doses. She only kissed the air herself. She hoped they were not offended, but she did not know them, nor did she feel that she even wanted to know most of them.

It transpired that there was one exception. He was a gentleman just arriving, with sunshine silhouetting him against the door as he strolled in. He was taller and younger than most of the men, with broad shoulders and a well-proportioned figure. He wore no wig, and his thick black hair was pulled back in a queue that shone with a smooth sheen as he bowed to her. Upon rising, an interested look flashed into his thick-lashed blue eyes. "Hello," he said simply, smiling down at her with a twinkle.

"You speak English," she observed, dropping him

a shy courtesy.

"Yes, thanks to my Oxford education."

"Oh? Which college, Monsieur?"

"Balliol."

"Yet you are French?" When she saw his profile, it was what she would call *parfait*. She marveled how God sometimes granted a man with such handsomely-formed features that she thought He must have taken great pleasure in creating him.

"Yes, I am a Frenchman, at your service. Since the others are all preoccupied, I must boldly introduce myself."

Genevieve smiled and said, "You have my leave."

"Thank you. I am Armand de Villebon." His voice and accented English thrilled her.

"*Enchanté.* I am Genevieve Lamar from London and Kent."

"I am enchanted to meet you, too, Miss Lamar." His kindly eyes smiled down at her, seeming to take her in without gawking all over her person as many other men did.

Genevieve wondered where her breath had gone.

Suddenly, a man struck his walking stick three times on the floor, echoing and drawing all attention. It caused a scurry of movement. The assembly of fashionables who were clustered around the staircase began to pair up. Judging by the hasty discussions that ensued, people were confused. Genevieve soon understood that the order of precedence was in chaotic question due to their arrival. Apparently the guests had all known their places, but now she and her mother belonged somewhere other than trailing at the end; but exactly where they did belong they had not worked out.

Genevieve said to Armand de Villebon, "I will wait until last. I do not like this fuss over us."

He looked surprised, and said, "Admirable. Shall we retreat and let them tussle it out?"

She gave him a grateful nod and backed away with him.

Sir Pomeroy was forcibly grabbed by Lady Bastwicke, who hissed at him, "Just make sure I'm ahead of that Jezebel, Madame Poisson. She thinks she is of higher rank than I am, but she certainly is not!"

Genevieve flushed with humiliation for her mother.

Sir Pomeroy, shooting Genevieve a longing look over his shoulder, remained ever suave, and squired Lady Bastwicke to the head of the line. He proclaimed, "Our new guest from England shall take the place of honor at this morning's *petit déjeuner*, shall she not?"

A woman near the doorway smiled in a frozen way as Lady Bastwicke swept past her and had to swivel sideways to enter the room. She turned to look over her shoulder, apparently glorying in her status at the front. She seemed to have forgotten all about Genevieve and Dorcasta.

Armand de Villebon said, "Miss Lamar, I truly must object to your taking the end of the line."

"I am happier here," she said, and thanked him. She motioned Dorcasta ahead of her toward an old man who was left without a partner.

Dorcasta took his trembling arm and stared back at Genevieve and Armand de Villebon.

He looked pleased when he escorted her in,

drawing interested attention from people taking their seats.

Genevieve enjoyed her bread and coffee at the end of a long table next to him. "Who of this company," she inquired quietly, "is the owner of this fabulous palace?"

He gave her an ironic look and whispered grimly, "No one here."

"Do the owners take *le petit déjeuner* in their own rooms?"

He leaned toward her to lift the cream pitcher. The chatter was not as loud as it had been before fresh plates of bread, jam, ham, and cherries had been delivered to all the tables, for most everyone ate with relish. He whispered, "Do you not know that we have all entered here by stealth?"

Startled, she stared at him. "What do you mean by stealth?"

He sipped his coffee. With the lift of a dark eyebrow, he assured her, "It's true. Not a single person here is known to the owner."

"What? But I thought my mother received an invitation. She showed it to the servant when we arrived."

"Oh, no doubt she did," he replied, offering her the jam, "but it could only have come from someone who is staying here illicitly."

Striving to appear normal so others wouldn't suspect their conversation, she asked quietly, "Do you mean that we are all here without permission?"

"*Exactement.*"

Incredulously, she stared at him. "This is wrong!"

"Yes, indeed." He eyed her levelly and with approval.

Chairs scraped as some people excused themselves to leave. Under cover of their mingled conversation and laughter, she asked, "Then why did you come here under these circumstances yourself, Monsieur de Villebon?"

He gave her a little smile and replied gently, "I need to know you for a day before I divulge my reason."

She almost laughed. "Why?"

"I want you to know that I wish to trust you already, but I must think on it."

"Think on what?"

"The wisdom of my telling you the answer to your question. I think perhaps a visit out of doors would be a good way to get to know you better. Would you like to accompany me?"

Genevieve, considering, said, "Perhaps later I can walk with you outside, but I have no idea what to do with my luggage right now."

Presently, he offered his arm, and they left the breakfast room. "Is that because you have not been allotted a room?"

"I don't like to even accept one because now I know we should not be here. I hate to be a party to this."

Quietly, he advised, "Play along with whatever your mother wants you to do. Trust me. I will wait outside in hopes of walking the grounds with you in about an hour, if you will? Just pass out of that door there, on the moat side."

"I will find the room I am allotted, unpack, and be there."

The prospect thrilled Genevieve to walk again with such a compelling man. He seemed so different from the others, but she must be careful, as Father had warned her. She must not run headlong to put her trust in strange men.

* * *

Having ascended to the top of *Le Grand Escalier*, she looked up in wonder. There was no end to the intricacies of design, even to the circular ceiling of the spiral above her.

Soon she stood beside her luggage in a bedchamber. When she opened the shutters, she had a lovely view of an expanse of green lawn, a moat straight below, and a forest at a pleasant distance beyond a balconied tower.

Just outside her room, her mother was pointing out to a serving maid her own bandboxes and directing Dorcasta to carry some of them. "I have a suite of rooms, furnished and allotted just for me in another wing entirely," she smugly declared. She had allotted a small whitewashed room with a bed on the floor to Dorcasta. It had no windows or other furniture but a rickety chair. Madam was already using the girl to fetch and carry for her, so it was for this plausible reason that she had taken Dorcasta along. Genevieve almost pitied her.

Sir Pomeroy Chancet hailed Genevieve just as she emerged from putting her own pleasant, sparsely-furnished bedchamber in order. She had found a key fastened with sealing wax under the old escritoire, so she locked her door. As he watched her do it, Sir Pomeroy looked displeased. He raised his gold quizzing glass to one eye, looked her over, and said, "We have a plan for a play this evening,

Genevieve, and we want you to play the innocent heroine. There will only be a few lines for you to learn. Will you come to our rehearsal at one o'clock?"

"No, thank you," she responded, throwing a long curl over her shoulder and heading for the staircase.

In dismay, he pressed, "But whyever not? You are perfect for the part."

"I don't wish to."

"You must! We have it all planned."

She challenged, "Who has it all planned, without my agreement?"

"Why, Lady Bastwicke, of course, and Madame Mortinette, and Miss Boil."

"That does it! I'm even less interested."

"Why?" Sir Pomeroy hurried to follow her, calling distinctly, "But I am to play the hero who gets you, and you are the only person I want in that part! I wrote the piece myself!" he crowed, as if that would convince her to leap joyfully into the role. He trailed her with loudly clattering heels, and called to Lady Bastwicke, who strolled ahead with a shorter male companion. "We *will* get her to do it!"

Lady Bastwicke queried, "Why wouldn't she?"

Genevieve's eyes flashed as she craned her neck to look back at Sir Pomeroy. "I told you I will not participate in that play, so stop lying and saying I will."

He grabbed her arm to detain her.

She shook him off with no finesse. "Stop your incessant grabbing!" she expelled.

He stumbled clumsily, and with a hurt look, whined, "But this is a play that moves from room to room, and I am dying to show you some secret chambers that I have found!"

Genevieve glared at him in warning.

As she saw that her mother's escort had walked off, Genevieve followed her, glaring back at her pursuer to keep him at bay. He finally halted when he saw the smiling Dorcasta hurrying and waving to waylay him.

Genevieve followed Madam toward the open door and outside. The sun-kissed moat, green grass, and majestic towers rising on both sides of them made Genevieve expel, "This is such a magnificent place!"

"Oh yes, I love being here," agreed Lady Bastwicke, squinting and shading her face from the sun with her fan.

"Mother, who invited you to come?"

"Why do you want to know? You're lucky enough to be here with me. And call me Madam."

"I wish to know because I heard that the owner is not even here."

Lady Bastwicke gave an odd little laugh. "That's true."

"Then how do we dare to be here?"

Her mother said defensively, "It would be empty if we were not here to . . . to keep it from becoming a home for mice and birds!—or vagrants, or all kinds of takings-advantage-of."

Genevieve put her hands on her hips and stared at her fidgeting mother. "So all the people I met are here without any right to be?"

"Don't be so censorious."

Genevieve pressed, "Including us!"

"We are here at Sir Pomeroy Chancet's invitation,

if you want exactitude, but the original party was arranged by Madame Mortinette, my best friend."

Genevieve decided to ignore that, for a squabble about him would only end in shouting. "I am only trying to understand. We are squatters here, then. No one has legitimately welcomed us, nobody lives here, not even servant retainers, yet all of us are taking the most shameful advantage of this magnificent château to . . . to what? Help ourselves to this glorious ambience in order to what, exactly?"

"To give this glorious château some life!" her mother finished blithely, moving away.

Genevieve speculated. "Have you been here before?"

"Not here, no."

"How long will we stay?"

Lady Bastwicke eyed her icily. "What does it matter?" Changing her tone as they spied a man in a white wig leaning on one of the curved balconies above, she fanned coquettishly at him and said, "That depends."

"Upon what?"

"Upon what everyone else wants to do."

"Everyone else? Your friends who think they can live here for as long as they feel inclined?"

"I have many like-minded, fascinating friends, as you have seen." She smoothed down her black star face patch in the mirror built inside her fan. "I must go to my room now that my trunks are there, and make myself ready for some amusement."

"What kind of amusement? Please explain to me what you plan to do here."

"Oh," her mother said expansively as she headed for the door, "whenever we get together, we perform theatrics like the one Sir Pom just wrote, and card parties go on all the time. We get up balls and musical soirées when the musicians are hired. You can be sure we are greatly entertained. It's so much freer here on the Continent than the events I am allowed to indulge in in London, that stuffy place!" The shadowed doorway swallowed her as she maneuvered her gown through it.

Genevieve slowly shook her head. This was the limit.

She hurried up the white stairs again to her allotted bedchamber. There, she perched on a little chair at the old carved escritoire and opened the drawers. Since she found nothing inside them save a dried-up burgundy rose and a crushed-up handkerchief smelling of old perfume, she went to find her own box of paper and pens from her trunk. She must report all of this to Arabelle.

As she dipped her pen in the ink bottle, she decided that it was far more important to write first to Father. She had promised him she would, and she felt it was vital to inform him of the inconceivable circumstance in which they now occupied the exquisite Château de Chambord.

When she was signing her letter, she heard a man's voice coming from somewhere outside her open window. He was saying in French-accented English, "Oho-ho, Regine, you are back with us! And you brought along your most lovely daughter. *Mais pourquoi* did you hide that fact from me? I found out that is what she is, you sly lady!"

Genevieve alerted, and went to crouch beneath the window where she could hear well.

"She is just a young thing," retorted her mother.

There she was again, wanting everyone—especially men—to think she was so much younger than she was.

"But not too young to marry, is she?" he asked, his intonation suggestive.

"Oh no," replied Madam. "As for myself, I married very young indeed. She is barely out of the schoolroom, as I was."

"Ah yes. I know very well that you married so very young. Too bad it is that you are married at all. But that makes no difference to you and me, no?" Then Genevieve heard sounds of tittering on her part and aggressive growls on his. She stood stunned.

"Yes, but what an impertinent *roué* you are!" Lady Bastwicke teased, and then emitted another shriek.

He quickly said, "Ooh, shush, someone might hear us."

"Who?"

"Perhaps that little child of a daughter."

"She is outside," retorted her mother.

"What does it matter where she is? Such a little one cannot affect our good times together, can she?"

Madam let out a series of escalating giggles. Was that a kissing sound before the scrape of shoes clattered away on the roof?

Genevieve stood appalled. Was her mother engaged in an improper liaison? It came to Genevieve as a lightning bolt of understanding that Lady Bastwicke had hastened here to France to reconvene with this sort of behavior. And dear Father knew nothing about it!

She added a postscript to the letter she had

written to him. She did not feel it traitorous to report to him that there were *débauchés* a-plenty here. Her loyalty was with her Father, not with her licentious mother.

With her sealed letter to him hidden in her pocket, Genevieve found her way back to *Le Grand Escalier* and descended. She heard voices. The people speaking were just below her, on the other tier of the staircase, apparently. In giddy stealth, keeping herself to the middle of each step, she tiptoed down until she could hear them just beneath her. It was Dorcasta who was asking someone, "So the people who own this place are not here?"

"Oh no." The voice was Sir Pomeroy Chancet's. So those two were now hobnobbing together. Genevieve flared her nostrils. He asked Dorcasta, "How could we possibly enjoy such splendid sport in such freedom if some tiresome owners were at home?"

Dorcasta laughed. "I see. This is where you all have good times, is it?"

"The good times are much improved now that your party has arrived."

Dorcasta's voice dripped with coyness as she said, "Why, thank you. We are very, very glad to be here . . . seeing you."

They were moving, so Genevieve made sure to keep herself out of sight while she moved correspondingly. She heard Sir Pomeroy say, "The main difficulty was getting our servants to pack all of our essentials to furnish our rooms, and the larders."

"Oh, really?"

"Yes, and we take care to bribe them not to tell anyone if they have to go buy us more food. Most of us make our servants sign contracts that they will not speak a word, on pain of dismissal without a reference. I did that with my valet and chef before we got here."

Disgusted, Genevieve descended quickly.

"This way!" said a middle-aged woman with a gap in her top teeth and a wild gray wig. "*Le déjeuner* is starting soon, so you might like to get some before it is depleted. I tell you, Mademoiselle, because I think you do not know how things go on here."

"*Merci*," said Genevieve. "Is it that time already? I appreciate your kindness." She needed to ask someone how she could post a letter, but something made her decide to wait until she found Armand de Villebon.

Genevieve thought she could partake of her *déjeuner* quickly and in solitude, but two brightly-dressed young men in white wigs—one short and one tall with skinny legs—sauntered in and joined her at the table. While they ate, they told her that one of their favorite pastimes was planned for the following day. The play was now postponed in favor of cards for tonight.

"Oh, good," Genevieve responded. She would not have to worry about joining the crowd, for the play was canceled and she did not play cards. "What is the favorite thing planned for tomorrow?"

The shorter man revealed that it was to be an auction.

"What kind of an auction?" she queried. "Do you buy things?"

Eagerly, the thin one told her, "Yes, we do.

Everyone brings an article from their luggage to sell. We bid on other peoples' not-so-necessary items."

The stocky man added, "It should be diverting to see what everyone brought along this time."

Genevieve, ever practical, asked, "Yes, but to whom does the money go?"

"To buy food and wine for our banquets."

"And musicians to play so we can sing and dance."

Genevieve thanked them for the news and left. She heard one of them calling to her, but she did not look back. She would not encourage those men. She felt relieved that they reported the demise of Sir Pomeroy's play, though.

She strolled outside and over the moat on the opposite side of the palace from which she had arrived. She looked back to take in the wide, majestic glory of the château and its clear reflection. Although she had not seen a clock, it felt like time for her rendezvous with Armand de Villebon.

Her heart skipped when she saw him riding a horse toward her. She stood where she was, adjusting the wide brim of her hat to keep the sun from her eyes. As he neared the stable end of the château, she expected him to veer off and put his horse away, but on he came. He wore a dark gray coat, minimal lace at his throat and wrists, and black gloves and boots. He lifted a hand in greeting long before they could hear one another. Genevieve felt glad when he sped up his horse and brought it to a smart halt before her. He flashed a white smile down at her. He seemed full of *joie de vivre.*

"Bonjour," she said, returning his smile. He looked so noble, mounted on his horse. *Be careful,* her mind told her romantic heart; *do not endow handsome men with wonderful qualities just because you want them to possess them.*

He dismounted in a smooth motion and said something to his horse.

"May I pet him?" she asked, admiring the animal's brown face and black mane, its large eyes gleaming.

"He would be honored, Mademoiselle Genevieve."

It was lovely to hear this man use her name. She spoke into the horse's nostrils softly, saying, "I've never known a French horse before. You are *magnifique."* She ran her hand carefully up the bridge of his nose. Since he did not flinch, she rubbed his warm forehead under his mane. When she would have stopped petting him, the horse pushed against her slightly, so she continued, pleased. "What is his name?"

"Gaspard. I see you like animals," Armand observed, his eyes twinkling.

"I love them."

"Where have you been with animals before?"

She told him about living on her father's estate, Bastwicke Chase in Kent, and of the farm animals at Fawnlake Hall, where she lived for over a decade with her uncle and aunt. "We girls had our own horses there."

He said, as they walked along, Genevieve leading his horse beside the moat, "I find that a lot of ladies abhor animals."

"Oh no, how could they?"

"They stay as far away as they can from smells and dirt, as I've been told animals consist of."

"That is what Dorcasta told me on the trip here," Genevieve said wryly.

"*Typique!*"

She gave Gaspard a hug and crooned, "Why, they're no dirtier than some of the people inside that château. In fact, he smells much cleaner."

Armand laughed. "True!"

Since he was so congenial, Genevieve told him how her family had followed Lord Chesterfield's habit of bathing almost daily since 1752, when she and her sister, Arabelle, had gone to live in London.

A window in the top story of a great curving tower opened, and a pale pink wig appeared, framing the face of Sir Pomeroy Chancet. He had obviously been busy at his toilette and was now clad in shimmering blue. "What is so fascinating out there, Miss Genevieve?" he called loudly. "Why was Monsieur laughing? Good thing Lord Chesterfield is not here, eh?"

She looked at Armand de Villebon, whose eyebrows rose in question.

Genevieve explained, "The same Lord Chesterfield I mentioned finds audible laughter *très vulgaire.*" She grinned at the amused Frenchman, and kept leading his horse toward the forest.

Sir Pomeroy jealously called, "You have not let me in on your secret, so I am coming down to discover what is going on between you two. You shall not lure Miss Genevieve from me, Monsieur! I have known her since I lived in London, and we are intimate friends!" He ended with cupped hands around his mouth, loudly demanding their retreating attention.

Genevieve only glanced at the sun-bronzed and powerfully-built Frenchman grinning and walking next to her. The window in the château clapped shut with emphasis. Armand chuckled. "What would you like to do? Make a run for it?"

Her heart leaped in agreement. "Yes!" she said, deciding to take him literally. "Run!" She raced, fleet-footed, toward the woods in the distance, leaving the vast white château behind. Gaspard readily picked up to an energetic trot, his black mane lifting and falling. Genevieve laughed back at Armand, who broke into a lope.

"Are you really concerned?" he asked as they ran. "I can handle Sir Pomeroy."

"I am sure you can, but let him be. He irks me. You heard him acting as if he owns me. He never has, and never will!"

"For how long has the fop bothered you?"

Genevieve ran faster through the waving grass. Gaspard seemed to love their escapade, so she had to hold him back from speeding ahead. Armand saw this, but he did not grab the reins away from her as most men would. He let her stay in charge of his horse, and she liked him immensely for it. Slowing to a walk on the forest path, she patted the horse's neck and said, "Sir Pomeroy latched onto me as soon as we arrived, and I see that he is still in cahoots with my mother. He did not succeed with my sister two years ago despite a most despicable chase, but for some unknown reason, Madam wants him for *me* now!" She grimaced horribly.

Armand laughed at her. "Why? He is so far beneath you in every conceivable way."

"All I know for certain is that she likes his big brown eyes! He flatters her daily, and she loves that more than anything."

"Don't most women?"

"No! Well," she amended, "I can't stand it from him." Recalling how she had succumbed to Shrubsole Curling's compliments, she dropped her lashes and admitted, "Oh, I willingly believed flattery in the past, and was foolishly taken in by it."

He looked at her curiously. "I am amused to hear you admit such a thing. Now I know I can believe whatever else you might say."

She halted the horse and met Armand's blue eyes. "By that, you are certain that you can?"

"Yes, I am." He smiled down at her as he came close, and Genevieve's heart swelled. He asked "Would you like to ride for a few minutes? I know you're not in a riding habit, but does it matter?"

Genevieve said, her eyes glowing, "How did you read my mind? I would *love* to ride Gaspard. This white dress does not hinder me because this horse and saddle are so clean." As he invitingly made a stirrup with his hands, she peered at the château through the branches, saw no one to witness them, and put her pink shoe into Armand's hands. She felt a thrill as he vaulted her up into the saddle.

Soon Gaspard was walking her along the sun-mottled forest path. She was distracted by the man strolling next to her, or moving ahead to hold a branch out of their way. "What do you do when you're not visiting here, Monsieur?"

He hesitated.

"You look as though you wonder if you should tell me. If you do tell me straight, no matter what it is, I shall know that I can always believe *you*."

He grinned and met her eyes. *"Touché!* After a day has passed, we will speak, remember?" So he was a man of his word.

She pulled Gaspard's head up when he tugged, trying to nip at long grass. "Let's not form bad habits," she told him with a pat on his neck. She suddenly remembered her mission. Plunging her hand through the slit in her skirt and down into her bag pocket, she withdrew her missive. "I have written a very important letter to my father in London. I pray that, if possible, you will dispatch it for me, secretly."

Seriously, he took it from her. "But of course. I will ride to post it as soon as you relinquish my besotted horse."

She put her hand on her heart. "I am so grateful!" She prepared to dismount, but he reached out and stopped her.

"Not that you have to dismount just yet," he protested. "Keep riding. We can loop that way and emerge near the walled gardens. We will speak leisurely there, and look into one of them as though we are exploring. Then I shall bid you an obvious *adieu* and ride away on this mission, leaving you to look at what sorry plants may be left."

Approving this plan with a happy grin, Genevieve suggested she dismount before they reached the clearing. When he lifted his arms for her, she glanced shyly into his face and let him swing her down, her white skirt billowing. Affected warmly by his touch, she said, "I am glad you have my letter because if I were seen giving it to you, my mother would inquire until we were all puce in the face who it is for, and what, exactly, I wrote."

"That sounds like a prospect to avoid." He regarded her reassuringly. "Now, shall we carry out our planned movements?"

"Yes." She was so tickled by their little charade that she cast him a brilliant smile. "Thank you for conspiring with me, Armand de Villebon. You know how to make a day . . . fascinating."

With a charming dimple in his cheek, he took the horse's reins from her. As they walked across the grass and found a door to a garden, they entered and saw purple, white, and yellow spring flowers blooming amongst old plants, dead and untouched. A waver in Armand's tone revealed his high spirits. "I like your cooperation, too. Now connive with me once more, and let me kiss your hand during our *adieux*. It will give me something to speed me along."

Patting her letter, which lay safely inside his waistcoat, he donned the hat from under his elbow with an air of departing politeness, then reached for her hand and kissed it. He was gone the next instant, having vaulted into his saddle and moved off in a polished movement of man and horse. His black hair hung down his back in a queue, matching the black-tailed horse. She wished she could paint this very scene against the grandeur of Château de Chambord. She watched the manly rider and his mount undulate smoothly away past the rounded corner of the château. She let out a long sigh.

As soon as she left the region of the walled gardens, she began what she hoped was a normal-looking meander around the side of the château where she had not been. When she closed the loop to arrive again on the moat side, she paused to admire the reflected vertical lines of windows and towers all across the palace. She did not look up at the roof, but scanned the upside-down mirror of the moat for the information she sought. There were people promenading on the roof and curving balconies, but no sign of her mother or Sir Pomeroy. When she changed her view, she saw his pink wig swiveling to and fro beyond the shining water. He was promenading on the ground, searching for her, no doubt.

She must high-tail it back into the woods as the only place to hide. She hoped that she could make it there before he saw her. Once on the forest path, she felt she had made an error, for she did not want to be waylaid alone by him. Before she could decide which direction to take, she heard a crackle of twigs underfoot nearby. She whirled.

From the mottled sunshine of the forest came a stiffly-walking old gentleman in a curled gray wig that fell to his shoulders. He used a walking stick and carried a few purple crocuses. Immediately upon seeing her, he smiled and made her a courtly bow with his leg forward and his wrist twirling the bouquet instead of the customary handkerchief.

She curtsied back. Judging him to be safer company by far than Sir Pomeroy, she made her way toward him. Spying that pink wig on its determined way in their direction, she said in French to the man, "Will you keep me safely by your side, Monsieur?"

Surprised, but with twinkling gray eyes, he promptly replied that he would love nothing better. He introduced himself as Comte Talon. "Is there anything I can do for you while I keep you safely by my side, Mademoiselle?"

"Yes, yes, do start telling me a story, or the history of this place. I want to be able to listen to you and ignore that pink wigged man over there, the one who has just ruined his hose on a blackberry vine," she whispered. She couldn't help peeking at Sir Pomeroy's anguished gyrations.

Cackling, Comte Talon glanced at the irate Sir Pomeroy stooping and trying to extricate his precious clocked stockings from the thorns. "I do know something of the history of Chambord," he said, guiding her in a path away from Sir Pomeroy as if they hadn't noticed him. "Francois Premier, King of France, built it in the 1500s as a hunting lodge. Is it not the most grandiose hunting lodge you've ever seen? He must have enjoyed showing off this enormous symbol of his wealth and power. He even invited his arch nemesis, Emperor Charles V, to hunt here."

Since Sir Pomeroy had finally detached himself from the blackberries, he looked too chagrined to face her with such ruined hose. He moved behind a tree.

Genevieve listened with great interest to the old Comte's monologue. She murmured in awe, and asked a few questions. Sir Pomeroy finally turned in exasperation and stalked back to the château, presumably to change his hose.

Presenting Genevieve with his flowers, the Comte said, "Excellent work! We are rid of him. He got what he deserved for plaguing you. Are you still interested in this history?"

"Most definitely!" she said, and meant it.

"Continuez, s'il vous plaît, Monsieur le Comte."

Relishing her interest, he explained that the King had given Chambord to Maurice de Saxe, a Marshal of France, as a reward for valor in 1745. "The Marshall installed his military regiment within those walls," the Comte said, casting a sad look at her. "Can you imagine such a travesty?"

Genevieve said that it sounded like a rough and risky use for a château of such beauty and grace. "I hope they were neat soldiers."

"Quite. For two years, Saxe threw sumptuous parties here."

"Why does he not live here now?" She could not understand why anyone would leave such a home empty, with the result that such a ragtag and bobtail party had made this their free hotel.

"Il est mort," replied the Comte.

"How long ago did he die?"

"Three years, I believe."

Boldly, Genevieve ventured to ask, "So, since he died and no one has lived here since, how did all of you get in?"

"Simply. Someone kept a key." He slid a look at Genevieve and added, "You should be grateful. That little detail is why you stand here now, gazing at all of that magnificence. I came along with my daughter who had the key, but only because I am in her care. I could not stay at her home alone. She took all her servants here, you see. I would have been left to fend for myself."

Genevieve smiled in understanding, and carefully asked, "Was this visit taken against your better judgment, Monsieur le Comte?"

His face turned into waves of wrinkles as he

grinned at her. "You want me to say yes, do you not? Well, dear girl, I was bored, and now I am not. What do you think? *C'est la vie, n'est pas?"*

* * *

Having graciously thanked Comte Talon, Genevieve busied herself with climbing different stairways, ending up all over the immense château.

She encountered people here and there, walking in the courtyards, coming out of bedchambers, hauling in luggage, conversing on stairs, and even setting up a card game on a beautifully-sunlit staircase landing. She ducked into the dining room before dinner and procured some ham, bread, cheese, cherries, a half bottle of sweet wine, and a goblet. She took them up to her bedchamber and shoved her heaviest trunk against the door after she locked it. She felt truly thankful to God that her room had a key.

When Dorcasta knocked a few minutes later, she declined her invitation. Madam wanted her to join them in a card party before dinner. Genevieve did not open her door, but told Dorcasta that she opted to go to bed early because she was exhausted. "Go and play yourself, if my mother wants you there." Dorcasta willingly agreed, and clattered off.

Genevieve had no idea what they did that evening, nor did she care. Her sleep was dreamless and she woke up rested. "Dear Lord," she whispered upon opening her eyes, "please show me what to do here, in this wrong situation. Thank you that I could send that letter to Father. Let it reach him quickly. In Jesus' name protect and guide me—and reward my messenger. Amen."

She opened her window and enjoyed the freshness, the birds twittering, and the morning light upon the white stone of the château walls to each side of her. Having dressed herself, she went down, and there, coming in through the immensely tall door, was the silhouette of Radford Laurence, Lord Ashby.

"Radford! Here you are, back from Chartres much earlier than I expected." She gave him a smile and a curtsy.

While bowing, he took her extended hand and kissed it. "I am," he said, looking up at her from under his brown eyebrows. "You are right on time to welcome me."

"It's nice to see you, but I can hardly welcome you to a place that is not my own, can I?"

"However it is, we meet again."

They were strolling toward an open door, and through it, she spied Armand de Villebon riding his horse. She wanted to run and ask him if he had encountered any trouble posting her letter. "Will you excuse me, please? I must speak to someone for a moment."

Radford hesitated, and peered beyond her shoulder. When Genevieve turned to look again, there was the horse's face, framed in the doorway. Radford asked, "Is that who you need to speak to, that horse coming in?"

She laughed delightedly. "Yes, Gaspard and I are friends!" She went to pet the horse's velvety nose.

Armand, still mounted, grinned down at her. He made her heart flutter.

"Good morning, Monsieur de Villebon. I have a

query for you."

"Fire away." He backed his horse out so she could follow it outside.

She looked earnestly up at him and whispered, "Is it on its way?"

"But of course, Genevieve."

"Oh, you are wonderful!" She clasped her hands in relief.

He looked amused and said, "Words to relish in memory when I am in serious doubt."

Genevieve slid him a wondering look, and then noticed that he glanced up toward the roof. There, amongst the elegant chimneys, her mother promenaded with a man. When he turned, she saw that, again, it was Sir Pomeroy Chancet. Now his wig was lavender. He spied her and waved his lace handkerchief enthusiastically.

Genevieve turned her back on him.

Armand growled, "Who does he think he is? Can I expect him to spy on you every day? Will he shadow the Lady Bastwicke in fear of us who can scare him away?"

Genevieve laughed hopelessly. "He is given constant encouragement by my mother. She knows I cannot abide him. I'm sorry, I shouldn't talk that way about a person, but my revulsion of him has a legitimate history."

"I have gathered that. Shall we walk my horse to the woods and remove you from his sight again?"

"Why not ride your horse right into the château? He could trot up and down any number of stairways, and enjoy himself as everyone else seems to be doing. He might even make it to the roof and scare away the guilty." They laughed together, and she petted the soft nose and scratched under his mane. "You would like that, wouldn't you?"

In the doorway stood Radford Laurence, observing them. "Ready, Genevieve?" he called pleasantly, gesturing her to join him inside.

Genevieve nodded, turned to Armand, and said quietly, "Please excuse me. A friend has just arrived from Chartres, and I should not abandon him."

Armand urged the horse a step closer to her and said low, "You must endure a lot, Genevieve. That is obvious by the fact that you felt you had to smuggle your letter out with me." He directed a glance upward.

Genevieve swept the château roof with a glance. She saw that her mother and Sir Pomeroy were still chatting and looking down at them from among the dense village of chimneys. Her mother beckoned her imperiously, but she pretended not to see. Instead, she nodded good-bye to Armand and took Radford's offered arm at the door. "Did you see your godson, Radford?" she asked.

"Yes, he was baptized the day I got there because he was coming down with a cold. He's a fine boy as babies go."

"I see. So you came here as soon as it was over?"

Radford smiled into her eyes. "I had to."

"Why?

"I could think of doing nothing else since we parted." He gave her hand a squeeze.

As he guided her inside, she saw that Armand and his horse were a distance away, but he was watching them.

CHAPTER 8

The Auction

As soon as they entered the T of the ground floor hall with the white staircase dominating the center, she and Radford agreed that they would like some coffee. Into the breakfast room they went, where someone's footman served them surprisingly good coffee and small pastries.

Radford asked, "How do you like it here so far?"

She looked at him in ironic wonder and said it was a fabulous place. "But it feels clandestinely wrong to be here," she confessed.

Just then, Lady Bastwicke and Madame Mortinette passed by the doorway. The latter backed up when she saw Radford. "Ooh-la-la, Lord Ashbee! Come and play cards with us! We need you, come, come! We have been looking everywhere for a man to play with us."

Lady Bastwicke added her entreaty. "You promised me on the way here that you would join a card party, remember?"

So off he went, making apologies to Genevieve,

who refused to join them.

When she reentered the central hall, she saw Sir Pomeroy almost tripping down the stairs in his sparkly-buckled shoes. He seemed to be in a rush. He called joyfully, "Genevieve! You are the most beautiful sight on site!" As he approached her, his hooded brown eyes roved all over her, which always angered her.

She kept walking. Where she was going, she knew not, but she kept at it with a fast, purposeful stride. She was soon at the immensely high door to the entrance courtyard, with him clomping loudly in his red-heeled shoes behind her. "You should not follow me," she said as though to a small boy.

"Whyever not?" I want to talk with you, Genevieve!"

"You should not follow me because . . . you do not have your hat!" she said over her shoulder, prevaricating. "I know it's not raining, but the sun might adversely affect the magnificent lavender hue of your wig." She hoped that, to such a fop, that made-up reason might work.

She went blithely out into the sunshine of the courtyard, where many other people were promenading. Apparently she had left him without a good reason to trail her. She headed to the door in the outer keep, through its shaded rooms, and outside into sunshine again. The door she had just closed soon opened behind her, and from her peripheral vision, she saw Sir Pomeroy peering out but staying in the shade.

To Genevieve's relief, the two young men she had encountered at *déjeuner* came sauntering along toward her. They doffed their hats and bowed to her.

She returned their welcoming greetings so that Sir Pomeroy would believe she had arranged to meet them.

The short one said, "Mademoiselle, if I may make so bold as to remind you, you have two hours to ransack your bandboxes and find something you can live without."

"Please explain why I should do that."

"Because we want you to come to the auction," supplied the skinny one, whose eyes were squinted upon her.

The round-faced one added, "We told you about it yesterday, remember?"

"Ah, yes, to provide funds for a feast, and to pay musicians?"

"For other amusements, too," said the tall one, gaining confidence from her interest. "It can be eye-opening to see what people bring to put on the auction block."

"All right, I will see what I can find." She saw the curls of that lavender wig in the doorway, so she turned back to the young men and asked them to escort her to find the auction room. As they willingly led the way, the three of them passed right by Sir Pomeroy skulking and sulking in the shadows. He quickly pretended he was languidly taking snuff. She was outraged that her mother wanted her to marry this specimen of vainglorious decay.

Genevieve did not deign to look his way, but followed the eager young men in a direction on the ground floor that she had not yet explored.

* * *

Two hours later, Genevieve was seated in the large salon among a buzz of voices and seat-taking. Servants carried in more chairs from their masters' and mistresses' bedchambers and from wherever they had set them up upon arrival. Obviously, all of these inhabitants had been obliged to cart their trappings of comfort here. It made for a motley collection of chairs.

Genevieve saw her mother seated near the front with Madame Mortinette. That lady wore too many face patches. The two of them were snorting with laughter as usual. Lady Bastwicke wore two face patches, dangling earrings that Genevieve had never seen before, and peacock feathers waving about in her gray powdered coiffure. Her friend had her hair powdered the very same gray.

Just as Dorcasta waddled in, trailing Arabelle's cherry red and blue flowered dress, Genevieve fumed with righteous rage. Had she taken Arabelle's complete London wardrobe along to wear as her own? She could not understand why Madam had let her, or encouraged her, whatever the case had been.

Genevieve felt like going to challenge her, but a servant stepped into the space between them and made her a bow. Genevieve recognized his amber-colored eyes. He was the servant who had helped them out of the coach upon their arrival. He held a thin book with a paper upon it. "Mademoiselle, may I have your name, please?"

"You need it for ... what purpose?"

"We register each person, and mark that they

brought an item to auction, or not."

"Is that the rule?"

"Yes, Mademoiselle."

She gave her name and said that yes, she did bring something.

He thanked her and added, "You may win one auction. Then, if no one else is bidding on an item, you may bid again on that one."

"I see."

He went across the aisle to take information from Dorcasta. She informed the servant that she indeed had something. Genevieve heard him say, "But I do not see a parcel with you."

"I know," she said coyly, "but I do have something to auction." When he looked under her chair and shrugged his shoulders, she redoubled her volume, apparently so he would understand her English. "I will keep it a *surprise*."

When the auctioneer with a white wig and a swarthy face took his place in front of the chattering crowd, he rapped for order on the marble floor with his walking stick. "I hope you have all brought your money," he said in French, beaming right and left upon the gathering.

They hushed, and the late arrivals were stopped by the servant and required to give their names before being allowed to find seats. Genevieve saw, at the end of the queue, the head of Armand de Villebon. He smiled at her, and she smiled back. Instantly, she felt relieved.

As the queue diminished to one person, the auctioneer cleared his throat and said, "If you have brought something to auction off, you may be here. If not, you must go and find something now, and then be readmitted if you wish to bid. You must buy one item, and only one, unless no one else is bidding on something after I call it twice. Understood?"

Murmurs of assent sounded around the room.

He asked if someone would like to bring forward the first contribution to the auction.

Sir Pomeroy rose instantly. "I have something special!" he announced, pivoting in mid-stride to look back at the audience. "It is something I am loathe to part with, but we must all sacrifice something for the good of us all, must we not?"

Lady Bastwicke tittered. She was swaying a transparent golden fan and casting smiles at Sir Pomeroy over it.

He pulled out an item from beneath his lavish wrist lace. When he lifted it up, all could see that it was a snuffbox. He announced, "This is silver, and it has a peacock painted in enamel on the top."

Madame Mortinette called, "Then how can you bear to give it up? It personifies you!"

Flirtatiously, he quipped, "Quite right! But I have another one that is even grander."

Genevieve found him looking straight at her. "The most deserving in the bunch of you is the one I hope will take possession of this . . . as she has, of my heart," he added, intensifying his gaze upon her.

Some men made crows of "Oh-ho!" and a lady nearby crowed, "Ooh-la-la!" It seemed that everyone in the room was looking at Genevieve.

She breathed heavily, striving to contain her ire. She was not going to bid on it. Did he really think she would be so gullible? He held the snuffbox aloft, moving it slowly to show it around, but with his suggestive smile urging her to bid.

Genevieve's ears buzzed, and she could not see very clearly, so chaotic were her emotions. She felt her cheeks on fire, but she hastily remembered not to move her hands or head one iota, or it would be taken as a bid. She said quietly but distinctly with a level chin, "No, *merci*. I do not sniff snuff. I prefer to keep my nose clean."

Everybody laughed.

Sir Pomeroy flushed vermillion under his white face powder.

Genevieve felt nervous at sight of his suddenly rigid stance, so she turned slightly and looked for Armand. He had stepped over the threshold and was regarding the registry paper that the servant held. "Wait here to resume your duties should anyone else arrive," she heard him say to the young man.

A few minutes later, someone bent over her. Startled, she looked up into Armand's face. "May I sit here for a moment?" he whispered.

She moved over immediately.

He said, chuckling, "That was rather a pointed statement by your would-be swain, was it not?"

Genevieve let him see her frustration. "Do you see what I go through?"

He grinned. "Yes. To so publicly aim an item at you did not show finesse as a suitor. A Frenchman would not be so clumsy. I am continually appalled, and baffled, by the behavior of some Englishmen."

That surprised a giggle out of her. "So am I."

"You must have rejected many advances from him for the dolt to take such a desperate action."

"I have! So did my sister before me."

"Is that so? But your mother likes him for her daughters?" He shook his head wonderingly.

Genevieve crossed her arms in frustration.

He said, "Let's see who wins that snuffbox of the peacock, since you are not enamored of it."

Bidding was moving fast, with Madame Mortinette and Lady Bastwicke bidding against each another. Soon a man topped their bids. Then Dorcasta's hand shot up, waving in Arabelle's red glove. "I bid all of my money," she called. She held up two golden coins for Sir Pomeroy and the auctioneer to see. She obviously didn't know what the French coins were worth.

Turning in their seats, everyone stared at the eager bidder. A young man made a catcall, and another said in English, "You want to give all zat money for zat peacock, Mademoiselle? Ooh-la-la, zat is foolish, no?"

Dorcasta stood up, smiling widely, still offering her coins to the auctioneer and Sir Pomeroy.

The auctioneer remarked that there could be no more bids until he saw how much the young woman was bidding. It seemed that the crowd unanimously wanted to see Dorcasta win. The auctioneer added, "Any new lady would win because this one admits that she is bidding all of her money. Not the brightest button in the box, are you?" In English, he called to Dorcasta, "How much is it, Mademoiselle?"

Dorcasta reddened, and rubbed the two coins between her fingers, causing them to fall with a clink and roll so that she had to bend down and try to retrieve them with too-long-fingered gloves.

Armand, observing, shook his head slowly and gave Genevieve a sidewise grin. She threw him a glance and squeezed her eyes shut.

After the gavel pounded, the auctioneer cried, "Sold! —to the young lady who is willing to give her all for your trinket, Sir Pomeroy."

Dorcasta sauntered triumphantly forward amidst the laughs and comments. She relinquished her money into the auctioneer's hand and turned to receive her prize from Sir Pomeroy.

His red smile was stiff as he relinquished it with obvious regret. The look he shot Genevieve caused Armand to quip, "That look could have sizzled a sausage."

Genevieve choked on a giggle, which made some of her tension dissipate.

Dorcasta, relishing all the attention focused upon her, turned back toward her seat, but ruined her promenade when she tripped on the hem of Arabelle's gown. She grabbed the nearest shoulder, which belonged to an elderly, frail-looking dandy. He clutched the girl, hung onto her for longer than necessary, and cackled up at her, showing missing teeth. After she tugged herself away and had nearly made it to her seat, she met Genevieve's eyes with a haughty look.

Genevieve and Armand locked eyes, and he remarked, "That one is new in society, I believe. What a murky pond to be thrown into. I wonder if she will want to keep paddling through it."

"I fear for her."

"Yes."

The auctioneer called for another offering, and Lady Bastwicke rose. Her wide skirt careened into chairs and hit peoples' knees as she strutted to the front. What was she going to give up? Genevieve wondered. It was a round box with a hinged lid and shells all around. Genevieve leaned forward and stared. She and little Lenora had made that shell box as a birthday present, suggesting that she keep her rings in it.

"Here we have fashionable hair powder," announced the auctioneer, who had looked inside and slapped away the powder that rose onto his coat. "It is presented in a box covered with shells, artistically arranged."

Lady Bastwicke simpered and gestured upward to her own newly-powdered gray hair, teased to a height grander than before. She said, "Every woman should powder her hair. After all, the men have done so for years—or worn wigs—and they look so fashionable that we ladies must make ourselves at least their equals." She tittered and made her grandiose way back to her seat amidst a few claps.

That compelled several women to bid, and the shell-covered box eventually went to a wiry lady whose hair was faded blonde, turning to gray. Genevieve thought that the powder might actually work well for her. More and more women were powdering their hair light gray, especially here in France. Genevieve suspected why the fashion caught on. Ladies found that they could camouflage their newly-found gray or white strands with—what else?—gray or white powder. They were also busy encouraging young women to powder their hair so that all ages of women would look more alike. Genevieve, like Arabelle, resisted such a ludicrous trend, not wanting gray or white hair, or the mess of powder. Father had his wigs covered pristine white each morning in his powder room, blown on by his valet through a bellows, while he covered his face with a cone and coughed prodigiously.

"*I* have something!" cried Dorcasta when the auctioneer called for the next item. When invited forward, she lifted the skirt of her dress very high, and instantly, young men made "Oho!" sounds and whistles.

The auctioneer inquired, "What is it that you have for us?"

Genevieve watched as Dorcasta maneuvered white linen with edgings of luxurious lace out from under the gown she wore. It proved to be a petticoat, and Genevieve recognized Arabelle's embroidery and sky blue ribbons threaded through it. She exclaimed beneath her breath, "This is the outside of enough!"

She excused herself to Armand, during which he quickly gave his hand to help her move past his knees. She went straight to Dorcasta and expelled in a loud whisper, "Dorcasta Doyle, I'm sorry, but you cannot auction that off!" She looked at the interested auctioneer and asserted, "A thousand pardons, Monsieur, but this belongs to my sister, and she will need it back. This is a mistake." She turned a probing look upon Dorcasta and held out her hand for the petticoat.

With a face red with guilty anger, Dorcasta stamped her foot. "We had to bring *something*, and I thought these clothes were now mine!"

"Pardon me, but that is not yours," Genevieve

added clearly in French so the others would understand. "I'm sorry, but that is not your petticoat to give. It was made with very costly lace for my sister, and she embroidered it. My sister will need this when next she is in London." Genevieve quickly translated her words to English for Dorcasta's ears.

Gulping, Dorcasta gave it up with a shove because otherwise she would have totally lost face in front of the whole company. "But I have nothing!" she quavered, trying to drum up sympathy.

Genevieve asked, "So that justifies theft?"

One of the men who had issued catcalls earlier quipped, "Auction off your own petticoat, Mademoiselle."

Dorcasta simpered at him. She decisively waddled toward the front, hitting her chin with her fist meditatively. "*I* know!" she said to the auctioneer.

"What is it you know?" he inquired superciliously. The way he regarded her, she was clearly on the level of pond scum to him now.

Turning to smile brightly, Dorcasta declared, "I will . . . sing!"

"Sing?" repeated the auctioneer. "How can you auction off a song? Who would buy it if everyone could hear it? Bah!"

Dorcasta, striving to sparkle at the crowd, said, "I will auction a song, and I will sing it to the winner." She added promisingly, "In private!"

There were excited sounds of "Oho!" from some of the men and women.

Genevieve deflated her lungs in a despairing sigh, and glanced at Armand. How could Dorcasta be so brash? She was now swiveling right and left, and watching the bidding rise from certain men in all parts of the room. Lady Bastwicke was laughing, fanning, and rooting them on.

Genevieve would have left, but Armand's hand caught her fingers. "I can guess how mortified you feel, Miss Genevieve, for I feel it myself. I have never seen the like. But stay. Stay for one more." He smiled imploringly down at her.

She melted at the reassuring twinkle in his eyes. "Only because you ask me, Armand de Villebon."

A pleased smile played upon his handsome lips. "Armand is enough, Genevieve, and thank you."

Dorcasta was clattering back toward her seat, and shot Genevieve a triumphant look. Galling her further, she decidedly came near and whispered loudly, "Thank you for telling me about my good voice. I can see that I am now most popular because of it." She flicked a coquettish look over Armand.

He said in French, "One can only hope that, when you are heard, it will be worth the money spent."

Genevieve choked on a laugh.

Dorcasta, who did not understand a word of French, nevertheless had the wind taken from her sails. She left them, wearing an uncertain look.

Genevieve said, "That was wicked, but I have to agree with you. She is incorrigible."

He murmured, "If she only knew how she just ruined her reputation."

"Yes; and my mother should not have let her come with us. She does not know what she is doing."

The auctioneer pounded his gavel and called,

"Now that our eldest and most distinguished friend, Monsieur de la Puy, has bought a song, we will have two more auction items before we pause for wine and cakes. So who will be next? How about you two in the back row?"

Genevieve crossed her arms because she was not keen to participate in such a lurid auction. But Armand gave an acquiescent bow of his head, and asked Genevieve if she would like to go first.

She declined, saying, "Please, no. You go, if you wish." She watched him as he strolled to the back and retrieved a bouquet of spring wildflowers from outside the doorway. Looking splendid, he walked with them to the front and said with a bow of his head, "*Merci,* Monsieur. Here is my humble offering." When enthusiastic bidding began on his flowers, he strolled back to his seat next to Genevieve.

She smiled and said, "Beautiful and tasteful," and bid once on his artful bouquet. Since the bidding among the ladies was fierce, she had not enough money to continue, and told him so with regret.

He shook his head slightly, conveying to her kindly that it didn't matter.

Dorcasta was gazing over her shoulder at him, smiling widely every few seconds, striving to catch his attention. Genevieve noted it with annoyance. Wasn't her money all gone? Seeing Genevieve's disapproval, Dorcasta's smile fell off. She looked into her drawstring pocket and actually called back to Armand, "It's just too bad that I haven't enough money, Monsieur. I only have small coin left. I want those flowers! They're put together so pretty—aren't they, Genevieve? But they are too dear now."

Genevieve made no response. How did she dare to chatter on and on?

The wildflower bouquet went to a man in a white wig in the front row, but Genevieve could not see who he was for all the heads in the way.

The auctioneer called, "Now it is the young lady's turn; our lovely English guest with the French name, Mademoiselle Geneviève. Have you something to offer us, *chérie?*"

She thought she might as well get it over with so she could leave. Despite all of the eyes following her, she went and gave him her neatly-wrapped paper parcel, retraced her steps, and sank into her seat, her heart pounding. Many people were still looking at her, the men in admiration. Two ladies were whispering behind their fans, and one of them pointed to Lady Bastwicke.

"Quel charme!" said the auctioneer. "She has tied this with a silk ribbon and decorated it with sprigs of dried lavender. It smells divine," he said. *"Mon arôme préféré!* What can she have for us inside? I am going to open it because I cannot help myself."

People laughed indulgently. As they leaned forward to see what he was unwrapping, Genevieve hoped it would favorably pass judgment. Though she did not like most of this crowd's actions or attitudes, she hoped her gift would not bring ridicule. The auctioneer lifted up her thin sheaf of creamy paper tied with another lavender ribbon, and in the bow that surrounded the pages, three strands more of dried purple lavender were arranged. Also tied into the bow was a drawing pencil.

"Ooh!" cried Sir Pomeroy. His hand shot up while he craned to look back at her with longing eyes. "I bid first and highest!" he declared, turning to the auctioneer. "It is an invitation to write her a *lettre d'amour!*"

"Dream on!" countered Genevieve clearly before she could stop herself.

That drew enthusiastic laughter.

She flushed, but kept her poise. She could feel Armand shaking with silent mirth beside her.

Peering back at her between bids, the sight of her disdainful composure seemingly made Sir Pomeroy more determined. Though he was rivaled by many others around the room, he topped everyone's bids with relish.

Genevieve rose before the bidding was over. She just had to get out of the room. Suddenly, she longed for the safe old life with Aunt Claracilla and her loving sister, Arabelle. And dear Father!—how she wished he would come and take her home. She would write to him again.

But would her mother take her back to London even if she begged? Would she ever let a mere daughter pry her away from this rollicking fun? She always appeared to be in alt amongst this type of rich but vulgar crowd. She laughed raucously, flirted with men, hit people with her fan, and said things behind it that brought such looks to peoples' faces.

Clutching her dear Arabelle's linen petticoat, Genevieve whisked past Armand, excusing herself, and ran lightly to the staircase. Soon she heard his whisper echo in the splendid acoustics of the hall. "Genevieve!"

She turned and looked down over the marble banister. He hurried toward her and asked, "Shall we promenade along the moat for a few minutes? I wish to tell you something away from all these ears."

"Yes!" she said. "Thank you." That was when she saw Radford Laurence, Lord Ashby in the shadow outside the door, from where he had apparently been watching the auction. She had not seen anyone's faces as she sped from that room. He raised a hand slightly, but she affected not to notice, and streaked for the door after Armand.

Armand took the petticoat from her arms and strode back to speak to the amber-eyed servant who stood in the doorway of the auction salon. Genevieve waited until he returned to her side, saying, "My man will keep it safe for you."

She breathed easier for several reasons. "I love this château," she said to him, "but . . . "

"But you do not love what is happening here?"

"Exactly."

He guided her hastily outside. "I, also, abhor it extremely."

"You do?" She really looked at him. "Then why are you here? No one brought *you* by force, did they?"

"Not by force, as you imply that you were, but I admit that there is a force that brought me here."

CHAPTER 9

A Clandestine Plan

Genevieve stopped at the moat's edge and looked up into Armand's face. He was so noble and arresting that she did not dare to look long and be caught staring.

He bent his dark head toward her and said earnestly, "I know that I can trust you, Genevieve. There is something I must do, and I want for you to have advance knowledge of it." He offered her his arm, and she placed her hand upon it. She felt slightly breathless, as if living in a dream. He escorted her alongside the moat and toward the green forest, which had become their place, it seemed. Fast-moving, billowing gray clouds came rolling toward them, darkening the sky.

"Our blue-sky weather is changing," remarked Genevieve as the sudden breeze lifted tendrils of her coppery hair into her eyelashes.

"Yes," he agreed, "and the weather must rapidly change inside."

She quizzed him with a look.

He said, "I have been deliberating whether or not to let you into my confidence, and I am happy to do so now because I trust you."

Genevieve brightened. "Why, thank you."

He touched her hand upon his arm and said, "I want to confide in you for your own safety."

"My . . . safety?"

"Yes." He looked back at the white beauty of the château. "On behalf of the owner of Chambord, I am investigating what is going on here. As you know, none of these people should be here."

"Then why were they—we—allowed entrance at all?"

"That is what I am here to find out. They are here *en masse*, and someone is the ringleader. Someone had a scheme, and got the château unlocked, or they could have broken in somewhere. There are thousands of doors and windows."

"When we arrived, I had no idea that the owner wasn't here as our host," said Genevieve. "Why does he not live here and watch over his property?"

"I don't yet know his reason. I was told that the new owner lives far away, in another country."

Genevieve said, "There is something very reckless and decadent about this. But my mother thinks that way. She cares not what—oh dear! I should not say any more." Genevieve put her hand over her mouth and searched his attentive blue eyes.

"I want you to speak frankly with me. Are you close to your mother?"

Genevieve told him briefly about how Lady Bastwicke had left her and her other children in

England with their relatives for many years, so she hardly knew her. She related how, less than two years ago, Madam had come back at the behest of her father, Lord Bastwicke. She told how she and her sister's upbringing by Aunt Claracilla and Uncle Trent had been based on love and the Word of God, and confessed to him that her real mother had nothing of those sources to offer, neither in heart nor in practice. "She is woefully worldly," concluded Genevieve with misery in her voice.

"Thank you for telling me. I sensed the difference in you at once. It only took a couple of minutes to see what she is. You, however, radiate goodness. That quality, Miss Genevieve, gives me the desire to protect you."

Genevieve experienced again that heart-fluttering feeling while she cast her eyes over his caring face. "You love truth and light yourself, I can see that."

"Certainly I do. The world is too full of darkness and deceit. It's like seeing God's rainbow when I see goodness in someone."

"If there is any goodness in me, it is not my own."

"I know who shines within you," Armand said. He put out his hand for hers and squeezed it. "Jesus."

"He is our Light," she said happily, squeezing his in return. She quickly turned and picked a little flower in their path. Armand picked a few more, and kept handing them to her as they walked. As they moved between tall trees and onto the path where she had walked with the old Comte, she whirled and said, "Armand! I know who has the key!"

He straightened up from picking. "You do?"

"Yes! Comte Talon confided to me that his daughter has one, and that is how they got in!"

Armand stepped toward her and grasped her arm. "He told you?"

"Yes! After you left with my letter, he came along in the woods and saved me from having to encounter Sir Pomeroy, who was heading my way. I asked Comte Talon to tell me all about this place, and how he happened to come here, and he did."

"It is amazing that you pulled that vital piece of information out of him. Ah, charm and beauty count for much! Well done, Genevieve!" Impulsively, he kissed her forehead.

Her heart skipped with joy. "So what are you going to do about the people squatting here?"

"I will halt it absolutely."

"I am glad to hear it! But they are so ensconced and settled. They have their furniture in the rooms they occupy, their food and servants in the kitchens, and their horses and carriages filling the stables. They even brought lap dogs, chickens, and birds, and I heard that musicians are ordered. Someone bought two cows from nearby for milk! I spied them in one of the walled gardens."

Armand said, "Yes, they have made it their own secret Versailles."

"I have not been to Versailles, but since the King retired there to get away from Paris, perhaps the simile is apt. May I ask what you plan to do?"

"Evict them."

"Just like that? What daring you have!"

Seeing her admiring side glance, he grinned.

"You are truly going to send them all away?"

"Yes. Every one of those culprits."

"When?"

"Tomorrow."

"Tomorrow! Oh, good! Are you the mysterious owner who lives far away, then?"

"No, I am not. He is Polish, and I do not know where he lives now."

"He will thank you, I am sure. How did it happen that you are the one to perform this mission?""

She and Armand stood looking back at the château, kissed now with other-worldly golden sun beams streaming from under the dark clouds. He said, "Our government committee in Paris sent me to gather evidence that this rumored invasion was truly occurring here, and, if true, to chase them all out. Today I gathered names to give them a record."

Genevieve, with dawning appreciation, exclaimed, "That was brilliantly done! Who would ever suspect the real reason we had to sign in to the auction? That was your idea?"

"Yes, and I have the authority to send everyone on the list, as well as any not on it, upon their way. I have most of their signatures."

"What if some did not attend the auction?"

"I will discover their names at the gate. My men will check everyone who leaves against the list, and add to it."

Genevieve cried, "Oh, what clever planning! I have felt so guilty being here, seeing the way those people dare to rollick and use this lovely place for their tawdry pleasures. I am excited by your plan, but it seems like a monumental and chaotic endeavor. What can I do to help?"

He tipped back his head and laughed. His eyes were gleaming on her as he said, "Your support is all I need to make this mission a success."

Genevieve colored faintly. "Just tell me how I can help you."

"For now, keep our secret."

"I will!" she said, hugging herself with anticipation. "I hope they take all of their trashy belongings with them, and leave this palace and the grounds in . . . pristine serenity."

"Amen to that. If they do not take everything, we will cart up the remains and bring it to the town market for people to take or burn." Armand cleared his throat, for two ladies were strolling toward them with parasols aloft.

"*Bonjour*, Armand," said the younger one, possibly forty years old, with blonde hair and smiling eyes. She wore an attractive lace cap with blue and gold ribbons floating from the back to match her gown.

"*Bonjour*, Tante Lavande," called Armand warmly. "Are you just arriving for the auction? It is in full swing." They kissed each others' cheeks.

"Oh, no, we looked in at it, but did not bring anything to sell, so Belle-mère wanted to walk instead." She seemed to look at him with a message in her eyes. Armand introduced the ladies. Smiling at Genevieve, Madame Lavande said, "We will go back in now because it grows too windy for our caps." In fact, the older woman was holding hers on.

When they had moved away, Genevieve asked quietly, "What about those ladies? Is one your aunt, and the other her mother-in-law?"

"Yes, Madame Lavande is my aunt by marriage.

She is with me on my mission. She took her mother-in-law here for the day on the pretext of being part of the crowd. She is observing, and will write up our report to the government about what is going on here."

"I see. What about the serving boy who is caring for the petticoat?"

"Jean-Luc is my servant. Soon my other men, who slept in rooms near the stable wing, will help him knock on doors and deliver notes of eviction. If these people see them, they're bound to assume my officials are other people's servants."

"My, but you are organized and clever! Who will wield the power to force everyone to leave?" Genevieve asked him, her mouth going dry at the prospect of the opposition to come. "Who is going to tell them?

"*You* offered to help," he reminded her, his dimple in evidence. At her incredulous gasp and stare, he laughed outright. "No need to look so terrified. I suppose I can desist from sending you to knock on doors."

* * *

Genevieve, revitalized by Armand's plan, returned to her chamber with nervous anticipation. There, outside her door, lay a wilting bouquet. She picked it up to find a folded creamy paper beneath it, tied with the same ribbon and lavender sprigs that she had brought to the auction. "Of all the nerve!" she expelled.

When she went inside and turned to close the door, she saw Sir Pomeroy hurrying her way from the shadows beyond the staircase. He had lain in wait for her! She snapped her door shut and locked it. How dared he think he could watch her, and then accost her at her chamber door? But that was his code of conduct with women, as she well knew.

She flipped open his note just as she heard a creak of the floorboard outside. Her heart jumped, the lock held, and she read,

> *Gorgeous Genevieve,*
> *First, I must tell you that I am utterly charmed by every sight of you. Truly, you are my ideal woman. Because I feel it is meant to be, I shall make bold to ask you: shall we join our lives and live in bliss? You would make me the happiest man in France—or in England, if you prefer. Your mother, as a Viscountess, has written me a letter of recommendation that may allow me back in England very soon. We are striving for that end so that I may keep you as my lovely wife in either country. In case you have qualms, I have won a great amount of money by my talent for cards, so we shall have no worries on that account. You see, I do not intend to gamble anymore. I already have a great inheritance and a château of my own.*
>
> *Tonight, I will come to you for your answer. Please, please make it favorable. We can then be married right here in France, and begin our ecstatic union. My ardor for you absolutely thrills me.*
>
> *Your loving*
> *Sir Pomeroy*

Genevieve shuddered, crushed up the paper, and threw it across the room. She must tell her mother to order Sir Pomeroy off the chase. She was likely the only person he would listen to.

Much later, she warily looked around outside her bedchamber lest he still lurked, but she only spied a garishly-painted old woman with an elegant walking stick and high hair leaving a bedchamber.

Genevieve searched for her mother for quite half an hour, up and down various corridors, traversing beautiful white landings with views out of towers, and grand sweeps of curving marble stairways. Madam was nowhere to be seen in any of the rooms that contained people talking, eating, playing the lute, singing, reading plays aloud in parts, or playing cards.

Genevieve was too embarrassed to ask the people where her own mother might be, so she just smiled or greeted them as she thought appropriate.

Finally, she returned to her bedchamber and went to the window to survey the grounds from there. She gloried to see the sparkle of water in the moat below, as now it reflected the pink sunset in a bright sheen. The dark clouds had passed on. She was high above the ground, and liked looking down the curve of the tower in which she was housed.

The countryside was lush and dotted with white and yellow narcissi, jonquils, and wild daffodils. The lawns and fields, the forest of varicolored green trees, and the smoke from kitchen fires in the distance wisped upward. She heard a horse whinny. The evening was so still that sound carried far.

Due to that fact, she heard voices. She paused near the open window. Of course! The roof! That was where she had seen her mother promenading before.

When Genevieve emerged from her door onto the roof, she gasped in awe. Slim towers and chimneys rose in higgledy-piggledy, ornate fashion all around her. It felt like a fairy story village as she walked between the varied heights and designs of them. Many had cupolas with elegantly-shaped windows. When she reached one of the gray conical towers, she heard her mother's voice.

There, in the shadow, she sat with a man. Genevieve hid where she could see, but not be seen. What was so odd to Genevieve was that, though it was daylight, Madam did not have on her customary wide gown with its six-foot farthingale. Instead, she wore a much-diminished coral-colored gown that seemed to have no supports beneath it at all. The stocky man's black wig was askew, and her bony right hand was kneading the back of his neck beneath his loosened lace jabot. He looked as though he savored it, for his eyes were closed.

Genevieve felt sick. She vacillated. Should she interrupt them at this embarrassing moment? What she wanted to do was back away unseen. But then anger sparked within her. How enraged would her dear Father be if he could see this?

"Mother?" she deliberately called, leaving aside the *Madam* she was supposed to use.

Lady Bastwicke's head spun around.

The man's eyes popped inelegantly. He began to straighten his clothes and surreptitiously move away.

"What is it?" snapped her mother. Her close-set eyes bored daggers into Genevieve.

"I wanted to . . . ask you something."

"Ask me later—tomorrow! Can't you see that I'm helping a friend in pain?"

The man had straightened his black wig with its double side curls, and was watching them with guarded fascination. He had a wide face, black brows, and deep lines down his cheeks. He appeared to be of less than middle height with broad shoulders, and he wore what looked like a brocade dressing gown over his shirt.

Genevieve, disgusted to the core, mumbled "Yes, *Maman*," and cast a look of disapproval from her to the man.

He gave her a bow of his head, but she could detect that her presence had diminished their day. She looked back before she entered the door in the chimney to descend. Madam was cajoling him with chirpy words, but she kept a vitriolic watch on Genevieve until she left.

Genevieve knew that Madam would not help her to get rid of Sir Pomeroy.

* * *

Radford, Lord Ashby stood among the throng of pre-dinner guests seating themselves in the dining room. Genevieve had missed out on the promenade of precedence, for which she was glad. He excused himself from four flirting ladies when he saw her. She marveled at how smoothly and politely he accomplished it. "Miss Genevieve!" he greeted her, smiling.

"Radford, you surprised me by your early arrival here," she said as she took the seat he held for her. She smiled at him, and then spied Armand de Villebon looking at her as he took a seat a few chairs away and across the table. He bowed his head in acknowledgement of her, and eyed her escort.

During the dinner, served inefficiently by a motley lot of different people's servants, she found herself distracted by the sound of Dorcasta's abrasive laughter. She was describing to someone how she sang for that "extremely old man" and then had the effrontery to point him out as he came into the room. "Then I discovered that he could hardly even *hear* me, so he had me go fetch his ear trumpet, and I sang straight into that!" She screeched in laughter, much in the style of Lady Bastwicke. "I am sure he cannot even hear me now," she added, waving coyly at the man.

Two young men across from her guffawed, but most people did not smile or understand. Then Genevieve saw that it was Armand and a few others to whom Dorcasta had related all that.

Trying to block them out, Genevieve focused her attention on Radford, and asked him how he found Chartres. He told her that the Cathedral was the best one he had ever seen, and that she should definitely experience it before she returned to England. "I found it much more appealing than the Notre-Dame de Paris. It has more light, is laid out beautifully, and the stained glass windows are astonishingly bright and varied. It has a pilgrims' labyrinth on the floor."

"I hope with all my heart that I can see it."

"Yes, and soon, or you might not have another

chance."

"True."

He asked, "Where is your mother this evening?"

Startled, Genevieve looked up and down the tables and behind her, but she was nowhere to be seen. "I do not know," she replied, unable to furnish excuses for her.

Watching her face, he asked, "Is it very trying to be here?"

"Yes, it is. It is impossible to look after one's . . . mother."

With a rueful chuckle, he took her hand and patted it, saying, "You, dear Genevieve, should never be burdened with such an office as taking care of her. Or of that other person she brought with her."

Genevieve happened to glance Armand's way, and saw him noting her hand being squeezed by Radford. She wondered what he thought. She gently withdrew her hand and reached for her goblet.

Radford asked, "Would you like me to take you away from here? I mean, if you're truly uncomfortable?"

"How would that be possible? What female would accompany me?"

"Miss Doyle, I suppose. She is rather a babe in these woods. She could benefit from your tutelage in everything."

It would be prudent to get her away from these people, Genevieve felt, but she did not like the company of Dorcasta. She said, "We know very little about her. She has made a swath of indiscretions through this motley crowd already.

There seems to be no limit to her . . . behavior." Genevieve surprised herself by speaking so frankly to him. "In London, she asked for my advice, but here she does not. I think she takes her tutelage from, well, others. She is useless as a companion for me even though Madam said she took her along for that purpose."

They heard Dorcasta's loud laugh again, and saw her energetically clink her goblet against a man's on her other side, causing wine to flip out of it.

"I see your point. You should not have to take on the burden of her. Pardon me for the suggestion. I did not think that through."

She met his eyes and said, "The best way for me to get along with her is to keep distant. I still wonder why my mother brought her along, because she doesn't enforce our companionship at all."

He said, looking at her in a puzzled way, "I have wondered if she could be her daughter."

"Her *daughter?*" Genevieve stared at him, aghast. "How could that be?"

Sideways through the door, wearing her grand farthingale again, Lady Bastwicke appeared, accompanied by the man with whom she had sat so cozily on the rooftop. Genevieve could hardly look at her. Could it be true? She breathed hard and barely met Radford's sympathetic eye.

"Come, Genevieve," he murmured, "let me escort you out."

"Yes, thank you." Genevieve let him pull out her chair, not waiting for a servant. She swept out of the long room on his arm, aware that many diners watched them leave.

Before they reached the doorway, she heard Dorcasta say, "That was my close friend, Lord Ashby." Then louder, as if the French, who did not understand her, were deaf, added, "He's a very *high Earl in England!* Of nobility!" she nearly shouted.

Radford, mightily abashed, muttered, "She must be drunk!"

As he led her out, Genevieve whispered, "Is that true? Are you her close friend, O Earl of Nobility?"

He looked extremely vexed. "No, of course not! The very idea!"

Genevieve's mind whirled, and what concerned her most was that Madam had been gone for so many years, but she wondered if she could possibly have had a child the age of Dorcasta. Every feeling revolted! If Dorcasta could possibly be her own half-sister, she would be appalled. She shuddered. To Radford, she whispered in the corridor, "It cannot be, for Arabelle is older, and very close to Dorcasta's age, so that makes it impossible. Arabelle was born ten months after my parents' wedding."

"I see. So much for my wild theory. I'm terribly sorry." He put his arm around her shoulders as they headed for the stairs. "Do you want a shawl from your room? I can take you part of the way there with propriety. Which way is it?"

Sir Pomeroy came running out from somewhere, and heard the question. "*I* shall take her there, Lord Ashby." Pompously, he added, "*I* know the way."

Genevieve glared at him. "How *you* know the way is nothing to do with me!" she expelled, and cast a darkling look at Radford. She hurried up the *Grand*

Escalier, turning her back on Sir Pomeroy.

Raising a dismissive hand, Radford said, "Sir Pomeroy, thank you, but we will manage." Genevieve noted how effectually he dismissed him with those few quiet words.

Radford stopped at the top of the staircase and whispered, "I am serious, Genevieve. If you want to leave, I can tell your mother that I'm taking you to see Chartres Cathedral tomorrow. It would give you a day away from here."

"Thank you, but I don't think so," she said, wanting to aid Armand in his mission. At Radford's crestfallen face, she said, "Perhaps another day, Lord Ashby."

He shook his head in polite exasperation. "Radford! Remember, Genevieve? I am Radford to you. You are Genevieve to me. No more of this Lord Ashby formality."

She smiled in compliance. "I remember."

He kissed her hand in English fashion, and left. He was on her mother's list of top eligible men. She liked him, and had almost gotten over her unease around him, but not completely. She still felt opposed to knuckling under to any man whom Madam suggested she marry.

She sighed, locked her door, undressed shakily, removed pins, and brushed her hair, cleaned her teeth, and crawled gratefully into bed. With thoughts jangling inside her head, she turned to prayer. She asked God to make all things right, and to calm her, and to give her a peaceful sleep. *In Jesus' name I pray for all to be well in the end, Lord. Show me what to do. Amen.*

PURSUING GENEVIEVE

* * *

When she awoke the next morning, there was a paper on the floor that had not been there the night before.   Another *billet* from Sir Pomeroy, she supposed.   Apprehensively, she picked up the folded page and hastily checked her door. The key was still turned, so no one could have entered. She looked up, and there, stuck in the window, was a sprig of wildflowers.   Someone had reached in from the roof walk and pushed in her note that way, to fall on the floor.   But who was it?   She opened the page.

> *Dear Genevieve,*
> *Will you please meet me for a quick word before you go in to breakfast? I will wait for you in the stable.*
>
> *A*

Her heart beat excitedly. She hurried into her clothes, choosing a pale aqua ensemble that she could fasten in front without assistance.   She arranged her hair and put on her tiny lace cap with the aqua silk ribbons and pink rosebuds.   She stepped into her pink shoes and hurried out, quietly locking the door.

When she entered the round stable's dim interior, the smell of horses and hay assailed her. She saw him silhouetted against the far window: Armand.

"I am here," she called softly.

Armand's horse nickered from a stall nearby, so she moved to pet his soft nose and say, *"Comment vas-tu, cher Gaspard?"*

His owner's smile was white in the dimness, and he surprised her by kissing her first on one cheek, and then more slowly on the other. *"Bonjour,"* he said, looking deep into her eyes. "You look beautiful!"

"Thank you." She felt uplifted. "It is a beautiful day that is dawning." She gave him a happy smile. Her cares of yesterday had dissolved for the moment.

"Will you come over here where we can talk? Do you mind this place?"

"Mind?" she echoed incredulously. "I love this atmosphere. I enjoy the smell of hay."

He smiled. "That's good. Have a seat." He gestured to a mounting block on which he had laid a clean saddle blanket. She thanked him and collapsed her panniers to sit upon it.

With his boot nearly touching her gown, he stood and leaned against his horse's stall and stroked Gaspard's face. "I have Jean-Luc, over there," he indicated the lad at the door, "ready to warn us if anyone comes." He lowered his voice. "I don't want any eavesdroppers while we talk."

Very interested, Genevieve whispered, "Is this about the plan?"

"It is, and I must implement it."

"How soon?"

"Now; this morning."

"Oh, my! What will that throng do when they're told?"

"They will pack their bags and hasten away if they have any sense at all."

"If they're reluctant, how will you make them go?"

"We will see what's necessary. First, I will have Jean-Luc and my other men deliver notes to them. I had them all printed last night in the village. Everyone will have to leave by tonight."

Genevieve, thrilled by his edict, asked, "Or else what?"

"Be reported, tracked down, or taken into custody in Paris. Those are my given orders. The government has sent a force of officers to haul them in, and they are assembled and preparing nearby as we speak. We don't want a big fuss here on these premises. Who knows if someone has brought a firearm and would decide to use it? I don't want anyone damaging Chambord."

"My word! It sounds like you have a great deal of authority."

Seeing her admiring expression, his lips curved and he admitted, "I do, which brings me to the reason I need to talk to you now. I do not want you in danger, Genevieve. You have come here innocently, and should not feel any adverse consequences from obeying your mother. Not that I would want her sent to prison, but she must leave as soon as she receives my notice."

"I hope she does. But how can I escape the same consequences as everyone else if she will not leave?"

"By escaping first," he said, looking her in the eyes. "I have taken your name off the list."

Genevieve was touched by his concern for her. "Escape to . . . where?"

"I will let you know as soon as I know."

"But if you should take me away from here yourself, is that not the sort of risqué plot that young ladies are never supposed to submit to?"

In mild amusement, he squinted at her through a fence of dark lashes. "In normal circumstances, that would be true."

"So you think I should individually go along with an escape plan?"

"Without a doubt."

Wanting not to be stupid again, she pressed, "Why are you so sure?"

"Because you are in immediate danger of a *marriage de convenance*."

"Convenient to my mother and Sir Pomeroy, you mean."

"It appears that way from all you have told me, and confirmed by what I observe. Does she want you off her hands?"

"You guessed it! Then she'll have a long stretch of freedom from marriageable daughters before she launches my little sister, Lenora, into the sea of matrimony. She is only seven."

Armand remarked with a look of regret, "You are not enjoying this period of your life, are you?"

Genevieve turned smoldering eyes upon him. "In some ways, it has been the worst."

"We must rectify that." He gave her hand a squeeze. "For now, I wish you would quietly pack up your things. Will you trust me to spirit you away from here? The list of squatters will likely be published in Paris, and the news will filter to London in no time. I am afraid your mother's name will be on it."

She looked at him and decided quickly. "Yes, I agree to support you."

"You will?"

"Yes. *Je suis d'accord.*"

His face lit up. "You are wise. Now, the quicker the better, for if we delay, someone might figure out what is happening and prevent you from leaving. We have to be clever and very subtle."

Genevieve whispered, "Did you know that yesterday Lord Ashby asked to take me to Chartres today?"

"He did? What did you say?"

"I did not agree because I want to stay here and help you. I didn't tell him that, though."

"Thank you, but I must whisk you out of here."

She tipped her head and eyed him with hope. "Then, when I go, I would love to see Chartres Cathedral."

He gave a short nod. "I wonder . . . what was Lord Ashby's reason for inviting you to Chartres?"

Genevieve hesitated. "He feels sorry for me because of my mother's and Miss Doyle's behavior, and has witnessed Sir Pomeroy's annoying pursuit."

"Is that all?" he asked her, hunkering down to look into her eyes. "Can you trust him?"

She wished she could gaze at Armand lovingly, but she could not sustain more than one tender glance. She lowered her eyelids and said, "Yes."

"Those are good reasons. This may help in our plan. Should Lord Ashby assist us, we can take turns conveying you somewhere that the others will not suspect."

"Where is that?"

He looked at her, considering. "Suppose I don't tell you. Then, if you are questioned about it, you will honestly say you do not know."

"Is that the real reason?"

He smiled. "Will you allow me to surprise you?"

That sounded exciting, so she took a deep breath and said, "I trust you." She said a quick prayer to God to make her trust well-founded.

"Wonderful!" He stood up, eyes glowing down at her. "We must get started. You pack, and I'll set my men to work. I will arrange something with Lord Ashby. How do you feel about all this?"

"It will be scary in a way, but never mind that; I shall be watching the reactions to the imminent upheaval. Let me know if I can do anything to help you, Monsieur de Villebon."

He leaned over and touched her cheek. "I will, Genevieve. Thank you for your cooperation. But please, call me Armand."

Buoyed with joy, she walked with him toward Jean-Luc, who was still silhouetted in the doorway, keeping watch.

The servant suddenly gave a loud stage whisper, "That Englishman is coming! If he sees you together, he might suspect something."

Armand motioned to her, and said, "*Continuez.*" She walked toward the open stable door. He ducked into a stall and hid behind his horse's head.

As she neared Jean-Luc, they locked eyes. Genevieve saw that the man who minced toward them was Sir Pomeroy. She decided to stay right where she was, in safety on the threshold, with the two supporting Frenchmen nearby.

With his tasseled walking stick twirling in one upraised hand, Sir Pomeroy called, "Ah, Genevieve! The most beauteous sight my eyes do feast upon! Did you peruse my letter?" He reached out to grab her forearm, but she moved swiftly back into the stable.

"Halt!" snapped Genevieve. "This is ghastly behavior, even from you!" She yanked away and fled.

He followed her, pushed her into a corner of the haystacks, and in a throbbing voice, said, "Will you, my darling, marry me at last? I have been dying for your answer, but I can never get near you anymore. Now, here I have to propose again, in this smelly stable!"

She ran, but he caught up with her again, and leaned to kiss her, his breath stinking of sour wine. She turned abruptly away, and in doing so, stumbled onto Jean-Luc's foot, for he appeared behind her. The servant caught at her shoulders to steady her. Then he planted himself between her and Sir Pomeroy. That one's face contorted with red rage under his lavender wig.

Genevieve said to him, "You know my answer! It will not change."

"But it must, please, Genevieve! Even your lady mother approves!" Sir Pomeroy angrily gestured Jean-Luc aside, saying, "Be off with you!"

Jean-Luc merely stood there, protecting Genevieve behind him.

"I said get going!" repeated Sir Pomeroy, pointing his stick toward the doorway.

That did not move the servant one iota.

"Now!" insisted Sir Pomeroy. "I need to talk privately with this lady! *Dépêchez-vous! Vous comprenez? Allez, allez!*"

Genevieve smothered a laugh.

Jean-Luc seemed to be even more deeply rooted to the spot, stony-faced.

Sir Pomeroy detected her amusement, and it fed

his anger. He turned a searing look upon Jean-Luc and unscrewed his walking stick with furious intent. "Maybe this will make you run!" He had uncovered a gleaming blade at the end of the stick.

Genevieve, frightened for Jean-Luc, grabbed at the swinging stick. She deflected it, but the blade flicked across her own neck. She gave a gasp of pain.

Armand immediately vaulted forward and wrested the weapon away. Jean-Luc lunged for the Baronet's knees. With a thud, he downed him to the stone floor.

Armand raised the sharp-ended stick and addressed Sir Pomeroy, who was trying to rise, his wig fallen off and his head grizzled short and graying and mercilessly exposed.

Jean-Luc kept a boot firmly pressed on his middle despite his gyrations

"You vile serpent!" came Armand's rich voice. "See what came of your violence? You have drawn blood from this lady's neck, and all because you demand that she marry you! Now get going! Stop persecuting her, or I will turn you into the French police. Jean-Luc, hand him his notice before he trots off."

Sir Pomeroy sputtered in furor. With pierced pride, he rolled over and grappled for his wig. Keeping his back toward them, he hastily adjusted it on his head. Genevieve knew he was utterly undone by their having seen his ugly, grizzled pate.

Jean-Luc riffled through a stack of papers in a leather knapsack hanging from a hook, and went to stand on the other side of Sir Pomeroy, facing him. He handed him the paper with his name written in black script.

While Sir Pomeroy was snapping it open, Armand returned to Genevieve, guided her farther back in the stable, and whispered, "How sorry I am that you underwent such pain! You were very brave. Here, I have handkerchiefs in my saddlebags. I just filled my canteen at the pump, so I'll wash that blood away before it gets on your dress."

As he did so, his touch was sure and gentle, and made Genevieve quite aware of his every move on her behalf. He murmured, "The blood keeps coming, so I must continue to swab it for a few minutes." He dabbed at her collarbone again and met her eyes with a guarded gleam, half questioning.

"I appreciate your . . . help." She relaxed under his ministrations, and a compelling feeling made her want to kiss his sculpted cheekbone so near to hers.

Armand was looking pleased with his task, and refreshed the cloth with cool water poured in a sparkling stream from his canteen.

Sir Pomeroy's raging silhouette appeared in the doorway again. Jean-Luc blocked him from entering. There was tense fury in every line of Sir Pomeroy's body as he challenged, "How can *you* tell *me* to leave this place?"

Armand said, "By the authority of the French government and the owner of Château de Chambord. It says so in your eviction notice, if you read it through. It's printed in both French and English."

"You cannot be serious!"

Armand looked at him from under a stern brow and said, "I most certainly am, and you must take it seriously. Be gone by tonight, or find yourself in irons."

* * *

Genevieve's mind raced as she forced herself to walk leisurely up the grand staircase past several gossiping ladies. She kept thinking, *I am going to leave Chambord . . . clandestinely!*

In her room, she put her vanity articles into her trunk and bandboxes. Down in the breakfast room, she felt giddy as, with a jumpy stomach, she ate a bit of bread and drank coffee at a tiny table by the window. Only a few people were breakfasting, and they were wondering aloud where everyone was this morning. One woman opined that they must be rehearsing the play for tonight.

Out in the central hall, Sir Pomeroy left a group of men and women who were looking harassed, talking fast and gesticulating. He had changed his breeches for clean ivory ones, and donned a pale apricot wig to match his coat and waistcoat. He wore a look of calculated charm and tried to kiss her on the cheeks as if they were meeting for the first time that day.

She warded him off and snapped, "None of that, please!"

He backed off and made her an elegant leg instead, smiling tightly for benefit of the people watching. "I only desist from closeness for the moment in this public place," he said loudly so they could hear. He followed her to the staircase.

Suddenly, he pulled her into the dark cavity in the center of it. He held so tightly onto her shoulders to keep her from moving that she squeaked in pain. He did not loosen his grip, but eyed the place on her neck that he had flicked red with the walking stick's blade. Before she knew what he would do, he appeared as though he would kiss her. He smelled of foul coffee breath and strong perfume.

Genevieve struggled. "What do you think you're doing?" she cried, and hit him hard in the ribs with her fists, as she could not move her arms any higher to reach his face.

He whispered angrily, spittle flying at her, "What does that man think he is doing, foisting eviction notices on us? Is he trying a huge trick, or what? I am not that gullible! If we have to leave, then you will come with me, and no more excuses!"

Genevieve kicked him on the shin. He hissed in air. She said vehemently, "I will not! –and he is rectifying a wrongful situation. We have absolutely no right to be here!"

She stomped on his shoe as he said through clenched teeth, "How dare you side with him? Ow!"

"Because he is in the right! Let me go!"

"No! I don't want to let you go!"

She looked at his lower portion, raised her knee, and said threateningly, "Take your hands off me or I will not hold back!"

Panicked, his grip loosened. She stared him down and squeezed out of the dark cylindrical center of the staircase and onto the white stairs.

"Genevieve! I am sorry!" he hissed, "but you know it was mistakenly done, to hurt you, that is. If you had not interfered with my punishing that blackguard of a servant, I would never have harmed *you*."

"But you would have hurt that serving boy! That sort of behavior I will never countenance from anyone!" She pointed at his face with emphasis and moved quickly up the stairs.

He whined, "I will never do that again since you don't approve of it."

"Good!" she threw back. "Now, scram!"

"Aw, come away with me, Genevieve!" he begged. "This is the time to leave, so let us go quickly! I will marry you! Is this not a wonderful opportunity? Let me take you away to my château tonight. We won't tell *anyone*!"

He is utterly insane if he thinks he'll persuade me, she thought. Yet perhaps she could gain some information from him at this juncture, so she asked over her shoulder, "Not even my mother?"

"Well, she *is* in our corner, so she will be vastly pleased no matter when she finds out," he said eagerly. He continued to plead with her in a charm-infested manner.

At the top of *Le Grand Escalier*, Genevieve knew that she would have trouble escaping from him into her room, so, with key in hand ready to shove into the keyhole she widened her eyes and peered with shocked eyes behind him. "Lady Mortinette!" she exclaimed, "Is that Sir Pomeroy's best wig you're wearing?"

That made him wheel around to look. Thereby, Genevieve made it through her door, snapped it shut, and locked it. She had left him peering at no one at all.

* * *

Within a few minutes, there came a scratch on her door. Since Sir Pomeroy always knocked imperiously, she thought it might be someone else, so she waited for a repeat. It came, and a female voice called in French, "Mademoiselle? Here is a note from Lady Bastwicke for you."

Genevieve, afraid of a ploy from Sir Pomeroy, thanked her and asked her to slide it under the door. A cream-colored paper squeezed through. Genevieve opened the sloppily-folded page and read, *Come to my chamber at once. Where have you been?*

She hastily opened the door a crack, keeping her foot against it as insurance. "Mademoiselle?" she called, since Sir Pomeroy was nowhere in sight. The small, white-capped maid returned and curtseyed.

"Who are you?" Genevieve asked.

The pale-haired girl replied that she was Madame Mortinette's maid, but that she also served Lady Bastwicke.

Genevieve asked if she would escort her to Lady Bastwicke's room.

"*Certainement,* Mademoiselle."

They went through a corridor and down a staircase, and eventually through a narrow bridge of a gallery with mounted heads of stags and deer and wild boars, lit on both sides with windows. This was built as a hunting lodge, Genevieve recalled. She wondered how old the animal heads were.

The maid opened a door with a salamander

carved into it. The motif appeared everywhere throughout the palace. She soon stood in a small anteroom. The maid said she would go ahead and announce her.

The instant the inner door was opened, Genevieve saw and heard Sir Pomeroy ask in an urgent tone, "But what shall I do to corner her? It sounds like it has to be tonight!"

"Yes, it does have to be tonight," Lady Bastwicke agreed, "because I am going with—"

The maid shut the door. Genevieve wanted desperately to hear more, but she was glad she had heard that Sir Pomeroy was planning to corner her, and that her mother was supporting him. Madam, however, was going somewhere with someone else.

Genevieve waited and thought hard. With Sir Pomeroy in the room, she was not about to enter it. The two of them might trap her there. When the maid opened the door, Genevieve stayed in the doorway eyeing Sir Pomeroy, who was pacing back and forth in an elegantly-furnished sitting room. Then he saw her.

Both he and her mother, who moved into view, looked at her guiltily, but Madam's expression changed. "Finally, Genevieve!" she said accusingly. "What took you so long? What is this I hear about someone ordering us all to *leave?*"

Sir Pomeroy was now gravitating toward her with a calculating look in his heavy-lidded eyes.

Genevieve, not to be distracted and caught by him, merely said in her direction, "I heard that, too. Let's go home now."

Lady Bastwicke wailed, "Of all the lunacy! We just got here!"

"I know, but we have to leave this château, so why not just go back home?"

"I am not going back to London because—" Madam suddenly looked at a loss for words.

Sir Pomeroy supplied, "Because you have been invited elsewhere."

"Yes, I have." She grabbed her enormous black fan and cooled herself defiantly.

"Where have you been invited, and who did the inviting?" Genevieve asked.

"It is to Tours, and you don't know the person."

Innocently, Genevieve asked, "Is it a man or a woman?"

"Go away now!" snapped her mother.

Hating to ask, Genevieve nevertheless inquired, "Was there something you needed when you called for me?"

Since Sir Pomeroy was edging her way again, Genevieve took a hold of the maid and kept her physically between him and herself, whispering in French for her not to worry; just stay between them until she could leave. The maid's blonde lashes fluttered in agreement, and she stayed firmly in place.

Lady Bastwicke replied, "Go find Dorcasta. I suggested she take a walk around the château with Lord Ashby, but I want you to give her another dress. This time, have it sized better for her. You can stitch some alterations in a pinch, can't you?"

Genevieve's heart sank. "I do not wish to give her a dress because she is ruining at least three of Arabelle's. I do not want mine spoiled as well. I need everything that I brought with me." She hated to sound selfish, but really!

"It is precisely because she is tripping over Arabelle's that she needs another one from you."

"Arabelle and I are the same height."

"You've grown?"

"Of course."

"Well, she complained that she can't go looking like that in front of Lord Ashby, or the other possible swains here."

Genevieve stared in disbelief. "Madam, why do you care that she appears well in front of Lord Ashby? Would she be a suitable wife for an *Earl?*"

The quick, conspiratorial look that passed between Madam and Sir Pomeroy mystified Genevieve, and since her mother did not answer, she backed out of the room. She was determined not to give her new clothes away, for Father had been so kind in taking her to have them made a month ago. Every article was necessary to her here in France, especially because she had no Bertha Blumm to see them laundered or pressed for her.

"She is in my charge, and . . . it is good to help the unfortunate," Lady Bastwicke answered, tacking her last words on airily.

Sir Pomeroy snorted.

Genevieve eyed her in amazement, for that kind of sentiment was absolutely unlike Lady Bastwicke. She never helped anyone.

She changed the subject. "Oh, and you may write to your father and say that I'm not coming home just now."

Genevieve regarded her mother with sad disparagement. She hurried to escape Sir Pomeroy's prowling look when he sidled toward her. She squeezed the maid's wrist in thanks, and ran through the trophy gallery and up the same hidden, spiral staircase and down the corridors until she reached her room.

There, she hastily wrote a letter to Father as instructed by her mother, but added a postscript that conveyed her own regrets that she had not been able to persuade Madam to return. She wrote that they were all being evicted from Chambord, and that she did not know what would happen. She, herself, was being taken care of by someone else and going to Chartres, she believed, while Madam was accepting an invitation to Tours. She asked Father to direct any letters to Lord Ashby in Chartres.

She quietly descended to find Radford so she could ask him for his address in Chartres, and to post her letter, because Armand was busy with important affairs. She saw Radford just outside one of the doors on the moat side. When she had asked him shyly for those favors, he smiled and asked, "Why not come with me, and we will send it on its way together?"

A bit stymied, she was distracted from replying by Armand striding purposefully with other men into the grand hall, their collective boots echoing. People were carrying things out toward the courtyard, and she could see through the enormous door that carriages were parked outside. Horses were being held, luggage was on its way out, and servants were packing things onto the horses and vehicles. People made their exodus in traveling clothes as well as day ensembles. Some of them chattered rebelliously, with derision, stress, and fear intermingled in rapidly-voiced French.

Genevieve expelled, "What a hullabaloo!"

Armand approached her and Radford. "It had better be an industrious hullabaloo, full of hauling and moving off of carriages all day long until Chambord is empty."

Curiously, she inquired, "Have they made a very troublesome fuss?"

"Ah, yes, some of them have. I care not how much they complain as long as they vacate and never come back."

Radford cleared his throat and said conspiratorially to Armand, "I am sticking to our plan, and will take Genevieve to see Chartres Cathedral to get her out of this mêlée."

"Thank you, Lord Ashby, but I will convey her myself tonight, after midnight."

Radford lifted his chin. "I doubt that plan would find approval with her father, Monsieur."

Armand asked, "Why not?"

"Because she should not go off with a stranger. She should go with her mother rather than you, don't you think?"

"But you just offered to take her yourself."

"Yes," said Radford, "but I am not a stranger to the family; in fact, I was one of their traveling party. I will escort her mother and Miss Doyle as well."

Looking dubiously at Genevieve, Armand asked, "Will your mother comply? Do you *want* to leave with her?"

Genevieve made fists at her sides and expelled, "Absolutely not! She won't come with me back to England, but has just announced that she is going to Tours. She did not divulge who invited her there.

Please, you must agree not to force me to go with her anywhere!"

Armand promptly said, "Do you agree, Ashby? Her mother would toss her, virtue and all, into the clutches of that handy dandy of hers, Chancet. They are hand in glove. Don't, I beg of you, think she should be forced to chance it with him!"

With obvious alarm, Radford said, "I see! No one should force you to go where he goes, Genevieve."

She shuddered. "I am grateful for both of your agreement on that point."

Armand leaned and said near her ear, "I will whisk you away before she comes to collect you." He was certainly masterful. It thrilled her because he was considerate at the same time.

She glanced at Radford. He was fingering his jaw, frowning and turning something over in his mind. He said to Armand, "I can take her earlier than you can, since I do not have to stay and see this evacuation done. You and your men have everything covered, correct? I am sure we agree that the sooner Genevieve gets away, the better."

He was right. She looked at Armand to see what he would say.

"Fine. You are our first option, Ashby, *if* she can get away with you at dusk without anyone seeing her leave. However, if that proves too risky, I will take her after dark as we planned. Then, my horse and coach will be almost impossible to see and follow."

Radford smiled in quick relief at Genevieve. "Splendid! I'll order my carriage for just after sunset."

Armand said, "I will have my man pick up her

luggage as she and I planned earlier. Genevieve? Is this all clear to you?"

"I hope so," she said, but knew it wasn't quite.

"Then go now and ready your things."

United in the purpose of her safety, the men made whispered plans while she hurried back to pack her comb, toothbrush, mirror, and lip salve into her reticule. All else was in her trunk and bandboxes. As she closed everything up, she felt uplifted by Radford's quiet insistence to whisk her away early, and she loved the intensity of Armand's outrage on her behalf. She had never felt such solicitude from other men; not even from Shrubsole Curling. He had not worried enough about what could happen to the two of them if and when Lord Bastwicke caught them eloping. Now she faced the unknown again, but oddly, it seemed as though the two powerful men were making sure they formed a solid plan for her benefit.

I need a strong man to help me in this life, she thought; *a man like the one who fought for dear Arabelle.* Her sister and the whole family were blessed by him.

As Genevieve hurried toward the staircase, Dorcasta came tripping down them. "I need to talk to you!" she called, her eyes darting at the men, who immediately moved away, talking low.

"What about?" asked Genevieve coolly, stopping in front of her.

"Don't let him get away," she said, eyeing them.

"Let who get away, for heaven's sake?"

Dorcasta emphasized in a stage whisper, "Lord Ashby!"

"Whatever do you want to detain him for?"

"I want him to take me to Chartres, but could you ask him for me?"

Lord Ashby heard her say his name, and glanced their way. Unseen by Dorcasta, he made a gesture to Genevieve to ward her off.

Genevieve followed his private signal and said, "No, I will not ask him for you. What right do you have to ask anything of His Lordship? Dorcasta, you grossly overstep." She turned away.

Dorcasta called over the banister in a sweet tone, "Oh, Lord Ashby!"

Radford and Armand sheered off to the courtyard. There, the motley stream of servants continued to carry more possessions out from several directions. A baby cried as it was carried out in a basket by the maid who served Madame Mortinette. Genevieve had not known anything about her baby.

Armand and Radford effected another consultation outside as she watched. Armand said something that made Radford look disappointed.

Dorcasta ran through the exodus of people to Radford. They spoke a couple of words, and then Dorcasta smiled flirtatiously and hurried back inside, past Genevieve, and down a corridor.

Genevieve hurried up the stairs with intent to lock herself in her room.

Armand vaulted up the stairs after her and rounded back out of sight of the ground floor. He whispered, "Will you be ready to leave with me by one or two o'clock in the morning?"

Genevieve's heart gave a skip. "Have plans changed again?"

"Yes."

"What brought that about?"

"That Dorcasta Doyle begged Lord Ashby to take her, and I told him to go ahead and do it."

Genevieve asked in consternation, "But, why?

"So you can come with me." He grinned down at her.

"I should say no."

"Will you?"

"No."

"Wonderful! I can personally see that you're safe. Shall we say the stable? I am afraid you will need to sneak out alone in order not to attract attention. Do not let that Dorca-tastrophe anywhere near you, or she will wonder what you are going to do. Don't answer any questions. Avoid all three of them like the plague."

Genevieve giggled. "I will. Can Jean-Luc come for my things somewhat earlier? Is that how we should contrive it?"

"Absolutely."

Genevieve said in an agonized whisper, "But Sir Pomeroy hangs around my room at odd times, trying to gain access when I'm there alone. He might be so inquisitive as to follow my luggage, and see in which vehicle it's stowed. That would give us away."

"All right, I have it. We'll put your luggage loosely on top of Lord Ashby's carriage, and make sure that he, or at least Miss Doyle, sees it and thinks that you two young ladies have your luggage packed together."

Genevieve looked at him admiringly. "Wonderful idea. Don't let Lord Ashby leave without transferring it to yours, though."

"I will make sure Jean-Luc does it. How will he know which are yours?"

"I can tie pink ribbons to each of my articles. There are only three."

"Excellent. We will only need to put one of them on the wrong coach to foil them." Armand cocked his head thoughtfully. "Does your bedchamber have a cupola or other access to the roof?"

"I actually have a door to a curving balcony on the moat side. I could unlatch it if I needed to."

"Marvelous. No one should be on the moat side tonight since all the packing into vehicles takes place on the opposite side. I'll send Jean-Luc to take your luggage out that way. How will I know which room is yours?"

Genevieve said, "It's Room 148, accessible one floor down from the roof. The number is painted above the door outside on the balcony walk."

"I'll have him knock, shall I?"

"Won't that attract attention if someone is on the roof nearby?"

Armand said, "He will be on the lookout. People should not be lingering there, unless they're coming out of their rooms that way, which would make no sense."

Genevieve still worried. "If Dorcasta Doyle rides with Lord Ashby to Chartres, where will she stay, being a young woman alone without Madam or me?"

He fingered the back of his neck and said presently, "That *is* a problem. Hmm. Now I think it's best if we persuade her to accompany Lady B instead."

Genevieve said, "I agree. But will everyone

concerned go along with that?"

***

"Ah, Genevieve, how cruel you are! Do you know what you do to me?" It was her vile suitor again, insinuating himself near her in the busy courtyard.

"No, but I see that you act the persistent villain with the wrong lady, so go bother one of those others there, waiting for their coach, whose eyes follow you. Go!" She did not explain that they probably disliked what they saw.

"Their eyes follow me? Truly? Which ones are they?

Exasperated, she urged, "Go find out!"

"But I don't want them; I want you!"

"Why don't you want those others, who might actually like you?"

"Because they chase me, and I prefer to do the chasing."

"Then go chase someone else before they leave this place and you never see them again. Your time is almost over." She glared into his eyes, let out a frustrated sigh, and then thought to ask him, "Why aren't you packing and rolling down the road? There are so few hours left, and I am sure you have many precious suits and wigs and glittering buckled shoes to safely pack up before they're offered in a pile to the villagers."

Alarm leapt into his eyes at her scenario. "Many people are leaving at the moment, but others, such as I, have decided to wait until after dinner. We must eat, and we will make it into a good-bye party." He gave an angry huff. "What a vile spoilsport is Monsieur de Villebon! I've a mind to punish him."

CHAPTER 10

Coaches in the Night

That evening, Genevieve felt nervous but eager to board a coach. If only she could truly elude Madam's and Sir Pomeroy's plans for her by this means. Pacing her room, back and forth, she was about to despair of Jean-Luc's ever appearing to take her baggage when the knock came on the outer door to the roof balcony. She flung the door open in relief.

There stood Sir Pomeroy.

She gasped, and tried to slam the door shut. His foot was inserted, making it impossible for her to close it. He cursed, for the door hit his toes very hard. "Are you ready?" he asked, trying to smile. "It's time to go."

Genevieve, pushing her shoulder hard against the door, struggled and eked out, "Why are you here?"

Irately, he said, "I know that your plan is to leave in Lord Ashby's coach, and if you think that will happen, I shall follow you. But we are traveling together, make no mistake, so get used to the plan that you well come in with your mother and me."

Genevieve, heart beating hard, contrived to say calmly, "Yes, I heard that was her new plan. Go call Dorcasta Doyle and get her settled first, will you? Poor thing, she might otherwise be left behind."

Sir Pomeroy said, "Fine, I'll go speed her on. The coach holds four. Lord Ashby need not be involved at all, so let's get rid of him. Servant, *garçon!*" he called. "Come here and deliver a message to Lord Ashby." Sir Pomeroy's tone changed, and he said angrily to the approaching servant, "Oh, it *would* be you! Fetch me another yokel! Be off with you!"

Genevieve heard Jean-Luc say, "I am not to be off at your word, Monsieur, for I obey the orders of my master only."

Sir Pomeroy demanded, "What are you doing here?"

"Making sure that rooms are vacated." Jean-Luc moved into Genevieve's view.

Sir Pomeroy turned and eyed him suspiciously. Genevieve saw that his foot had shifted and she could quickly shut the door if she wanted to. While Sir Pomeroy eyed Jean-Luc, she lifted her hand, showing five fingers, and saw Jean-Luc nod imperceptibly. She slammed and bolted the door.

"You *will* be mine!" Sir Pomeroy shouted through the door. "I have vowed many times to marry you!"

"Marry me? Why?" she retorted loudly through the window. She knew it sounded foolish to Jean-Luc that she should deign to answer the horrid man, but she thought he should know what was occurring here with Sir Pomeroy so that he could tell Armand.

Sir Pomeroy put his mouth to the window, so she jumped back. His words came clearly. "I have told you some of the reasons, but there are dozens more. It will all come out when we are married. I shall traverse *Le Grand Escalier* and also this rooftop until I see you emerge, and then I will propose to you romantically on my knee. Again!" His voice had a ring of finality to it. "I am quite rich, after all. I will keep you in beautiful dresses."

Genevieve thought perhaps this was the moment to fish for the mysterious details of his present life. "How did you become so rich after being exiled from England for your crimes?"

"Do hush! No one who matters to me here knows about that insignificant episode of my life, so kindly do not spout my past in that audible voice."

"How did your fortunes change, then?"

"Someone left me an inheritance after I helped him win a lot of money at the dice."

Genevieve asked curiously, "How did that person die?"

"Since you are to be my wife, I will tell you. The person from whom he won a fortune called him out."

Genevieve cried, "He dueled? Did he die in the duel?"

"Yes. He was woefully rusty with his sword."

"Why, that makes me jump to the conclusion that the dice were loaded and he was suspected of cheating. Why else would his opponent challenge him to a duel after a dice game?"

There came a silence. The door handle moved but the key was still firmly vertical in the keyhole.

She pressed, "Have I hit on the truth?"

He whined, "I'd like to come in and explain, Genevieve."

"No admittance to this lady's chamber. You know that!"

"It wasn't cheating," he explained lamely.

"Whatever you say. So, as a result, what kind of a fortune did you inherit? Had you sat him down beforehand to make sure he put you as a benefactor in his will?"

"We *mutually* agreed, since I was looking after his crumbling little château while he was in the Auberge for three months. He said he was grateful, had found that his only close relative had died there after an illness, and I tactfully suggested that, at his age, he might do well to put his own affairs, coupled with what his old brother had left him, in order."

Genevieve, shaking her head, asked, "How old was he?"

"Fifty-nine."

"So, now that he is dead as well as his brother, did you receive all their money as well as the crumbling château?"

"I did!" he said enthusiastically. "Why can't you open this door so we can talk more closely? You get to live in the château with me when we are married. Just think! A little French château! –with a tower!"

"If it's crumbling, who cares? It's probably freezing in the winter, and full of mice. Will the money last your whole lifetime?" Genevieve knew she must sound concerned about his ability to provide for her in order to get all the facts, so she shamelessly kept up her queries. She was gaining a lot of information this way.

"Certainly it will, as long as I stay lucky at my games. Now do you see why I am a suitable suitor for you, my delectable Genevieve? You can be my princess in the tower."

"Does my mother know all this?"

"Oh, she does, she does. She has been my confidante, and she now reveres my worth," he added pompously.

Genevieve corrected, "Your monetary worth, you mean." She sank onto her trunk. She felt rather shaky from her continued grilling of Sir Pomeroy, but she might as well ask another blunt question while she had the chance. She turned her face toward the door. "Are you richer than, say, Lord Ashby?" She hated the way she sounded, for she reminded herself of Dorcasta.

In a great loud voice, he proclaimed, "I believe I am one-and-a-half times richer! I hope."

"Oh, my!" called Genevieve, pretending to be impressed. Maybe he would think he had her interest now, and would trust her, and leave. "And to think how we all thought he was very rich indeed!"

"Oh, but I am richer!"

She did not believe him. She called matter-of-factly, "Well, rich man, I am busy, and you must get busy, too, packing your movable riches back to your crumbling abode."

In a sing-song voice, he promised, "I shall see you soon, and will be hurrying for the ecstatic times to come!"

Emitting a huge, weary sigh, Genevieve went to her farthest window and saw a star twinkling in the dark sky. She dwelt on heavenly things, and felt peace beginning to seep back into her flustered mind.

There came a knock at her door that led to the central staircase. Her heart beat fast as she made no reply, hoping Sir Pomeroy was not trying again from that side. The rapping came again, and was accompanied by Madam's voice saying, "Why does she lock her door? Genevieve! Are you in there?"

She decided that if her mother did not know, she would stay silent. She tiptoed to lie on her bed so that if Madam had a key that miraculously worked in her lock, she could pretend to be asleep.

As soon as the clicking footsteps receded a bit, Genevieve streaked to the door and put her ear against the keyhole.

Lady Bastwicke was saying, "Just be cleverer than she is. Yes, do lie in wait for her here on the stairs, and when it is dark, which it will be soon, I shall send a note to her room to summon her to mine. I will say that I need my forehead rubbed for my headache before we travel. Blow out that candle."

Genevieve's thoughts roiled with anger. There came a soft knock on the outer door. Thank God! She tiptoed across the room. She smiled with joy, and her spirits soared. One glance out her window confirmed that it was Armand himself who had come for her. He had surely heard from Jean-Luc that Sir Pomeroy had been here. She fumbled to open the door, and there he was, smiling down at her.

"I've been worried about you and that prancing swain," he whispered.

"Yes, he's been pestering me. My mother, just now, at that other door, came with him to coerce me to leave with them, but I didn't answer." She smiled at him in giddy relief. "My things are ready."

He looked around him and whispered, "Do you have more luggage than this one trunk?"

She nodded, and pointed to the two bandboxes. Her reticule was draped over them.

"That's all?"

She nodded.

"Well done!" He backed out the door and beckoned Jean-Luc. The men took her articles as Armand whispered, "My coach is ready, and so is Lord Ashby's."

Genevieve pressed his arm and said, "I cannot go with him because Sir Pomeroy said he plans to follow his coach in case I sneak off with Lord Ashby. He was here and told me so."

"That is unfortunate, but we must outwit him. Since Miss Doyle's luggage is on Sir Pomeroy's coach, we will put one of your bandboxes on it as well. I'll hide the rest of your baggage in my coach. Then, under cover of darkness, I will grab your bandbox back."

"In whose coach will I ride?"

"I am afraid you will need to start out in Lord Ashby's."

Her spirits fell. "But that puts me into Sir Pomeroy's plan. He said he will take me from Lord Ashby's coach by force if I don't ride with him and my mother."

Armand locked eyes with her in the dimness. "Don't worry, Genevieve." He moved close, took her hand in his strong, warm one, and lifted her chin with the other. "That cannot be allowed to happen," he assured her. "Let Lord Ashby take you off before Sir Pomeroy is even ready."

"And you must leave later?"

"Yes, midnight is the deadline, and I must lock up here. With my men, we will ascertain that everyone is out, with all their animals and chattel with them. With hundreds of rooms, it might take us hours. Now I must be off before anyone spots me here with your luggage."

They smiled in camaraderie. She followed him onto the balcony and back into the center of the roof. She watched his broad shoulders disappear into the nearest ornate doorway. She marveled again how like a small city it was up here, with some huge chimneys shaped like wine bottles, and myriad decorated spires pointing skyward. She thought what a perfect place it turned out to be to hide one's movements. Armand had disappeared in seconds.

She let out a long sigh, and wondered how her escape would transpire. Would Sir Pomeroy really do what he threatened, with her mother's sanction? Would he lie in wait for her on the stairs? She dared not take any of the chimney doors, for it was dark now, and a candle would show her progress. She did not know her way without light. The only staircase she felt familiar with was the double helix *Grand Escalier.*

* * *

She shivered with nervous excitement as she pulled her silk shawl over her head. It was dark green, which she had chosen because it would cover her coppery-gold hair in the darkness. It must be time; twilight had passed, and they had agreed that she would leave after the first stars appeared. She saw two more of them beginning to brighten.

What would she do if Sir Pomeroy proved true to his threat and waited outside her door to grab her? Her part of the escape plan must be performed now. She had prayed, and now reminded herself that she must believe. Worry was the opposite of faith.

She set her door key into a drawer and opened her door carefully, but even its little creak made her wince. Listening, she heard nothing. She swished out, not bothering to risk another click by shutting it. Step by quiet step, she moved to the top of the white staircase whose pale steps look ghostly white against deep shadows.

She saw him! Sir Pomeroy's white wig was advancing up the near staircase. How could she outrun such a determined man? How could she get to the stables without his catching her?

As she streaked on tiptoe to the top of *Le Grand Escalier*, she suddenly remembered that it was a double one. She had to find the other top to the staircase in the dark. She hurried in a semicircle, leaving the top of the first staircase behind. Sir Pomeroy's tread quickened, but she hoped he had not seen her. She kept running clockwise. She was rewarded—thank God!—by the top of the other staircase. Her feet flew down it. She held her breath when she saw him pass across from her, revolving up around the grand spiral while she circled downward. She took the middle of the steps that were stacked beneath his. She wished she could thank Leonardo da Vinci for designing this saving feature so that she could descend on one level as Sir Pomeroy ascended on the other. Now, even if he spied her, it was impossible for him to reach her.

She slipped at the bottom because of her desperate speed, but recovered and streaked across the hall on tiptoe. She kept to the shadows and avoided the rectangle of floor that shone in the moonlight from the tall, open door. He might look down over the balustrade and see her now unless he was on the other side. But she must have foiled him, for she heard nothing behind her.

She dashed out of the shadow, through the door, and into the courtyard. There, she sped to the open door in the outer keep, past straggling, complaining people, and hurried through the building. Outside, she turned right and ran to the round one-storey stable wing. Seeing light through a doorway, she made that her destination.

Activity abounded. She could see coaches and carts and silhouettes of people, and horses being led and hitched. Servants were issued orders, and everyone seemed flurried and irate.

Inside the stable, the smell of animals and hay made her almost wilt with relief. She saw the movement of a man's head in a queue, silhouetted against a hanging lantern, so she made her way closer, keeping in the shadow of a stall until she could ascertain who it was.

"*Qui est-ce?*" It was the low voice of Armand as he turned toward her.

"*C'est moi,*" she said breathlessly.

"Well done! I'm glad you're here." Looking alert

and pleased, he grasped her hand and pulled her with him, past a few horses in the stalls, shifting or munching. "Did you have any difficulty?"

Genevieve admitted that Sir Pomeroy had been lying in wait for her, but that she had taken the alternate rung down *Le Grand Escalier.*

Admiringly, he said, "That was brilliant, Genevieve!"

She basked in his smile. As they moved outside and toward a black coach highlighted in the moonlight, he added, "You are the most intelligent young lady I have ever met."

He took her hand and led her away from the château, across the pale sheen of grass, and onto the gravel path that the moon shone upon with silvery light. She squeezed his hand with loving, grateful pressure.

Glancing back, she saw that there were lights burning in only three windows, one high in the château. Genevieve sadly admired the grandiose and overpowering majesty of the palace with its graceful curving towers of silvery white; and beyond, the phenomenal roof city of spires and ornate chimneys that she had just left.

He detached his saddled horse, Gaspard, from where he was tied, and held his reins while he handed her into a coach and tucked in her gown. Through the window, she gave Gaspard's soft nose a stroke and said, "Good boy!"

Armand gestured the groom down from his standing perch on the back of the vehicle and gave him a leg up onto Gaspard. She heard him quietly tell the driver not to light the carriage lanterns until they were at least a mile away, if he needed them at all, but to try and drive without them. He was to make all speed to Beaugency.

She craned her neck and watched Armand run to a second coach in the deep shadow of the nearby trees. She had not even noticed it because it was so well concealed, with four dark horses hitched to it and a quantity of baggage on top. She could only perceive it now because it moved forward by one turn of the wheels until the moonbeams showed the curved shape of the coach body. Armand spoke to someone inside.

She was astonished when he returned and vaulted into the coach and landed in the seat opposite her. The wheels moved and picked up immediate speed, heading down a long avenue lined with trees.

"You are coming along?" she exclaimed. "But you are needed here to see that everyone leaves. You told me so."

"Yes, that is true. I will come back. I just need to make sure you escape from that weasel. Aha! It is just as I thought." He was peering back intently through the window.

"What is?"

"He is after us."

"Sir Pomeroy?" Genevieve clutched the seat and her heart thumped.

Armand rubbed his hands together. "This is going to be fun!"

"Fun!" echoed Genevieve, aghast.

"That character must not succeed. I have a plan in motion, literally, right now. Let him follow!"

"What are you doing?"

"Let me explain when I need to. I want to keep Radford's coach in sight. Ah yes, he is behind us, but ahead of Sir Pomeroy."

"You spoke with Radford in the coach back there?"

"Yes. He still wants to take you to Chartres."

"Oh! *Am* I going to Chartres?"

"Yes, you are. It is a good distance from here, but I believe it to be the safest place for you to hide."

Genevieve did not know what to think. She was on tenterhooks as the cantering horses sped them wildly through the dark. Her heart did somersaults. With Sir Pomeroy pursuing them so closely, what could happen? If Armand abandoned her to return to Chambord tonight, she might again be open prey to that roué.

"A relative of mine lives there," Armand was saying.

Genevieve blinked. "Where?"

"In Chartres. She promised to take you in."

"Is she expecting me?"

"We arranged it as a possibility. Here is a message I wrote to her." He groped within his waistcoat and handed her a folded, sealed page. "Should you lose this, the address is 4 Rue des Béguines. Or, if that isn't safe, meet her in the back of the Cathedral near the U shaped *bas-relief* that depicts the life of Christ. That is the second plan, should your pursuer prevent you from entering that address. It would be easier to hide in the cathedral."

Genevieve thanked him somewhat shakily. She looked back with her nose to the window, but could only see the moonlit treetops they were dashing past. She tucked the paper into her bosom.

The driver called suddenly, "Monsieur, someone

is overtaking the coach behind us!"

Sure enough, they heard rapid hoof beats growing louder. Genevieve studied Armand's moonlit face in alarm.

"Whip 'em up!" he commanded out the window. The driver did so, and veered around the outer gates at speed, throwing Genevieve sidewise against the squabs.

"It's Sir Pomeroy, isn't it?" she asked. "I am sure he is raging." She prayed fervently that Armand would keep her safe from him and Madam both. She braced her feet on the floor and grasped the seat as the coach veered left, and jounced and bounced her on her desired trip to Chartres. Never could she have imagined any of this.

If only she could have tried to escape a most horrid and undesirable marriage in a manner more genteel. What would Father say about her traveling with a man, and without a female companion? Those were pointless qualms now, but her train of thought persisted. What would he think of his single daughter's going off in the dead of night across the French countryside with a virtual stranger, leaving her mother behind? She shuddered, and tried not to think of all the ramifications of her actions. She would explain it all in detail to Father one day—*if* she emerged unscathed.

Armand said, "I see Ashby's coach passing Sir Pomeroy's again."

"Oh, good!"

"Try not to look back. I would hope that your pursuer would think you are in Ashby's coach, not this one. Perhaps he might catch a glimpse of your head as we round that bend ahead." Armand quickly moved from his seat to the spot next to her. He pulled her head gently onto his shoulder. "This way, you have less chance of being seen," he said into her hair.

Genevieve giggled.

He chuckled, too.

"You are something of a rogue, Monsieur de Villebon," she said, with her cheek snuggled into the fine wool of his *justacorps*.

"I'm glad to be one at the moment," he returned. "Tell me, why did you and your mother come here to Chambord, if you don't mind my asking?"

Genevieve found that, here in the intimate darkness, she could quite easily let her words on that subject roll out. "She received an invitation from Sir Pomeroy, and then she recruited—no, *urged*—Lord Ashby to accompany us part of the way. I swear that he knew nothing about this party at Chambord beforehand, nor would he have approved this whole lurid scheme."

"I believe that to be true from what I've observed of his character so far. But it is Sir Pomeroy Chancet whom she wants as a son-in-law, and not Lord Ashby? Why? He seems a most demented choice."

Genevieve lifted her head and said, "His history regarding my family is utterly despicable! I have no notion why my mother encourages him. She talked of his new fortune, however, so that must be why. He informed me that his inheritance is one and a-half times more than Lord Ashby's."

Armand's crowed, "So that's it! But I have wondered why he and Lady Bastwicke often have their heads together."

"Yes, it's odd, and I find it mighty suspicious, except that she seems to easily control him, and he doesn't appear to mind."

The coach was slowing, and Armand alerted, admonishing her to put her head down.

"Where?" she asked.

"In the crook of my arm."

She obeyed, and felt the movement of his muscles as he strained to look back.

"We are crossing the bridge at Beaugency."

"Now what?" she asked from her prone position.

He put his hand on her head and caressed her hair as he said, "We're determined to lose Sir Pomeroy. I sincerely hope Radford is sharp in his part of the scheme." He stroked her hair some more, causing her lovely bliss, and said, "Genevieve, try not to be alarmed. One or both of us may have to leap out of this coach very quickly when I see our chance."

"I am ready," she assured him. She pulled her hem up so her feet were free of possible tripping and said, "I am glad to have nothing to carry. What will happen to my luggage? Not that I am worried about those things," she added. She was feeling buoyed up and romantic, and was sorry to think that her desperate escapade with Armand de Villebon might soon end. Would she ever see him again?

"We will see to everything, including your luggage, the best we can," he promised.

The horses halted next to a door flanked by windows at which candles burned. He said, "I hope you don't mind, but I need you to crouch down on the floor until I come for you. I'm throwing my cloak over you. Do not move, even if someone opens the door."

"I won't."

The coach rocked slightly, and the door clicked shut. She heard a horse snort, and the coach in which she lay moved forward a bit. Then Armand shouted, "Radford! Go around to the back! Quick! Here he comes!"

Genevieve bit her lip and prayed. Next, she heard ringing hoofs go by, and within seconds, the clatter of an arriving vehicle and many horses. The coach she lay in jerked forward and made a sharp turn. She heard Armand being left behind, calling, "Sir Pomeroy Chancet, of all people! Where are *you* headed?"

Oh, dear God, she prayed. *Save us!*

Her coach kept curving and slowing; and then, before it stopped completely, the door opened and a hand felt inside, first upon the seats, and then it hit upon the cloak piled on her back. She gulped, and held her breath in fright.

CHAPTER 11

Scandalous

Since Armand had warned her not to move, she lay still as a statue.

"Where is she?" asked a male voice in a whisper.

Her pulses pounded in her temples as two hands plucked at the cloak, lifting it, letting evening air in upon her. She was caught. She lifted her head to face the inevitable. She would fight him to the death!

"Genevieve, hurry! Come with me, quickly!" the voice urged in a tense whisper.

She saw no white wig gleaming in the moonlight.

"Who are you?" she demanded, sitting up.

"It is I, Genevieve." When he moved close, she saw that it was Radford.

"Oh!" she breathed in relief.

"You thought it was Sir Pomeroy?" He's at the front end of the inn. We are at the back. You are to hop into my coach and away we'll fly!"

"To where?"

"Chartres."

"Does Armand know?"

"Of course he knows, he ordered it. Come on, no time to lose."

She went. Running, holding onto his hand, she hit her shin painfully on the coach step in the dark, landed rather hard inside, and breathlessly righted herself. In vaulted Radford after her, and away their coach rumbled, down the alley, into the street, and back over the bridge.

"Why are we crossing back?" she demanded suddenly.

"So that Sir Pomeroy will not find us. If he figures out that you have been moved to my coach, he will fly hell-for-leather in the same direction we've been going."

"I see. This is clever. When will we continue to Chartres?"

"My driver will circle through a few streets, and then, when perhaps a quarter hour has passed, we will continue on in our original direction."

"When will we be there?"

"If all goes well, the day after tomorrow."

Genevieve sat still, thinking. "So we will sleep . . . where?"

Radford said, "Armand de Villebon recommends we stay at a place he knows in Huisseau-sur-Mauves. He supplied us with a French coachman who knows the route and the places."

"I see." *Now* what would her father think? Her scandalous situation grew worse and worse: two nights on the road, alone with another man? Her respectability was a thing of the past, if anyone found out.

Radford said, "I know this is not the done thing.

However, Armand and I have no intention of telling anyone about our method of spiriting you away, or even that we were responsible."

"But how will we explain any of this if we are forced to?"

"Since I am to deliver you to a lady in Chartres, we can concoct the fiction that you left Chambord with her."

"Oh? Was the lady really at Chambord?"

"Yes. Armand will be back there on his fast horse to evict any stragglers from the premises, so this dash here with you may go completely unnoticed."

Genevieve nervously objected, "But Sir Pomeroy saw him just now, at the front of the inn!"

"Did he?"

"I heard Armand call and ask him quite innocently where he was bound."

"Did you hear where he is bound?"

"No. Is he still at the inn? And where is Dorcasta Doyle?"

"Why do you ask *me*, Genevieve?"

"Because I thought that you and she kept tabs on each others' whereabouts recently." Genevieve still felt irked at the memory of Dorcasta's pursuit of him. How dared she raise her sights to a Peer of the Realm? For an intimidated little miss from the country, she certainly had grown in brashness and aggressive behavior.

Radford, having given his coachman orders to flee at top speed, settled himself in the coach facing forward next to her. As they vibrated over cobblestones and flagstones around the town, and then on the open road to the countryside, he kept looking back through the small window between their heads. Finally, he said, "I think we've made the switch with success. I see no pursuer on the road."

Genevieve sighed and tried to relax. "My question, My Lord?"

"Was it about Miss Doyle?"

"Yes. Where is she?"

"I thought she was with Sir Pomeroy."

"Is my mother with them?"

"That I do not know."

They rode in silence for a time. Genevieve wondered what to say. She had never imagined that she would be rolling rapidly through the night on an escapade with Lord Ashby, but here she was. She wondered how Armand was proceeding with his project, and whether he was finding any recalcitrant individuals to deal with. She voiced those thoughts to Radford.

"I would be surprised if he found anyone amenable."

"However, they all should know that they were doing wrong."

"True. But I have come to see that many people do not give wrongful actions much weight. Rather, they revel in such rebellious caprices."

"Do you mean that a hardened heart feels no prick of the conscience?"

"Something like that," he replied. "I believe that there are many people who overrule their original better judgment."

"I do, too. They are perhaps tender in the beginning, but with each foray into some little sin or vice, the tenderness toughens up. The feeling of wrong-doing becomes less and less, and eventually the sin bothers them no more." She stifled a yawn.

He said kindly, "You might like to doze for awhile before we get to our night's lodging."

"Yes, I will. Thank you." She closed her eyes and tried to snuggle into some semblance of relaxation against the corner squabs. She thought of how recently she had lain on Armand's arm and felt such pleasant sweetness there.

"Are you comfortable?" Lord Ashby asked.

Genevieve jumped.

He said, "I am sorry to have startled you. I believe you must have already dropped off to sleep."

She contrasted his apologetic manner to Armand's protective and unabashed way of pushing her down out of sight when she was in danger of being seen. She marveled at his boldness, and even more so, her shocking enjoyment of lying with her cheek on his person, feeling his fingers caressing her hair. She was certain that Lord Ashby would never impose upon her physically in that way.

She knew no more until he roused her from sleep, saying, "We are here, Miss Genevieve. A bed awaits you."

She rubbed her eyes and saw that they were halted in a dark village street. As he assisted her out of the carriage, she looked up and saw, nearby in the moonlight, huge curved walls and conical towers edged in pale light. Stars twinkled in profusion above them. "What place is this?" she asked, enjoying the romantic sight.

"Huisseau-sur-Mauves. Here you can sleep more comfortably for the rest of the night."

She felt lethargic as he guided her with her arm

tucked into his. Her yawns were huge, and she had to cover them often as the landlord and maid guided her up stone steps to a bedchamber.

Before Lord Ashby left from the room, he said, "Here are your bags from the coach. I will say good-night, Genevieve, as I see a tray of refreshments awaits you there on the table. To guard you, I shall be in the next room." He pointed to an arched door near the fireplace. "Knock loudly or just come in at any time should you need to."

That sounded well, but also scandalous. "Are we safe, do you think?" she whispered, and started to move to the narrow window facing the street.

A quarter hour later, while she was eating in her room and Radford in his with the door open between them, they heard a rattling of wheels and horse hoofs and wheels clattering loudly below.

He dashed into her room and said, "Stay back from the window! That could be—" He left off and pulled in the shutters until they were almost closed. He peered between them. "Blow out your candle!"

She did so.

"Deuce take it!" he said under his breath. "It's Chancet's coach, all right!"

"Oh, no!" expelled Genevieve. "What do we do now?"

"It's a good thing our driver moved our coach out of sight. Perhaps, if we're lucky, they will not know we stopped here."

Before long, they heard the sound of Lady Bastwicke's voice through the floor below, trying to convey, in French, that she needed their best room. She was told that they had no more rooms available. She fired off a string of invectives, citing her title and that of Sir Pomeroy Chancet, English Baronet. It seemed to do no good. She kept on, but her awkward French was failing her, and Genevieve, her heart in her throat as she listened, prayed that they would not discover her here.

The landlord remained immovable, and directed Monsieur and the English lady to an inn at the end of the street.

Genevieve whispered, as their voices diminished, "Can you see if Dorcasta is with them?"

"She is, unless that silhouette I see in the coach is a serving maid."

Lord Ashby pulled the shutters all the way in and locked them. With a sigh, he took Genevieve's hands in his and said, "I think we better move on."

"I agree. Let's go!"

"Good girl. When we think they're settled into that inn yonder, we will take our careful leave."

"Again," said Genevieve.

Running across the walled courtyard with him, she held onto his hand. He solicitously guided her toward the carriage, woke the coachman who was sleeping inside, and apologized to him for having to relinquish sleep for some hours longer. The coachman didn't seem to mind because Radford slipped him more money.

To Genevieve, he said, "He is proud to serve not only us, he said, but also Monsieur de Villebon."

"Yes, I heard him. That is fortunate. You know quite a lot of French, then, My Lord."

"I traveled around France two years ago, and picked up a bit more than I had learned from my tutor," he admitted. "Where did you learn so much?"

"Aunt Claracilla taught Arabelle and me, and we had a French governess for part of that time. We actually enjoyed it because it was almost all conversational. I never could have imagined to what use I would put it."

* * *

After their successful, quiet departure, they spent uneventful wee hours traveling by the light of the moon and the coach lanterns. She slept. The driver veered off the road into a grove of trees some time before dawn, when the sky was still gray. She and Radford got out to walk a little, as did the coachman, taking turns with the groom to hold the horses.

When they continued their journey, which put them much farther along than if they had stayed to sleep, Genevieve saw, as dawn approached, a flat plain with a dark, imposing shape upon the horizon. It was, without doubt, a cathedral. The sight thrilled her. It looked massive and grand as it pointed a tall spire toward the sky. It, alone, dominated the plain of fields that stretched as far as the eye could see. The closer they rolled toward it over the next hour, the more detail she could see. It rose from the midst of a considerable town, which finally appeared. Surprisingly, she saw that the spire soaring toward Heaven split when she viewed it from a different angle on their journey. It was, in fact, two mismatched spires. "How awe-inspiring it is!" she exclaimed to Radford.

"Yes, Chartres Cathedral has two unique spires."

"From here, they look stunning together." When

they eventually reached the town and saw the cathedral towering over the rooftops, she could see that it was dark gray, immense, and very ornate. Streets and houses clustered around it in all directions. The sun had just appeared, casting a golden glow over the rooftops. East windows reflected the sun in shimmers like liquid gold.

She asked, "Have we eluded them, do you think?"

"I hope so. By traveling all night, we made remarkable speed, and the flat roads helped the horses immensely."

"This is good. I feel so far away now. Do you know what I mean?"

"You were far away from London at Chambord, too; in fact you're closer to home here."

It was not what she meant, but she let it go.

The coach bore them over the flagstones into the narrow streets. Spring flowers grew brightly in window boxes, shutters opened to reveal lace curtains, and people emerged from their houses, most of them with baskets. She smelled bread baking.

Radford yawned behind his hand and smiled. "Are you as hungry as I am?"

"Probably hungrier!"

He nodded.

The coachman halted the horses as Genevieve stared at another church to her left. It was ancient and magnificent, with gray flying buttresses. It rose so near at hand that, when she emerged stiffly from the vehicle, she was only a stone's throw away from it.

She turned back to the house where the groom sounded a door knocker. From the floor above them, two large shutters flew back against the wall. A blonde head appeared, beneath which smiled a pleasant lady's face. Genevieve smiled happily in recognition, for she had seen her walking with the older woman under parasols at Chambord. Armand had introduced them. Madame Lavande told them to come in; she was sending her servant down to unlock the door.

Having climbed winding stairs, Genevieve was soon seated in a first floor house with white plaster and ancient brown wood half-timbering made of tree limbs on the walls. Between the kitchen and the dining room, the light passed through a stained glass window depicting Chartres Cathedral.

Madame Lavande welcomed them with smiles and kisses on both cheeks. Genevieve gave her Armand's letter, and said she had met her briefly at Chambord, with her mother-in-law.

She told her young maid to run and buy freshly-baked bread. Madame Lavande explained that the *boulangerie* was just around the corner. She served hot coffee to them, read the letter, and asked Genevieve and Radford to explain what their escape had been like.

After hearing the details, Madame Lavande was appalled. "Does your mother know that you had this importunate suitor, Sir Pomeroy Chancet, threatening your peace at every turn?"

Radford replied for her. "Yes, but she may not know what he did last night, nor how we evaded him."

Genevieve said, "But Monsieur de Villebon and Lord Ashby, here, very adroitly maneuvered to throw Sir Pomeroy off our scent. But he and my mother came frightfully close to discovering us last night anyway."

Radford cited Genevieve's wish to see Cathédrale de Chartres if at all possible.

Madame Lavande nodded and said, "I will take you to the Cathedral tonight after dark."

Radford said, "Thank you, Madame Lavande, but I am happy to take her there myself, as she and I discussed."

Madame Lavande looked from him to Genevieve and back again. "I see it is your wish, Lord Ashby, but I think it is dangerous for either of you to risk being seen together by those who chase you, don't you think?"

* * *

The bells woke Genevieve. It was glorious change-ringing of many large bells from the nearby church with the flying buttresses. Madame Lavande said it was the church of Saint-Pierre. The beautiful sounds swirled all around, wafting one after the other, from every window, making Genevieve marvel in the richness that kept resonating. She went out to the sitting room feeling joyfully transported.

Madame Lavande looked up from her letter-writing and smiled. "Did you sleep well, Genevieve?"

"Extremely well, thank you, Madame."

"So you like the bells?"

"I have never heard any so melodious, or so near. The sounds swirl in, around, and through me!"

"Do they make you happy?"

"Oh, yes; uplifted."

"That is good. You were looking too full of worries when you arrived, *ma petite*, that sleep and bells and food are what you needed, no?"

"Yes, and I thank you kindly for your lovely care of me. Has anyone knocked at your door while I slept?"

"Do you mean, in pursuit of you? No." She made Genevieve rest and eat during the whole day. She did not so much as let her look down out of the windows where she could be seen from the square unless she stayed back in the shadows.

Genevieve felt grateful for her protection, but restless. She wondered what was happening, but heard nothing, for Radford had said he would not approach this house during daylight lest it give away her whereabouts.

That evening, Madame Lavande accompanied Genevieve to the Cathedral, both of them cloaked in dark hooded capes. They walked up the hill between the high houses, the projecting floors to some of them casting dark shadows in the narrow lanes below. Two servant boys veered off another way, carrying their minimal luggage on a roundabout course.

Soon they emerged in sight of the Cathedral's front face. It took Genevieve's breath away— La Cathédrale de Chartres! It rose grander and more overpowering in its spectacular beauty than Genevieve had ever imagined. Its two towering spires were different designs and offset from one another, but she liked the artistry of their pairing. In between, above the high arched doorway, was a round window of stained glass. Lit from within, the colors looked so vivid and glorious that she would have stood staring upward at it for much longer had not Madame Lavande taken her by the arm and drawn her along.

"I have no words," breathed Genevieve. Madame Lavande nodded in agreement. Once inside, they walked past the seated worshippers, past banks of flickering candles toward the back of the Cathedral where less light penetrated away from the bright area of flickering candles.

Genevieve whispered, "I remember that I am to linger near a *bas-relief* depicting the life of Christ."

"There it is," said Madame Lavande. "Good. Let us stay here so your pursuers will not see you, if they come in. I shall be watching," she whispered. "Find a place to duck into should I sound the alarm."

"What is your alarm?"

"Ah, let me see . . . I shall knock over that little chair."

"You are daring," said Genevieve. "You will draw all eyes upon you."

"Better than on you," she replied, and smiled.

"*Merci*," said Genevieve, and pulled her hood over her forehead to shadow her face. She began to study the life of Jesus as sculpted in Biblical figures.

It took some time before she had made her way around the U shaped progression. By the end, she felt very touched. "Thank you, Jesus," she said softly. Her heart swelled with gratitude over what He had done for her.

In the distance, a man's figure with a white wig detached itself from an influx of people coming in through the front door. He minced across the labyrinth on the floor, nearly tripping over a man who was crawling around its path on hands and knees.

Genevieve's heart jolted. Who could mistake that dandified gait? It was Sir Pomeroy Chancet, peering from side to side.

Panic-stricken, she hurried to an iron gate across from the beginning of the life of Christ. She opened and closed it silently, and ducked behind the partial wall that made it a small worship spot. While her pulses pounded in her temples, she prayed that he would not find her here.

She heard a chair clatter to the stone floor. Yes, Madame Lavande had spotted him, too. Genevieve had described him in detail.

Minutes ticked by. She heard footsteps. She pressed her hands to her thumping heart, and dared not breathe.

Sir Pomeroy's voice came alarmingly near as he queried of someone, "Have you seen a young lady with blondish reddish hair?"

"Je ne comprends pas," a woman replied. It was Madame Lavande, disguising her voice to sound like an old lady who did not understand him.

Frustrated, he left, his heels clicking until the sound died away.

Genevieve made sure that her curls were well back and hidden beneath the hood when she, after ten minutes, rose shakily to her feet. As one leg had gone to sleep, she leaned against the wall to recover, and that was when she heard a feminine whisper. "It's time to leave!" said Madame Lavande with urgency.

"I'm here," Genevieve whispered back, surprised

at how her voice carried.

"I will not approach you in case that man is still in here, lurking and watching. Stay hidden for a moment."

Genevieve shivered.

Madame Lavande whispered, "I will go out the staircase of curved steps that leads up to the street in back. I saw that the gate is ajar. Follow if you see me beckon once I'm up on the street level."

"I will."

"Keep your face in shadow. Stoop like an old woman as I am doing. Speak French with a different voice if anyone accosts you."

"*Oui,* Madame." Genevieve waited, and watched her ascend the shadowy staircase. When it seemed that the coast was clear, she waddled slowly after her. Only a few strangers could see her from the chairs in the distance, so she hurried up the half-circle steps. Outside, the sky was dark over the city, and lamps were being lit. She saw Madame Lavande's cloaked figure beckoning her.

Next, she was motioning wildly from kitty-corner across the street, so Genevieve hurried. When she reached her, two horses and a small, curvy carriage came to a halt beside them.

Genevieve grabbed her companion's arm in panic. "Is that Sir Pomeroy?"

The door of the vehicle opened, and it was with great surprise that she saw it was Radford who held the door open, his gloved hand reaching out for hers. She managed her skirts, collapsing her panniers, and moved over to make room for Madame Lavande next to her and across from him. He had a concentrated frown between his brows.

"Sir Pomeroy was in the Cathedral!" Genevieve expelled with her hand to her breast.

Radford said, "I know. I saw him go in."

"Does he recognize us, do you think?"

"I'm watching, but so far, I cannot tell. There's only a horse cart in sight, but you never know. Blast! —here he comes!"

Genevieve had to lean on Lord Ashby to see out his window. She, too, saw the white wig against the dark stone of the Cathedral's north face, looking their way and moving with purpose. She gasped. "Yes, he is vaulting into that coach that just drove up!"

"Sir Pomeroy Chancet, that roué!" cried Madame Lavande. "He is chasing you still, *ma pauvre chérie!*"

"Yes! And if my mother is with him, there will be no excuse whatsoever for my not going with them."

"Get down and stay hidden under your hood!" Madame Lavande said. "If he only sees my face at this window, I doubt that he will follow us."

Radford suddenly said, "I will give this coachman instruction to race on ahead. I will walk back and lead Sir Pomeroy off the trail by telling him that I have just parted from Madame Lavande, who is going to my friends' home at the other end of town. I will not confess to having seen you, Genevieve. Will you ladies be all right together with this coachman and groom from Chambord? They assured me that they have their instructions to convey you to safety. I have to leap out now, while I can."

Genevieve looked at him with gratitude. "Yes, we must trust. If you're willing to do all this for me, then I thank you, Radford."

The door clicked shut, and the coach jolted forward. Madame Lavande locked their door and put her legs over Genevieve, spreading her gown to cover her. Genevieve kept her palms on the floor, and her knees together, balancing herself as the vehicle bumped and shuddered and swerved around corners.

Madame Lavande touched Genevieve's shoulder and said, "I think that Lord Ashby has feelings for you."

In her muffled position on the floor, Genevieve silently considered her words.

"Do you not think so?" persisted Madame Lavande.

"I think it is possible, but I do not really know. What is happening? Is there a pursuit?"

"I see nothing yet. I only saw Milord talking to the blackguard, but we are out of their sight now for several minutes." Madame Lavande suddenly snapped, "That swine! How dare he think he can foist you away and marry you?"

"He has my mother's sanction, that's why."

"Bah! What kind of a mother is she, anyway?"

"A very determined one. But where are we going? I thought we were returning to your house. It feels like we are no longer in the town."

"We are in the country, speeding north. Armand wrote me that we must get you out of Chartres with all speed if we spied that man who prances when he walks. There is danger of your being actually forced into marriage if you stay here. We must fly through the night. Armand wrote that our coachman has the directions. I do not know what they are."

CHAPTER 12

The Hidden Château

Fly through the night they did. It was nearing daybreak when, upon a flat country road formerly resting in a peaceful silence that not even a rooster had broken, their carriage rolled between fallow fields, turned some corners, and stopped. For some time, Genevieve had watched a gray steeple growing larger. Behind a row of trees, house roofs appeared around it.

While the tired horses shook their harnesses, her view to the left showed a high brick wall with a round inset hole. When she opened the window, she heard the double coos of doves. "How soothing that sounds," she said to Madame Lavande. "Just listen." Inside the hole, she saw cross hatching, and knew it was the dovecote.

Madame Lavande, rousing and stretching delicately, opened her eyes. "Yes, it sounds heavenly. Did you sleep all through the night?" she asked. "I am ashamed to ask you, because I did."

"I slept for the past few hours. We have a good

coachman and horses."

"Are we stopping here, I wonder?"

Genevieve said, "I do not know. Oh, look, we have a pink and red sunrise." The sunbeams streaked upward in a fan shape across the eastern sky, throwing rose color onto the clouds.

From the farmyard to which the dovecote belonged, a dog ran barking at them, which caused a rooster to wake up and crow. Presently, a tan-skinned old man strode briskly from a stone barn, past a long house with half-timbering high on its walls, and three roof gables. Removing his dark beret, he replied respectfully to the coachman and pointed to a high wall to Genevieve's right. Treetops towered above that wall from the inside.

The gate in it consisted of arched raspberry-colored wooden doors fastened in black iron. They were topped and surrounded by alternating brick-and-stone work and accented above by an ornate cut-out design.

"What is he saying?" asked Genevieve. "I couldn't hear."

"We are to walk in through that gate, but the coach is not to come in," said Madame Lavande.

"What is this place?"

She smiled broadly. "It sounds like our destination. Me, I would willingly sleep again in a comfortable bed. I believe it will be in this place. And you, Genevieve?"

"Oh, I couldn't sleep now. I am wondering what has happened in Chartres, whether Lord Ashby headed Sir Pomeroy off of our trail, or if he had to fight him."

"Do not worry. We are here, and we shall go

through this gate. Just look at the height of these walls. Surely we will be safe inside, *ma chérie.*"

When the groom opened their door to the fresh, cool morning, the ladies unfolded themselves from the coach, and smoothed their hair and clothing. They walked to the doors, one of which swung inward a minute after the farmer knocked upon it five times. He bowed low to the ladies and gestured them in.

The view that met their eyes took Genevieve's breath away. It was not an inn, as she expected, but an ancient château! Round, pale red towers rose majestically with crenellated tops. It was a feast for her eyes, and gave her a euphoric feeling she had never experienced before. "Oh!" she expelled. "I am in a fairytale paradise!"

"Oui, c'est magnifique!"

They stood gazing in awestruck wonder. It was a square château of great dignity and charm. Behind it, in a green lawn, stood a chapel with a steeple, and to their right, against the wall, a long orangerie with trees visible behind full-length arched glass windows.

"I have never even imagined any place this secluded and beautiful!" breathed Genevieve.

"Nor have I, and I have seen many châteaux. Genevieve, I see that you and I are to stay in safety here."

"We are?"

"Yes, here inside that locked gate and inside the château, certainly, for do you see any other place?" She smiled happily and led Genevieve exuberantly forward.

Genevieve actually skipped for joy as they went.

"Oh, I wish my sister, Arabelle, was here!" Genevieve felt transported to a place where her soul could rest, and her body and mind could revel in the serene, exquisite beauty. She looked around at the low, clipped hedge design, and beyond, where an avenue of tall, bordering trees disappeared into the distance. How marvelous it would be to ride a horse through there, shaded from above. In the distance, a herd of red deer took fright at their presence, and bounded away, showing their black and white tails.

As the ladies approached the moat, Madame Lavande said, "Your mother and Sir Pomeroy will not be able to harm you here."

Genevieve breathed a heartfelt sigh of relief. A feeling of liberty flowed through her as the beauty rose close in front of her. "Who owns this romantic, walled-in château?" she asked. "Why are we so lucky to be sent here?"

She had not heard a thing but the birds' dawn chorus, it was that peaceful. While gazing at the park and up at the two crenellated towers that flanked a bridge with two small arches beneath it, she heard a clink and a slight creaking sound. She had assumed that they would walk over the narrow drawbridge that led to a small door, but to its right, a wider drawbridge was lowering over the moat. Genevieve smiled delightedly at her companion. Down came the wood structure with a handrail, and settled into place.

"We must be expected," said Madame Lavande, looking pleased. She gestured Genevieve to step onto it first.

At the same time, a pounding came from the gate

behind them and echoed on the castle wall. Genevieve met Madame Lavande's eyes in sudden questioning. "O Lord, help us! Could it possibly be my mother?"

"No, certainly not. How would she know where we are?"

Before them, an old manservant approached them from an arched tunnel on which deer antlers hung. He removed his beret and bowed to them. In French, he asked, "Who are you, please?"

Genevieve told him, fearful that it would not mean a thing to him, and that they would be turned away.

He didn't catch their names, and had to be told again by Madame Lavande in a loud voice near his ear, with her pointing toward the gate, telling him not to admit those who were knocking. The pounding at the outer gate continued. The man nodded his head, passed Genevieve on the drawbridge, and headed for the gate. The cacophony soon included a woman's high-pitched voice, shouting, "*Aidez-moi!* I must get in to get my daughter back!"

Genevieve turned in terror toward the gate. "It's Madam! Oh no, no, no! What can we do?"

Madame Lavande said, "The old servant will not let them in."

A lad of about fourteen came running out of the inner courtyard. With alert eyes pinned on her face, and then Madame Lavande's, he asked, "Are you Madame Lavande and the English lady, Miss Lamar?"

"Yes!" they cried in unison.

"Please to come in." He bowed quickly and said,

"I am Thibaut; at your service."

"Merci, merci!" Genevieve moved after him, shooting a wild look over her shoulder.

Madame Lavande told the boy emphatically to keep away the woman pounding at the gate. She turned to Genevieve, "Is that not right? You do not want to see her?"

"Right!" Genevieve added earnestly to Thibaut, "If you cannot deny the fact that we are here, at least hide us, and do not let her in, please!"

Madame added hastily that it was someone pursuing Genevieve to harm her. "Keep that woman out!"

Thibaut's eyes danced. He asked, "Is that the one I see coming in through the gate?"

Sure enough, Lady Bastwicke had gained admittance by the old servant, who had gone to do his duty as gatekeeper, having misunderstood Madame Lavande completely.

Lady Bastwicke stood there eyeing the castle with great surprise. Then her eyes pinned on Genevieve.

"Hurry, Thibaut!" said Genevieve, "can you keep her out?"

Madame Lavande exclaimed, "The nerve of that despicable woman! Thibaut, she will do terrible deeds to her daughter! She will make her marry a profligate man!"

The servant boy asked Genevieve, "You want me to keep her away from you by any means?"

"Yes!" both ladies cried.

"I will!" he declared, and moved with purpose.

Madame Lavande said intensely, "All is over for you, Genevieve, if she reaches you now! This is not good!"

Genevieve drew herself up and called to Thibaut, "How do you lock people out?

"By wheeling up this drawbridge, Mademoiselle." They could hear his hands operating something metal.

Madame Lavande cried "Wheel it up quickly, before she reaches it!"

Lady Bastwicke, her wide russet skirt swaying, made her angry way toward the drawbridge. "Genevieve!" she shrieked. "You are my daughter! Get back here at once!"

Genevieve saw a white wig appear through the gate across the lawn. Desperately, she urged Thibaut to act quickly. "Do not let her or that man in, no matter what they say!"

Thibaut, grasping a black iron wheel, nodded at her and turned it rapidly. Soon Genevieve was thrilled to see, in the nick of time, the end of the drawbridge rising, rising, and behind it, her mother, her cap ruffles quivering, staring open-mouthed up at the lifting bridge.

"Genevieve!" she screamed, "make him lower that this instant!"

Thibaut, eyeing the last of Lady Bastwicke, grinned and continued to raise the drawbridge until it closed neatly into place. *"Voilà!* I have locked her out. She cannot get in." He gave the ladies a bow and a flourish.

Genevieve clapped him jubilantly. But then she alerted. "What about that little drawbridge? Is the door locked on this side of it?"

"Yes, I bolted it. Do not fear, Mademoiselle." He went to peer through a small cross-hatched window. Chuckling, he said to them, "I think, with that wide dress, she cannot fit between the chains anyway. She can get stuck if she tries it sideways."

The ladies laughed nervously. Genevieve almost wilted with relief. "What a good man you are!"

A loud knock sounded suddenly next to Thibaut on the narrow door to the small drawbridge. It was followed by the angry voice of Sir Pomeroy shouting, "Let us in!" He had fit through where Lady Bastwicke could not.

Thibaut asked, his eyes glinting, "Can I give him a scare?"

Madame Lavande instantly said, "Yes!"

The next thing they knew, he was turning another wheel. From outside, they heard a yelp and an angry outcry. Smiling while watching through the peep hole, he halted his motion and cast a mischievous glance at Genevieve. "Do you think the tipped drawbridge he is standing on will frighten him away? Perhaps a little higher?" He turned the wheel more. There came a screech from outside. "Enough, enough! Put it down, you—villains! Do you want me to fall into the moat?"

At that, Thibaut laughed aloud and looked sidewise at the ladies. "Don't temp me!" He whirled the wheel backward as quickly as he could. They heard a yell and a *clunk*.

Genevieve heard the welcome sound of Sir Pomeroy's heels beating a retreat. Madam could be heard issuing acrimonious threats at them all, interrupted by Sir Pomeroy's discordant censure.

Still watching through the little window, Thibaut reported, "They are running away!"

Madame Lavande moved swiftly and pulled the boy into a hug as she gushed, "Thank you, thank you, our good man!" She peeked out the little window herself.

Genevieve added, "Thibaut, you're our hero!"

He smiled and said, "I am happy to serve you."

Surrounded by the high inner walls and the sense of momentary salvation, Genevieve stretched out her fingers and showed how they shook. "How unnerving!" she breathed. Collapsing against the solid stone wall in the courtyard, she expelled, "I have never done anything like this in my life! She has intimidated me mercilessly for two years."

Madame Lavande gazed at Genevieve with sympathy and admiration. "You courageous girl!"

"Yes, but she is still out there. She will hate me forever, and take her revenge."

"On her own daughter?"

Thibaut cleared his throat. "*Now* what can I do for you ladies? Would you like to go inside?"

Genevieve nodded gratefully. They followed him across the cobblestone courtyard which was surrounded by high walls with windows in several stories.

They could still hear Lady Bastwicke shouting invectives and threats in great fury, but the sounds were diminishing.

Madame Lavande said, "Yes, but will she lower herself to scream there all day long? She has no dignity."

"Who knows what she will do?"

"Another one with no dignity is that importunate swain of yours."

Genevieve moaned. "Will he never give up?"

Madame Lavande touched her cheek sympathetically and said, "It is time for us to go inside and talk to the mistress of this refuge. I will ask her for secure sanctuary." She turned to Thibaut and fired off several questions, to which he replied that the Comte was not at home, but the Comtesse might still be in bed.

Genevieve said quietly, "I hope her chamber was not on the drawbridge side and that her window was not open, or she would be slumbering no longer."

Madame Lavande expelled, "Will that woman never stop her caterwauling? *Vraiment horrible!* Thibaut, is your mistress likely to see us?"

"I will have her informed of your arrival now, Madame Lavande." He led them up a step and into a long, wood-paneled drawing room. Thibaut indicated that they sit, so Genevieve sank onto a turquoise velvet settee beside a golden candelabrum where the light shone warmly and lit the golden frames of ancient portraits.

Thibaut strode away down the room and disappeared through a far door.

Genevieve said, "This is a sweet and noble place! I feel like I've come to Heaven. Oh, but why did my mother have to spoil it? It felt like the Devil pounding at the door of Heaven. Will anyone be able to oust her from the grounds?"

Madame Lavande said, "If necessary, I will pay Thibaut well if he and anyone else who works here will escort her out and keep her out."

"Thank you for that. But what will she do? I can't stay here, hiding forever, can I?"

Madame Lavande shook her head. "Let not your

heart be troubled."

That made Genevieve think of that Bible passage that went, *Let not your heart be troubled: ye believe in God, believe also in me. In my Father's house are many mansions: if it were not so, I would have told you. I go to prepare a place for you. And if I go and prepare a place for you, I will come again, and receive you unto myself; that where I am, there ye may be also.* She sighed and said, "Yes, I'm thankful that, in this present mansion, we have a temporary refuge. There is a far better one to come."

Thibaut returned, saying, "My mistress will see you shortly. Wait here, please."

Madame Lavande asked when the master would be home.

"I do not know, but possibly tomorrow or the next day, Madame."

Genevieve wondered, "What if my mother waylays him, charms him, and comes in with him? She will take me away with her by legal right, and try to forcibly wed me to that scoundrel."

Thibaut stood and thought for a moment. "If I hear him arriving, I will run up to the tower battlements and call a warning to him. I will watch out for those two before I let down the drawbridge."

Genevieve and Madame Lavande both voiced their approval of this plan, but indicated that Thibaut should pass on loud, precise instructions to the elderly servant who had let in the intruders.

Genevieve asked, "May I come into the tower with you then, Thibaut? I need to see and hear what happens."

PURSUING GENEVIEVE

* * *

It occurred that, while a serving maid appeared to call them into the mistress's presence a quarter hour later, Thibaut dashed into the room and breathlessly called to Genevieve. "He comes, Mademoiselle! He is early!"

Genevieve quickly told Madame Lavande to go and meet the lady of the house. "I'm going with Thibaut." They left on the words, he leading her up a circular staircase inside a tower.

When they emerged into the topmost room, she dashed to the window under the crenellations. There was a well-formed man wearing a black three-cornered hat striding toward the castle, followed at a loping, awkward run by Lady Bastwicke, with Sir Pomeroy Chancet taking up the rear.

"Yoo-hoo! Wait up, Monsieur!" called Lady Bastwicke. Genevieve had rarely seen her so undignified. She had a sick feeling, fearing that the Comte would be taken in by Madam's pleas. Apparently the old servant in the beret had not yet heard the message to keep them out.

The man under the hat turned toward Madam, and she and Sir Pomeroy rushed to face him.

Sir Pomeroy, summoning up manners, made him a leg, bowing.

Lady Bastwicke merely said, "I have seen you before. Weren't you at Chambord?"

"I was, Lady Bastwicke. What, may I ask, are you doing here?"

"I—I came for my daughter."

"Your daughter? Why, where is she?"

Lady Bastwicke pointed grandly. "In there!"

Sir Pomeroy smiled up at the man and declared, "Monsieur de Villebon, I am to marry her and take her home to England, but how can I do it if she is in there?" He, likewise, pointed at the impregnable château. "If you are admitted there, we will come with you." He beamed ingratiatingly and twirled his handkerchief.

Genevieve put her hand on her thudding heart and felt extremely glad to learn that it was Armand, of all people, whom they pleaded with. She was extremely surprised and grateful that he was here.

"Indeed," he drawled. "Why is she in there, Sir Pomeroy? Does she know you are here?"

"Ah . . ." he prevaricated, glancing wildly at Lady Bastwicke.

Lady Bastwicke snapped, "Of course she does! She saw us, and then the drawbridge raised up to keep us out? She is a horrid and uncontrollable girl!"

Sir Pomeroy turned and really looked at Madam. "Horrid and uncontrollable? That is not how you have described her to me."

"Oh, hush! Horrid to run from you, I meant, and now she won't do what I command." To Armand, she said, "She and a strange lady had a servant lock us out as soon as they saw us coming!"

Armand drawled, "*Did* she, now! I find that most interesting."

Thibaut decided the moment was right to speak, and with a questioning look at Genevieve, to which she nodded enthusiastically, he called down across the moat, "Comte de Villebon!"

Armand swiveled and looked up at the tower. So

Armand was a Comte! He had never said a word about his nobility. It was a joy for Genevieve to see the handsome face beneath the hat looking up at her.

"*Oui*, Thibaut?"

"I am instructed to tell you, Monsieur le Comte, that a young lady is in danger from those people, and we have given her and Madame Lavande refuge."

There came a screech from Lady Bastwicke and she shook her fist upward although it was doubtful that she could see Thibaut. Sir Pomeroy folded his arms in a black-browed pose.

Armand looked amused, but those two could not see his face.

Sir Pomeroy suddenly spotted Genevieve, who quickly drew back. "Genevieve!" he cried. "I just remembered; I have a letter here for you. I must give it to you in person."

Genevieve rolled her eyes in exasperation. It must be a love letter full of his lewd longings again.

Armand snatched it neatly from his waving fingers and said, "Thank you. I will deliver it."

Sir Pomeroy, open-mouthed, turned furious, but Armand had tucked it away inside his coat by then.

Genevieve silently cheered him.

Lady Bastwicke suddenly changed her attitude entirely. Eyeing him, she began gushing about the impressive château, the moat, the clipped maze-like garden to the west, the pink roses climbing up the wall, and ended with his handsome waistcoat.

"It is but a functional suit that I wear, Lady Bastwicke, but thank you."

Attempting to tuck her hand into his arm, she

gave him a ghastly smile and asked, "Will you kindly see if they'll give us tired travelers a cup of coffee inside?"

Thibaut called loudly, "Monsieur le Comte! Your Mother needs you, and she also needs quiet. She cannot accept those visitors anytime today."

Armand looked up and nodded at him, whereupon Thibaut pointed at Genevieve and made gesticulations that resulted in Armand's turning back to Lady Bastwicke.

He said, "*Je regrette*, Madame. My mother is not well. I must attend to her." He smiled genially and herded them back toward the gate despite their sputtering. "I will escort you out." He did so with amazing dispatch, while Genevieve rejoiced, watching his masterful, nonabrasive technique.

Madam's back was stiff, but she had no choice but to go, so she waddled along in her huge gown that rode a little lopsidedly.

It hit Genevieve then. *His mother*, he had said. His mother was the chatelaine of this château!

Sir Pomeroy turned unexpectedly, and ran back to peer up, trying to see Genevieve. "What a minx you are! You escaped at Chambord and somehow in Chartres. Now you think you're safe by fleeing in there, over that drawbridge." He smiled, his lip rouge prominent. "I find you are full of surprises. You only grow more desirable."

She groaned and turned away.

Thibaut was eyeing at her. "A *poursuivant détesté?*"

"The worst!" she said from the heart.

"The Comte will chase him out."

"Oh, didn't he arrive just in time? But you were wonderful at saving me today, Thibaut. *Merci beaucoup!*"

"*De rien,*" he said, slightly flushing. "I must hurry to the drawbridges."

"What is this place called?"

"Château de Villebon."

Genevieve caught her breath. "In truth?"

"Yes, of course."

Armand could be heard calling Thibaut.

"*Oui,* Monsieur le Comte?"

"Lower the drawbridge until I can jump onto it, will you?"

"Consider it done," the boy called, and he clattered down and around the tower stairs.

Genevieve peered back out at Armand, her heart full. She watched as the drawbridge lowered until it was nearly down, whereupon he jumped lightly to its top and ran down it into the castle. Soon the end rose again and closed with a *clunk*.

* * *

Armand strolled into the long drawing room and saw Genevieve pacing. He smiled at her, propped his hat onto a statue's head, and strode to her, smiling and then kissing both of her cheeks.

The words burst from her mouth. "You are my hero!"

His eyes gleamed joyously. "I am? How did I achieve that?"

"By achieving our escape, for sending us here, and for escorting my mother and Sir Pomeroy out. You worked miracle after miracle." She put her hand on her heart. "I feel safe in here with you." She should feel ashamed of such gladness, but this was a war she must fight to the end, or lose.

Thibaut entered the room and said to Genevieve, "Comtesse de Villebon is ready to receive you now, Mademoiselle."

When they were ushered into a sitting room, a slim and pretty dark-haired lady sat before them, moving bobbins of white thread upon a cushion, creating intricate scallops of bobbin lace. Madame Lavande leaned toward her, watching. Both women looked up and smiled.

Armand presented Genevieve to his mother, the Comtesse de Villebon.

"Welcome, Mademoiselle Genevieve." The corners of her eyes crinkled becomingly as she smiled. Genevieve went shyly to kiss her cheeks. She was a lovely woman with graceful black eyebrows. Dimples appeared when she smiled, and there was irrefutable evidence that she was Armand's mother in the thick, dark eyelashes and the shape of their smiles. She wore a fashionable purple and white print *robe ronde* and a bobbin lace choker. Genevieve felt a real welcome from her, and her tension dissipated.

As they presently drank coffee from round porcelain cups and ate bread with jam, the recent frenetic happenings were poured into Comtesse de Villebon's ears. The brouhaha at Chambord and ever since were described in turn by Armand, Genevieve, and Madame Lavande. The Comtesse expressed her amazement at Armand's mission at Château de Chambord. She tactfully told Genevieve that she sympathized with her plight and all that she had gone through to avoid Sir Pomeroy Chancet. "I have heard of him," she said with a lift of an eyebrow.

Startled, Genevieve said, "You have?"

Armand, setting down his cup, prompted, "What did you hear, *Maman?*"

"That he swindled money and an estate from a distant cousin of ours in the Auvergne."

"Swindled!" exclaimed Genevieve. "He told me that someone willed him everything out of gratitude."

"Not so. I have another relative who expected to inherit, but he receives nothing now unless he takes legal action. Sir Pomeroy Chancet lived with our late cousin for awhile, and now Sir Pomeroy Chancet has it all."

Genevieve and Madame Lavande locked widened eyes and made outraged noises.

Armand said, rubbing his nose thoughtfully, "The rightful heir has grounds to have that investigated."

* * *

Armand left the ladies, saying he wanted to go discover where Sir Pomeroy and Lady Bastwicke were, and learn their immediate plans.

The Comtesse said to Genevieve, "Come, let me show you where you will sleep tonight. Armand brought your luggage. My maid is showing Madame Lavande to her room, so come with me." Up the stairs they went, to a bedchamber with a bed draped in aqua and gold, the silk bed curtains falling elegantly from a high pinnacle. "This we call *La Chambre Royale* because several Kings of France have slept here."

Genevieve breathed, "It has a fairy-tale feeling.

Do you truly want to give it to me for the night? You do? Oh, thank you, Comtesse!"

"Thibaut, please carry her things in here," she said as she spied him bearing bandboxes. She turned back to Genevieve. "Ask Armand to take you to the chapel. You look like the kind of lady who would appreciate it."

When Armand returned, he said he would be glad to show her. Genevieve walked with him over the cobbles of the castle courtyard, through the arched tunnel with the antlers on both sides, and over the lowered drawbridge that spanned the glittering moat. She had enjoyed breakfast and a nap in the royal bed, and had woken much refreshed.

She said to him, "I am wondering how you went and came back in with my mother and Sir Pomeroy outside your gate. Did they see you? It seems that they would have accosted you, and followed you back in here."

"They never saw me because I rode out and back in through a gate at the far end of the deer park."

"Did you discover where they are?"

"Yes, Thibaut went with me and scouted the village. He saw them at the inn."

Genevieve continued to admire Armand's strategies in dealing with troublesome people, and his modesty about everything that he accomplished. She said, "You impress me, Comte de Villebon."

"Please, call me Armand, as you are my guest, and I do like calling you Genevieve." The way he smiled at her gave her a flutter inside.

In the chapel, it was bright with sunshine.

Armand went to the organ and played a happy-sounding French hymn for her. It went well in the ambience of stained glass windows and gold. As he sang in French, she hummed along, and at the end, she said from the heart, "Thank you, Armand. You filled this chapel with life. It feels like a blessed place."

"I always play when I come in here. If I go into churches or cathedrals that are empty and silent, it doesn't feel the same. They are meant for the Word, spoken or sung, and only then do they come to life."

"I so agree! A place of worship needs a sermon or prayers or music sung to praise God and our Saviour; otherwise, it's only walls and decoration. How often do you have services here?"

"Each Sunday."

"Do you play the organ then?"

He smiled somewhat sheepishly. "How did you guess?"

"Because you are so adept at it, and I find, more and more, that you are unconventional. You could be a high-and-mighty kind of man in your position, but you don't act that way."

Armand laughed. "High-and-mighty? Me? Not so, Genevieve."

"But you are the Comte de Villebon, are you not?"

"Yes, I inherited the title. It was my father's, but he never strutted around playing Comte because he also inherited the title from his father. We have not been used to lording it over our people. That would be pointless and arrogant. We are grateful for our blessings, and we are here to serve others."

Genevieve smiled at him. "That shows, not only in you but also in your mother."

"Do you know people who enjoy lording it over others?"

She rolled her eyes. "Of course I do. Many people in English society have a modicum of that spirit, or are saturated with it. My own mother is endowed with a generous share, as you have seen, and Sir Pomeroy seems neck-and-neck with her now. My mother married into the aristocracy, but she was not born to it."

Armand's lips twitched. He eyed her sidewise as they walked outside onto the lawn.

Genevieve, looking with wonder at the château towers from the back, said, "That's curious."

"What is?"

"There are round towers at the other three corners, but that tower is offset, more toward the middle, leaving this corner sharp. Why is that?"

Armand shook his head and said, "We have never figured that out."

"Has this storybook château been your home all your life?"

"Yes, I was born here." He suddenly recalled something, reached inside his *justacorps*, and handed her a thick letter. "This is for you. I took it from Sir Pomeroy."

"Yes, I saw you." Genevieve looked at the handwriting. "Oh good, it's from my father!"

"Ah! So it's not from Sir Pomeroy, then?"

"No, or I would drown it in the moat. Please excuse me if I read this now."

"Of course. Come take a seat in the orangerie."

She accepted with delight, and sank to a chair in

the warm sunshine inside the long brick building. Long arched windows provided light for the budding trees and plants. Armand waited outside.

The red wax seal had already been opened. It appeared to be the last page of a letter addressed to Madam, her mother.

In her Father's handwriting, she read:

> *This is of urgent importance. I am under obligation now to inform you, Regina, that there is one outcome to the Marriage Act that inadvertently affects you and me. I would have preferred to tell you of this in person, but since you are not here, I must write to you with this sobering news.*
>
> *First of all, recall how, when we met, you told me that you had been married for a short time, your husband had died, and left you with a child on the way? I hurried to marry and save you, as you begged me to do—and which I did do, out of compassion more than sense—only to discover that none of that was true, for you had not married nor were you expecting a child.*
>
> *Because of that hasty marriage, we must now pay a life-altering consequence. We were married by a clergyman in Fleet Street, one whom the Marriage Act Committee grilled thoroughly last week and found utterly invalid as a clergyman. He now sits in Newgate Prison.*
>
> *The outcome, Regina, is that your and my so-called marriage was not a valid marriage at all. Our union is made null and void by*

the investigations into the clergy occasioned by this new law, and by the subsequent discovery that our clergyman was a sham. We are not married in the eyes of English law.

I can do nothing to change this. You would do well to come home and make your plans.

Bastwicke

"What?" Genevieve exclaimed aloud. She let the letter fall and stared in alarm at Armand.

He hurried in through the door. "Your news has struck you hard. What is it? What can I do?" He took her hand, hunkered down, and searched her face.

Pushing the pages at him, she gulped and said, "Please read that."

At one place in his reading, a frown pulled his dark eyebrows together, and at another, they skyrocketed.

Genevieve's thoughts whirled. She wondered what on earth would happen next. No wonder her mother had been screeching to get at her. Was she planning to race back to England after reading this unfathomable news?

CHAPTER 13

Violent Passions

Genevieve said a fond good-bye to Madame Lavande because it was time for her to return to Chartres. "How can I ever thank you for everything you have done for me?"

"Bah! It was a great pleasure to be with you, and a never-to-be-forgotten adventure. Not so much fun for you, but now that my good nephew, Armand, is back, he will protect you from Sir Pomeroy's *idée fixe*. Surely that is what my good nephew will do."

Genevieve blushed slightly, hoping that would prove true. She trusted him. That thought came to her with clarity.

After seeing her off, Genevieve was relieved to see that Thibaut locked the outer gates to the secluded park of Château de Villebon. She said, "I feel safe and secure in here."

Armand, walking toward the front of his pale red château with its four rounded towers flanking the drawbridge, said, "I am so glad you do. Will you walk with me down the riding lane?"

"Yes, I'd love to; it is so inviting."

When she asked him how the eviction of Château de Chambord went, he said he had concluded it, and left his team to clean up the mess. "They should be done in a few days. I came away and left the project in good hands. I had something far more important to do."

"May I know what that was?"

"Securing your safety, Genevieve." He smiled sidewise at her and offered his arm. She placed hers upon it, feeling privileged at the close proximity in which he kept her walking beside him in the shaded lane. Its trees grew in uniformity on each side of the long, grassy bridleway. She looked high above them to the new leaves on the branches that occasionally met in the middle. Her heart sang with the birds that twittered. "It must be a treat to ride through here," she said, and sighed.

"It is."

"Armand, can we talk about the bizarre news that my parents are not married?"

He looked at her seriously. "Yes. That is troubling indeed."

Genevieve told him about how her father had worked long hours for two years with Lord Hardwicke and others to draft the Marriage Act. "Now that it is approved and passed into law, this result has happened to my father's own marriage!"

She thought with regret about how she, his daughter, had tried to elope. If she and Mr. Curling had succeeded, they could have had just such a clandestine marriage in Fleet Street as her father's and mother's had been. How provident it was that her stupid plan had been halted by dear Father.

"Thank you, God," she whispered, giving credit where credit was due.

"Pardon?"

She looked up at Armand and said, "I'm sorry. I was just—"

"Thanking God. Do you want to tell me what for, or is it intrusive for me to ask?"

Genevieve looked up at him, saw the concern in his eyes, and melted. "It is something I choose not to speak of now, but I have much to thank Him for."

"As do I." He had a soft light in his eyes, shining through his dark lashes. "I am so glad you're here."

"I am, too. This is the most serene place I have ever been, and more beautiful than anything in my imagination."

He squeezed her hand, which still held his arm. "You gratify me, Genevieve." He sighed. "Let's discuss what we should do next."

"I must go back to London, Armand."

"I suppose it's inevitable."

"My father might need me. He and Madam are now in crisis."

"Yes, they are. You're right. I am just wondering if you would grant me the office of escorting you there."

* * *

"See to it, Armand," said Comtesse de Villebon, smiling at her son, "for Genevieve needs your protection. And on the way, if you have the chance, I applaud your idea of seeing that Sir Pomeroy Chancet is arrested before he escapes to England. I assume, from the many ways he has harassed Genevieve, that he will sneak out of France and follow her to England."

Armand said, "He is why I must escort her to her father. I cannot let her ride in the carriage that her mother will occupy. I will alert the officials to apprehend him so he cannot leave France."

Genevieve said, "He had to leave England in a hurry for crimes he committed in London, so I doubt that he will be allowed back into the country."

"Oh? That works in your favor, then. But suppose he tries to slip in under an assumed name?"

Later, walking around the château in the twilight, Genevieve said to him, cautiously hopeful, "Armand, is it right that you said I don't have to travel with Madam? She would make the journey most nerve-shattering for me."

"I agree. What do you suppose she will do now that she has learned that her marriage is null and void?"

Genevieve shook her head wonderingly. "I have no idea. This is unprecedented."

* * *

A little later, looking at the formal garden's elegant green hedge pattern, she remarked, "To grow up in this château as a little boy, you must have had wonderful times, playing everywhere, Armand." She saw red deer grazing in the distance.

"Oh, yes. My friends and I ran up and down the tower stairs, acting out all kinds of stories. We hid and chased, shot our bows, and rode our ponies. We fell into the moat a few times. I inadvertently learned to swim that way. We made ourselves a little raft and toppled off of that."

Genevieve laughed. "That drawbridge was a spectacular surprise when I saw it descend for us, and again when it rose. Did you often vault onto it as it was going up, as I saw you do?"

"Yes, and didn't my practice came in handy?" He grinned.

Genevieve smiled, her eyes misting with feeling. "Thank you for the part you played so diplomatically on my behalf. You have been doing that for me since we met at Chambord."

"No thanks needed." His eyes glimmered into hers again, giving her a shiver of delight. He became more and more exciting to talk to. He was so attractive in his good-humored way that she found herself shyly looking away lest her admiration should show too blatantly.

They moved on to talk about the journey Genevieve needed to make to England on the morrow. Armand said, "I will go to spy on Sir Pomeroy Chancet tonight, and find out what he thinks his plans are."

"Good; I do not want him joining us on the journey. He is a conniving creature, so he may have found a way to sneak back into England by hiding behind my mother's skirts."

* * *

"How could this have happened to our family?" Genevieve said aloud. She startled herself awake.

Soon realizing she had been dreaming, she relaxed back onto the pillow. She lay looking up at the long aqua draperies above her. She was a guest in the royal bedchamber in Château de Villebon! She felt reluctant to leave.

She said a prayer to God to fix what appeared to be an insurmountable problem. If indeed her dear Father and Madam were not married, what would happen? He was Lord Bastwicke, and naturally Madam had thought, for all these years, that she was Lady Bastwicke. She acted accordingly. Apparently now she was no such thing. She was Arabelle's, Genevieve's, Lenora's, and Jerome's mother, but if she was not married to their father, who were they?

Genevieve sighed dismally, and rose from the bed, replacing the bedclothes neatly. Here she was in the enchanted, secluded, and serene Château de Villebon, so she wanted to enjoy every last minute, ignoring all negative thoughts.

She rang for a maid, who came smiling into the room with a curtsey. She had slept in the next room in order to be available for any wants Genevieve might have. It appeared that the girl named Babette had been awake and ready for some time.

While Genevieve was being helped into her traveling ensemble of pale aqua with teal accents, Babette supplied her with the information that Comte de Villebon had already partaken of his *petit-déjeuner* and was choosing his horses. When Genevieve made her way to a window, there she saw the coach below, shining clean, awaiting her at the end of the drawbridge.

"It will be hard for me to leave this place!" she said to Babette.

"*Oui.* It is the loveliest place I have ever seen in La Belle France."

"Where do you live?" Genevieve asked as she received her *caleche* from Babette, and placed it carefully over her coiffure.

"In the village yonder. I believe the lady from England and the fancy-wigged gentleman are staying at my father's inn."

"They are? Oh, my. Will you do me a favor?"

"*Oui,* but of course."

"Go home and listen, and ask questions of your father, and find out if those two English guests are going away to England together, or going their separate ways. It is vital for us to know. Please find out when they will leave."

Whisking off her apron, Babette smiled and said, "Yes, Mademoiselle Genevieve, I will ask permission and do it for you now." With a curtsy, she hurried away.

As Genevieve breakfasted in a charming little room with the Comtesse, she learned that Armand was her only child, and that she loved him dearly. She did not seem to cling to him, though, but said that since he returned from Balliol at Oxford, he had been very busy keeping the estate, for they had many tenant farmers, and properties in Villebon and beyond. At one point, Genevieve felt a bit startled to hear that sometimes they had dinner parties here, and young men and ladies of French society from as far as Paris and Chartres attended them.

Genevieve's heart felt odd, so she blurted out,

"Does Armand love any of those young ladies?"

The Comtesse checked for a moment, cocked her head, and said, "I do not know, exactly. He dances with them, and they flirt with him, and issue him many invitations. He has only accepted a few of those this past year since my husband died. Usually, he claims he is too busy here. I think he gives that reason to the ones he does not care to encourage."

Genevieve slowly let out her breath. She realized that she cared very much whether or not he loved one of those ladies.

Armand entered the room, smiled at her, and went to kiss his mother on both cheeks. *"Au revoir, Maman."*

Then he turned to Genevieve and kissed her in the same manner, touching her cheeks with his lips in real kisses. Her heart beat faster when his smiling eyes looked directly into hers. "We shall be off to England now, Genevieve, if that is still what you want. Are you feeling all right?"

She couldn't feel better except for her thumping heart, so she said, "I am feeling wonderful this morning, thanks to your kindness. This was the loveliest place in which to wake up. *Merci beaucoup* to both of you. But are you sure you want to travel to England, Armand?"

"Absolutely; I will not throw you to the wolves."

Babette entered the doorway. Genevieve beckoned her. "What have you discovered?"

With great portent, Babette said, "The woman is going to England this morning, and the man is going north, also. I do not know if it is to England or not because they have two coaches waiting."

Genevieve locked eyes with Armand. "Where is he going, I wonder?" she asked, and thanked the maid.

Armand looked rueful, and moved to pull out her chair for her to rise. "Who knows? We will be off, *Maman*. I do not know when I will be back. I will write to you."

The Comtesse accompanied them through the arched entryway and onto the drawbridge. There she kissed him lovingly. "I know you will see this young lady safely to her father's house. May God go with you."

"*Merci, Maman.*"

Genevieve felt a burst of emotion toward the lovely woman, and hugged her, and felt her kisses on both of her cheeks. "I have loved being here, meeting you. You made me feel so welcome and cared-for."

"Please come back," urged the Comtesse. Genevieve felt sincerity behind her words.

"How I would love to!" It seemed unlikely, though.

Traveling the road across the flat countryside with its fields stretching in all directions, Genevieve pondered the experiences she had had at Château de Villebon. It seemed like a dream, that private château behind high walls, secluded from the eyes of the world. It had seemed like Heaven on Earth. How had she been so blessed to be given sanctuary in that loving home?

Its owner was now riding beside the coach, escorting her to London, of all things. It all felt miraculous.

They had reached the outskirts of a village an

hour or so later, when another coach approached with cantering horses just behind them. Armand gestured his driver to pull over and let them pass.

Genevieve felt the coach body sway as the coachman pulled up under a tree. There was some shouting, and Genevieve wanted to put her head out to see who it was, but she knew it was prudent to hide.

Presently, Armand came to the door, opened it, and said to her, "I am afraid we have to take up a passenger."

"What? Who?" asked Genevieve, suddenly fearful.

"That Miss Doyle."

Genevieve collapsed back into her seat and sighed, "Oh, no!"

"I am sorry. Here they come."

She sat up, moved things off of the opposite seat, and took a deep breath.

Dorcasta sauntered to the open doorway, her snapping eyes roving over Armand. She smiled hugely and offered her hand for him to aid her. "Oh, could you lift my gown hem, please, so I can find that little round step with my foot? This skirt is just too long for me, isn't it?" She giggled.

Armand motioned for the groom to do it, at which Genevieve rejoiced. But why did she have to be afflicted with Dorcasta again?

She heard Armand say, "So what will you do, Lord Ashby?"

Genevieve put her head out the doorway to see Radford. He smiled and replied, "I will come with you. I will let my coach with our baggage follow, and hire a horse to ride, as I see you are riding."

The men continued talking of their plans. Armand stood taller, with his broad shoulders and long black coat, breeches, and boots, his dark queue, and white ruffles at his throat and wrists. Like Armand, Radford carried a tri-cornered hat under his elbow as was the custom for gentlemen. He looked lithe in his midnight blue coat and breeches, lace at the neck and wrists. His brown hair formed a queue in which a silver buckle gleamed.

Genevieve could hear Dorcasta breathing next to her, and saw her staring at the men with an artificial smile pinned on. Genevieve backed away so they wouldn't look like two silly misses ogling the attractive men.

Dorcasta gushed, "They are both the most comely men I have ever seen! Which would you pick?"

Genevieve rolled her eyes and snapped, "That is an inappropriate question!"

"Well, I don't mean we can exactly pick and get the one we like best, but we can go after them and try, can't we?"

"Dorcasta!" said Genevieve sharply. "Stop overstepping!"

"But your mother said I am to make myself attractive to gentlemen, and they will fall for me. But I have to use my feminine wiles."

"Oh, my word!" exploded Genevieve under her breath. "So that is what you do? Try to seduce all the men, hoping one will fall for you on that slim of a basis? You think that you only have to fawn over them, and strive to seem attractive?"

Dorcasta's exuberance gradually deflated. "I

don't know what you mean."

Genevieve realized that the girl had no conception of real worth in a person's character. With her, it was all superficial. She had been confirmed in her shallow views by coaching from Madam, a leader of superficiality in that tawdry society of hers.

Radford approached the ladies. "I am glad to see you safe and well, Genevieve. We will be on our way. I just heard that Sir Pomeroy could conceivably appear behind us. There is no other side road we know of, so speed is of the essence."

Armand loomed near and said, "Lower your shades if you hear horses and wheels from behind. If that happens, your driver has orders to whip 'em up. Ashby and I will hide with our horses until they pass."

When they were bowling along at a spanking pace, Genevieve asked Dorcasta how she came to be in a coach with Lord Ashby, and on her way back to England. "I thought you were going with my mother to Tours."

"She saw Lord Ashby in Chartres, and told him to take me."

"Why did she not take you herself?"

"She said she wanted the fastest coach available to get her back to London, and she would eventually have you with her, so there was no room for me in it. Plus," Dorcasta preened, "she wanted Lord Ashby to take me for another good reason."

"What good reason?"

Dorcasta blushed slightly and said, lifting her chin, "She said that he might be smitten with me. I think he is."

"He is?" echoed Genevieve, scoffing privately. He had not acted like he was a few minutes ago; in fact, both men had ignored her.

Dorcasta clapped her hands together. "Oh, yes!"

"Can you tell me on what you base that idea?"

Dorcasta gestured in circles as she said, "All the walks and talks we had at Chambord, of course; and my singing, and, well, you know," she pressed Genevieve's knee. "Smiles and looks, and the fact that I show him how I admire him in everything.

Genevieve eyed her and murmured, "Mmm, so that's what you go on."

After a few ticks, Dorcasta said, "Well, he didn't exactly ignore me, you know."

"How can a man ignore a woman who is *making herself attractive* to him, as you describe your technique? He would have to be a stone statue not to react in some way, especially if he is a proper gentleman, and you are doing it right in his face. Lord Ashby is always polite." Silently, she added, *So stop annoying him!*

Dorcasta used her practice of wide smiling, nodding, and agreeing with everything Armand and Radford said. This she did the whole way, whenever they stopped, or were face-to-face with the gentlemen. Genevieve could see that Radford was slightly entertained by her. She wanted to kick him for it. Was he really that shallow that he couldn't see the artifice Dorcasta practiced so shamelessly on him?

It made her think: Did some men even wonder about the real woman inside when they were under the barrage of artillery like Dorcasta tried to fire his way? Frustrated, she thought about her Father when he was under such a campaign from her mother years ago. Did he succumb because of her determined coquetry? She still employed such wiles with other men.

Watching, Genevieve felt relieved by Armand's bland treatment of Dorcasta no matter how she smiled and simpered and flattered him. When she suddenly laughed loudly to grab attention back onto herself, he did not flinch or even look her way. Genevieve hung onto that gratifying observation. It said much for his character.

Lord Ashby, however, acted so tolerantly toward her, and even smiled at her, which rewarded Dorcasta's efforts and encouraged her to a high degree.

Except for the sight of Armand on his horse, it was a trying journey for Genevieve. It was through Dorcasta's flow of self-interested chatter that Genevieve learned that, even though Aunt Claracilla invited her for a Sunday afternoon coffee with the Vicar and a few young people once a year, she did not seem to appreciate it. She expressed no indication of affection for Genevieve's aunt, saying she hardly knew her. She said the parties were inane and the young men local yokels. "I've learned that about them now."

Growing angry, Genevieve bluntly asked her, "Why do you turn your nose up at the kind of nice young men my Aunt Claracilla knows? Why do you now aspire to men who are impossibly high above your station?"

Dorcasta stiffened and said, "Lady Bastwicke told me I ought."

"Yes, and look where my mother is now, with all

of her scheming and conniving to better herself! – and to better you as well! She has no husband because of behavior akin to yours years ago. Do you think that you will continue to bask in her . . . influence?"

Dorcasta looked shocked, and sat silent for quite some time. Her jaw came up presently, and jutted out as she looked fixedly into the distance. Despite what Genevieve had said to make her think, she continued her chase after both noblemen. When they reached the north coast of France and waited for the packet so they could cross the Channel, Genevieve had had more than enough of Dorcasta.

When they stood in sight of the shore, waiting to board a boat at Calais, the sea was blue with wavelets, the sky cerulean, and white clouds formed in high piles with dark gray undersides. While Genevieve tied her *calèche* ribbons under her chin against the rising breeze, she turned to look back at *La Belle France* in overwhelming regret.

There, in the distance, a cloud of dust rose from a vehicle on the road. A dark coach and horses grew larger, divided, and became two vehicles approaching fast. Genevieve was the only one who saw them, for the others were in the inn or the inn yard where they would leave the horses and vehicles.

As usual, Dorcasta followed the men. Genevieve had not joined them because watching that girl's actions made her ill. Therefore, when she ascertained that the coaches approaching were of some quality, she headed toward the inn. Before she could get there, the first coachman pulled up his horses. The door flew open, and out jumped Sir

Pomeroy Chancet. He ran for her, grabbed her by the waist as she ran, and dragged her back toward the coach, saying, "Ah-ha! My lovely one, my delicious Genevieve, my own at last!" He smelled of liquor, and held her so tightly around the ribcage that she could hardly breathe.

She tried to scream, and achieved some repeated sounds of "Help! *Aidez-moi!*" but he manhandled her without mercy. Her panniers, which she always pushed down when entering such a narrow space, caught and held her outside the coach door. "Stop pushing me!" she yelled into his face. Since his hold had loosened, she turned and screamed, "*Aidez-moi!*" as loudly as she could toward the open inn window. There, she saw Dorcasta staring. The girl did not move, but kept standing there gawking as Genevieve grappled desperately with Sir Pomeroy. "Help! Armand!" she screeched.

The courtyard door plummeted open. It was he! After him came Radford, both on a run.

"Thank God!" she cried. "You're in for it now, Pomeroy!"

Through gritted teeth, he growled, "No, I'm not!" and depressed her gown on one side to maneuver her pannier and push her in.

Genevieve kicked backward, cracking him in the shin with her heel. He yowled.

Armand yanked Sir Pomeroy off of her, and Radford jerked one of his arms behind his back.

A flash of light reflected off a metal blade that Sir Pomeroy was pulling out of his vest with his other hand. He struck out here and there with the dagger in his struggle with the two men. Armand soon clamped him by an arm across his neck, causing his white face to turn puce.

Radford breathed heavily and dodged Sir Pomeroy's flailing arms with the dagger flashing. Suddenly, Radford looked stunned. Genevieve wondered if he had been hurt, and soon saw, by his whitening face and reddening coat, that Sir Pomeroy had stabbed him. "He got me!" cried Radford as blood spread over his waistcoat. He staggered back, gasping, "He stabbed me! Look out, Armand!"

In suppressed rage, Armand growled something into Sir Pomeroy's ear, causing him to cry, "No!"

"Then drop it!"

The bloody dagger fell, ringing, to the flagstones.

Appalled, Genevieve shot Sir Pomeroy a fierce glare and ran to Radford. His chest was all red by then, so she grabbed his lapels and strove to hold the fabric tightly together against the blood, but that didn't help. "Let's run to the inn," she said, "because you need care right now!" She cast a desperate glance at Armand, but his back was turned as he manhandled the struggling Sir Pomeroy.

"Th-thank you!" said Radford, stunned and shaken.

"Put your arm around my shoulders, and try to hurry with me."

They had taken but a step when the slowing clip of horses' hooves veered into the inn yard, and the second coach pulled up beside them. The horses' coats gleamed with sweat.

Moving resolutely toward the inn, Genevieve could not pay the arrival any mind, but kept going, supporting Radford's arm over her shoulder. She was aware that drops of blood were falling along their path, and she worried over how badly he was wounded. Who could possibly treat him before a doctor could be found?

As she moved with her shallow-breathing burden, she heard Lady Bastwicke's voice behind them. She yelled accusingly at Armand, "You let Sir Pomeroy loose right now!"

Armand called, "Why should I do that? He stabbed Lord Ashby with his dagger!"

Genevieve, turning to glance back over the half-door, saw her mother make the fastest exit ever achieved from the coach door. She marched angrily to where Armand held Sir Pomeroy and hit him across the face with her fan sticks.

"Ow!" yelled Sir Pomeroy, his eyes popping wide in pain and dismay. He tried to jerk away, but Armand pushed him straight before him, saying to Lady Bastwicke, "I am conveying him to the lock-up, where the French will take care of this murderous blackguard."

Lady Bastwicke snapped, "Murderous? Do it!"

"No! Regina!" howled Sir Pomeroy in high-pitched alarm. "Remember our plan?"

She turned back and advanced like a sweeping square shovel and shrieked into his face, "You are the biggest fool in nature! I never, in my wildest dreams, thought you could injure a Peer of the Realm! Or any *gentleman!* How dare you? These men are good husband material! You are lower than a snake's belly! Yes, lock him up! For good! Torture him in there!"

Sir Pomeroy stared wildly at Genevieve as Armand guided him forcibly past her inside the inn. With his wig askew, he gobbled, "I did it because I—I want *you*, Genevieve!"

Armand growled something menacing at him, and pushed him forward.

Dorcasta hovered in the parlor, her eyes wide upon the wounded Lord Ashby.

Genevieve told a servant to run and get water and a tourniquet, and have someone dash for a physician. She said grimly to Dorcasta, "Stop staring, and move aside!" Genevieve helped the ever-heavier Radford onto a *chaise longue* and laid his shoulders gently back.

Dorcasta exclaimed, "Oh no! He's bleeding!" She put her hand to her mouth, gagged, and turned away.

Radford, his face white, murmured, "Sorry! Don't want to upset the ladies," and tried to cover his wound with both splayed-out hands.

"For goodness sake," said Genevieve, "pay no attention to her! We must stop the flow." She dug into her bag pocket and yanked out two lace-edged handkerchiefs. She hastily undid the long row of buttons on his waistcoat and lifted up the bloody cotton shirt. A tremor went down her spine at the sight of his bleeding gash. She applied both handkerchiefs onto it and held them there firmly with her palms. "You, Dorcasta!" she commanded. "Make yourself useful!"

"What can *I* do? I can't look at blood!"

"Run out there and bring that dagger back. I see it still on the ground. Pick it up by the handle, but do not wipe the blood off! Do you understand?"

Dorcasta was looking terrified, and did not answer.

Radford looked at Genevieve, his eyes watching her face in weak adoration. It gave Genevieve a frisson of surprise, and made her momentarily self-conscious. She turned to see if Dorcasta was moving.

Since the useless girl still stood there, frozen, staring at the inert Lord Ashby with her hands over her mouth, Genevieve cried, "Dorcasta! Now! We need to keep the evidence! I cannot leave to go get that dagger, but you can–unless you'd prefer to do what I'm doing? Just press your palms here—"

"I'm going!" expelled Dorcasta, her face flushing red. She stumbled out the door.

Radford said softly, "Thank you, Genevieve."

"Does it hurt unbearably?" she returned, examining his face, which now had dots of perspiration on his upper lip and forehead.

"Not . . . unbearably. You're holding it, and your warmth and nearness help me."

Genevieve looked at him with compassion. "I hope I'm not hurting you worse, but until the doctor comes, this is all I know to do."

"It's right."

A vehicle rattled into the yard, and she stretched to look, hoping it was the doctor. She had inadvertently loosened her pressure on his wound, and the blood flowed around her fingers from the sopped linens. She grabbed the edge of a tablecloth that she could just reach on the nearby table. All she could do was jerk it in hopes that the articles on top would fare well. With a clinking of metal and a tinkling of glass upon the floor, the tablecloth released. She piled folds of it onto Radford's wound and pushed hard on them.

He was watching her weakly, a smile hovering over his lips as he sweated.

The door opened, and Genevieve felt grateful for the distraction of Dorcasta sashaying in with the weapon, followed by Armand. He still clamped and pushed the furious-faced Sir Pomeroy with arms behind his back. Apparently he had not found a secure location in which to lock him. Lady Bastwicke lumbered in on their heels, issuing angry invectives at Sir Pomeroy.

"Hush!" cried Genevieve to the lot of them. In a quieter tone, she said over her shoulder, "Lord Ashby is suffering, so he needs peace!" She said sternly, "Sir Pomeroy, I want to hear why you took to violence. Why did you grab me and try to force me into that coach? More importantly, why did you stab Lord Ashby?"

He seemed to welcome the chance to unloose his cork, bottled up as he was. "I want you! I mean, for my wife. They were all going to prevent it, and I love you!"

Lady Bastwicke stamped her foot and jeered at him, "You do not! You only love yourself."

Genevieve, eyeing her mother in disbelief, felt it important to have her own say. She lifted her voice to be heard by all in the public room, even the maid behind the counter. "I find it amazing that I have to even say this, but wanting someone and loving them are totally different things, Sir Pomeroy. You *want* because you lust!"

Aghast, his mouth fell open, but nothing came out. He looked the picture of guilt.

She had a captive audience, so she continued, "You want to *take* everything for yourself. Many people"—and she cast a look at Dorcasta and her mother in turn—"want to take, take, take! They want something, or someone, or glory, or attention. They need to vaunt themselves. That is vainglory." She looked around at her stilled audience, and added, "I believe that loving, on the other hand, is giving. Giving love is the opposite of all the 'I want' motives you can think of."

"How do you know that?" spat her mother. "You're insinuating about us, and making that all up."

Having had her say, Genevieve ignored that, turned away to inspect Radford's wound, and saw that he was eyeing her intently. She noted with worry that he bled more profusely, for the tablecloth, too, had turned red through its folds. She moved to put a fresh area onto it.

Radford quietly said, "Answer your mother, Genevieve."

Thus, surprisingly urged, Genevieve looked over her shoulder at each of the others in the room. "I know that *God* is love. We know that He loved us all so much that he gave us his only begotten Son. And Jesus gave his life for us. Isn't that double proof that loving is giving?"

Armand said, from where he was tying Sir Pomeroy's wrists together, "Amen."

Radford croaked out, "I agree."

She saw a strange look on her mother's face. Dorcasta was eyeing Lady Bastwicke as well. Then everyone seemed to fix on Sir Pomeroy. He hung his head.

Everything happened in the next minute: the doctor arrived to take over from Genevieve, praising her for her good ministrations. Three magistrate's men, who had finally been located, hustled Sir Pomeroy out, headed for the gaol. Dorcasta gave up the dagger to them at Genevieve's reminder, and the ladies were told, by the frightened landlady, that luncheon awaited them in the small parlor.

The doctor and Armand stayed with Lord Ashby.

For once, Lady Bastwicke sat quiet, ignoring her food, but drinking the wine.

Genevieve wondered what Madam had ever lovingly given to dear Father. How would she fare with her habitual grasping attitude when she faced the loyal man who was now her former husband?

CHAPTER 14

The Painful Crossing

"Genevieve," said Lady Bastwicke, "grab his hat." Armand and the French physician were moving Lord Ashby out of the inn by carrying him on an old door that the landlord had kept in his stable.

Dorcasta cried, "I will get it!" and snatched it from the hat tree. She cast a triumphant look at Genevieve.

Genevieve rolled her eyes.

Dorcasta skipped after the cavalcade, holding her skirt high, and walking next to Radford. Now that he was bandaged and in a clean shirt with his waistcoat buttons fastened, she beamed and chattered at him. She perched his tricorne hat on her own head.

Genevieve doubted that Dorcasta's childish cavorting would prosper with the painfully wounded Radford. His eyes were closed, and he looked white around the mouth. She prayed.

* * *

They were sailing, with Calais receding and England not yet visible across the English Channel. The sky was filled with fast-moving clouds, the wind and waves were moderate, and the men declared it a good day to make speed.

Lady Bastwicke felt ill. Dorcasta emerged from the companionway up to the deck and reported that she required Genevieve to go down to her cabin and attend to her.

"Dorcasta, I am attending to Lord Ashby. Will you see to Lady Bastwicke yourself, please?"

Dorcasta stood her ground. "She does not want me. She told me to trade places with you."

"Why?"

"I do not know." She actually nudged Genevieve aside and leaned to where she could see the recumbent Lord Ashby's face.

"I will go see her for a few minutes, but only since he is asleep. Do not wake him, whatever you do. Sit a distance away, do you understand?"

Dorcasta gave her a darkling look.

Something must have occurred between Madam and Dorcasta, thought Genevieve, as she hurried to her mother's cabin. Lady Bastwicke was leaning back against cushions, her hair still a ravaged mess from the wind. She looked at Genevieve sourly. "Shut the door."

"How are you feeling?"

"Terrible! What do you expect?"

"Is it *mal de mer?*"

"Yes, I am seasick, but I am mostly furious! Why he had to go and make up a weird law about marriage that now *dissolves ours!*—why, I could kick him in the teeth! Worse!" Her face twisted and her hands made a strangling motion.

"Madam! Father did not realize it would cause this unforeseen outcome for you! Besides, there was the original factor: the clergyman who was not real, and had no power to perform marriages!"

"So what in blazes am I supposed to do now? This is unbearable!"

Genevieve was bewildered by how best to advise her—if any words from her even mattered—for Madam never took anyone's advice. "I think it would be best not to rail at Father at all when we get home."

"Not rail at him?" echoed Madam, sitting up straight, her nostrils flared. "Are you insane? He deserves to be horse-whipped!"

"No, no, do not say such things! He wrote that he never foresaw that your marriage would be revealed as ineffective. But since it is, you and he will need to find the solution. Can you not marry again in the legal way?"

"What? Let all of London know that we are not married? And have those stupid, idiotic Banns called in church—in public!—to see if anyone else in the world has an objection to our marrying again? Then go through a wedding with him now, at this stage? O-ho, we would be the laughing stock of all of Society, and the subject of hot gossip for years to come! Oooh!" she fumed, "He just better not be telling anybody!"

Genevieve, struck by the picture she had conjured up, saw that it was certainly scandal-fodder, likely above and beyond what Madam chewed upon so often with her friends. She said consolingly, "Father wrote in such a tone that I believe he is keeping it a secret."

"He just better be! He should *never* tell anybody, and neither should we! We can go on as before. Nobody will know."

Genevieve could not think what to say to that. Her father would know, and he never cheated at anything nor deceived anyone.

Madam sat up and said angrily, "If you don't tell a soul, not even Arabelle, we can get through this."

"But what if Father needs everything to be legal?" She foundered for a reason. "For the purposes of his Will, for example."

Madam alerted, like a hen with a gimlet eye upon her. "So that's it!"

Genevieve protested, "No, no, of course that did not figure into the Marriage Act. We have not spoken with him yet, so we must wait to hear what he says. We will see him soon, so please try to rest both your body and your mind. Tell me if I can get you anything to make you feel better right now."

"Nothing will make me feel better!" Lady Bastwicke eyed Genevieve for an instant. "Get my fan. It's stuffy in here."

"I can open the porthole, too, if you like."

"No! I hate sea spray. Just the fan."

Genevieve bent and lifted the large painted fan from where her mother pointed. When she opened it by means of untying a ribbon and flaring it out, a paper dropped to the floor. It was folded long and thin. Genevieve picked it up with her back to her mother. As it opened slightly, she saw, in black ink, the handwritten French words, *Bon débarras.* Mercy! Who was bidding Madam good riddance?

Genevieve slipped the paper back in, closed the fan, and placed it on her mother's lap. She stayed, hoping to find out who had written it. She stowed some bandboxes into a corner and shot a glance her way.

Lady Bastwicke drew herself up, curiously read the paper, and stiffened with rage.

"What is it, Madam?"

"You! Get out now. Men! I hate every last one of them! Never true, never loyal! The world is full of hypocritical, grasping creeps!"

"Who have you found so, Madam?"

"Never you mind! You think people are your special friends, but they never are in the end!"

Genevieve murmured, "Like Sir Pomeroy, for example?"

"He is but one in a long line!"

Genevieve said she was sorry to hear that, but as she left, she was glad to breathe the refreshing sea air wafting down the companionway. *Oh, dear God,* she prayed, *please help us out of all these troubles.*

When she gained the deck, there, seated near Lord Ashby's bench was Dorcasta, laughing affectedly and waving her hands about. Radford was looking blanched. His eyes were half closed, his head lolling to the side.

Fury coursed through Genevieve. She went straight to Dorcasta, grabbed her by the upper arm until she yelped, and set her aside. When she saw Radford's eyelids drop, she expelled, "Lord Ashby must rest! I told you not to wake him! He is in pain, and he doesn't feel the pain *while he sleeps!*"

Radford smiled up at Genevieve with misty eyes.

Dorcasta saw it. She set her jaw and said, "But cheerful thoughts and chat are better, I thought. I was taking his mind off his pain, wasn't I, Lord Ashby?"

Genevieve lifted her eyes heavenward and gave Dorcasta a dismissive wave. "I will take over now. You may go."

Angrily, Dorcasta made a beeline for Armand de Villebon, who was conversing with the Captain of the boat.

Genevieve felt her heart catch at sight of Armand. He was so admirable in his integrity and temperament. He was speaking amicably to the Captain, and they both laughed.

"So," rasped Radford from below her, recalling her attention.

She looked down at him, and sat on the bench that Dorcasta had dragged next to him. "Yes?"

"Thank you for contriving this moment for us to be together, without her."

She had not meant to contrive it, precisely, but she let that pass. "Does your bandage feel supportive enough?"

Radford tried to reach for her hand, but winced.

"Don't move, Radford. What do you want?"

"You, dear Genevieve. May I ask you a question? I feel chagrin because this is hardly the setting."

Genevieve's mouth went dry.

He managed to grip her hand. "Will you marry me, Genevieve? You are absolutely the best woman on this planet, I am now convinced. I love you, and appreciate you, and I know that you would make me the happiest—so sorry, I mean to say, I would do my best to make *you* happy."

She felt a bit cruel, but she had to say, "Those are kind words, but you are wounded, and must not think past your recovery, Radford."

He sighed and looked sadly at her. "You are not in love with me, then?"

Genevieve, hurting while saying it, answered him quietly. "I like you, I respect you, and I want you to heal quickly. Can you sleep again, and try to forget everything else? You are overtaxing your mind."

"How can I sleep, Genevieve, with you here before me?"

This was the man who used to intimidate her. She marveled. Her heart was now refusing the Earl of Ashby, who wanted her to become Lady Ashby and make him the happiest of men. That troubled her greatly. She did not want to hurt him, for he was too nice to hurt. She liked him, but did she love him?

Though she had felt fearfully in awe of him, she found that the apprehension had dissipated. It had become more pleasant to speak with him. Even though she appreciated his gentlemanly demeanor, his soft-spoken nature, and the mildly funny things he said at times, she did not feel fascinated by him nor inspired to do things with him. She realized that his temperament did not give her a wish to adventure with him nor to feel joy just looking at him. He admired her, but he did not excite her, so what was she to do?

Dorcasta's laughter trilled loudly. Holding the green skirt high with one hand, the plump girl promenaded down the slightly swaying deck, clutching the arm of Armand de Villebon and affecting laughter. She was pretending that the boat wobbled her off balance.

Genevieve fumed.

As soon as they drew near, Armand detached Dorcasta and threw a melting look Genevieve's way. Of Radford, he asked, "Is your pain any better or worse now?"

"I wish I could say better . . . but it's quite a bit worse."

"Let us trust that you will not be jolted much on our overland journey to London."

Genevieve said, "Perhaps we should establish him at Bastwicke Chase, which is in Kent, instead of the longer journey to London."

"Can we do that?" asked Armand, his face brightening. At Genevieve's nod and smile, he asked, "Would you prefer it, Radford?"

Genevieve expelled, "I think he fainted!"

When they had revived him with Lady Bastwicke's smelling salts beneath his nose, Dorcasta declared decisively that she would sit with him. She shot Armand a huge smile, her chin cocked, apparently willing him to notice what a caring person she was.

So Armand invited Genevieve to walk with him. She capitulated, but only for the reason that Radford might stress himself again by asking her to marry him. It was best to leave him. As she walked with Armand beneath the taut white sails towering above them toward the bow of the boat, he pulled her hand more securely through the crook of his arm.

He said, "I am relieved that Sir Pomeroy is locked up at last. The French will not be lenient with him for stabbing a Peer."

"Even an English Peer?"

"They will not put up with it." Armand looked down at her, and relaxed into a smile. "You have helped Lord Ashby a lot."

"Not really."

His eyebrows rose in question.

Prevaricating, she said, "He seems depressed in addition to suffering pain. I feel guilty that I may have weakened his condition by something I said. That may be why he fainted."

"How could you possibly have caused that? Men don't faint because of words." Armand eyed her curiously.

Under his gaze, she found it difficult to think or explain. His inquiring gaze rested so tenderly upon her that she wanted to melt against him and tell him all her troubles.

Dorcasta was screaming, "Genevieve! Monsieur de Villebon! Come back here!"

They hurried. When they got to where they had left Radford lying on the bench by the stern railing, not only had he tumbled down onto the deck planks, but Madam was sitting where he had lain, her huge skirts whipping in the wind and her hair all over the place. She was waving her skinny elbows and blithering, "Pick him up! Pick him up before he rolls into the Channel!"

Armand dropped to Radford's side, securing him and asking, "Can you bear it if I lift you? Please move aside, Madam. Make room, Miss Doyle! Why did you fall, Ashby?"

Madam cut in, "Where were you? He fell off the bench with that last high wave. Drat this boat, and the sea, and this confounded wind!"

Genevieve said, "Madam, it would be safer if you went below." She asked Radford, whose eyes blinked slowly as he seemed to take her face into focus, "Did that fall hurt you terribly?"

Radford just looked at her, almost as if he comprehended nothing.

Armand said, "If you young ladies will hold onto him, I'll go get him more coverings and a softer pillow, and something with which to tie him so he doesn't fall off again." They had kept him on deck because it would have hurt him too much to be maneuvered down the narrow companionway and around corners into a tiny cabin. This fall had probably done him no good, but he did not admit it.

Genevieve felt his forehead. It was warm, even in the wind. "You are feverish! Dorcasta, I'll hold him while you run for cold water and a towel to put on his forehead. Yes, you! Now!"

Lady Bastwicke remained. She clung to the rail in nauseated misery. Genevieve gestured her to leave, but she did not budge.

Sighing, Genevieve bent over Radford and said, "Everyone is hoping to help you bear this."

He grappled for her hand and held it, but could not speak. With his other, he clutched his ribcage.

Genevieve's heart pounded in sympathy. She felt so helpless.

Armand came up the companionway carrying a blanket and an armful of cushions. He paused in his tracks as he looked at Genevieve and Lord Ashby.

Genevieve welcomed the distraction. "Thank

you, Armand. I'll put one pillow under his head if you'll lift him." She wondered what he thought of Radford's grip on her hand, and the way he kept gazing up at her as they tried to make him more comfortable.

* * *

"I expect your mother, the former Lady Bastwicke, will not want me to leave her now," opined Dorcasta, watching the sleeping woman snoring in her cabin.

"Now that what?" asked Genevieve irately, having just poked her head in.

"Now that she needs me near. You know the trouble that your father has made for her."

Genevieve drew herself up in outrage. "There is no trouble of my father's making!"

Madam woke up with a jerk. Seeing Genevieve's angry face and Dorcasta's cringing, she inquired irritably, "What are you yelling about?"

"Dorcasta is blaming Father for causing trouble, and she doesn't even know how fine a man he is, nor does she know anything about the matter."

Dorcasta diminished into the corner. She cast surreptitious looks at Lady Bastwicke.

Genevieve asserted, *"Does* she?"

Lady Bastwicke replied, "All she knows is that, because of that idiotic Marriage Act, he has apparently dissolved his own marriage to me! But you keep mum, Dorcasta, or you will have me to deal with!"

Genevieve cried, "That is not true! He has only just discovered that your marriage wasn't legal!

Don't blame him!" With her hands in fists, she left them and ran up to where the salty sea air could blow through her head.

CHAPTER 15

Chaos at Bastwicke Chase

The boat arrived at Dover beneath the towering cliffs of white chalk. It was not soon enough for the seasick Lady Bastwicke. She lifted her head from her pillow in the stuffy cabin as the anchor chain rattled. She moaned and complained, and demanded that Genevieve arrange her hair.

As Genevieve toiled, backcombing the matted gray and orange hair, and pinning it up and back into a neater coiffure, Dorcasta returned, saying Monsieur de Villebon was sitting with Lord Ashby.

Madam ordered her to fetch gloves and her *calèche* from the bandboxes already on deck. "Do not touch my jewels!" she warned the girl severely.

Dorcasta shot her a frosty look and threw some gloves onto the bed. Apparently the two were not on such marvelous terms as Dorcasta had pretended. That one's cheeks actually flamed red when Madam said, "It is time for you to go back to your home, so be sure to give our coachman your village name. Do not even think that you can overlook that and come along with us, Miss Doyle. Your adventure is over."

She pointed at Dorcasta's person and said, "Furthermore, you will need to clean and send those articles of clothing back. Address them to Bastwicke Chase, as that is our country estate. My eldest daughter can collect them from there if they're not too ruined. Do it sharp, do you hear? I would take them from you now, but I highly doubt that you have anything else suitable to wear. Am I right?"

Genevieve could see that it galled Dorcasta to reply, but she said, "Madam, you gave these to me, and *you* can attempt to take them off me!" She stomped off in Arabelle's green traveling dress, holding up the soiled hem in front while the back trailed and caught in the door when she tried to slam it. She turned angrily and kicked it behind her, slamming the door again with emphasis.

Lady Bastwicke expelled, "Well! What a witchy little misery she turned out to be!"

Startled, Genevieve asked something that had been bothering her ever since they met the girl. "What did you expect of her, Madam?"

"Expect of her? I needed her to keep you company in France. She didn't. She just went after the men."

"You wanted her to keep me company so that you could have fun at Chambord without me in your way? You thought we would be girls together, busy with our own silliness? But she stuck by you, avoided me, and flirted with all the men in sight."

"She should have been grateful enough to do everything I told her to do. She avoided you because you were the one the men admired, not her."

Genevieve said carefully, "But did you not instruct her to go around striving to attract men? Was she not a better pupil than I?"

A guilty look flitted over her mother's face. She recovered and gave a sharp laugh. "I suppose she was. I am still upset with you over that. But it was a golden opportunity for that chit to get herself a husband, yet I wonder: Why did she not achieve it?"

Genevieve felt like saying that she ruined herself by all her vulgar behavior, and by aiming far too high.

Madam suddenly asked, "How is Lord Ashby? Is he recovered yet?"

"No, of course not. He is in great pain, and has a fever."

There came a knock at the door, and through it, Dorcasta called, "I am sent to tell you that we are disembarking."

As the ladies gained the dock at the foot of the town of Dover, they could see Armand in an inn yard, supervising the laying of a stretcher crosswise from seat to seat in a coach. It would give Radford a place to lie flat until they reached Bastwicke Chase. Servants arrived carrying a feather mattress and blankets.

"Drat that Sir Pomeroy!" snapped Lady Bastwicke suddenly, stamping her foot.

Genevieve looked at her in astonishment. "You say that about your pet with the big brown eyes?"

"Genevieve! He stabbed a Peer of the Realm! Who can countenance that?"

"No one can support his stabbing anybody. I

agree with you wholeheartedly about him. I only wonder that you continued to befriend him after what he did to Arabelle and Father and me. Why did you like him so much?"

As they moved toward the black coaches parked against the background of the white cliff, Lady Bastwicke said, "Because he flirted, and he was fun to have around."

Genevieve added, "He gave you lavish compliments. But it was more than that, was it not?" She had to get to the bottom of this. "Why did you take me to France, Madam? Did it have anything to do with him?"

"Yes, of course. You rejected every man on my list. I decided you would marry him. That was then."

Genevieve shook her head. It was ludicrous. "I know," she said with a deep sigh. "That became obvious when we arrived there. But why did you want me to marry the likes of *him?* He has such a criminal history with our family! He is banished from England for those reasons, and he had no money. You keep telling me that money is so important in a man."

Lady Bastwicke looked at her slant-wise. "He has money now, and I learned of it awhile back."

"Many others have money, so why would you throw me, your own daughter, at someone so full of vice?" Since she got no reply as her mother minced toward the coaches, Genevieve added, "I doubt that he got it legitimately, or did he?"

"He did not. He told me all about it. But that's water under the bridge, and there's nothing anyone can do about it. That old man is dead, and he doesn't care who has his money, and Sir Pomeroy needed an income badly. His *château* would have been a good place to stay while I'm in France. He can't come back to England, even if he was pardoned for his crimes in London by marrying you, because now he got himself into worse trouble for stabbing Lord Ashby. He can't legally have that estate or the money now, and will probably rot in gaol. He turned out to be completely useless!"

Seeing that her mother was about to end her diatribe by peeking into the coach into which Armand and servants had carried Radford, Genevieve grasped her arm and faced her. "Tell me, why did you invite Lord Ashby to come to France with us?

"Just realize, Genevieve, that you need all the options you can get. You do not know how to entice men. The more choices I threw in front of you, the more chances there should have been to get you married off!" With sparks of furor, she hissed, "So say yes to him if he asks you, before he dies! Get his money and his title while you still can, you brainless girl!"

* * *

Armand secured a private parlor for their refreshment at an inn, directed the preparations for three coaches' departure from Dover, and saw that baggage and horses were in place by one o'clock in the afternoon.

The road west led through downs of new spring grass shaded by budding leaves in the orchards and hedges. The coaches joggled their way through the

Kentish villages and bowled along the open road. The conical towers of oast houses rose here and there near their hop gardens. Genevieve's father had hop gardens on his estate, and traded them and his filbert nuts in London.

She missed Father. Her head whirled in turmoil, and her heart ached with her marriage proposal dilemma with the wounded Radford. How she needed Father's advice!

Dorcasta said suddenly, as they swerved around a corner, "I can hardly wait to see Bastwicke Chase."

"Why is that?" asked Genevieve, glancing at her mother snoozing to see if she would react to that presumption. Genevieve's lap was covered by her bronze quilted gown and wooden farthingale. She tried to make herself comfortable, but it proved a heavy burden that poked her no matter which way she squirmed.

Dorcasta cast her eyes upward and said, "Oh, I have heard of its glories, and if it's anything like Château de Chambord, then I will be the happiest girl in England staying there. Your family is so rich."

Genevieve retorted, "It is nothing like Chambord, and why do you think you will stay there? Did you not hear my mother say we would deliver you to your own village?"

"It's beyond that, I think, maybe, and I need to nurse Lord Ashby." Dorcasta folded her arms with determination.

"I thought you said you were from Rye? That is not on our way, but south on the coast. To get there, you should have parted from us at Dover. And, what do you know about nursing?"

"Lord Ashby himself wants me near. I can just ask people what to do if I don't see what to do immediately. You can help me, and I will pick it up quickly."

Genevieve did not think Madam would put up with the girl any longer, and in that, she was in perfect accord with her.

Leaving that irksome situation aside, Genevieve made herself ready to alight from the confines of the coach. Outside, she shook out her clothing and looked up. The sky was bright blue and the narcissi and jonquils yellow and bobbing in abundance around the house at Bastwicke Chase. The diamond-shaped glass glinted between leaded panes in the three-storied mansion. She breathed a sigh of gladness to be back.

There stood the coach bearing Radford, halted in the *porte cochère*. Servants were herded out by the butler, old Hawkins, his white wig glowing in the sun. His craggy face crinkled into a smile when he saw Genevieve. She waved and smiled at him.

Madam admonished her, as always. "You do not wave at servants! How many times do I have to thrash it into you? You ignore them unless you have an order for them. They are not your *friends*." She walked on regally, and the servants bowed and curtseyed to her as she mounted the steps.

"But I have known dear Hawkins all my life," Genevieve returned, unrepentant. He *was* her friend.

Armand caught up with them, so she hung back to say, "Welcome to Bastwicke Chase, Armand."

"Thank you, Genevieve. Have you lived here all your life?"

"No, but I did when I was little, and also part of the past two years. I spent many years with my Aunt Claracilla and Uncle Trent a few miles from here, at Fawnlake Hall. That was when Madam was in Europe for an extended period."

Pausing in the shadow of a column before entering the wide doorway, Armand asked quietly, "All that time she was not here with you?"

"She did return a few times, for short visits."

"Hmm. Do you have brothers or sisters other than your older sister, Arabelle?"

"Yes, a little sister, Lenora, and a brother, Jerome. They are seven and five." She leaned closer to him and whispered, "Two of my mother's visits were to give birth to them, nine months each following her previous visits." She blushed and looked away, then flicked a quick look at his face. It was awkward, but she wanted him to know.

He nodded seriously. "I see." As they entered the hall, he asked, "Who raised them, then?"

"A faithful nurse who has since died. They have a young nurse now who is devoted to them. When Arabelle and I were reunited with the little ones in London, we taught them lessons ourselves, played with them, took them on outings, and kept them happy. Father was there, you see, and we all went to church. It's easy to spend time with them because we love them. Right now, I miss them so much. I hope you can meet them."

He smiled. "I very much wish to."

That made Genevieve suddenly more cheerful.

* * *

Twenty minutes later, Lord Ashby lay in a guest chamber near the top of the stairs on the first floor. Shafts of sunlight slanted into the darkened room when Genevieve walked in. She drew each long brocade curtain aside to let in some light, and saw a manservant, Giles, seated in the corner, keeping watch over their afflicted guest. He rose and bowed to her.

"How is he, Giles?" she asked, moving toward the black walnut tester bed and looking between the blue bed curtains.

"I don't rightly know, Miss Genevieve. He has been quiet except for a few attempts to sit up. Too painful for him, I think."

Genevieve gazed at Radford's face with its brown eyebrows and eyelashes darker than ever against his pallor. "We must let him sleep." She knelt, put her forehead down on his bed covering, clasped her hands together, and prayed to God to help him.

She felt the bed move, and then a groping touch upon her head. When she looked up, Radford was gazing at her with shining eyes. "Genevieve! What are you doing? Dare I hope that you are praying for me?"

She nodded. "Yes."

He caressed her forehead with a fevered hand. "That is good. It gives me hope."

Rising, Genevieve called to Giles, "Wet a cloth with cold water and bring it here, please. Then, we need ice chips from the big block in the ice house. Tell the kitchen to fill a bowl with them. Bring more linen to wrap it in."

"Yes, Miss Genevieve." He handed her the wet cloth, and hurried away, leaving the door open.

While arranging it on Radford's forehead, she said, "You have a fever, and that concerns me."

He gripped her forearm and said, "That does not concern me as much as my goal does."

"Your goal? What is that?"

"You, as my wife, before I die?"

Genevieve gasped. "What? You think you will die?"

"That is up to God, but my heart misgives me, as Shakespeare put it. I want to marry you, Genevieve, for you are the most ideal woman I have ever had the pleasure to know, and—" He faltered and winced; then fell back with his eyes closed.

Panicked, Genevieve took his head in her hands and shook it gently from side to side. "Wake up, Radford!"

It worked; his eyes opened.

The door creaked, and in walked Lord Bastwicke. His size blocked out most of the long window's light behind him so she saw only his broad-shouldered silhouette. "Father!" she cried, running to him. "Thank God you're here!"

She was scooped up by his strong arms. "Genevieve! My precious!" he boomed, squeezing her in a hug and kissing her temple. "You cannot know how relieved I am to have you back."

"I am overjoyed to be back with you! But come see poor Lord Ashby. He is not doing well. He fainted a moment ago."

"What can we expect after he was run through? I heard it all from a Frenchman downstairs."

"Armand de Villebon is his name." she said.

"Yes." Father looked at her for an instant before

he drew near the bed. "Lord Ashby! I'm here to see you, young man, so wake up and take notice."

Genevieve grinned, and watched to see if her Father's genial humor would cheer Radford at all.

He lifted his head a few inches. The damp cloth from his forehead fell onto his face. Father grabbed it off. Radford's heavy eyelids lifted, and a little spark shone in his eyes. He eked out, "Lord Bastwicke. How are you?"

"I don't know, quite frankly. I just arrived from London, expecting to ready things for everyone's arrival tomorrow. As soon as I entered my house, I heard that everyone was here already, and that you are prone in this chamber with a nasty dagger wound."

Radford's gaze moved longingly to Genevieve, and he said, "Lord Bastwicke, may we talk briefly?"

Father said, "Genevieve, go find something to do for awhile, will you please?"

"Yes, Father, I will make sure the doctor was called." As she left, feeling uneasy, she heard him ask Radford what he could do for him.

Her mother was walking with clicking heels upon the wide, square balcony mezzanine surrounding the staircase. "Genevieve, there you are. Come here."

She went to stand before her with hands folded and eyes questioning.

"Let us go into my boudoir; we can't talk here."

Genevieve followed her, asking, "Has the doctor been called?"

"Of course. He should be here by now." Once inside her rooms, her mother went straight to the mirror, examined her face, and groped through some glass containers. She applied a rabbit's foot full of white powder to her face, and followed it with swirls of rouge upon her bony cheeks. She was about to redden her lips when she caught Genevieve's eyes in the mirror. "What are you staring at?"

"I am only waiting to hear what you want to talk to me about. Would you like me to arrange your hair since Bertha is nowhere to be seen?"

"She is still in London, drat it, so do your best. Give me that pick."

Genevieve handed her the two-foot-long enameled pick. She grabbed it and hurriedly inserted it into her high coiffure and scratched her head with it in several places.

As Genevieve removed pins and combed the top layer of the tangled hair, Lady Bastwicke declared, "We are in an intolerable batch of troubles here! One is that your father has apparently arrived. He has not yet seen me, but I have to be ready to face him. I will not have him saying we aren't married anymore! That is ludicrous! He must forget about that idiotic Marriage Act, and tell his equally lunatic committee that the whole idea was a gargantuan mistake, and it won't work! Of all the insanity, to declare his own marriage void! If he thinks he's going to unload me that way, he has another think coming! He is a daft and malicious man to even try it!"

"Madam! Do not cast such wrongful aspersions upon Father!"

"Whyever not?" She spun about to face her, fire in her eyes.

"Because they are not true. I think you ought to

be as nice to him as you possibly can, not drive him away with a malignant attitude."

Lady Bastwicke sucked in breath through her teeth. "Malignant? What insolence!" she exploded. "You evil girl! Out!"

Genevieve knew she had gone too far. She set down the comb and gladly left the room, her heart pounding. What solution could possibly transpire from such rancor?

As she stood clutching the wood balcony railing, she saw, coming into the hall below, Armand de Villebon. He looked up and smiled at her, then suddenly looked concerned.

With a warming heart, Genevieve beckoned to him.

He vaulted up the staircase. "At your service, Miss Genevieve. What's wrong?"

"Don't *Miss* me."

He looked at her innocently from between his black lashes and said, "But I do miss you. Downstairs, I rattle around like a pea in a drum. What can I do? I see that you're upset."

She sighed. "I am. Oh, there goes Giles with the ice. Wait a moment, Giles. My father is with Lord Ashby now. Please wait until he comes out and then take the ice in and administer some to His Lordship's forehead. Wrap it in the linen."

Giles said, "I will, Miss Genevieve, but Miss Doyle said she is coming up to bring His Lordship some broth."

Dorcasta appeared at the bottom of the stairs, stopping to bunch up the green skirt in one hand. Up she came, striving to keep a full bowl from spilling.

Armand pulled Genevieve gently away and murmured, "Let her go. What can I do to help you?"

Genevieve asked, "In what way?"

"In any way. All ways, if possible." He gazed down at her with tender questioning.

Genevieve could not reply, for Dorcasta was passing by them, smiling widely at Armand and ignoring her.

The door to Radford's room opened and, as Lord Bastwicke came out, Dorcasta slipped in.

From across the landing, Lady Bastwicke emerged sidewise from her rooms. Apparently the sight of the three of them before her made her blanch. She lifted her pointed chin, causing her peacock hair feathers in her coiffure to wave. She said loftily to no one in particular, "I must see how Lord Ashby is," while totally ignoring Lord Bastwicke.

It was not a promising tone for Madam to take in her present situation, thought Genevieve. She could at least have greeted the man she wanted to retain as her husband.

* * *

Later, in the morning room between Lord and Lady Bastwicke's wings of the house, Genevieve stood quavering in her heart while staring at her mother.

Lady Bastwicke said in a hard tone, glancing uneasily toward the door, "You heard me! Your father told me that he overheard you receive a marriage proposal at last! *You* will become Lady

Ashby! Think of the high leap in your fortunes! I know he has a castle somewhere."

"What do you mean, Regina," boomed Father from the doorway, "by saying that she *will* become Lady Ashby?"

"Just what I said! Didn't you hear Lord Ashby ask Genevieve to marry him?" As he frowned at her, Madam coyly sidled up to him and clutched his arm. "Is it not marvelous news . . . dear?"

He growled menacingly, "Has our Genevieve accepted him?–without consulting me?" There was the sound of distant thunder in his voice. "So far, I only know his feelings, as he told me himself after she left the room."

"I have not replied to him," Genevieve assured her father.

"Intolerable girl!" her mother exploded. "What are you waiting for?" Then, looking at Lord Bastwicke and back at Genevieve, she simmered down her tone considerably. "You will be pleased to be Lady Ashby, Genevieve. Husband," she said, swiveling back to him with a horrific smile, "it's as good as settled with that tragically-wounded Earl. Why would she even think of turning him down?"

Lord Bastwicke said severely, "If my daughter is coerced into a marriage—wounded Earl or not—I will not allow it! Genevieve, come with me."

He drew her by the hand, and down the corridor toward the front of the house. In an oriel window seat, he bade her sit. He paced back and forth and finally said, "She was forcing your hand?"

"Trying to, Father. It is her *modus operandi.*"

"Were you about to give in?"

"Not to her, Father."

A smile of relief relaxed his face. "That's my girl! Nothing of this sort can ever again be settled without parental approval. In this case, mine!" He gave her a level look from under his black eyebrows.

She jumped up and hugged his broad form, and smelled the outdoor breezes on his wool waistcoat. Fervently, she said, "I am so glad you came in when you did. I did not know what to do, truly, because I don't want to wound Radford further. I have been in such turmoil of heart, Father. Radford, whom I like, has begged me to marry him since his injury, but I have not known what to say."

"If you do not know what to say, say nothing until you feel sure. How glad I am that you did not commit yourself in words without thinking it over or telling me, or you would have instantly betrothed yourself to him."

Genevieve's shoulders sagged. "I know, I am careful in what I say, Father, but it seems so . . . cruel to deny him his dying wish."

"He may be dying, but he may still live. But he's a good fellow: steady, titled, and wealthy."

Genevieve sighed. "I feel so ill at ease when Radford declares passionately that he loves me."

"What unholy pressure you are under. You do not have to decide today."

"It's hard to withstand when people are so domineering, or in such need."

"I know." He looked into the far distance. "I learned never to be a friend to someone—or to marry—out of pity. I have done both."

Hearing such a confession astounded her. Gingerly, she asked, "How did your marriage come to be, Father? Will you tell me so that I understand?"

He sighed heavily, looked around to make sure no one else was listening, and said, "It was a case of my pleasing her, just as you are drawn to do for yonder Earl. She was captivating when she was young, and knew just how to go about enticing a young man like me, clueless about women's wiles. I had just lost a beloved father to illness and attained his title. I had only my sister, Claracilla, who had already married and moved to Fawnlake Hall, and an ailing mother almost gone as well. I was susceptible to the first young lady who gave me attention. She said all kinds of flattering things to me, and I soaked them up like a dry sponge."

"Was she kind to you back then?"

He shot her an ironic look. "I thought she was in love with me. Whatever it was, we were off to be married by a vicar she said was her cousin. She said that she desperately needed me because she had been married and widowed, and was in a delicate condition. I was sorry for her."

Genevieve cried softly, "So you married her for that reason? Oh, Father!" She whispered, "So Arabelle is not your true daughter then?"

Father gripped her arm firmly. "Yes, she is, do not worry about that. The story turned out, after our wedding in Fleet Street, to be completely false. She was a virgin bride, but had concocted the story to make me rush to marry her. Apparently she wanted me for my new title, my estates, and to beat her sisters to the altar. She was in competition with them for some reason." He made a sound of disgust. "We had Arabelle a year later. The best things that ever happened out of our marriage were you children.”

“Oh,” said Genevieve, shaken. “I hate to ask this again, Father, but I am grown now, and we confide in each other. Are all of us truly your children? Even the little ones? She was gone from you—from us—for so many years that Arabelle and I have wondered about it. Sorry to ask, Father.”

“Yes, I have to honestly say that they are all my children. She came back twice, and twice again in the correct time for their births.”

“I thought so, but I am so glad to hear you confirm it. Why did she keep leaving?”

“She said that she is not the motherly type. She had to go to France and Switzerland, where she felt at home with her special friends. They understood her, apparently. Too many stuffy people in London, she said, and unbearable boredom here at Bastwicke Chase.”

“But what will happen now, Father, since your marriage to her is dissolved? Will she go and stay away for the rest of her life?”

He shook his head slowly. “That remains to be seen. This is a perplexing dilemma.”

Genevieve tried to read his expression to discover how he felt, but he slapped his hands on his knees, stood up, and walked away to Madam’s chamber door. There, he knocked. The maid admitted him.

Before long, she heard her mother’s sharp voice berating him with bitter blame and invectives. Out he came, looking furious. He strode toward his own wing of the mansion, punching one fist into his palm.

Father’s dog must have heard him from the hall

below, for he came bounding up the stairs and stopped upon his master's feet, looking up at him with a dog smile and a wildly wagging tail. Lord Bastwicke rubbed the yellow Labrador's neck vigorously with both hands. "Good dog, Vesper! You, at least, are my loyal ally. Let's go!"

Armand emerged from Radford's bedchamber just as Genevieve leaned her head upon her hand lachrymosely in the window seat. Her heart lifted at sight of him. Approaching, he asked, "Do you want company, Genevieve?" His questioning look touched her as he moved cushions aside.

"Yes, your company," she replied, close to tears. He put a golden velvet cushion on her lap and sat down. She hugged its silky softness to her bosom and added, "This is a serious situation with my father and mother."

"So I gather. Is it a fact that they are no longer legally married?"

"Yes, now that the new act was passed and the bogus clergyman exposed, they are not."

He looked seriously taken aback. "I have not heard of such a situation, ever."

"It is due to the new law, which now affects illegal weddings retroactively. My mother was the one who recommended that supposed vicar back then. He was a cousin of hers, and bogus. I wonder if she knew that."

He shook his head and asked gravely, "Will they, ah, marry again?"

Genevieve tried to choose her words, but after a look at his kind eyes, she blurted out, "Father did not say. It did not sound to me as though he is certain. I thought my mother would come home and be extra sweet to him, and although she tried, she demonstrated a few minutes ago that she cannot keep that up." Genevieve passed a hand over her forehead. It ached. "I am worried."

Armand reached over and passed his hand over her forehead several times until she truly felt better. She sighed. He was so caring. She was afraid she would let go and weep in front of him.

* * *

The doctor had declared that Lord Ashby was so much worse that he sincerely doubted that he would live long. The wound was infected, and he had a lack of knowledge or medicine to do anything more about it.

Feeling struck with remorse by this news, Genevieve went to see him with more ice. She hoped to alleviate some of his fever, at least. As she approached the bed with a wavering candle, Radford's eyes shone intensely upon her, and he smiled weakly. The thought flashed through her that it would be the kindest thing to give him the parting gift he so peculiarly desired before he left this life. After all, it would be in name only, and not for long, if what the doctor and her eyes told her were probable.

Radford croaked, "Will you marry me, Genevieve? I love you so much!"

"Why do you want marriage now?" she put to him softly.

"You mean because I could soon be gone?"

She felt helpless to reply, and made a business of lighting another candle. Giles, the vigilant servant, had moved close with a cloth bag full of the ice chips, and as he reached to place it on His Lordship's brow, he glanced at Genevieve with concern.

Radford held the ice bundle in place as he tried to draw her closer with his other hand, saying, "But if God should let me live, I could wake every morning and look beside me, and there you would be!" He smiled up at her with feeling, and moved the ice pack onto his chest.

Giles left discreetly.

Genevieve wanted to take her hand out of Radford's hot grasp, but did not do so for fear of offending him.

"Say yes, Genevieve!" he urged. Then quietly he said, "If I do die, you will have an inheritance from me, and you can be free of . . . all that tyranny you're living under."

So he meant her mother. Genevieve thought fast. Was she prepared to live her whole life with him should he recover? She prayed in her heart for swift help, and then put her hand on his hot, damp forehead. "Oh, Radford, I will . . . th–"

She had not finished saying that she would think and pray, because the floorboards creaked and the door, which Giles had left ajar, crashed open and hit the wall.

In swept Lady Bastwicke, hurrying toward them, screeching, "What fabulous news!" To Genevieve, she declared, "So you *will* marry Lord Ashby! I heard you say you will! Hurrah! Run and tell your father! Tell him to come here and congratulate his future son-in-law! Hurry scurry!"

Genevieve, her heart pounding, objected, "I

hadn't finished—"

Her mother maintained joyously to Radford, "I heard her say *I will!*"

From the pillows, Radford said, "I heard her, too, but I do not know what Genevieve was going to say after that, if anything."

Madam brushed that aside, saying, "It does not signify. Your private moment is over for the moment. That's what happens when a Peer of the Realm becomes betrothed."

CHAPTER 16

Triumph and Turmoil

Armand was standing near the front door downstairs, setting aside his hat, when Genevieve burst out of Radford's chamber and fled down the staircase. Tears nearly obliterated her vision, but she needed to get away.

"Genevieve!" he said, startled.

She ran away from him until she reached the window at the end of the corridor. There, she grabbed the long powder blue velvet curtain and swirled it around her as she used to do as a girl when she needed to hide.

She heard his footsteps coming. "What is the matter?" Soon, she felt his touch on her back through the velvet.

"I am locked in now," she admitted, and sniffed repeatedly.

"Where are you locked in?"

"Into the future that my mother wants for me!" She felt herself turned bodily around as he unwound her. Emerging, she covered her face and looked at him through her fingers.

He bent and looked through them into her eyes, asking, "Why? What happened to you?"

"My mother—my mother heard Radford ask me to marry him, and as I started to say, 'I will . . . *think* and pray about what to do,' she only heard the first two words as she came in and loudly whooped that I had just agreed to marry Radford by saying *I will!*"

Armand's eyes widened, and then he frowned darkly. "What a sham! So she thinks it's valid because she says so?"

"Yes! What's more, Radford is happy to accept it."

"Did you tell them it was not what you agreed to?"

"No, yes, I tried to, but I had no chance of being heard because Madam chattered on and on, right over me, to prevent my denying it. I suspect she could see it in my eyes, but she's determined to accomplish it."

Armand stared at her, dark pupils wide as he turned over the situation. His fist clenched.

Genevieve sank to the window seat. He sat beside her and said earnestly, "They must not continue in that misconception, Genevieve, if you did not agree."

With a sigh, she said, "Yes, but you should have seen how Radford relaxed. I felt like I took a huge amount of pain off of him, Armand! Oh no, here she comes!"

Lady Bastwicke descended the staircase with the housekeeper in tow. She said over her shoulder, "We have a celebration in the family today. Have the servants bring special treats up to his room so we can all congratulate Lord Ashby on his betrothal." Catching sight of Genevieve, she strode toward her and Armand. "What are you two doing here like this, together? You may leave her now, Monsieur de Villebon, and go back to France, for she is betrothed to Lord Ashby. He's a British Earl."

Genevieve gave a wet sniff and groped for her handkerchief from under the ruffle on her forearm, finding nothing.

Looking stony, Armand stood and foraged inside his coat and pulled out a handkerchief, which he gave to Genevieve.

She said waveringly, "Thank you, Armand," in a pitiful voice, and touched the linen to her eyes and blew her nose on the pleasant-smelling linen.

Lady Bastwicke said warningly, "That is Monsieur de Villebon to you, Genevieve. You are not on intimate terms with this man, this Frenchman. In fact, you are now a foreigner in our land, are you not, Monsieur?" She gave him a smug side glance with her chin high. Without waiting for an answer, she left them, side-stepped her way through a door, and snapped it shut. They could hear her sharply calling instructions to servants.

Genevieve, flushing with shame, expelled, "That was terrible!"

"Not to worry. I believe she is still sore at me for what happened at Chambord and Villebon."

"Yes, and she will never cease from vulgarity. Is she so blind that she cannot see how horrendously she controls people, and abrasively runs roughshod over us all?"

"I believe she is partially blind, but of an extraordinarily mighty will. But you are different,

Genevieve. Children do not have to mirror their parents, and very often they do not." As fresh tears fell from her eyes, he took the handkerchief from her and applied it tenderly. "I greatly admire how you turned out, Genevieve."

Madam reappeared, scowling, her forefinger pointed at Armand. "Monsieur, did I not tell you to leave? I'll have no more of you! You ruined our pleasure at Chambord, and treated me abominably at Villebon!"

To Genevieve's admiration, he said nothing.

That seemed to enrage her. "How dare you! My daughter has got herself a rich and titled fiancé!" With a withering look at Genevieve, she spat, "Miraculously!" With that, she shot him a superior look and headed up the stairs. "What you need to do now is disappear!"

The seconds ticked, and Genevieve looked at Armand and said, "See?"

"And you do not want this marriage, Genevieve?" He reached for her hand and said, "Shall we go elsewhere to talk?"

"Gladly. I know where." He accompanied her as she slipped behind the grand staircase and down the servants' corridors, winding back and forth to where an aroma of baking apples filled the air. "Let's get some of those apples and take them with us," she proposed.

He smiled when she led him into the kitchen. She secured hot apple turnovers in two towels, took the basket from the cook with thanks, and asked Hawkins, the butler if she might have a bottle of raspberry cordial and two goblet from his pantry.

With refreshment thus secured, Armand took the

basket. "Brilliant idea." Out they went, through the door that led through the kitchen garden and the outer gate into the filbert orchard. They hurried beneath the spreading old limbs with their green baby leaves illuminated by the sunshine. There was a gap where three trees were missing in a row, and there, Genevieve indicated that he set the basket on the round top of an iron table made of curlicues. There was a collection of ornate iron chairs, two of which he pulled close. They seated themselves facing a stack of seasoned straw bales onto which an old archery target was affixed. "Who shoots here?" he asked.

"I do, and Arabelle does. I mean, we did."

"And will again, I hope. It's a pleasant pastime."

"Yes, it was."

He asked, "Why only in the past, Genevieve? You must not give up your pleasures in life."

She sighed in misery and said, "But I will have to go to Ashby Castle and live all the way over there in Somerset, and how will Arabelle and I ever do such things as this together again? She lives not far from here."

Armand said, "But since you did not agree to marry the Earl, surely your father won't let you be forced into it—will he?"

"That's what I do not know."

"And that is worrying you the most?"

"Well, that, and also the fact that I know I would make Radford happy if I did marry him."

"Even if he dies of this infected wound?"

"Especially if he does. It would make his last days on this earth . . . happy, he said. It's the reason he is quite desperate. I think he feels he will not live long."

Armand changed his position, shot a puzzled glance her way, and asked carefully, "What if he does live?"

Genevieve covered her face with her hands, overwhelmed by the enormity of the prospect. "Then I would be his wife . . . for my whole life!"

"What a risk!" he marveled.

Spying a movement in the distance, Genevieve saw her sister, Arabelle, in a pink gown passing through light and shade, coming toward them. Then, noticing the two of them, she slowed and stopped. Backing up, she left in a hurry before Armand saw her.

The tension of silence mounted, so Genevieve asked him, "Shall we eat our apple turnovers?"

"Yes. It might give you strength and fortitude."

She blurted out, "You are a strength and fortitude-giver in my life right now. I think God sent you."

Swiftly, before she knew what was happening, he lifted her hand and kissed it.

Genevieve, through wet eyelashes, stared at him in wonder as she recovered. She watched him as he turned his broad back and lifted the food and drink from the basket. With a flourish and a cheerful smile, he opened the cloth wrapping and laid her pastry in front of her. It was warm, and oozing with baked apples and the aroma of cinnamon.

They smiled at each other after their first bites.

"*Superbe!*" He set the goblets side by side on the table, and uncorked and poured from the cordial bottle. He presented Genevieve hers. "*Bon appétit,* Ma'mselle. I hope this will make you feel better." A few minutes later, he said, "If you speak to your father, perhaps he will understand. We must obliterate this ridiculous problem of yours."

"But you heard my mother. She will stick to this and not let go. I know her. Things must always go her way."

"However," he pointed out, "she is legally no longer married to your father, is she?"

"That's what Father maintains, yes."

"Then how can she be so dictatorial?"

"She is still my mother, but you make an interesting point. Logically, she should be very nice to him, and agreeable, don't you think?"

"Absolutely. Pleasing him should be her utmost goal, as you advised her early on."

When Genevieve and Armand emerged from the orchard, they heard Madam's voice. It was coming from the open window above them, where she was pacing back and forth and gesticulating to someone. "So how would we *live* if we're not married?"

"What do you mean, what will we do *if?*" asked Lord Bastwicke. "We are in that position now."

"Is this for real? You aren't just trying to scare me for some spiteful reason?"

Lord Bastwicke's voice rumbled, "I do not think as you do, Madam."

"Oooh! You're vile!"

Genevieve and Armand heard a crash, tinkle, and an "Ow!" from the recipient of her aim. Genevieve shrank back in mortification, and almost tripped. Armand steadied her.

"Bastwicke, I want to know what you are going to do to fix this!"

"Do you care?" he asked. "How often do you live with me, anyway?"

"That's because you're so boring."

"Fine; I'm boring. You prefer your fun. You may go. You always do anyway."

"I had my fun for a little while, but we were ousted by that devious Frenchman, so it wasn't very long."

"Oh? Is that the only reason you returned? It was not, then, because I asked you to? Your presence before me now had nothing to do with the dissolution of our marriage?"

"No! Yes, I did! Can't you see? Here I am!"

"Yes, here you are, but seemingly full of vindictiveness. Come back; we are not finished, Regina!"

"Oh, but until you turn things back the way they were, we are!" A door slammed.

Genevieve felt such a mixture of chaotic emotions that when she looked at her fingers, they were shaking.

Armand took both her hands in his warm ones and held them, saying, "So that is how it stands. Your father is in a quagmire."

"She should be nice to him now—much nicer than she has ever been before. I am going to tell her so. Again."

"You do not fear her anger toward you? Apparently she throws things."

"I do, and I don't. I shall take Arabelle with me."

Armand looked at her with approval. "Use your wisdom, and do your best. That is all you can do, Genevieve."

"She is a thorn in everyone's side, but how would

it be if she had to be outside of this family? And what if we children would possibly not be considered legitimate anymore?"

Armand said, "Those are some rather alarming thoughts. I will talk to your father, shall I?"

"About?"

"I will inquire what would happen to you all if he and she do not remarry."

"Yes, thank you." With a full heart, Genevieve boldly stood on tiptoe and kissed him on the cheek. As she ran ahead of him, she looked over her shoulder and sent him a relieved and loving smile, and a little wave.

He looked enchanted.

* * *

"Arabelle, will you please come with me?" Genevieve took her beautiful dark-haired sister by the hand and led her along the arched corridor to Madam's door.

"Why are we going in to her?"

"Because I think we should convince Madam that she needs to try extremely hard to reconcile with Father. Don't you see? She is fighting with him so viciously when she needs to be sweet to him. How is she ever going to win him back when she's constantly yelling at him?"

"I so agree. It makes me sick." Arabelle followed Genevieve into the room where her mother was lying on the bed, her white face powder ravaged by tracks which could only have resulted from tears.

"Madam?" called Arabelle softly.

"What do you want? Both of you here? I did not

summon you. Go away!”

Genevieve sat down on a bedside chair, and Arabelle pulled one closer for herself. “We want to talk with you.”

“What about?” She sat up and motioned a maid away. After the dressing room door closed, she persisted, “Out with it! I’m not feeling well.”

Arabelle said, “We know you’re not, Madam. This is all very distressing for you. That’s why we came to see if we can help in some small way.”

“You girls? Help *me*? I don’t need help in small ways, I need a huge miracle.”

Genevieve nodded. “We think this is a terrible thing that has happened, your not being married to Father anymore, or at all. No one could have foreseen this. But to get out of this quandary, perhaps it would help if you would be very . . .”

As Genevieve faltered under her mother’s intensifying glare, Arabelle supplied, “Very loving to him, we mean.”

“After what he’s done?”

“Yes!” the sisters responded.

“Why on earth should *I* be nice to *him?*”

Genevieve, feeling bolder, said, “Be respectful at least, because that’s the way to catch him back.”

Lady Bastwicke (that was) stared ludicrously at her. “*You,* Genevieve, are telling *me* how to catch a man? Huh! How dare you, when you hadn’t the least inkling of how to do it yourself! What high impertinence!” Angrily, she snatched up a closed fan and threw it at Genevieve.

“Ow!” Genevieve fingered her temple, left the fan where it fell, and escaped from the room. She would not submit to such treatment, not now nor ever again. Arabelle threw the hurtful fan on Madam's bed and followed her sister out.

"Did success attend you?" asked Armand as the young ladies hurried onto the mezzanine.

"We only succeeded in enraging her," Genevieve admitted helplessly. "This Proverb keeps coming to mind: *Pride goeth before destruction, and an haughty spirit before a fall.*"

Arabelle said, "It's just too bad for her, but what the Bible says is true." She looked at Armand and added, "Genevieve, I met Armand de Villebon earlier. Armand, are you privy to all this family trouble? I am sorry and ashamed, if that is the case."

"I only want to help," he said, smiling kindly.

Genevieve drew Arabelle along with them, and put her hand through Armand's offered arm. She led them down the wide staircase and stage-whispered to him, "Have you talked to our father?"

"I have, yes. Let us repair to a more private place, shall we?"

Genevieve led them to the ground floor reception salon where visitors were directed to wait when they called, and closed the door. "What did you say?" she asked him eagerly.

"I asked His Lordship if the case were true; that his marriage was dissolved, and he said it is. I asked him how he could rectify the situation, and he said that they would need to call the Banns in his parish church for three Sundays in a row, giving the congregation or anyone present the chance to speak up if there is any just cause why the two of them could not be re-wed."

Arabelle drew an astonished breath and locked

eyes with Genevieve.

Genevieve said frankly, "I don't know about objections from other people, but we sisters know that there is plenty of just cause why Father would not *like* to remarry her." They had all heard the Bastwicke fight.

Arabelle said, "She would absolutely hate the public exposure of all this."

"True!" Genevieve added, "But, as galling as the Banns would be for her, she has to go through the first and even more difficult task of convincing Father to marry her again."

Arabelle's eyes widened. "I don't know how she will ever do it. She lit into Genevieve violently for suggesting that she be loving toward him."

"Armand, what else did you and our father say to each other?" asked Genevieve, appreciating how he was trying to help.

"He also quoted something. It was, let me see if I can say this correctly in English, *It is better to live on the housetop than with a brawling woman in a . . . large house*, I believe."

Arabelle said, "Yes, close enough," and locked eyes significantly with Genevieve.

Armand added, "Surprisingly, he admitted that, though he cares deeply for you, his children, the thought of having her back in the house every day feels like jumping off a precipice into—ah, well, I shouldn't say."

"Armand, we want to know. What was his word?" pressed Genevieve.

He looked at them each in turn, and said, "Hell."

CHAPTER 17

Questioning Love

Genevieve hurried to find Father. He was in his library, just sitting at his escritoire, his forehead in his hand and his wig hanging on the fire screen. At sound of her entrance, he did not grab it, nor did he appear to even hear her until she stood next to him. He stirred, looked up at her, and blinked.

"Ah, it's you, my precious. You walk so quietly. Hand me my wig, will you, please?"

Genevieve did so, feeling the heaviness of his contemplation.

When he had covered his short gray hair with his white wig with the luxurious sausage curls on each side, he looked at her and asked, "Is there something I can do for you, my dear?"

"Is there something I can do for you, Father?" she countered solemnly.

"No."

They looked at each other, and he said, "Sit."

She settled herself onto his knee. "What are you going to do about your marriage, Father?"

"That is the big question."

The door swung open, and in walked Madam in a fresh gown of peach and burgundy stripes with short burgundy feathers spiking up from her natural light red hair. She had re-powdered her face, which was now very white. These signs told Genevieve that Madam had bathed and washed her hair powder out. She said, "Lord Ashby wants you, Genevieve. Hurry scurry!"

Lord Bastwicke said, "I thought I left him falling asleep a few minutes ago. Why is he awake already?"

"I was just in there," she said, touching her side curl and simpering toward Lord Bastwicke. "He's awake."

"How is he to heal if we bother him every few minutes?"

She declared, "If Genevieve goes in there, he will feel better." She moved about the room, picking up a round glass paperweight and hefting it in her palm.

Genevieve winced. Was she going to throw it? Nevertheless, she said, "He would do much better to be left alone, to sleep."

Anger flared in Madam's eyes, but with a visible effort, she controlled her voice and said, "After you answer his summons, he can sleep. Go now and see what your fiancé wants."

Genevieve looked at Father, who had risen when Madam had entered. He stayed standing, but a good distance away. Now he gave Genevieve a nod of dismissal. She realized that it was likely that he felt the need to talk with Madam now that she was not yelling. He was not focusing on the issue of her and Radford.

Genevieve left. She wondered, with every lagging step, if any good would come of either conversation. She was afraid that both could result in courses that would change their lives, and most likely for the worse.

When she entered the invalid's chamber, the curtains were again drawn shut against the sunny day. She tiptoed toward the black walnut tester bed with its single candle burning on the side table.

"Genevieve! How nice of you to come and see me." Radford's voice was quiet but glad.

"Are you not supposed to be sleeping? You should not have so many interruptions to your healing rest, but my mother said you wanted to see me."

"She did? That was . . . thoughtful of her." He gave a small cough, and gasped in pain.

Genevieve found his choice of word peculiar. *Thoughtful?* She knew then that he had not sent for her. She decided she would stay for a few minutes anyway, not to seem rude. Already he looked better, smiling at her.

"Has your pain diminished at all?"

He reached for her, and she hesitantly went closer and relinquished one hand to his. "Yes, for his moment, it has gone away," he said, but he looked drained and his skin was hot.

"I wonder if a cool bath would help. Giles can arrange it right away," she decided.

"No, not necessary now, Genevieve; but later, when the servant returns. I only need you."

She reached and yanked the bell pull anyway, and wet a cotton towel from the bowl of ice and put it on his forehead and another one on his neck.

Gazing up at her, he grasped her wrist and said, "I am a sorry kind of suitor, Genevieve, but I retain my wish to present myself to you. I keep thinking that, if I should not recover from this stab, I would like for you, as my wife, to have everything that I can give you."

"Oh, Radford, stop talking like that."

"Pardon me, but I am serious. Will you indeed marry me, dear Genevieve? Before I go?"

"You may not be going, Radford."

"Then, until death us do part?"

She trembled with apprehension to give him either answer. To stop his gaze from reading her nervous face so intently, Genevieve stooped and picked up a handkerchief lying in a damp ball on the carpet. She smoothed it out to discover that it was familiar. It was a handkerchief of hers, embroidered in her golden stitches, Copperplate style, and forming the quote, *Be still, and know that I am God.* How odd to find it here.

Hating herself for ignoring his direct question, she nevertheless plunged ahead to ask, "How did this get here? It's mine, but I have not seen it since before we went to France."

"She must have brought it with her." Radford was lying back again, looking deflated. "She mopped my brow with something."

"She? Who?"

Just as he said, "Miss Doyle," Genevieve remembered. When Dorcasta had had no handkerchief in the coach as they left for the musical evening in London, Madam had told Genevieve to give the girl one of hers. She had never returned it. "When was Miss Doyle here?"

"A few minutes before you came in, and after your mother left. Dorcasta said she's coming back after she takes some . . . refreshment. You can see her then." His voice diminished. "The doctor was here, and gave me laudanum for the pain."

"Then go to sleep, Radford," said Genevieve soothingly, pulling his bedclothes carefully up around his shoulders.

His eyes were slits as he watched her. "This is what I see as such a blessing, dearest Genevieve. You, helping me. All through life. No more loneliness. My brother is so happy; he has such a loving wife."

She felt distinctly uncomfortable, and could make no reply. Poor Radford. It was a revelation to hear that he was lonely. She could change his life in this instant if she but said yes to him wholeheartedly and tried to return his love. Someone in a book had said that love was something you could choose to give. Was that true? All she could do for the moment was to whisper as she walked toward the door, "Thy will be done, O Lord."

"What did you say, Genevieve?"

She could not stay, or evince a reply.

* * *

Armand sat between long curtains in the window seat where the sun shone. He folded a paper, put it inside his coat, and came to her. "It was time I wrote to my mother," he said. "But what did you just say?" he asked as he quietly closed Radford's chamber door behind them.

"I was praying. For God's will to be done."

"That's the best thing to do. There's a lot to pray about."

"Never in my life has there been more." She poured out to him, "I have so many worries, and I forgot who is in charge. When I found this handkerchief on the floor by his bed, I saw how I need to believe these words that I, myself, embroidered. Look." She showed Armand the script.

He nodded and said seriously. "God will lead you, and your father, and all of us. We must trust Him, and also do what He shows us to be right."

"Sometimes it's difficult to know what that is, though, isn't it?"

"For a time, yes. Can you try to just trust?"

Genevieve nodded, looked up at him, and murmured, "Do you believe that loving is giving?"

"Yes."

"Then, what do you think? Are we each to give of ourselves as a way to show love? Even if we don't think we feel it very much?"

"We are instructed to give to those who ask *if* we are able. Not of necessity, but of a true heart."

Genevieve looked up at the pastel mural on the domed ceiling. "But what if a person in need wants you to do something badly, but only ever talks of how much it will benefit *him?*"

Armand said quietly, "Such as, *You will make me the happiest of men?*"

"Exactly that. Here is my question: is he giving love, or only asking for another to give love to him?"

"Who knows, but the main motivation sounds like *Please me.* If a man says to a woman, *Marry me because you will make me the happiest of men,* I view that as self-serving, just as you told us all in France. Such a man does not think to make her happy first; he wants to feel love *from* her. He is not saying that he will do all in his power to give her happiness, but he will gladly take it, and expect it. When some men say *I love you,* they mean *I love what you will do for me.*"

Genevieve smiled at him in appreciative wonder. What a man! Aloud, she said, "In other words, *Out of the abundance of the heart, the mouth speaketh.*"

"What a good reminder."

"Thank you, Armand, for your understanding."

* * *

It was feet on the staircase that interrupted them. A dark curly head ascended from below; Dorcasta Doyle! Genevieve thought she had been sent away by Madam. What gave her the right to stay in this house? Genevieve let out a huff, trying not to let Armand see her exasperation. But one look at him, and he burst out in a helpless laugh. "How inevitable," he said under his breath. "No moment is complete without *this* intrusion."

That made Genevieve grin. They shook their heads together, then turned to the intruder and put on sober, questioning faces.

She shot them a black look, but did not say a word of greeting. She took a small tray that she had been balancing on one hand while holding up the green wool skirt to mount the stairs. So she was still wearing Arabelle's outfit that was steadily becoming a bedraggled wreck.

Armand lifted his eyebrows at Genevieve and went to open the door for Dorcasta. "Miss Doyle," he said, and gestured her into Radford's room. After she haughtily passed by him, Genevieve motioned for him to follow her. He nodded in mock solemnity, as though they were on an espionage mission. He cupped his hands around his ear and put his ear to the crack in the doorway.

Genevieve giggled. She decided to tiptoe behind him and listen, too.

"I've brought you something to eat and drink, My Lord!" Dorcasta sang out, inviting thanks by her tone.

Another door clicked open across the way, and out came Madam with rouged red lips and cheeks. She had added a black crescent moon patch to her left cheek and a triple-stranded pearl necklace encircling her throat. "Genevieve, what are you doing lurking there? You look as if you're eavesdropping."

"Do I?" she stage-whispered, and nodded. "Where are you going, Madam?" she inquired quickly to deflect her from continuing her questions.

"Going? Nowhere. Nowhere fast!" she added, clomping by, pressing the door lever, and turning sideways to enter the bedchamber. "Get in here, where you belong. Monsieur de Villebon, I expected you to have left for France by now. Dorcasta Doyle! What are *you* doing here?" she yelled with rancor.

Genevieve gestured helplessly to Armand and

followed in her mother's wake, boldly taking his wrist ruffle and tugging him after her into the room. Startled, Dorcasta tilted her tray and caused a goblet and a plate of pastries to slide off onto Radford's bedclothes.

"Ow!" issued from deep in the pillows. They had landed hard on his shins.

That made Genevieve angry. She hurried to the bedside, brushing past the apologizing Dorcasta, and asked, "Radford, did that quick movement of yours cause any more blood to flow?" She moved aside the deep V neckline of his night shirt so she could see. "Sure enough!" There was blood showing on the outside of his bandage. "Dorcasta, move away! We must call the doctor back."

Armand said, "I will go for him. Your butler will give me directions." Gratefully, Genevieve nodded and watched him stride out of the room.

Madam shouted at Dorcasta, "Clean up your mess and get out! What in blazes are you doing in here, anyway?"

Dorcasta moved close to her and stuttered confidingly, "I—I was doing what you—you once told me, Lady Bastwicke." She whispered, "Giving the man attention!"

Madam's close-set eyes seared into her and she hissed through clenched teeth, "Not *this* man, stupid! He's taken!"

Dorcasta said in a whining tone, "I didn't know that. At least, I didn't think Genevieve liked him *that* much."

"Hush, you back-stabber!" expelled Madam.

Dorcasta flounced out, calling at the door, "Do not worry, Lord Ashby! I will be back, as promised!

I will keep all of my promises to you, unlike some women."

Madam scowled furiously, but in came Lord Bastwicke, and it amazed Genevieve to see how quickly Madam turned an actual smile up at him and touched his hand in passing. But her back was ramrod straight as she made her exit to follow Dorcasta and fire more darts of vitriol at her.

Father's black eyebrows shot up, and he looked at Genevieve in bewilderment.

Outside the open door, Lady Bastwicke had her arms akimbo above her enormous skirt, confronting Dorcasta.

Dorcasta was saying, "Aren't we supposed to keep our promises?"

Madam threw back, "That totally depends upon what they are in the first place! Why?"

"Then you have to let me by so I can go back into his room."

"Have to? How dare you?"

"I promised Lord Ashby that I would *marry* him someday!"

"*What?*" Lady Bastwicke's voice slammed at her like a thunderclap.

Dorcasta jumped out of reach and asserted, "I did!"

"Then why did he propose to Genevieve?"

Dorcasta simpered at Genevieve whom she could see watching them. "Maybe because he mistakenly thought that *I* turned him down."

Lady Bastwicke snarled, "You did no such thing! As if you would ever turn down a Peer of the Realm with bags of money and lands and a castle! As if he would ever propose to the likes of stupid little you!"

Madam turned her grand figure around and, seeing Father looking at them, checked. She rearranged her wrathful face by twisting her lips up into a smile at him. "My Lord! Send that extreme troublemaker away. I am afraid that she tells lies, and I have taken her to France and given her every advantage, but now that our time is through, you must make her go. Away!" She smiled again, her teeth looking crooked and yellow between her orange-red lips. Behind that baring of the teeth, Genevieve saw the fire in her eyes that smoldered in tamped-down furor.

"What did she say?" barked Lord Bastwicke. "I heard something about a proposal?"

Dorcasta nearly tripped as she dashed to him for help. "Yes! It's me who promised Lord Ashby that if ever he needed a wife, I will certainly be it."

Skeptically eyeing her, he threw back, "My word! Young people today, no sense of propriety! Did he agree to that?"

Dorcasta hesitated, keeping her chin up but not meeting his eyes. "He didn't say no?"

Madam instantly turned Dorcasta by the shoulders and pointed her to the stairs. She opened her mouth to revile her, but then, glancing up at Lord Bastwicke, she said in a milder tone, "You are not promised then, Miss Doyle? You may leave now."

Genevieve returned to the room and approached the bed. "Radford, before anyone else comes in, may I please ask you: did you ever agree to a marriage with Dorcasta Doyle?"

He stirred, clutched his chest, and blinked up at her several times. "Of all the things to ask me,

Genevieve," he said wearily. "Why would I do such a . . . daft thing . . . as that?"

"So you did not? Even after she *promised*, as she says, to marry you if you wanted to?"

He tried to rise, but she pushed him gently down by the shoulder.

"Not a chance," he expelled, trying to find a less painful position.

Genevieve felt a form of relief. Then she wondered why. If those two were betrothed, it would have been an end to her dilemma.

"Why did you ask that, Genevieve?"

"Only because she is telling my parents that she *is* promised to you."

With an effort, he opened his eyes wider. "Then I am sorry to tell you that there are some people in this world who . . . lie and deceive. There are . . . others . . . who are true." She felt him grope for her hand. When he squeezed it in his hot palm, he emphasized, "Such as you."

The doctor came in at that moment, and Genevieve left, her mouth dry and her heart thumping.

* * *

Genevieve went outside, seeking her Father. She found him petting Vesper on the lane to the hops garden. "Father!" she called. The dog alerted and bounded toward her, arriving with his tail swinging and his face smiling. Before he reached her, she commanded, "Vesper, sit!"

The dog did so, his brown eyes glistening up at her and his tongue lolling. "Good dog." She petted his smooth head and he wagged faster. She leaned down to hug his soft ear against her cheek. "Father," she said, looking up at his approach, "there is something blessed about a dog. They always cheer us up."

"How true. Vesper is good at that. And he loves to obey."

Genevieve thought, *I don't always love to obey.* She said, "I need to ask you something, Father."

He bent down and scratched his dog around the neck. Vesper wagged his whole hind end and licked his face. "What is it, precious?" Father hunkered down to the dog, which now lay on his back, presenting his tummy to be scratched.

"I need to ask you if you approve my marrying Lord Ashby."

"I see nothing wrong with him, provided he recovers. Do we not like and trust him, and call him by his first name?"

"Yes, but though I like him now, I do not believe I love him."

Lord Bastwicke looked away. "Well, I didn't love Regina, either. I think I know how you feel, but in the long run, does that really matter? Some of my friends who married for love are quite unhappy now, years later."

Genevieve stared at him. She had long suspected the truth. "Doesn't it matter, Father?"

He turned his face toward the mansion, and his large-nosed profile gave nothing away. When he straightened up, he reached out to her.

She put her hand in his large one and they walked, Vesper eagerly taking his place on his master's left, keeping pace with them. "You will have to decide. It matters more to women than to men, I believe. With busy men, work takes a great deal of our effort and thought and energy. Perhaps with ordinary women, they have the same hours of occupation in their days, but with ladies of Society, it is not enough. They have time to kill, and they can often feel lonely. Their thoughts turn to their husbands, from whom they seek love and admiration, and sometimes even companionship. My sister, Claracilla, and her Trent have such companionship. I have come to see that houses and lands are not enough."

"With Madam, that seems to be true."

"It is true. She has had enough, she said, of a dull stick of a husband," growled Father, "so she went to the Continent to live a life of amusement. I believe she craved constant admiration most of all."

"Yes, and still craves it."

"You saw that in France, I suppose?" he asked, looking intently toward the hop garden.

Genevieve debated what she should reveal to him. "At Château de Chambord, I did not see her often. She spent some time with a woman friend, giggling behind their fans, and also . . ."

"Go on. Were there men?"

"One whom I saw her . . . talking with a couple of times." Genevieve quickly switched her tack. "You are so good to her, Father. I truly don't know why she doesn't find that more than enough."

"Because she does not love me."

"Whyever not?"

He sighed. "Likely because I do not praise her all the time."

Genevieve boldly queried, "But who *does* admire

her? What is anyone to genuinely praise her for?"

"I don't know. She could be quite entertaining in the beginning. I married her because she said she needed a husband, and fast."

Genevieve felt bad for him.

"But it transpired that it was certainly not true, but by then, she had *successfully hooked a large, gleaming fish,* as I heard her boasting to her sister."

"That was such a wrong thing to do! You are such a giver. I have seen that she is a taker! –a grabber, in fact!"

He said nothing for many moments as they curved to walk over the grassy lawns, circumventing the house.

Genevieve, furious at all the injustice to her father, who was an honest, considerate man, cried, "So what do we do? Will you keep on giving, and remarry her?"

His white wig moved from side to side as he shook his head in perplexity. He looked to be experiencing a deep depression.

Genevieve stepped back and petted Vesper's head. "What will *I* need to do, Father? Give of myself and say yes to Lord Ashby even though I don't feel the same love that he does?"

Father looked lost in thought. Genevieve stood there, petting a concerned dog while her heart beat like his tail was doing against her dress.

Lord Bastwicke said, "Pardon? You were saying that you don't love Ashby? Well, good luck with that because very few people of my acquaintance find that elusive commodity."

Genevieve was appalled by her Father's change of attitude, but felt that he was under the influence of his own dark predicament, and had lost his usual joy of living. "Arabelle married for love," she said wistfully.

He turned to see where Genevieve was looking, and there came Arabelle, looking like a beautiful painting with pink ribbons cascading from her hat and twirling among her dark curls. She emerged from beneath the portico and passed between the columns. When she saw them, she smiled and came their way.

"What do you think each of us should do?" Genevieve hurriedly asked, moving forward to link her arm with Arabelle's. "Father, please tell her what you told me about how our mother hooked you into marriage."

Lord Bastwicke cleared his throat, said, "She knows. Come on, Vesper, let's go," and waving his hand above his head, called back, "I'm fed up with the subject. I'm going shooting."

Arabelle sadly said, "I have often wondered if there was any scrap of love in their marriage. Father tries hard, though, and I feel sorry for all the patience he has had to employ."

Genevieve, watching his large form veer off with the eager dog, said, "Father has a lot of love in his big heart, so I think he has covered it all of these years by being good to her. But she's not nice back, nor appreciative of him."

"No. It's a pity, and such a waste of precious time."

"She clings so tightly to the wrong outlook. She should stop being so obsessed with herself and with the impression she's making on others. She should quit being so competitive for attention."

Arabelle said, "She gets attention, all right, but does she realize what people are thinking of her?"

Genevieve said, "I just wonder what Father will do. Will he remarry her or not? If not, what will happen to all of us? Who will we be?"

Arabelle's dark eyebrows lifted. "Since I am married, I shall remain who and what I am; but you and Lenora and Jerome would be motherless."

Genevieve interjected, "We have been motherless most of our lives."

"I know. Aunt Claracilla was our mother in love, but I wonder if—"

"You wonder if we would be called legitimate daughters since our parents weren't really married in Fleet Street all those years ago."

Arabelle shook her head slowly. "It's hard to say what people would think. But, you know what?"

They smiled at each other and said, "Who cares what people think?"

Genevieve added, "We shall go ahead with that attitude, shall we? But I have a greater dilemma, and I see both sides."

"Tell me," said Arabelle, leading the way to the bench beneath a leafless old walnut tree.

So Genevieve told her about Radford's dire need for her to accept his proposals.

Arabelle said, "I am really surprised that he is so insistent. I thought he was generally polite, and kept his dignity."

"Yes, but he is wounded now, and dosed with laudanum, and talks of having me as his wife until the end."

"As if the end is near, you mean?"

"I get that impression." Genevieve took a deep

breath and let it out in a sigh. "But he could be wrong."

"I can see why you're distressed. Do you love him?"

Genevieve exclaimed, "See? That's what you care about the most!"

Arabelle looked startled. "Shouldn't I?"

"Yes! I feel it's the most important thing. But Father said that only a few people he knows have love for each other in their marriages. He talked as if it's something we can hardly ever expect."

"Oh, Genevieve, I don't agree!"

"You have the best husband ever, and he loves you so much that we can see it every time you're together."

"I know. I am blessed. I pray fervently that you will be just as blessed."

* * *

Radford reached out his hand to Genevieve. "The Bishop I have summoned will marry us here in this house. I will write to him, my dear."

Genevieve gasped. "But Father said the Banns have to be called in church! The new law, remember? People cannot marry quickly as they used to do."

"Your mother said that the law has not gone into effect yet. Genevieve, if we hurry, we can do it! I don't often ask things for myself, but this means so much to me. I could die as the husband of the most wonderful young lady in this world. And then, I will see you in Heaven forever after that . . . even though we will not be married there." He dropped his head back against the pillows, but kept his glistening eyes trained pleadingly on hers.

"Radford, that is not possible because my father said the new law is now in effect and being enforced. A Bishop coming here cannot perform a marriage without those Banns being called for three weeks in a row. I'm sorry, but it's true. Ask my father, not my mother."

He looked downhearted.

She went on, "If I said yes to your proposal," and she held up her hand at his eagerness, "but I am only saying *if. If* I did, how do you see us in, say, a month? And, in a year?"

He licked his dry lips, so she gave him a water glass. After he drank, he said, "In a month, I see us at Ashby Castle, and in a year's time, too."

"Doing what?"

"Loving each other. I care nothing for the rest."

"You sound like a reader of novels and poetry."

He lowered his eyelids and smiled. "I have become a romantic of late. Ever since my brother, Simon, fell in love and married, I have observed what an exalted state that is. I feel it myself now, and understand it. If only you could love me as I love you, Genevieve! You cannot imagine how much I would like to have you as my wife. Oh, what a dream! You would make me the happiest man alive."

Was he reaching for a last chance at his own happiness before he died? Or was he determined to live through this crisis, and keep her at his castle, and bask in what love she would be compelled to give him in return for all of his passion for her? She seriously doubted that she had such selfless fortitude in her being as Father demonstrated.

Her mother came clattering into the room. "Cooie, Radford!" she called, "are you up? Oh, Genevieve, you're here; that's splendid. What are you talking about?"

"I was seeing how he fared after the doctor left. I am leaving now, to let him sleep."

"No, you stay. Otherwise Dorcasta will barge in."

"Madam," said Genevieve heavily, "she will barge in anyway."

Laughing affectedly in Radford's direction, Madam said, "Well, just keep her from bothering him. She is nowhere near as refined as you are, Genevieve. She might shake his arm and hurt him worse. Shall we do you the favor of keeping her away, Radford?"

He glanced her way and uttered a heartfelt, "Yes!"

"Well, I have magnificent news, since I just talked with my husband. Next Sunday, in London, we will call the Banns in church for your marriage!"

CHAPTER 18

Lay Down Your Life

As soon as Genevieve descended to the ground floor, she spied Armand. Turning away, she endeavored to hide her face from him. She pushed open the door to the salon. It had a comfortable chair with a hood upon it. She dashed into that, for it hid her from the door. Why wouldn't her tears subside? She needed her handkerchief, and was still grappling for it when he came in. She knew it was him by the way he quietly clicked the door shut behind him.

With the French pronunciation, he said, "Geneviève?"

Wetly, she responded, *"Oui?"*

He approached until he stood at her side, regarding her. He dropped to one knee, took her hand, then tugged away her handkerchief and dabbed at her eyelashes.

"You're so often doing this," she mourned. When she opened her eyes, he was looking at her with a hint of amusement mingled with sympathy. She couldn't help but giggle.

"It seems that it is necessary. What is the matter now?"

"Everything!"

From out in the entry hall, they heard, "Come quickly, Genevieve! Where are you? Genevieve!" It was Madam.

Genevieve instantly alerted.

Armand strolled to the door, opened it for her, and whispered, "Shall I come with you?"

"Yes. Perhaps. I don't know!" she wailed softly.

His look spelled determination, and he followed.

Dorcasta expelled, "I will *not* leave this instant! I am affianced to Lord Ashby as of days ago!"

Madam scoffed, "How is that possible? You're lying!"

Dorcasta said belligerently, "I am to marry him as soon as the Vicar gets here because it is agreed and settled."

"Impossible! He asked Genevieve to marry him many times over!"

"Let's go ask him then," said Dorcasta, and flounced away up the stairs.

When they all reached Radford's bedside, Lord Bastwicke was there to witness Radford's whispered reply. "I thought she was Genevieve!"

An explosion of wrath came from Madam, and she let Dorcasta have it with recriminations, ending with, "What a vile, sneaking snake you turned out to be!"

Dorcasta yelled back, "You're just jealous because I am going to marry this Lord—especially because you are no longer married to one yourself! In fact, you are nothing! Your children are bastards, and you are not Lady Bastwicke anymore! I bet Lord Bastwicke made up the new law just to get *rid* of you!"

At the sight of Lady Bastwicke filling her lungs, she plummeted out of the room.

Lord Bastwicke growled, "Is that so!" He strode after her and pointed to the stairs. "Out of my house!" he roared.

She scuttled, with shoulders hunched like a cowed possum, down the middle of the stairs, tripping on the hem of Arabelle's gown. At that moment, Arabelle herself stepped into view at the bottom. Dorcasta fell and tumbled noisily down the remaining stairs. When she had kicked and struggled herself to a sitting position, she put her hand to her forehead dramatically and moaned. Taking her hand away and staring at it, she screamed, "Blood! I am hurt!" Turning, she yelled up the stairs at Lord Bastwicke, "You made me cut my head! I'm probably going to die!" She snatched the handkerchief that Arabelle offered her.

"Who are you?" asked Arabelle curiously. "You are wearing a dress that looks familiar to me."

Madam clomped to the top of the staircase and sneered down upon Dorcasta. Furiously, she informed Arabelle, "She stole your clothes in London, and has ruined three of them. Dorcasta Doyle, you—you ungrateful wretch! You get what you deserve! I shall be surprised if *any* man will want to marry you now, as you will very likely carry a scar to mar your visage until the day you die. Forget any privileges I bestowed upon you because of your aunt! I am positively *through* with you!"

From her bedchamber window some minutes later, Genevieve looked down and saw the hired dogcart arrive. Soon, Dorcasta waddled toward it. There she went, clambering onto the step, half tripping and hatless. A servant pushed a small trunk and bandbox with loud clunks, into the boot, knocked on the carriage body, and the single horse moved forward. The old carriage left tracks in the light gravel. *They will soon be covered over*, Genevieve thought.

To Arabelle, she said, "I did try to help her at first, but soon she didn't need me at all. I'm sorry, but I'm glad she took your abused green dress because I I never want to see it again. Too many bad memories are attached to it. I am only sorry that you had to lose it. I will order you something new."

Arabelle moved next to her at the window seat and watched the vehicle disappear down the tree-lined lane. "That hardly matters. What does matter is that she behaved like a sorry excuse for a female."

"I cannot pity her. She brought everything upon herself with her self-aggrandizing behavior, all through France and back here."

"I marvel that she thought she had any right to propose herself as a wife to Radford–a Peer! That was outrageous on every level."

"Yes. How quickly she evolved from timid to vainglorious."

Arabelle lifted an eyebrow and remarked, "You said she had a vicious attitude toward Madam all of a sudden."

Genevieve opened the leaded window for air, and turned. "What's so ironic is, she learned all of her arrogance and her social aggressiveness from

Madam herself."

"Yes, and I just asked Madam what she meant by a debt to Dorcasta's aunt."

"What did she say?"

Arabelle looked portentous. "Apparently, before Madam was married, Dorcasta's aunt, who was a friend of hers, introduced her to Father. I feel that there could be more to the story, but she gave me short shrift."

"I'm amazed that she told you that much," murmured Genevieve.

* * *

That evening, Radford rasped, "Ah, Genevieve, I have lain here thinking and dreaming, and knowing I must speak to you again. I love you," he said. While she stared at him with apprehension, he gazed fervently up at her without blinking and asked, "Will you hurry and marry me before I die? I *am* going to die, you know."

Genevieve glanced, wide-eyed, from Arabelle to Radford. "You must recover, not die!"

"I knew you would say that," he said, "but I feel it. God is calling me home."

Arabelle, with a supporting arm around Genevieve's shoulders, asked him, "Do you know this for sure?"

"Yes, I do."

"How?" she countered gently.

He touched an open Bible on the bedclothes. "I saw Jesus."

"You mean, in your mind's eye, while reading the Word? I agree; we always see Jesus in his Word."

"I saw him with my eyes."

Genevieve's mouth made an O. His eyes were shining. "When?"

"Just before I rang the bell. He appeared, standing beside that armoire, and he was rising from the floor very slowly, and all the while He was smiling at me. I cannot describe it! So pure and loving! I felt so exalted. My troubles will soon be over. I am going to Heaven, and I believe it will be soon!" His head fell back onto the pillows, and he gazed radiantly up at Genevieve.

She and Arabelle were squeezing one another's hands. Genevieve asked him quietly, "So if it's not too wrong to ask, why do you need me to marry you? If Jesus is taking you soon, I mean?"

Radford smiled. "Because, dear Genevieve, I love you. I not only wish to give you my name, but also an inheritance that passes from my late mother to my wife. I thought that you might possibly need it, with things so uncertain now between your parents. Who knows what will happen with their marriage, now dissolved?" He watched her with hope. He was not asking her for a long lifetime's happiness for himself. He wanted to confer on her a blessing he had power to bestow.

Genevieve groped inside her sleeve lace for her handkerchief. She touched it to Radford's eyes, for small shining tears had appeared at the outer corners and were tracking down his temples. She found herself blinking her own tears away. Taking a deep breath, she said, "At last, I think I understand."

He awaited her concurrence. If she said yes, he would be so glad. He could live his allotted time and be joyful, not worried or straining to persuade her for an answer. If she said no, he would be sunk into disappointment. Could she do that to someone for whom Jesus lingered near, as he fervently believed?

She looked at Arabelle, who was watching her with a question in her loving eyes. Genevieve knew her sister remained her support no matter what she decided. But, as Genevieve knew, it was up to her alone.

No, that was not right. She was never alone. With her hand still clutched by Radford's fevered one, she sank to her knees and put her forehead against the silken coverlet. *Dear God*, she prayed silently, *please show me clearly now what to do. Do not let me make a mistake. You know what my heart feels, but Thy will be done. In Jesus' name I ask for Thy answer. I will abide by it, if you give me strength. Amen.*

Pulling her dress out from under her knees with some difficulty, she rose to her feet. She realized what she must do, and she would do it.

She looked into Radford's expectant eyes and said softly, "Yes, I will, Radford. I want your last days to be happy."

* * *

Lady Bastwicke came in and broke the mood. Sensing something, she asked, "What's going forward?"

Armand, appearing behind her, looked curiously at Genevieve.

Radford pulled himself up with renewed strength and beamed, pulling her down closer until there were but six inches between their noses. "Thank you, thank you, *thank* you, my love! You don't know what this means to me!"

Genevieve tried to smile, but her hands had gone ice cold, and she felt overwhelmed by the enormity of what she had done.

Armand kept quizzing her silently in a most troubled way.

Arabelle said, "Let us leave them, Madam. They need to have some time together before we fuss with our congratulations, don't you think?"

Madam cried, "No, no! Genevieve, are you happy now to marry Lord Ashby? Finally?"

"I have consented, yes." Genevieve wished she had not sounded so coerced, but she realized that she really had been. She felt Radford kissing her hand. Her mother was swaying around, whooping loudly and gushing.

The door plummeted open and halted at Armand's boot. Father strode in. "What's all the noise about?"

His former wife declared proudly, "Lord Ashby finally has our daughter's *yes* answer confirmed!"

"No!" breathed Father. Shooting Genevieve a sharp, questioning look, he moved toward the bed, saying, "Well, this is a surprise, Genevieve. How are you feeling, Radford?"

"Wonderful! Blessed! My prayers are answered!"

"Hmm! When do you think to marry, then?"

Radford looked up at Genevieve and asked her, "As soon as possible?"

Lord Bastwicke said, "As soon as that. You will need to call the Banns first."

"How do we begin, Lord Bastwicke?" asked

Radford.

"Three consecutive Sundays in our family's parish church in London, you need to declare your mutual wishes to be married. That gives us and anyone else the opportunity to hear it, and to give a reason why your marriage cannot take place, if that be the case."

Radford eked out, "Then we will be in church . . . next Sunday." He was gripping his bandaged side.

Genevieve locked eyes with her Father and pulled her arm out of Radford's grasp. She took Arabelle's outstretched hand and left the room with her.

She dared to meet Armand's eyes because she felt rather sick. It was like slamming the door on his caring, loving face. Yes, she realized: *loving!*

Now her life was tied in knots. "Help me!" she whispered urgently to Arabelle as soon as the door clicked shut behind them.

* * *

When they reached the herb corner of the kitchen garden, Arabelle snatched a lavender stalk from last summer and gave it to Genevieve, apparently to be soothed by the remaining scent. "It is so touching that you agreed to marry him after hearing that Jesus is soon to take him home. I felt why you had to say yes. But Genevieve, dearest, why are you asking me to help you now?"

Genevieve sank onto the stone bench and said, "I don't know. You heard why I said yes. He obviously needs me for a little while."

Arabelle put her arm around Genevieve's

shoulders and crooned, "You are so good! Oh, Genevieve, I can see that he needs you, but what about *your* feelings? Do you love him?"

"I don't . . . think so," she admitted, putting her face into Arabelle's neck and taking deep breaths. "No, not him."

"There, you are speaking honestly. But why should you make a sacrifice so monumental?"

"Because the Bible tells us that greater love hath no man than that he lay down his life for his friends," replied Genevieve wetly. "If I remember right, you were about to sacrifice yourself to a much worse kind of man before all went right for you."

Arabelle sighed. "Imagine your bringing that up now. But you're right. For me, it was a frightening time, and I don't recommend that you ever do the same. But now you have, in a different way."

"I know. And I—oh, but here *he* comes! Oh, Arabelle, what does he think?"

Arabelle really looked at her.

The gate squeaked and Armand came through into the garden, having spotted them through the iron grillwork.

Arabelle turned to smile at him. Quietly, she asked Genevieve, "Do you want him to join us?"

"I doubt that we have any choice. Oh, if only!" Genevieve straightened her posture and lifted her chin, sniffing and trying to look normal.

Armand came to stand before her. He looked deep into her eyes and held them captive. "Why did you do it, Genevieve?"

Taking a deep breath, she said, "Because he is so miserable, and he declared over and over that if I married him, it would cheer his last days on this earth. He has seen Jesus. Yes, really! I am touched that he received that sign that he is near the end."

"I see." Solemnly, Armand walked away a few steps, turned, and paced back in his long leather boots. "So you don't believe Ashby will recover?"

Genevieve lifted her hands and shrugged. "How can I possibly know? I am just telling you what he told us, and what I was moved to do, after praying about it."

Armand hunkered down near the ladies' spreading gowns. He touched Genevieve's forearm in gentle emphasis as he asked, "Suppose, just suppose that what he said he saw was something wishful from his fever, or the laudanum, or a dream, and he believes it to be real. I am not saying that I doubt him, but we all know that he could be in a delirium some of the time. What then, if you marry him, and he recovers and lives a long life? Will you be . . . happy with that?"

Genevieve glanced over his face, and found it impossible to look into his eyes. "I . . . I would be his wife, then, for as long as he lives, I expect. I would have to do my best if I vowed to God and him and everybody."

There was a long silence.

Sounding slightly exasperated, Armand said, "You don't sound overjoyed by the prospect."

Despite herself, Genevieve giggled wetly. "No."

Arabelle looked at her in surprise.

Genevieve said, "I have prayed to God more fervently than ever before, so I must now trust Him to show me his will."

Arabelle rubbed her back and said, "That is wise,

my dear."

"Is it?" asked Armand. "Was there love in the picture on your side? Or are you praying for that, too?"

Arabelle intervened gently. "Radford loves her; there is little doubt about that."

"Yes, I suppose he thinks he does," he returned crisply, "but what does Genevieve's heart feel for him? If he loves her, why does he require this of her?"

Genevieve stood, looked Armand straight in his handsome face, and said, "This is not about *Genevieve's* heart." Feeling choked, she left the garden in a blinding hurry. By the time she had reached her favorite spot at the edge of the orchard, tears were streaming from her eyes into her hair.

Oh, how she loved and longed for Armand! She sank onto the moss-covered log in despair. She could only admit to herself that she had wished *he* had asked her to marry him, for she would have exuberantly said yes. Then, if Father would have agreed, she would not be suffering with this chaos in her heart.

But Armand was a French Count who was surely destined to marry a noble French lady; one who would live in his exquisite château with him. There, they would raise a family of beautiful French children who would love playing in the moat.

* * *

Lord Bastwicke and Armand de Villebon rode the

horses through the holloway and into view of Bastwicke Chase, having been to the village to give the horses a good gallop. They were healthily flushed with their exertions. When they had crossed the circular drive in front of the *porte-cochère* and cantered to the stable, Armand dismounted and handed his reins to the groom who came running. Another stable boy dashed to secure His Lordship's horse.

Having thanked the groom, Armand walked into the shade and asked, "Your Lordship, I am wondering what you will do about your marriage situation."

"My whole family is wondering that." Lord Bastwicke pulled off his coat, shook the dust off, and slung it over his shoulder. "Even I am wondering that."

"Pardon me, but have you discussed it with Her Ladyship recently?"

Lord Bastwicke gave a huff. "How can I discuss it with her when one minute she is railing at me for the ludicrous law I strove to pass, and the next, she is fawning over me like some silly chit trying to catch a stranger for a husband?"

Genevieve, strolling toward them ahead of Madam and Arabelle, paused. Madam called to them, "Is this not a perfect place to stroll of an evening? I declare, it is more peaceful than our London square, which one never strolls in, and so pleasant when peopled by such, er, tall and good-looking men." She gave a flip of her fan and eyed Lord Bastwicke blatantly over it.

Father looked flabbergasted. Madam moved to take his arm, but it was awkward for them to walk together because her wide gown hit him with every step they took.

Genevieve saw Armand's eyes flicker, and when she met them behind her parents' backs, they shared a look of suppressed mirth. Arabelle, too, covered her mouth as the three of them followed the pair up the slight slope toward the mansion. Up on the first floor's central window, a curtain moved. Genevieve was surprised to see a man silhouetted there. "Who is that?" she asked, shooting Arabelle a quizzical look. "It doesn't look like any of the servants."

As they neared, the man was gone, but as they entered the house, there, at the top of the grand staircase stood Radford Laurence, Lord Ashby, looking frail with his hair hanging loose from his usual neat queue, and his coat on over his night clothes. Upon spotting Genevieve, he smiled down at her and made a little bow of his head.

Arabelle called, "Aren't you supposed to be in bed, Radford?"

"I feel so much better now that Genevieve is my willing fiancée. I'm tired of bed."

Genevieve's hand tightened on Arabelle's arm. She suddenly felt weak. Was he recovering?

Arabelle turned and appealed to Armand to escort Radford back to bed. Genevieve hung back, for, on the steps outside, Father and Madam were arguing in scarcely-lowered voices.

"We *must* be married again!" she hissed. "We've already been so, for years. There's no question about it, so why do you hesitate?"

"If we do marry again, we must have the Banns called." Father, surprisingly, used the word *if*.

Radford looked stooped as Armand guided him back to his chamber, cajoling him in a friendly way, reminding him that his wound needed to be kept still if it was going to knit together properly.

Radford complained, "I know, but I am sore and stiff from lying there. No position feels comfortable anymore."

"I know what you mean," said Armand. "Perhaps one of the straight chairs will be good for a change."

Genevieve was grateful that Armand took Radford in hand because the burning looks of love that Radford had seared over her made her feel guilty. She moved into the salon and dropped into the hooded chair. She covered her face with her hands and stamped her foot.

Lord Bastwicke came into the room and said, "May I join you, Genevieve?"

"Yes!" she said, glad that it was he. "Are you alone?" she whispered. She gazed at him with heavy eyes.

"Yes, your mother went to sulk. We all have our problems!" he said, bouncing his bulk onto the settee. "Even you, I presume."

"What is yours, Father?" she asked quickly, wanting him to tell her how he felt about everything that concerned his marriage.

"Your mother wants me to marry her again, but without the Banns."

"But you must definitely call the Banns?"

"Oh, yes, the Banns are Law, so that is how it must be. I know that, in the eyes of God with the vows I made to Him, we are married until death do us part." He sighed and looked at her. "I must maintain that vow, morally and legally." He lifted his hands and dropped them. "This does seem monumentally ridiculous. All my work has brought me more murky trouble than I could ever have imagined."

Genevieve leaned forward and looked into his dear face. His thick black brows drew together above his troubled eyes. "Yes, Father, I do so sympathize. Your achievement was very good and needful. But is her aversion to calling the Banns your main worry? Or is it the other difficulty?"

"What difficulty?"

Gingerly, Genevieve asked, "The inkling I have that maybe you do not wish to remarry her."

Silence fell in the room. Then he blew out a heavy sigh. Genevieve patted his hand and waited. After a bit, he drew in a noisy breath, stood up, and walked away, saying over his shoulder, "She is a parcel of trouble. I have often been at my wits' end knowing what to do about her."

"I know, Father. That is, I've seen some of it."

"But what about the scandal? She keeps drumming that at me, in between bouts of fake adulation. It makes me sick!"

There came another knock at the door, and Arabelle poked her head in, asking, "May I come in?"

Lord Bastwicke said, "Come on," and went to put his arm around Arabelle's shoulders. "Be thankful for your loving marriage, my dear," he said, and kissed the top of her head. "You are the blessed one."

Arabelle, quickly grasping the subject on his mind, said, "I have prayed so much for yours, Father. But she will not change, will she?"

"No. Who ever changes?"

Genevieve said, "Father is concerned about the catastrophic uproar it would cause were he not to renew their marriage, but his conscience tells him he must retain it before God."

Arabelle said, "Yes. Madam is terrified of being left adrift in Society. What would people do, and how would she live if she ceased to be Lady Bastwicke? She said that much to me this morning."

"Right," said Lord Bastwicke, "for there is no affection in her for me, or for anyone but herself at this point. I wonder if she even cares for her particular cronies."

Genevieve said, "I have seen that they come and go."

"If I do legally marry her, it will be because I vowed before God, and for the sake of you, my children. I will try to be a good husband to her to the bitter end." Scratching the back of his neck, head down, he left the room.

"Dear Father!" expelled Genevieve.

Arabelle said, "Yes indeed. Poor you, too. You have sacrificed yourself, even though you do not love Radford. I see that you have the most loving, caring heart, or you would not have consented to his wish. You are doing a beautiful thing for him . . . but I still worry."

"What worries you?"

"That you are giving up the love of your life for Radford."

Shakily, Genevieve asked, "What do you mean?"

"Armand!"

"What about him?" Genevieve evaded her eyes

and studied her fingernails.

"He is obviously the man you prefer, Genevieve."

Genevieve looked up. She had always been frank with Arabelle. "Ye-es," she said, her voice quavering. "Much prefer!"

"Then why are you set to marry anyone else? How could he possibly think that you care for him when you announce that you are going to do this foolhardy thing at the beseeching of another man?"

"You are so severe with me!"

The door swung open, and their mother lumbered in, knocking down a vase from a table with a crash and a tinkle. "What are you calling foolhardy, Arabelle?" she demanded as the water dripped onto the parquet.

Genevieve hurried to soak up the water with her handkerchief and restore the sweet-smelling white hyacinth into the vase.

"Well?" insisted Madam, arms akimbo as she glared at Arabelle.

Arabelle moved to Genevieve's side. "I feel badly for Genevieve."

"Why? She is marrying Lord Ashby, of all people, which should make you very happy!"

"But she does not love him! *Do* you, Genevieve?"

Madam cried, "Love! What in the world do you think marriage is, Arabelle? An opera?"

"It's love!" expelled Arabelle, her eyes sparkling.

"No, it isn't! In reality, it's bettering oneself, and securing a high place in Society. Besides, men don't care about love, as you romantically call it. All they want is a certain excitement, and when that's over, well, it's over. The woman needs the compensation of money and jewels and travel—and freedom to enjoy one's own friends and pursuits."

Arabelle, eyeing Madam sidewise, added, "And what do you do if you should lose all that, and have no love either?"

"Get out!" snarled their mother, pointing to the door with a shaking forefinger.

The girls fled. Genevieve whispered, *"Touché!"*

CHAPTER 19

Calling the Banns

The next morning, the servants assisted Lord Ashby into Lord Bastwicke's landau. The whole party made their way to London in three coaches and a baggage cart. They had barely seen their things unloaded in Bloomsbury Square before it was time for a soup, bread, and cheese supper thrown together by the startled, unprepared cook.

Genevieve hurried to the nursery to quietly peek at Lenora and Jerome. They were breathing softly in their little beds side by side, with Fanny reading by the fireside, already in her nightrail and cap. Genevieve thanked her for such wonderful care of them.

She then went to her chamber, where Arabelle was stowing some things from her trunk into the armoire. Relishing the return of her sister to her side of the great bed, Genevieve recounted her experiences in France until huge yawns overtook them. At last, she curled into a ball with a pillow behind her back, prayed the *Lord's Prayer*, and fell asleep before she finished it.

The next thing she knew, it was Sunday morning, and the sun shone through all the eastern windows in Bloomsbury Square.

"Wake up, Genevieve." She felt Arabelle gently nudge her shoulder.

Genevieve pulled the covers tighter around her shoulders, moaning, "Oh Arabelle, I don't want to!"

She heard the heavy creak of floorboards and the sharp rap at the door before Bertha Blumm barged in with her usual hot water pitcher, calling, "Up, up, you slugabeds! Only an hour and a quarter before the carriages for church line up. Jump into your bath, Miss Genevieve, and you in the next one, Arabelle. I hear this is a banner day."

The Banns! Today was the first of the required three. Genevieve moaned, and wound herself into a tighter ball.

Bertha called, "No time to waste!"

As Arabelle slowly moved her legs out of the covers, Genevieve forlornly followed suit and stumbled toward the screen, dropped her nightrail, and sank in. The warm water soothed her.

Bertha added, "It's a shame you ladies cannot wash your hair because it will never dry in time."

At the dressing table when Genevieve's shoes, stockings, and chemise were in place, Bertha brushed her hair with careful strokes. She stared blearily at her reflection as Bertha pinned most of her hair into place at the back of her head. She looped it around, forming a large chignon, stuck in more pins to form a few curls, and said, "No time for tighter ones since you didn't think to put curling rags in last night. This will have to do. You next, Arabelle."

"Don't worry, Bertha, this looks good," said Genevieve with a sigh.

In the mirror, she watched Arabelle take steaming cups from a maid who held a tray of pastries. She brought it to Genevieve, who said, "Thank you; set it on the bed. It's just what I need." With her first quick sip of coffee, she burnt her tongue. The day was not beginning well. She knew she would suffer some pain every time she ate anything all day. But she devoured a sweet pastry anyway.

When they were seated inside the coach that was to follow their parents', Genevieve said to Arabelle, "Pray with me that God's will is done, not mine. Not just Radford's or Madam's wills, either."

"Yes, of course. God is watching you; never forget it, Genevieve. His eye is on the sparrow, and are you not worth far more than many sparrows? He knows whenever a hair falls from your head," she added with a touch to Genevieve's hair, "so never fear, He knows all about this, and will take care of you."

"I know I am to trust. When I pray, year after year, for his will to be done in my life, I must believe and trust that it *is* being done, right?"

"Yes."

Genevieve laid her head on her sister's shoulder and continued, "The fact that Radford saw Jesus coming for him gives me such a serious resolve to do what must be right."

Arabelle patted her hand, but said nothing for the rest of the ride to church.

When they arrived, people thronged the portico of St. George's, Hanover Square, with a few men and children sitting or walking between the six Corinthian columns. Genevieve remarked in surprise, "Look! Is Madam trying to hide behind Father?"

Arabelle gave a soft chuckle and said, "It certainly looks that way. Do you suppose she is avoiding people because of what may happen?"

"Do you mean her having to endure the Banns? Or not having them read at all, leaving her marriage dissolved?"

"I pity her either way. Whatever is Father going to do? Has he decided?"

Genevieve shrugged. "He hasn't told me, but he talked gravely about his vow to God, and to her."

At the top of the stairs, she saw Armand's handsome dark head and broad shoulders half hidden by a column. He was supporting Radford to walk in. Her heart sank. This was going to happen.

When the service was over and the last hymn notes died out from the magnificent organ, a cleric announced that the new Marriage Act had become Law, and would now be practiced for the first time in that church.

Thus began Genevieve's hazy nightmare. Radford's hot, clammy hand gripped hers at the altar as they stood facing the row upon row of people staring at them in utter fascination.

Words from the cleric made her pulse drum loudly in her ears. "Lord Ashby, bachelor, here present, wisheth to join in wedlock with Miss Genevieve Lamar, spinster of this parish, also present. If anyone knoweth any impediment to their marriage, let him now speak before her parents, friends, and this congregation."

While there had been a clearing of throats, whispers, and even a giggle after the word *spinster*, Genevieve heard no voice reply until the cleric told Radford that they could resume their seats.

He then asked Lord Bastwicke, "Was that right?" and Father replied that it was. "Now, it is our turn," Father told him.

"Excuse me?" queried the surprised cleric. "Whose turn would that be, Your Lordship?"

Father held up his forefinger as an indication for him to wait. He returned to their front pew and took Madam's hand, drawing her to her feet. While she let loose a fuming breath, he smiled at her and said low, "Genevieve has done it, and so can we. Come, it's the only way. We once made our vows before God, so let us honor them until death us do part."

Madam lifted her chin, lowered her eyelids, and went with him, her huge purple gown rustling in the silence. The congregation proved extremely attentive, agog to hear what it was all about.

With a smile, Lord Bastwicke spoke in his deep and easy voice, "Since this new Law came into effect, we—"

Lady Bastwicke interrupted in her high pitched voice, "We think it is a good idea to demonstrate by example how this is done so everyone learns." She smiled and nodded at people, her hair feathers waving.

Lord Bastwicke was taken aback, but cleared his throat and waited until the smatterings of chatter subsided. He explained that a discrepancy had surfaced in their marriage process, so he and his lady wife thought it best to "do it all again" just to make sure that all points fit the new Law.

Madam corrected, smiling stiffly, "We would just like to demonstrate the new Law."

So Lord Bastwicke and his former wife spoke their intention to marry. Someone laughed at the back when the cleric read from his instruction paper, terming her a *spinster*.

Madam grabbed Lord Bastwicke's arm as she tripped on the step, and instead of resuming her seat, marched down the aisle and outside with her head held high, pulling him with her.

* * *

Genevieve moped through the following week. She spent most of her time playing and reading with Lenora and Jerome up in the nursery and out in the garden. She strove to concentrate on little lessons for them outside the schoolroom. She felt that she needed to spend as much time with them as she could, for she could be married soon and transported away to live at Ashby Castle.

Radford was installed in his town house, and reportedly, Armand was staying at a hotel nearby. How odd it seemed to Genevieve. He had come by nearly every day to bring them news, for he made it a daily practice to breakfast with Radford. Armand's most recent report was that Radford was walking a little without help, but he still felt pains that made him double over. He was also unable to keep most meals down.

Genevieve sometimes opened the front door to him herself, waiting nearby, but other days she hid, because it was increasingly difficult to see him and not weep. She loved that beautiful, kind Frenchman so much.

Saturday evening, as Genevieve strove to prepare herself mentally to go through the Banns again, she dragged her feet up the staircase. When she passed her mother's bedchamber, she heard a familiar male voice that she had not heard since before her trip to France. She stood stock still, listening. Could it be? She knocked and pushed the door wider and, sure enough; there stood Shrubsole Curling, her former elopement partner and Madam's sometime hairdresser.

He caught her eye in the mirror and his demeanor brightened. "Why, it's Miss Genevieve!" He turned to admire her up and down.

Her mother looked around, her pointed nose in the air, and said, "You may go, Genevieve; I don't need you—unless you need your hair put in curls tonight? In fact, that is an idea because Bertha is not here, and what will you do in the morning if your hair is not prepared? All those people will stare at you again."

Genevieve said, her voice acting oddly, "Mr. Curling?"

Shrubsole smiled widely, his horsey face looking gaunt and his nondescript hair still in its scraggly queue. "I will be happy to oblige, Your Ladyship."

Genevieve soon realized, from the banter that her mother tossed his way, that she had told him that tomorrow was Genevieve's and Lord Ashby's second time to call the Banns in church. She explained the new practice of law to him as though she were knowledgeable about it. She extolled how well Lord Ashby had stood in front of the congregation beside Genevieve despite being in pain from a dagger wound inflicted on him in France.

She turned to remark, "Genevieve, you looked far weaker than he did, I must say. I wonder if anyone there believed that you actually *want* to marry him. Shame on you! What will people think if you don't put on a radiant face tomorrow?"

Shrubsole alerted with curiosity. He eyed Genevieve's flushing face. He dropped the comb and ducked to retrieve it. While slowly rising, he whispered near her ear. "Tell me why."

As she headed for the door to escape, her mother called, "Genevieve, he's ready for you. He can do it in your room."

Genevieve felt a stab of unease, but soon reminded herself that Madam knew nothing about her and Mr. Curling's aborted elopement.

When he lifted Genevieve's long hair and began to brush it, she wondered how she could endure their proximity. She could tell that he reveled in it, but she wished him miles away. No longer did she like him. It struck her that she never had admired him. He had been more like a playfellow in a guilty prank. She felt how immature her infatuation had been, for he had nothing to commend himself in his manner, education, or manliness. Of the latter, he seemed to possess but a sparse share.

"I wonder if you're happy," he said low, after a glance at her face in the mirror.

Genevieve gave him a quelling stare, but no reply, and dismissed him, saying that she could roll her own hair up in rags.

* * *

At the next calling of the Banns, Genevieve watched in amazement as Madam promenaded up the aisle, dressed too extravagantly for church, with Father walking just to the back and right of her tomato red gown. Again, they stated their intent to marry, and the new people in the congregation whispered their questions along the pews. Those who had heard it before had brought more people to witness the spectacle of the married Lord and Lady planning to remarry. Therefore, Genevieve's and Lord Ashby's announcement paled, for which lessened attention she felt grateful.

Radford said to her as they resumed their pew, "Dear Genevieve, thank you. Just one more time, next Sunday. I pray I will make it that far."

She could not reply. She tried to take deep breaths, but was constricted by her corset. When Armand came to aid Radford to his feet and escort him out of the church, he eyed her with loving concern. The congregation was on its feet, leaving. He came to her while someone was congratulating Radford, and asked, "Genevieve! Are you feeling ill?"

At her nod, he told Radford to sit in the nearest pew and he would be back. To Genevieve, he said, "Let me help you out of here," and offered his arm. She readily grasped it. He walked her very slowly, touching her hand while trailing the people shuffling out of the aisle. "Tell me," he said quietly, "why you are so anguished, Genevieve."

Her heart began to pound. He was so near, and he looked so loving and sympathetic. She broke down and said, "What if I told you that I do not wish to marry him?"

Without hesitation, he said, "I would believe you."

"What I just said is true."

"You are doing this to please your mother, and also out of pity for him; is that right?"

"I'm doing it for him alone." She let out a breath of relief that she had the chance to confess that fact.

The clergyman appeared in front of them, coming up the aisle after saying good-bye to parishioners at the door. He asked if he might escort Lord Ashby out, and give him a few words of encouragement. Armand told him it was a kind thing to do, as Lord Ashby had still not recovered.

To Genevieve, Armand said quietly as they walked down the outside steps toward her carriage, "I will be in touch. I must take him home to his bed."

She said, "You are the kindest man ever, to take care of him. I cannot imagine why you should stay here in England and do so, when you have that incredibly lovely castle in France to live in, with such an adorable mother." Her eyes became moist as she thought of all that beauty and serenity. Casting an eye on her own mother preening for people from her open coach door, Genevieve added to Armand, "You are so blessed to have her. The atmosphere of your home is so loving, Armand."

She felt him squeeze her hand. "Thank you, it is true, Genevieve, but I am here to see you through. Ah, your father comes."

So she cast Armand a heartfelt look of tender

gratitude, and took the solid arm of her dear Father, and tried to calm herself.

CHAPTER 20

Out of the Mouths of Babes

Genevieve stumbled through the following week as though she were sleepwalking. Arabelle had had to go home, so Genevieve went often to the nursery, giving lessons in manners and etiquette to Lenora and Jerome, and reading to them from the Bible in the back garden when the sun shone. Lenora made designs with flower petals and Jerome made his toy horses hide in the uncut grass. She opened the Bible many times a day because she needed its comforting words more than ever these days.

The children greeted her with whoops and hugs each time she appeared in their domain. She squeezed them, kissed their soft cheeks, and combed their hair, all of which helped to steady her. They loved her attention. Their nursemaid, Fanny, was also buoyed up and grateful for her help with the little ones. Genevieve sent her off to relax or go out as she chose for a time every day.

On the Saturday before the last Banns, Lenora

looked up into Genevieve's face after being kissed in the morning, and asked, "Have you been crying?"

She could not lie, and especially not to her perceptive little sister. "Yes, Lenora, I have."

"Why?"

Genevieve decided to reveal all. They were sisters, after all. "Because it worries me so much, what I am doing, calling the Banns with Lord Ashby when maybe I shouldn't have agreed to marry him."

Lenora's eyes widened. "You shouldn't? Whyever not? Because he's not well yet?"

"That's not it. He said he saw Jesus, and that it means he will go with Him to Heaven soon. But he wants me to marry him first."

Looking awestruck, Lenora thought about that for many ticks of the clock.

Genevieve sank onto the settee and pulled each child into her arms. Jerome put a cat onto her lap, so she had to disengage her arms to keep its claws from puncturing her gown. As she put the cat onto her shoulder and her cheek against its fur, she said, "The marriage might be of very short duration unless he makes a miraculous recovery."

Lenora objected, "But he loves you lots, right?"

"I think so; yes, he says so."

Jerome looked up into her eyes and inquired, "Do you love him?"

Lenora, too, was all attention.

"I . . . don't know. Probably not . . . enough." She thought of Armand de Villebon's beloved face at their last meeting in the church aisle, and said, "No. I honestly don't. Not as I should."

Lenora said stoutly to Jerome behind her hand,

"She should not marry him."

Jerome looked inspired and said, "Because he's not the Prince! Not the right one." Having declared that, he picked up the cat, who purred loudly as he stroked it.

Genevieve looked at him in wonder. He sounded decisive, just like their Father. To Lenora, she said, "Where does he get such thoughts?"

She bounced on the seat. "From me! I tell him stories, and one of them has a Prince who is nice to the Princess, but he isn't the real one, and she has to tell him no, you must leave me."

Jerome cut in, "Then she hopes and waits a little while for the real Prince, the strong one, who gallops from his castle on the other side of the lake and gives her things she likes."

Lenora said importantly, meeting Genevieve's eyes significantly, "And loves her! And then she loves him for being so nice."

"Oh, I see. You're a smart little storyteller."

Lenora cuddled Genevieve's hand against her cheek, and kissed it.

Jerome, who was nearest the door to the landing, suddenly said, "Madam is calling you, Genevieve!" He opened the door, and they all heard her stringent voice.

Genevieve reluctantly rose at the repeat of her name, promising to return as soon as she could. She descended the grand staircase. There she was, motioning imperiously and hissing, "Hurry scurry!"

"What is it, Madam?"

"Here is our drawing room full of people, all agog about our double Banns-calling, and I am sick of fielding all their questions. Come take your part!

Help change the subject."

Genevieve nearly panicked. "What can *I* do or say?"

"Just tell them that Lord Ashby is promised by his doctors to recover soon from a sword wound he received defending your honor. I've told them that already, but it will be better believed if you say it with pride. Hint at how much you love each other. Then they won't think we're forcing you to marry so high of a title. Get in there, now!"

Appalled, Genevieve moved automatically to the glass to lick her palms and smooth back stray wisps on the sides of her hair. She was startled to see Welford, the footman, opening the door and Armand de Villebon's manly form strolling in.

Her face infused with joy. He locked glad eyes with her in the mirror as he handed his hat to the footman.

Lady Bastwicke had already rejoined her guests, so Genevieve turned happily to face Armand, and curtseyed.

He smiled, drew her near, and kissed her on each cheek, saying, "*Bonjour*, Mademoiselle Genevieve. I much prefer our French style of greeting."

"*Bonjour*, Armand. Thank you for appearing at this moment. I need rescuing!"

"How so?"

"Madam bids me go in there," she gestured to the room full of chatter beyond the draped doorway. "She commands me to tell how much in love I am, and how I will marry the Earl who fought a duel in my honor and took a grievous sword injury. How can I possibly do that?"

Armand laughed helplessly. "I'm sorry, but if you

do not feel any of that is true, don't say it, Genevieve."

"Even though my mother commands it?"

He looked steadily into her eyes. "Will you let her control your voice and your decisions all your life?"

"No!"

"Then begin here as you mean to go on; with fortitude. I saw you reveal your courage in France."

"Yes, but it's hard to defy her immediate demands. She is so insistent, and must always be obeyed *tout de suite*."

"I realize that, but now is the time to do what is best for you. You live your life, and she lives hers—not that of her children, I would hope."

Genevieve felt empowered by his words, by his presence, and by the need to spend time with him. "Then come this way. We shall repair to the breakfast room. Welford, send us some coffee and sweets, if you please." She smiled at the young footman who was always in her corner. He went, looking glad, having heard their conversation.

Genevieve called after him, "If she demands you fetch me again, tell her I am entertaining a noble guest."

"Yes, Miss Genevieve." He bowed his head to them both, and left with a smile on his lips.

* * *

"This is pleasant," remarked Armand as he lifted his round coffee cup and looked out the window at the garden with its bobbing narcissi and trees in new leaf. "I am glad to see the strain lessened in your lovely face, Genevieve."

Surprised, she said, "It is only for the moment, I'm sure." She set down her cup, added another lump of sugar, and stirred. "How is he today?"

"Radford? Better, he says, but I wonder. He is still a disturbing gray, but makes a real effort to converse."

"What does the doctor say?"

"Very little. He comes every day to change the bandage and check his ongoing fever, but goes away looking bleak."

"Oh." Genevieve fiddled with her spoon and then looked into Armand's face. The light from the window played across his blue eyes, making them glisten between the black lashes. Her heart swelled painfully.

They spoke of the Banns that had taken place. He asked, "Were you surprised by your parents' calling the Banns for themselves?"

"I was astonished. I believe Father sprung it on her at that moment in church. The sermon was moving, so I think the Spirit must have confirmed Father's will to do what is right."

"Very likely. It was interesting what she said to try to explain it. But what counts is that they are now united in their goal."

"Did you have any influence on my father?" she asked, suddenly struck by the possibility.

"Who knows? We did talk about it."

"What did he say to you, and you to him?"

"Well, he exclaimed over what a quagmire they were stuck in, and I asked him what he could possibly do. He said that Lady Bastwicke had declared that she would not stand in front of the world for the Banns, but that she would not stand for them to be unmarried, either."

Genevieve shook her head slowly. "How did *he* feel?"

"He told me that, although she is a difficult woman, he married her in good faith. He intends to keep his vows to God and to her, for better or for worse. He said that had not changed with him; but the emotional rack he went through had only been a hindrance to his decision for awhile."

"Oh, my noble Father! I cannot imagine his leaving her in the lurch. But I know he suffers, and it was probably a compelling temptation to cry off. That was likely why he procrastinated in revealing his decision to her."

Armand murmured, "Your father is a man of integrity. I respect him highly."

"Yes, his words are always solid and moral."

"To speak morally is to speak intelligently."

Genevieve smiled at him and agreed. "What do you think the congregation thought of Madam's pretending that she and he were only demonstrating the Banns?"

Armand shook his head slightly. "Some of the people might believe it, but I doubt that they all do."

"Yes, I fear she will suffer endless questions, and be the subject of malicious gossip for weeks to come, even though she gave a somewhat convincing argument. They still have to marry somehow. I just hope she treats my Father well after all of this."

"Come," he said, rising and reaching for her hand to help her up. Genevieve loved how he took charge of her, often by physical means. "If I accompany you into her drawing room, will you go? This would be on your own terms, mind you. Don't say what you don't feel."

"Thank you," she breathed, and went with him, arm in arm. Since she was no good at hiding her feelings, she suspected that he saw her adoration of him in the look she gave him.

* * *

Sitting next to him on a settee at the far end of Madam's noisy drawing room a quarter hour later, she could concentrate on nothing but his nearness. When a woman asked her a question, she did not hear or respond.

Armand chuckled.

"What?" she whispered at him sidewise.

"Ignoring people now? That woman asked you how you liked your time in France."

"Oh?" She turned to the lady staring at her from under a high-piled gray coiffure adorned with purple feathers. Genevieve formed a smile and said, "It was the most interesting trip of my life."

"Did your mother behave herself there?" inquired the next woman, peering from behind an enormous blue fan. She winked at the first lady.

Genevieve just smiled and nodded. Turning back to Armand, she said, "I can't forget that I am promised to my sister and brother. Want to come visit them?"

Armand whispered, "Absolutely. We've stayed long enough, and thankfully, she hasn't come to the subject of your, ah, engagement. Excuse us," he said to the women, and they made their escape past Lady Bastwicke, who was in the middle of a loud anecdote. Her eyes followed them and she frowned briefly, but Genevieve hurried out and up the stairs. Armand, chuckling, took two steps at a time until he caught up with her. "You're fast!"

"I've learned."

Up in the nursery, Jerome came running as soon as the door opened. Lenora was at the low table with the nurse, Fanny, poring over a card puzzle. Lenora whirled around, upset her stool, and, ran forward, shouting, "Genevieve! You brought the handsome Prince! Yippee!" She clasped her hands together and beamed up at him. "We met you once, but had to come upstairs too soon." She stamped her foot.

Armand, grinning, made her a bow and chucked her under the chin. "I'm delighted that we meet again, Miss Lenora."

Jerome hugged Genevieve around her waist. She picked him up, and plunked down onto the settee with him, kissing his forehead and petting his dark silky hair.

Armand took Lenora by the hand and sat next to Genevieve. In the distance, Fanny smiled, curtseyed, and left by another door.

Lenora promptly made use of Armand's knees as a chair for herself and said straight into his face, "I need to talk to you."

"Talk as much as you want," he said genially.

"Alone!" she whispered, casting an eye at Genevieve.

"Then I'm curious to hear what you have to say, Miss Lenora. Where shall we go for this *tête-a-tête?*"

"In there," she pointed to an arched door.

Armand winked at Genevieve as the girl slid off his lap and tugged him away.

Lenora directed him into a dark closet, the storage room for their rocking horse, bathtub, and toy coach.

Genevieve giggled and said to Jerome, "How will he fit?"

Jerome said, "Look, he has to duck his head way down."

The door closed on them after some thumps and a clatter of the copper tub to the floor.

"They're in the dark," said Jerome knowingly, hunching up his shoulders and grinning.

"Whispering," added Genevieve.

When they emerged some five minutes later, Armand wore an unreadable countenance, while Lenora looked wise and secretive. Smiling widely at Genevieve, she skipped toward her and declared, "We have a secret, and we won't tell!"

CHAPTER 21

The Final Banns

The next day heralded the third Sunday of calling the Banns. Genevieve worried without ceasing, except when she fell to her knees at her silk settee, laid her forehead onto a cushion, and prayed. Never before this month had she known what it was to *pray without ceasing*.

When she walked through the church doorway and saw Radford near the front, watching again for her arrival, she could not force a smile back at him. His eyes glittered unnaturally. When she reached his side and sank to the pew, she saw how flushed he looked, and asked, "Are you feeling worse?"

"Much better since you arrived, darling Genevieve," he breathed. He took her hand and kissed it. She could feel how feverish he continued to be, even through her glove. He had not improved.

She said, "Excuse me, you need help right now, so I'm going for a doctor, Radford." She scanned the milling congregation for any sign of a doctor she could recognize. Spotting none, she continued walking toward the back, where she encountered Father. She told him, "Radford is very hot and ill. This cannot go on, can it?"

"If he wants to be here, he is putting the matter above his health. Let him go home and to bed when it's done. I'll send my coachman for a doctor now." He motioned to the balcony, and his coachman stood up and nodded, leaving his seat.

Genevieve noticed that Father had a damp forehead himself, and she wondered about his feelings on this final day in which he renewed his commitment to stick with Madam.

She hurried toward the door and breathed deeply between the columns on the top step. People looked at her curiously, and while she was trying to ignore them by retying her cloak ribbons, a familiar feminine voice behind her said, "You don't really want a sick man, do you?"

"What?" Genevieve looked back into the face of Dorcasta Doyle, who was angling her chin defiantly, her eyes squinting belligerently at Genevieve. "I bet you love somebody else," she continued, "and you're not even happy to be betrothed, are you? Otherwise, you would be snuggled up beside Lord Ashby, and smiling. What a waste!"

Touché, thought Genevieve.

"Don't worry," pronounced Dorcasta, jabbing a sharp forefinger at Genevieve's arm, "I will take him off your hands."

"Oh? How can you do that?" She expected her to say she would challenge the Banns. "If you do challenge the Banns, you must have an ironclad reason or you'll go to prison."

"I will?" She opened her eyes very wide. "Well, I'm not going to do that then."

"How do you plan to take him off my hands, as you put it?"

"By going up there to sit by him and tell him what I just said to you. He will then marry *me*, see?"

Genevieve laughed low. "Go ahead and try it! I don't think you'd be that cruel, though."

Genevieve stared in disbelief as Dorcasta shot her a defiant look, flounced into the aisle, and waddled all the way to the front. She turned into the pew where Radford sat hunched. Smiling widely, she bent to kiss him on both cheeks, French style, for all the congregation to see. She then appeared to assail the startled man with a barrage of words in his ear, and settled herself importantly next to him as the organ began to play.

Genevieve, conscience-stricken, was about to go up after her and seat herself dutifully on Radford's other side to conclude their Banns, when a coach rolled to a stop at the bottom of the steps. The person to emerge was Armand. He turned to help someone out. She was astonished to see that it was Lenora.

"Genevieve!" she called excitedly. "I'm in a secret with Armand!"

He admonished her quietly. She covered her mouth with her hand, but her eyes remained lively upon him, and then revolved portentously to Genevieve.

"What in the world?" Genevieve queried as they neared her. She darted a probing look at Armand. As he approached her, she breathed, "I am in such a quandary!"

"Over what, exactly?" he whispered.

She let the latecomers pass by and then asked, "How can I marry him, just out of pity?"

"You have just said it. How can you?"

Lenora tugged at Genevieve's hand and whispered, "If you don't love *him,* do not marry him!" She shook a forefinger up at her frowningly.

Armand took Genevieve behind the column, away from prying eyes, and said, "I am ready to take you away from this impossible situation, if you should say the word. You mean it for the very best reason, but you are depressed because of it, Genevieve. It will not be your doing if you do not sacrifice yourself; it will be mine. Look, my carriage awaits. I'm here to whisk you away."

A groom stood next to its door, holding a fur rug, ready to place it over whoever entered.

Genevieve broke her reserve and said, "Oh, Armand! I want to go with you, so badly! But I must go and talk with Radford. I can't just leave him!"

Lenora crept into view, looked eagerly from her to Armand, and gave a little jump. "I'll go do it! He likes me."

Genevieve eyed her confident face and laughed weakly. "Oh, Lenora! You wouldn't."

Armand nodded encouragement to Lenora.

Stymied, Genevieve stared at him. "No, really!"

Armand's attention shifted suddenly to something inside the church. When Genevieve looked, Dorcasta was leaning toward Radford, talking into his ear. Genevieve saw that Radford's neck looked stiff as he apparently tried to move away from her. Armand asked, "What is she doing to him?"

"Coercing him to marry her, as she told me today that she would."

Armand's eyebrows shot up. "What? But that's ludicrous!"

Lenora piped up, "Girls shouldn't do that! I'm going to tell that Dorcasta what she cannot do!" With her bent elbows pumping her along, she ran up the aisle before Genevieve could stop her. She locked widened eyes with Armand.

The music ended, and they heard Lenora admonish in a clear, ringing voice, "Dorcasta Doyle, if you plan to marry him when he already asked my sister, that's a big mistake. He has to ask you first. Otherwise, you're behaving loose and improper."

Genevieve's jaw dropped, and Armand laughed.

There was a flutter of shocked whispering and chortling behind gloved hands. Genevieve backed out of sight before people should turn around and see her there, the fiancée that was, seemingly sending her little sister to cry off.

Armand pulled her around a column, and with a swift lift, had her cradled to his chest, descending the steps before she knew what was happening. He maneuvered her into the carriage, his dear face near to hers. In he slid after her and the groom threw the soft fur over her knees.

"Stop!" she cried.

"Now what?" he asked, looking concerned.

"Oh, Armand," breathed Genevieve, her pulses pounding. "What are you doing?"

He smiled and leaned forward. "It is my highest aim in life to see you happy, and the happiest I have seen you was at Château de Villebon. May I take you back to France with me, darling Genevieve?"

She stared at him. Her heart thudded as she let his words sink in. "Armand, do you truly want to take me away from all this? But, why?"

"Because I love you, Genevieve. You must marry no one but me. I live only to make you the happiest of women. It breaks my heart to see you like this."

She closed her eyes in monumental relief. "Yes, yes, yes, you are the only man I must marry!" She cried, "I didn't know that you loved me!"

"You didn't? Oh, but I do, Genevieve, ever so fiercely!"

* * *

Genevieve's head swirled with new thoughts and sensations as Armand gathered her into his arms and kissed her. "Oh Armand!" she exclaimed with stars in her eyes. "Thank you! But before we go, I feel just horrible that we've left him there in Dorcasta's—"

"Clutches? We will hear eventually if she succeeds in starting up new Banns for her and His Lordship, but I sincerely doubt it."

"She has audacity, which mushroomed since she went to France with us. It is culminating in what she is doing at this moment in church. What should we do?"

"Would you like to leave all this behind, and marry me?"

"I would absolutely *love* to marry you!" Genevieve

confessed, and then began to cry.

With great concern, he inquired, "Why are you crying, dear Love?"

"Because I was so afraid that I would never, ever hear you say what you just did. My life was going to be darkness, but now, it is full of hope and full of light!" She gave him a dazzling smile from her full heart. "Oh, but look, here comes Father!"

"Good," said Armand. "I want to ask him."

Genevieve eyed him for a second, smiled, swiped at her tears, and beckoned her father over. "Yes, we must always treat him with all respect and honesty."

Lord Bastwicke approached them. "Genevieve?" he said after Armand had lowered the coach window.

"Yes, Father?"

"What are you doing? You are not sitting in church for the Banns to be called for the last time, Genevieve. The hymn will soon end. Lenora is acting very oddly, sitting beside me and behind Lord Ashby, keeping her lips tightly shut. Does she know something I don't know? It's alarming to see that Miss Doyle hanging onto Lord Ashby in your place."

"He looked suspiciously from her to Armand under his eyebrows. "I say!" he said, really looking at the two of them in the coach's interior. "Would this be an *elopement,* Genevieve?" His words sounded like a menacing knell, reminding her of her first perilous attempt.

"Not without your consent, Father. Oh, but I couldn't do it! I'm sorry to disappoint you and Madam, but it was not right."

Leaning his arms on the bottom of the window,

Lord Bastwicke demanded, "What was not right?"

"Agreeing to marry Radford!—out of pity. I do not love him. I love . . . Armand de Villebon, here present!" she added in a rush, and felt herself glow with the truth.

Armand smiled handsomely and said, "I love her, Lord Bastwicke. May I have your permission to marry her?"

"Ah! This is a perplexing dilemma."

"The third Banns were not called. Surely that counts for an unfinished bond to wed?" Armand put to him.

"It is certainly unfinished. Let's see, how shall we deal with this unforeseen situation?"

"Oh no!" breathed Genevieve. "Here comes Madam! Quick, Father, what do we do? She will try to force me back! But I need to say good-bye and ask Radford to forgive me. After that, will you let us leave without my having to stand for the Banns, please, Father?"

Madam had descended the staircase on the arm of a man, and left him with a little wave. She was soon next to Father's shoulder, rasping at Genevieve, "What on earth is keeping you, Genevieve? How can you risk being so late for your last Banns? They're singing the last hymn! Radford is looking around for you, trying to fend off that encroaching Dorcasta, and Lenora is patting his cheek. He looks utterly stymied! You idiotic girl! Get back in there and put him out of his misery!" She tried to elbow Father out of the way, thrusting her hand onto the coach door lever to open it.

"Regina, let it go," said Father firmly. "Genevieve has changed her mind, but she wants to talk once more to Ashby."

Taking an outraged breath, Madam exploded, "What? Genevieve, come inside right this second and claim him before Dorcasta succeeds in her evil plan to oust you and take him for herself! She said she's going to be of higher rank than me!"

Genevieve rolled a wide-eyed look of fear at Armand.

He whispered into her ear while Madam stared at them, "You go in and do what you want to do. I want to ask your father something. But don't go agreeing to marry Ashby, my love." He leaned back and gave her the eye.

Genevieve nodded gratefully, and looked at her mother, pretending to submit.

"Hurry scurry!" Madam took her by the forearm and pulled her up the stone steps until they were between the entrance columns. Genevieve glanced back down at the men talking through the coach window, and worried. Yanked into the church by Madam's insistence, she saw, at the front of the church, Dorcasta apparently trying to lift Radford to his feet. He swayed and fell back onto the pew.

Genevieve's anger flared. She brushed past her mother and hurried up the aisle while the people were singing. In front, she attacked Dorcasta with, "What are you doing to Lord Ashby?"

She whirled guiltily. "Go away! He must marry me, not you!"

"It won't work that way," she said to Dorcasta. Genevieve hastened to gesture Lenora aside so she could sit on the other side of Radford. To him, she said, "You look exceedingly in need of your bed. The doctor is on his way. Are you in terrible pain?"

He reached out a shaking hand toward her, grasped her fingers with clammy cold hands and said, "Genevieve, my angel, my love! Thank you for coming to say good-bye. Thank you for being so cooperative and kind to me. God bless you always! I will go with Jesus now."

She gasped, and watched his eyelashes lower. Then he leaned toward her until his cheek rested on her shoulder. He sighed happily. As her heart thumped loudly in the sudden quietness after the hymn's "Amen," his grip on her loosened.

Footsteps sounded, and Armand's face swam before her wet eyes. He gently took Radford's shoulders and straightened him. After feeling his neck and wrist and listening to his chest, he said reverently, "Jesus came for him indeed."

CHAPTER 22

Lenora's Fairy Tale

That afternoon, Genevieve hurried around her chamber in Bastwicke House, opening drawers and flinging armoire doors open.

Lenora came in, watched her for a minute, and asked, "Did Lord Ashby already go to Heaven?"

"Yes, Lenora, he did."

"He was my friend," she said, and began to cry quietly. "He fed me an ice at that ball a long time ago when I was little."

Genevieve stopped her packing, drew her sister to the settee, and cradled her in her arms. "I know he was. You will be sad to have him gone."

She sniffed wetly and met Genevieve's eyes. "But I will see him again in Heaven, won't I?"

"Certainly you will."

"What is he doing now?"

"Sleeping in Jesus. Remember the little girl in the Bible who died, and when Jesus got there, everybody in the house said He was too late to help her?"

"Too late to help her because they said she was dead?"

"That's what they said. Do you remember what Jesus told them?"

"He said, *She is not dead, but sleepeth.*"

"That's right. And those people laughed him to scorn."

"That was so rude."

"Yes, but then what happened?" Genevieve smoothed Lenora's blonde curls behind her ears.

"Jesus told the girl to arise, and she did!" Lenora clapped her hands.

"Yes, and do you know why? Because when the children of God die, they go straight to sleeping in Jesus' loving care until Judgment Day. So, you see, it was easy for Jesus to raise her up again because she was in his care. He is always, always with us."

Lenora nodded and wiped her eyes with her sleeve ruffle. "I am glad that he is safe with Him."

"Me, too. Life was too hard for him to bear at the end, with so much pain, so he was taken home." Genevieve rocked her warm little sister gently.

Lenora murmured, "No more pain." Another minute passed. "What are you going to do now, Genevieve?"

"Would you like it if I married Armand de Villebon?"

Lenora jumped up to face her, infused by astonished joy. "Oh, yes, I would! Are you really going to?"

"Yes!"

"Did he ask you?"

Genevieve laughed. "Yes, of course he did."

Lenora looked knowing.

Genevieve asked, "Can you tell me your secret with him now?"

"Yes, because you know it now."

"What was it?"

"I told him that you are so nice to people that you were going to marry Radford just because he was dying to marry you. But," she shook her finger, "you didn't know that you should wait for True Love."

"Do you mean you told Armand about the wrong Prince and the Right Prince?"

"Yes, I did. I said that you loved *him*."

Genevieve marveled, and scooped her little sister in a warm hug. "You are a true and loving sister, Lenora! Thank you so much!"

* * *

"Lenora, I have to hurry now."

"To do what?"

"Finish packing before Madam comes home tonight. Otherwise, Armand and I might not make it out of here without a huge fuss."

"Is he taking you away tonight?"

"Yes." Genevieve got up and tossed stockings and night rails into her open bandboxes. She gave some handkerchiefs to Lenora, who flung them in.

"Where are you going?" Lenora climbed up the steps to the bed and clutched Genevieve's arm, looking her in the face with worry while she was trying to fold an embroidered petticoat.

There came a knock on the door. Genevieve called, "Enter!"

In came Armand in all his glory, dressed for

traveling, and smiling bewitchingly at them.

Genevieve gasped, and with her hand on her heart, said, "I never expected you to enter this room!" *Except in my dreams,* she added silently. "Armand, please tell Lenora what Father said about calling the Banns in France."

Armand picked Lenora up, touched her nose, and said, "O Partner in Secrecy, I am here to tell you that our plan is working beautifully."

"It is?" Lenora looked eager to hear more.

"Yes, indeed. Your Father told me, in strict confidence—and I can tell you because I know what a great secret keeper you are—that I can whisk your beautiful sister out of this country and into mine, where there are no delays such as Banns to keep us from marrying—as soon as we wish!"

Lenora's mouth made an awestruck O as she took in the great news. She squealed, threw her arms around his neck, and kissed his cheek with fervor. "Oh Genevieve!" she crowed, looking ecstatically down at her from her perch, "I'm so glad you finally know that Armand is the right Prince!"

* * *

"Que la grâce, la miséricorde et la paix de Dieu notre Père et de Jésus-Christ notre Seigneur et du Saint-Esprit soient avec vous maintenant et toujours. Amen." The wedding ceremony in the chapel at Château de Villebon concluded.

Genevieve handed her bouquet to Arabelle and turned back to smile up at Armand. He lifted her off her feet, and his lips impressed upon her how deeply he loved her. She mingled with his kiss in liberating joy. Yes, grace, mercy, and peace from above were truly theirs. Her heart felt ready to burst with love and thankfulness.

With moist eyes, she clung to Armand's hand and turned to face the onlookers seated in the sun-streaming chapel.

There was Father, looking proud and pleased next to the Comtesse de Villebon. Next to her, Aunt Claracilla beamed, with her hands clasped and lifted in thankfulness to God.

Lenora jumped up and down in her seat, clapping her hands and smiling in triumph. She took great pleasure in having her secret with Armand result in such a romantic fairy-tale wedding.

Jerome smiled excitedly next to her. He stood up and smartly saluted Armand, and received one in response from his new brother-in-law.

Genevieve received a wink from Madame Lavande, for they had shared peril and joy, and now had a loving bond.

The rest of the festively-dressed congregation consisted of Armand's friends and relatives, who filled up every seat. Some of the men formed a half circle, standing around the back walls.

Madame de Villebon was the first to kiss Genevieve and express her heartfelt thanks for marrying her one and only son, whom she treasured so dearly. Genevieve smiled into her kind face and told her how privileged she felt, not only to marry him but also to gain such a loving *Belle-mère.*

* * *

As Arabelle and Genevieve strolled in their youthful, elegant gowns of palest aqua and pink toward the château, Armand had a drove of gentlemen walking next to him, talking exuberantly, slapping him on the back. A man halted his progress with the bride by grasping Armand's arm and launching into an anecdote. The other men were soon laughing, and another man began to add to the story. The sisters had a chance to pause together beside the reflecting moat under the castle towers.

Putting her nose into her bouquet, Genevieve inhaled blissfully. Finally, she asked, "Why did Madam not come?"

Arabelle made a wry face. "Oh, Genevieve, she stayed in London, explaining that she is in the throes of planning her own Renewal of Marriage Vows, as she creatively calls it. She has decided to make a grand event of it!"

"No! Really?"

"She said their private ceremony will be followed by a ball somewhere, and she is ordering a glittering gold and silver gown with a fan to match. With a mirror in it."

Genevieve laughed helplessly. "Of course."

Arabelle added, "But to be frank, she let slip the truth of why she wouldn't come. She bitterly resented that you are gaining such a noble French Count as your husband, and that you 'caught' him on your own, against her dictates. After all, he was the villain who ousted her and her friends from Château de Chambord. And to top that, Genevieve, you get to live here in Château de Villebon, where she was not admitted. For these reasons and more, she would not come," Arabelle said, taking Genevieve's hand. "But look out, for I bet she will show up unannounced to visit you someday, dragging along some of her friends to cavort with. Better keep the drawbridge up." The sisters laughed.

Inside the Royal bedchamber, Genevieve placed her white rose bouquet into a vase of water and smiled at Arabelle. "It's probably best that Madam didn't come. I wouldn't have wanted any negative looks or words to sour this fabulous day. Instead, it is a blessing from God how everything has turned out. Everything!"

Arabelle hugged her, Genevieve kissed her cheek, and Arabelle wiped tears away. "I'm so happy for you, Genevieve! So many prayers answered."

"You must stay here as long as you can, and come back often."

"I will, and I'll bring my love with me."

"Yes, he and Armand will hit it off splendidly. Can't you just picture them cantering together down that ride between the trees?"

"Oh yes. And you and I spending time exploring all of the rooms in these mysterious towers! Have you seen inside them all yet?"

"No, but what fun it will be! We must take Lenora and Jerome into them all, and have Armand tell us what he and his friends played when they were boys."

Arabelle smelled the rose bouquet and asked, "Can we take flowers and fruit from the orangerie? I'd like to embellish this room for you."

"Ask Comtesse de Villebon. I'm sure she'll say yes. It's all more than I could ever, ever have hoped for, or imagined! Thanks to God on high!"

Arabelle said, "Yes, but aren't you Comtesse de Villebon now?"

Genevieve stared at her.

Arabelle laughed and said, "Lenora and Jerome think they're living in a fairy tale here. She keeps telling people that her sister married the right Prince! It doesn't matter if all these French people don't understand her because they all smile at her, pat her cheeks, and kiss her."

Genevieve smiled and said, "Jerome was awestruck by the moat. Lenora assured him that he can play Knight and Lady with her. Oh, aren't they going to have fun? The week will go too fast!"

Father cleared his throat in the doorway. From his coat, he pulled a letter. "This may not be the most appropriate moment to distract you with news, Genevieve, but do you want to hear it?" He was repressing a peculiar look that she could not quite understand.

"Absolutely, if it's good. What could it be?"

"Your mother has reported that after we all left the late Lord Ashby's funeral and you 'eloped' here with Armand, a few days passed, and this letter came. It is addressed to you, my precious. Read it after I tell you the rest."

"Yes, Father," she said, receiving the folded paper with the seal already cracked open.

Lord Bastwicke continued, "Incidentally, that Miss Doyle said she wanted to get her hair done by Lady Bastwicke's hairdresser, but Regina said that would only happen over her dead body because she was not loaning Bertha Blumm to her. But that girl found out from the footman that when Bertha was gone, your mother called in one Shrubsole Curling." He gave Genevieve a speaking glance.

Genevieve looked at him with rueful interest. "And?"

"Miss Doyle looked him up, struck up an acquaintance, and has since eloped with him!" Father's eyes were as determined as could be.

"My, oh my!" Genevieve responded.

Arabelle gasped and crowed, "She went after *him?*"

Father growled, "I wonder if she'll bother to call the Banns." He shook his head dolefully. "I'm going to follow that one because if they try to marry without proper Banns, it will not take." He gestured. "Read your letter. Your mother obviously opened it."

Genevieve drew Arabelle closer so they could read it together. It was a statement, written in an erratic hand and signed at the bottom by "Ashby" with an ink splotch after it. It stated simply that, other than Ashby Castle, his inherited estates, and his title, which would pass to his brother, Simon, he left all of his independent funds to Miss Genevieve Lamar. It concluded with his heartfelt thanks and his wishes for God's richest blessings upon her and her future.

Genevieve stood speechless.

Arabelle locked eyes with her. "What eloquent proof that he loved you!"

"Father," wailed Genevieve, "should I feel guilty?"

He instantly frowned. "No! Accept it and be grateful. Your heart was in the right place, and you were prompted by a need to help him, ready to sacrifice your own wishes; your own life, in fact.

Just thank God, I say, because He prevented you. Man proposes but God disposes; something like that."

Arabelle squeezed her sister's shoulder and added, "He took Radford to Heaven. What could be better than that?"

Genevieve nodded, refolding the paper. She went to the table with the looking glass above it, put the will into a little drawer that was now hers, and took the silver comb, a gift from the Comtesse, to her side wisps. Father and Arabelle left the bedchamber with the aqua bed curtains gracefully swooping from a coronet on the ceiling.

Genevieve wondered why they left so suddenly and silently, but when she looked at the doorway, there was Armand, gazing at her with love in his eyes. He clicked the bedchamber door shut behind his back. He drew her into his arms. Her heart began to skip and pound.

"My darling Genevieve," he said, "I long to stay in here with you, but *Maman* is waiting for us to be seated at the table to begin our wedding feast."

Genevieve felt him backing her gently toward the King's bed, laying her down onto her back, and moving close to her. She looked into his face above hers and asked, "Is this how we get ourselves to the banquet?"

Grinning, he ran a finger across one of her eyebrows, down her cheek, across her lips, and then impulsively kissed her. In loving seclusion with only him, she wanted fervently for their kisses to continue. At last he raised his head and said with regret, "I'm afraid this must be all for now."

"Yes," she sighed. "Will we really occupy this

enchanting fairytale room?" she asked him, feeling languorous as he pulled her to her feet and close to his rapidly-beating heart. "Your mother told me that Kings of France have stayed here."

"Only the best for my own Queen Genevieve." He kissed her and said, "It is my wish, my privilege, and my pursuit to make you happy here, with me."

The End

Thank You from the Author

My dear Reader,

Thank you for reading this book! I loved writing PURSUING GENEVIEVE, and hope you were engaged by the adventurous pursuit of Genevieve.

If you enjoyed this book, I am delighted. I would be so grateful if you, my reader, would help me in any of these ways:

1. **Tell your friends** about the book.
2. **Post a review** on your book store's website.
3. **Ask your library** to order it.
4. **Buy THE ROGUE AND THE ROSE,** or any of my other books.
5. **Visit https://mellyoraashley.com** to sign up for email announcements of my next books.

I appreciate your support so much!
Your Kindred Spirit,

Mellyora Ashley

Scan this QR code to visit Author's website: mellyoraashley.com

BONUS: Read on for a preview of

THE ROGUE AND THE ROSE

England and Wales, 1822

CHAPTER 1

The Rogue

"A gentleman does *not* take such liberties!" cried Celia, the Countess of Mallet, with uncharacteristic rage. She kicked Lord Smeaton so hard that she caught her foot in the sheet and tumbled off balance over the edge of the bed. Borne to the floor on a landslide of bedding, she woke up, sat up, and blinked at her bedchamber. There was no one there. Relief drained through her. He was only a nightmare! Last night in the garden, he had been all too real.

Picking herself up, she pushed long blonde strands of hair out of her eyes, and made her way across the soft carpet to the oriel. Rainbow shafts glittered through its beveled edges as she swung the window open and filled her lungs with the morning air. The back lawn of Mallet Manor glittered in dew as though diamonds had been scattered down. This beauty was hers . . . but not for long. Not unless she made that unspeakable sacrifice.

Only a month left! She gripped the windowsill until her fingertips whitened. *Only a month to find a husband!*

Over the Cotswold Hills, pink streaks brightened the sky, and a wood pigeon poured forth his melody. Celia dropped her head to her arms. "Dear God, help me!" she prayed aloud. "I don't want to marry anyone. I cannot do it! As you know, Lord, I don't even like any of those men, much less love them!"

Across the still air came a faint tattoo. She shaded her eyes and gazed beyond the stream, the fields, and the treetops. Nothing marred the scene.

There it came again, the drum of hoofs. As Celia stared, a dark-caped rider burst into view, riding a magnificent black horse. The masculine silhouette galloped past a bright yellow field and over the arc of the stone bridge. There, the hoof beats changed to a hollow clip that echoed off the garden walls. The horse and rider disappeared. Their sound halted on the paving stones just outside the iron gate.

Why   did   they   stop   there?   she   wondered.

Messengers always trotted up the front drive and delivered their missives to Hews, the butler. Only her servants used the courtyard entrance.

I must see that proud head, those strong shoulders, she decided. *What a powerful jumper he must be; what a gallop he had.*

In her lacy night chemise, she ran to the turret across the room. There, milky-blue glass in the window emulated sky and clouds, preventing her from seeing out. She pushed the latch but, rusted from rain, it would not open. She twisted hard, but to no avail. With a determined will, she gave a mighty lunge. The window jerked outward with a loud screech and catapulted her torso over the sill. With a tingle of terror, she caught herself from falling to the flagstones three stories below.

With her waist on the sill and bare shoulders out of the window, she suddenly knew that someone's eyes were upon her.

There stood the black-caped rider, watching her through the curlicues of the gate. He stood like a vision she had conjured up during her studies of Prince Rupert, but this man emanated masculinity that she had imagined in lesser dimensions, but never, ever seen.

He shaded his eyes against the morning sun and lifted his hat to her.

Why? she wondered.

With a touch of cool breeze upon her skin, a sudden suspicion seared through her. She glanced down at herself, and could have screamed in vexation. She was wearing only a flimsy chemise!

Mortified, she scrambled to squeeze herself back through the window. She grappled for the casement, and, with a banging of elbows, finally got herself inside. Shaking, she sank to the floor.

"Ohhh!" she moaned. "This is worse than any nightmare!" Recalling his smile of admiration, she yanked up her bodice and cried, *"That horrid rogue!"*

For details about
THE ROGUE AND THE ROSE, visit:
https://mellyoraashley.com

Glossary

Abigail – A lady's maid.

Belle-mère – Mother-in-law.

Calèche – A woman's large folding bonnet, named for a carriage. It resembled a long covered wagon hood with curved supports.

Déjeuner – Luncheon.

Échelles – French for ladder. A form of bodice decoration where ribbon bows, often diminishing in size from bosom to waist, decorated the center front of a gown's stomacher.

Escritoire – A French writing desk, often of an elegant design, with drawers and compartments.

Farthingale – An extensive framework of hoops, usually of whalebone, worked into cloth, worn to extend the skirts of women's gowns at the sides.

Idée fixe – Obsession.

Jabot – A frill of lace worn at the neck of a shirt, cascading over the top of the waistcoat; often tied on with ribbons at the back of the neck.

Joie de vivre – Joy of living.

Justacorps – Men's outer body-coat, reaching to the knees, worn in the 17th and 18th centuries.

Modus operandi – Operating mode.

Parfait – Perfect.

Panniers – Side hoops to hold out the skirt of a

gown, made of reed or whalebone. They were covered with cotton or linen, and the two halves tied together in front and back. They could be collapsed by the wearer for sitting in chairs.

Petit déjeuner – Breakfast.

Petticoat – An underskirt of rich, decorative fabric, visible in front under the gown's main skirt. When gowns were no longer designed with an open front, the petticoat became an undergarment.

Porte cochère—In this book, a porch roof projecting over a driveway at the entrance to a house, providing shelter for those getting in and out of vehicles.

Poursuivant détesté – Hated pursuer.

Queue – A hanging tail of hair at the back of the head, secured by a ribbon at the nape of the neck. It was sometimes contained in a bag.

Robe à la française – A lady's gown with a fitted waist in front, flowing loosely over a hoop at the back and sides. Sleeves ended in a cuff at the elbow, with wide lace flounces showing from the chemise undergarment.

Viscount – (vi-count) A member of the fourth order of the British peerage, ranking between an Earl and a Baron.

Viscountess – (vi-countess) The wife of a Viscount.

About the Author

Mellyora Ashley enjoyed her job as an executive secretary, but as a few years passed, she longed to write her romantic novel. Her husband urged her to stay at home, raise their sons, and write. Her first book, A LADY IN DISGUISE, was published by Kensington in New York.

Photo by RJ Studio

Besides writing her books, she is a playwright, director, and an award-winning costume designer for theater and opera. She was editor of a Christian publication, and taught a college class called "Write to Delight."

Mellyora loves to travel in Europe, where she thrills to see the realism of her book research. Visiting and exploring with her friends there, she finds stunning locations and inspiration for her Regency and historical novels.

She writes for the love of sharing her stories with you.